Vamp
Call of

Book Two

MW01076129

Yvette Bostic

Acknowledgement

I'd like to start by saying, while there are some references to places and events, any similarities to specific people are purely coincidental.

I hope you enjoyed the beginning of the *Call of the Elements Series* by reading Magister's Bane first. Don't start with *Vampire's Crucible* or you'll be truly disappointed. I had a blast writing this tale and allowing the characters to run wild with their own stories. I hope you enjoy reading it just as much.

Book 3-Elemental's Domain is scheduled to release October 15, 2019. It's now available on pre-order.

I want to say thank you to the people who've helped me throughout this process. My husband has been my encouragement, as well as the perfect sounding board and first-draft proof reader. I could not have done it without his positive attitude and patience. Thank you to my wonderful editor, Hannah at Between the Lines Editorial (www.btleditorial.com). She is an extremely talented young woman who's also a joy to work with. And thank you to Aleksandra Klepacka (https://www.facebook.com/AlissandraArt/), the very gifted young artist who created my cover art. Thank you to my very gracious beta readers. Your comments and opinions about the characters, events and time lines make all the difference!

And last but not least, thank you to my readers! You're the reason I continue to write.

The Light in the Darkness Series:

Light's Dawn: A Novella

Light's Rise-Book 1

Light's Eyes-Book 2

Light's Fall-Book 3

Call of the Elements Series:

Magister's Bane-Book 1

Vampire's Crucible-Book 2

Elemental's Domain-Book 3

Stay tuned for more....

Prologue

Braden's new smoke gray Mercedes pulled up in front of the Sanguis Hotel and Casino, the headquarters for the vampire council. The humans pushing their way through the revolving doors made his lips curl. The constant rush to spend their money both disgusted and pleased him. Without them, his financial empire would crumble, but their spontaneous decisions driven by irrational emotions grated Braden's nerves. They would always cut off their nose to spite their face, regardless of the consequences.

"Do you want me to wait for you?" Gordon asked from the driver's seat.

"Yes," Braden replied. "I don't expect this to take long."

"Should I have the jet on standby to return to London?"

"No, I still have business with a half-breed." Business he would thoroughly enjoy.

Braden opened the passenger door and stepped into the hot, dry air typical during Nevada's late summer drought, something he didn't have to suffer in London. But a certain mage was here in the desert. One he was anxious to meet.

He quickly made his way through the casino to Jack's private office, ignoring the suggestive looks of several ladies and a few men. His desires would soon be satisfied. He could wait. Being eternal gave him patience humans were incapable of understanding.

Assuming his usual air of disinterest, he pushed open the door to the office without knocking. Jack would be suspicious if he did otherwise and Braden had no intention of drawing his attention.

"Brother," Jack said, not rising from the leather chair at his desk. "I'm glad you could make it so quickly." He waved his hand at the two chairs facing him. "Have a seat."

Braden crossed the space and dropped into the nearest one, leaning back and crossing his legs. "What is so urgent that couldn't be handled on the phone?" he asked.

"I'm worried about Sergey," Jack said without hesitation, which wasn't news to Braden.

"What has our Russian friend done now?"

"There are whispers that he will betray me," Jack replied.

Braden didn't miss Jack's raised eyebrows or the way he leaned forward in his chair. Did his brother suspect another traitor? Possibly. Jack wasn't stupid.

"I haven't heard these whispers," Braden said, concealing his lie with ease. "While Sergey's region is difficult to manage, he does it very well. His own personal rewards have been quite substantial. I'd be surprised if he decided to throw all of that away just to defy you."

Jack leaned back again and steepled his fingers. "Those were my thoughts as well. All our regions could say the same, with the exception of Simon. But Sergey failed to capture the mage."

Braden waved his hand in the air and smiled. "I believe your little mage needs a different approach, brother, which is why I volunteered to find her."

"And what have you found?" Jack's voice lowered with his impatience, and Braden's smile widened.

"She is with a vampire and currently running from her partner who tried to kill her."

"Is she?"

"Yes, I believe I can persuade her to join me," Braden purred. "I will exploit her father's gifts, just as you planned."

"What makes you think you can convince her to join us?" Jack asked. "And will there be enough time to train her to use her gifts?"

"Is there anyone I haven't been able to persuade?" Braden draped his arm over the back of his chair. "As long as we continue on our current timeline, she'll be more than trained. I'll convince her to embrace her darkness and use it to its full potential."

Jack smiled. "Very good. And our illustrious queens will leave her to us?"

"Yes, I've already secured that promise," Braden replied.

"Perfect." Jack rubbed his hands together. "Make me a weapon that even the fae cannot ignore."

"It will be my pleasure."

Chapter 1

I stared at the long, metal warehouse in the valley below. The sun's rays reflected off its shiny surface, making me glad for my dark sunglasses and wide-brimmed hat. They'd been a gift from Logan, the man standing next me, to protect my ridiculously pale skin. His own ball cap shaded his features but didn't hide his exhaustion. While the sun wouldn't kill him, long exposure to it weakened him greatly.

"Why are we standing out here in the sun?" I asked, watching his eyebrows meet and the long bridge of his nose wrinkle. "This can't be comfortable for you."

"Something isn't right," he replied, his attention focused on the metal building and mine on the dark circles under his hazel eyes. "There are too many cars."

"Then let's come back after dark," I suggested. "There's no point standing here letting the sun bake our brains."

"It'd be nice to know who's taking up so much of Jonathan's time," he said, apparently ignoring my attempts to alleviate his discomfort and mine.

"Then let's find some place in the shade." I fanned myself dramatically with my hand, but he continued to ignore me. "Fine."

I huffed and scanned the high desert stretching out in front of me. Jonathan Smith, the man who'd taken in the magical world's outcasts and half-breeds couldn't have picked a more remote location for his compound. It was the perfect hideout for his super-secret-squirrel-society. Tall cliffs protected the northern side, sloping down to the east and meeting the only entrance in and out. Rocky hills covered the southwestern side, providing little shade from the setting sun. In two hours, the oppressive heat would give way to the desert's chilled night.

A group of thorny shrubs hung out over three large boulders just down the hill from me. It wasn't perfect, but it was better than exposing my delicate skin to the blazing ball in the sky. I shifted in that direction, knowing Logan would see me. His hand settled on my shoulder, and I smiled.

"They're certain to have look-outs, and rocks sliding down the hill followed by a little girl will definitely be noticed," he said, turning me around to face him. I craned my neck back to look up into my favorite eyes.

"Then you should run really fast to that group of shrubs," I said. "Carrying me of course, because I'm not running really fast." I motioned to the welcoming shade just below us, and he followed the direction of my pointing finger. I knew he would argue just as he knew I was suggesting it for his sake.

"I don't need a mother hen," he growled.

"Could've fooled me," I countered, putting my hands on my hips.

"I've managed the last forty years without you."

"Yes, but now you're stuck with me, and I'm tired of watching you wither away in this heat."

He opened his mouth to reply, then snapped it shut. I gasped as he scooped me up and dashed across the fifty yards within seconds. I barely had time to flatten my hat against my head before we arrived in the shaded alcove.

"I need to learn to tell you no," he hissed.

"No, you don't," I chimed, lacing my fingers around the back of his neck. The boulders behind us blocked out the sun, casting shadows across his face. "At least you can watch your friends now without being discovered."

He lowered me to the ground, a grin spreading across his face. "Try not to find any snakes or scorpions."

My eyes widened. I hadn't thought of that. They'd be hiding from the heat as well. I peered beneath the shadowed ledge but didn't see anything moving. They probably wouldn't move until I sat my skinny butt on the ground. I picked up a brittle stick and started poking around beneath the boulders. A few spiders and long-legged bugs scurried away, but nothing else emerged.

Logan chuckled and I whipped around, brandishing my tiny stick. "What's so funny?"

"There's nothing there. Now sit down and get comfortable," he said, the little smirk I'd always found irritating spread across his face.

"And what makes you so sure?" I narrowed my eyes at him and he laughed.

"Only humans refuse to recognize a predator among them, princess," he replied, his smirk turning into a full smile.

I knew a pair of fangs hid among those pearly whites. I'd seen them twice, but today he was just Logan. My friend and somehow bonded-partner-thing that I still didn't understand. I crossed my ankles and sat down, folding my legs in front of me. He turned his back to me and continued staring at the three black sedans parked in the front of the building below.

His white t-shirt stretched across his shoulders and tucked into his khaki cargo pants. His lean, muscular build matched his easy-going and patient attitude. It was hard to believe he was a vampire. I'd always assumed they were heartless beings incapable of any emotions, but Logan had proved me wrong. Still, he reminded me frequently that most other vampires were *exactly* what I believed. He tried to pound it into my head that everything they did was for their own selfish ends. They were incapable of compassion, and loyalty was born of the commitment they received in return. It had nothing to do with honor, love, or friendship.

Interacting with Logan on a daily basis made it hard to believe.

In the last few days, I'd tried many times to discover why he was different but couldn't get an answer from him. Rather than tell me he didn't know, which I knew was a lie, he changed the subject. That tactic would only work for so long. It pissed me off more than anything else and cemented my determination to find an answer. I thought he would know that and just give in, but apparently not.

The muscles across Logan's shoulders tensed, pulling the fabric tight, and an uneasy feeling seeped through our bond. I squinted down at the building. Several men dressed in black suits emerged from a side door and wasted no time getting into the waiting vehicles. Two people remained at the entrance, but I couldn't identify them from our hiding spot. I assumed one would be Jonathan, though.

"Don't move," Logan murmured.

The tension in his voice silenced my sarcastic remark. Billows of sand and dust rose behind the three vehicles as they raced towards the canyon's exit. I leaned forward to watch them go.

"I said don't move," Logan hissed, his body completely motionless in that way only vampires could achieve. "They'll be looking for any sign of surveillance and I have no desire to be a target."

My body froze, half leaning forward. "Who are they?"

"Braden, a member of the council, and his entourage," he replied. Of course, he could see them with his super-vampire-sight. But that meant they could see us, too.

"Why would he meet with Jonathan?" I asked, almost afraid of the answer.

Logan didn't reply as we watched the clouds of dust disappear.

"Can I move now?"

"Yes." He took a step backwards and sat down next to me, folding his long legs beneath him.

"Does Jonathan know I'm with you?" I asked, hearing my voice quiver. The vampires had to be looking for us. They couldn't be happy about the Magister's fate. Her death took away the vampires' access to more mages.

"No," Logan replied, still focused on the building below. The two people at the door disappeared inside and he turned to me. "He doesn't know I'm coming either, which isn't unusual. I don't have the typical nine to five job."

"No, I suppose not." I picked at a loose thread on my jeans, thinking before my next question. Logan had been working with Jonathan for decades, and I didn't want to push him away by accusing his employer of selling him out. "Can we trust Jonathan?"

A long sigh drew my attention to my vampire. I thought of him as mine because our lives were tied together. If one of us died, so would the other. I was also denying an attraction to him. Okay, not really.

"I thought I could, at least with some things," he replied, pulling his ball cap from his head. The long black hair on the crown of his head fell across his face. He ran his fingers through it, pulling it back into a loose ponytail before replacing the cap. "I thought we were on the same side when it came to the mage-vampires."

I frowned remembering my first conversation with Jonathan. "He told Kellen and I that he had a small group of vampires on his side."

"When?"

"Just after our fight at Victor's," I replied. "Jonathan was waiting for us at Kellen's. He said he had the European mages, several groups of shifters, and a small group of vampires allied with him." I forced myself to maintain eye contact with Logan as I remembered the rest of the conversation. I wasn't ready to share the part about Kellen's mother and the Europeans' assumption that Kellen and I were more than just partners. "I'd assumed Kellen told you."

Logan's eyebrows rose for a second then narrowed and met in the middle. "It's possible Jonathan meant the mage-vampires we'd been recruiting." He pulled his gaze from me and looked down at the metal warehouse. "But, I'm not sure."

"Did you really not know about his visit?" I asked.

"No, neither of them told me, even though there were plenty of opportunities in the two weeks that followed."

The old 'Kellen' ploy. Tell only part of the story and leave the rest for later. Maybe. In my partner's defense, though, my vampire had never told us about his working relationship with Jonathan Smith. Kellen had even asked Logan if he knew Mr. Smith, and he'd sat right there in the kitchen and evaded the question without anyone noticing.

But Logan saved me from the goons Kellen sent after me. There was that.

"We should be at full strength before going in there," I said, thinking of my weakened vampire.

"As much as I don't appreciate you pointing out my weakness, I have to agree." He turned back to me and his hazel eyes shifted colors with his mood. "We'll wait until dark, then make a decision."

"Why can't we go back to your place?" I asked, thinking of food, water, and a cool shower.

"It would take nearly an hour in my exhausted state," he replied, lying back and lacing his fingers behind his head. "And I'd have to carry you all the way back. It's only two hours from sunset. I'd rather wait."

He closed his eyes and that irritating smirk played at his lips. It didn't take us an hour to get to Jonathan's. It was more like thirty-five minutes. He knew I would feel the lie and said it anyway. But he had a point; he was tired and he would have to carry me. A four-hour walk for me turned into a thirty-minute run for him.

Stupid vampire.

Two hours was a really long time to sit and do nothing. I didn't even have a cell phone to distract me, and I wasn't tired. I laid back and mimicked his pose, lacing my fingers behind my head. The reddish-brown striations on the underside of the rock ledge were interesting. Not. What the hell was I going to do until sunset?

I rolled to my side, cradling my head on my arm, and stared at Logan's profile. His forehead wasn't long or short, but just the perfect length between his hair line and thick brows. His nose had a slight bump right between his eyes before smoothing out as it pointed towards his lips. His long, dark lashes brushed against the pale skin beneath his eyes. I wished I had eyelashes like that, but no. I was stuck with barely-there lashes that no one could see because of my white hair.

Three diamond studs pierced the top of his left ear, which was now partially covered by his hair. When we'd first met, he embraced a true gothic appearance, but I noticed it fading a little more every day. He no longer wore cut up black jeans and black t-shirts. While the top of his hair was still really long, the sides were no longer shaved. Was he growing it out for a reason? It would make sense for him to change his appearance. I wasn't the only one on the vampire council's hit list.

"You realize it's impossible to sleep with you staring at me," Logan said, not opening his eyes.

"Do you realize I've never seen you sleep?" I countered. "I'm always out before you and you're always awake long before me."

He peered at me through his eyelashes, then rolled to his side and cradled his head in his palm. "Most people don't need ten hours of sleep." He didn't even try to suppress that insufferable smirk of his.

"Neither do I," I huffed.

"Sure you don't." He brushed a strand of hair away from his face with his free hand. "Come on, let's go." He rolled out from beneath our rock and stood, extending his hand to me.

"What happened to waiting for dark?" I asked, crawling out after him. How did he do it so gracefully?

"You're obviously not tired and can't entertain yourself while I sleep." He pulled me to my feet then scooped me up like a sack of dogfood. "Let's just get this over with."

The desert flew by as we raced down the hill to an uncertain welcome.

Logan stopped just short of a narrow door on the back side of the metal building we'd been surveying and lowered me to my feet. Before his hand reached the shiny knob, the door swung open.

"Logan." A tall woman with dark blond hair slid out the narrow opening, closing the door behind her.

"Elaine," my vampire responded with a nod.

"You cannot be here." She glanced at me. "And neither can she. Take this and meet me at the blue house in twenty-four hours."

I stared at the smartphone she forced into Logan's palm. Fear raced down my spine.

"I had better not recognize either of you," she said, opening the door and disappearing into the dark interior. It closed silently behind her.

"Well, shit," Logan whispered.

"I guess we should've called first," I said, "or waited for an invite."

Logan leaned against the building and pulled his hat from his head. "Yeah, that's a long run for nothing."

The phone in his hand vibrated, and he flipped it over, revealing a single-worded text: "Leave."

"Wow. And here I thought they were allies," I whispered. "Is that phone safe?"

"We're endangering them by being here, but Elaine wouldn't return the favor by giving me a trackable phone," he said, extending his arm out to me. "I need to get a better form of transportation."

"I'm sorry," I mumbled, suddenly feeling guilty about making him carry me all the way back. "If I had two pennies to my name, I'd buy a car."

He grunted and flipped me up on his back. I wrapped my legs around his waist and arms around his neck. As we raced back across the desert, my mind whirled with 'what ifs' and 'Holy shit what do we do now?'

Chapter 2

As soon as we arrived back at Logan's house, he collapsed on the sofa in his sparse living room. Guilt churned in my gut. I'd become a physical, mental, and financial burden to him. He didn't need to buy food before I arrived and only needed a car for long road trips. I assumed he rented one or maybe borrowed one of Jonathan's. Carrying me around in public wouldn't be an option for either of us. I needed to find a way to contribute or leave. I couldn't expect him to completely change his life for me.

I kneeled at the side of the sofa and unlaced his boots, then pulled them from his feet. My efforts to lift his legs onto the couch resulted in several grunts from me and a growl from him.

"Don't pamper me, woman," he mumbled, rolling over and pulling his legs onto the cushion.

"Whatever."

Stupid men, even as vampires. I stood and looked around the small room containing only the sofa and a round dining room table with two wooden chairs. A meager kitchen filled the opposite corner, with only the bare necessities in the cupboards. Logan's place wasn't really a house. It was one of those completely off-the-grid homes. The previous owner blasted a hole in the side of a cliff and filled it with furniture. He did a pretty good job of framing out the exterior door, but the only windows were in the front, which limited air flow. It also lacked heat, which left the stone rooms cold.

The only thing good about the place was its water source. I was pretty sure the guy stumbled on it by accident. A natural spring flowed from the rock at the back of the cavern, supplying a commodity that everyone else had to have delivered. I wasn't sure if Logan or the other guy installed the solar panels, but I was grateful for them regardless. Cold showers sucked.

I made my way to the only bedroom, which also housed Logan's library. Bookcases covered three of the four walls, all of them filled with books. I perused the titles, looking for something about the different supernatural families. I knew about the mages because I was one. Victor's clan introduced me to wolf shifters. Then there were the vampires. *Maybe that's where I should start.*

My new connection to Logan made little sense to me. He'd told me as much as he knew, but parts of it still left me in the dark. Apparently, certain elements had to be in place for a bond to be created.

Exchanging blood. Check.

Having sex. Check.

Pre-existing affection for each other. Check?

It was there, but where the hell did it come from? I wasn't attracted to Logan before all that, was I? He was funny and polite, but his vampire side terrified me. Something else was missing, but I still didn't know what.

The vampire bond must have been nearly non-existent if it required the vampire to actually care about the person he or she bonded. Or they just didn't want it to be widely known so they came up with a ridiculous requirement that only the most ignorant would believe. I might as well throw myself into that group of stupid, because I believed. How could I not?

I stared at the shelves in front of me, not really seeing them as my thoughts wandered back to Mr. Smith's compound. Which one of the council members had been there? Logan said his name was Braden, but which one was he? I remembered each of them from my interrogation at the hotel after they kidnapped me, and they were all terrifying, even the one sitting off to the side who appeared disinterested in the entire affair. Maybe he scared me the most. The others wore their hatred and disgust openly, but that one hid his true feelings. I shivered involuntarily. I'd have to ask Logan which one was looking for us.

I reached for a book on the history of Transylvania, my hand stopping on the thick leather spine. In the meeting with Kellen and Jonathan a week ago, Jonathan had said he had a small group of vampires on his side. Could he have meant one of the council? That's stupid. Council members would only be the most loyal to the vampire cause. But, why would this Braden guy show up at Jonathan's compound to just talk? Unless Jonathan was in league with the vampires and his whole story about wanting to stop them was a bunch of bullshit.

Too many questions and no way to get answers. I wondered if Logan had a computer. My time might be better spent searching for a new hairdo. The tall woman, Elaine, said she better not recognize us, which meant a disguise. At least that was something tangible that I could achieve. Only it wasn't. I didn't have any money, so I'd have to rely on Logan to pay for it.

That needed to change. I'd never been able to do more than keep from starving, but at least I did it on my own. I hated relying on someone else for even my most basic needs. This whole situation sucked beyond belief. Except for Logan's company. That was kind of nice. *Get a grip, stupid.*

I left the book in its place on the shelf and looked around the room. A bed, tall wardrobe, and two low dressers occupied the space. The trunk we took from Kellen's rested on the floor beside the wardrobe. I knew it was empty because I'd unpacked my things and stashed them in one of the dressers. Unless there was a secret desk that pulled out of the bookshelf, there was no place for a computer.

I wandered back into the living room, but I knew there wasn't a computer out there. I'd only been here two days, but the space wasn't big enough to hide anything. The room served as living room, dining room, and kitchen. A stacked washer and dryer took up a corner in the kitchen, so there wasn't even a laundry room.

I turned in a slow circle and ran my fingers through my hair. I couldn't stay cooped up in this small space with nothing to do. Anxiety I hadn't realized I harbored bubbled to the surface. My heart started racing and my breaths broke into short gasps. What the hell? Did I all of a sudden get claustrophobic? That didn't make sense. I'd been here for two days already. But we'd been busy and hadn't stayed inside. And Logan hadn't left me alone, but I wasn't alone right now.

I looked over at his long body stretched out on the sofa. He'd rolled over again, now lying on his back with one arm thrown over his head. My anxiety settled just a little, making me frown. I did not need a man to keep me calm. I'd lived without them my whole life, but here I was walking across the room and standing over him.

I shook my head and kicked off my shoes, then crawled into the tiny space next to him. He moaned and I poked his ribs, forcing him to scoot over. He wrapped his arm around me and I nestled my head just beneath his collar bone.

"Are you comfortable yet?" he mumbled.

"Yep, thanks."

I pressed my hand against his chest and sighed. All my anxiety seeped away. Well damn. I hated that I depended on him and I really needed to work on being away. I shouldn't need him by my side in order to function. This was stupid.

I sighed again and drank in Logan's delicious spearmint. Really stupid.

Chapter 3

I woke up in exactly the same place I fell asleep. My neck ached, and the arm I'd been laying on was completely numb.

"Well, shit," I muttered, pushing against Logan's chest and sitting up on the edge of the sofa. My fingers refused to move and tingles rushed up and down my arm. "Oh, that hurts."

My vampire pulled me back against him and wrapped his hands around my arm, massaging it with his long fingers.

"I wondered how long you would sleep," he said, rubbing life back into my blood-starved arm.

"What time is it?" I mumbled.

"Two in the morning," he replied, releasing my arm and wrapping his hands around my waist.

I leaned against him trying not to enjoy his warmth against my back. His finger traced a circle around my belly button, igniting desires I didn't want to feel. Yeah, right.

"Any ideas for disguises?" I asked, lacing my fingers in his in a futile attempt to put out the fire.

"Of course," he replied. "I have a friend who can take care of everything, but I need to find out how soon she can meet us." He pushed his hands lower, deftly releasing the button on my jeans with his long fingers.

"Logan," I whispered. "We shouldn't keep doing this." I tightened my grip on his hands, but it was useless.

"Doing what?" he asked, his voice dropping in volume as his hands continued their path.

I wanted him and he knew it. His coy little question didn't fool me. My traitorous hips rose to meet his fingers and I moaned. We couldn't keep doing this. Every time we had sex, my need to be near him deepened. He had to feel it as well, didn't he?

"I gotta pee," I said, wriggling out of his grasp and falling off the sofa.

He chuckled as I raced towards the only bathroom. I would've hit him if I thought it'd do any good. But it wouldn't. He might have actually liked it, which didn't ease my frustration. He drove me crazy, both emotionally and sexually.

The bathroom was probably the nicest room in the whole house. The natural spring ran from the wall into a tiled basin. Logan explained the storage container and pump and whatever, but it was really just whatever to me. I understood none of it but appreciated the small beauty in an otherwise plain house.

I leaned against the small cedar counter and stared at my reflection in the mirror. So much had happened to me in the last couple months. There was very little left of the young woman bouncing between jobs and struggling to get one meal a day.

"How did this happen?" I asked myself.

"Beats the hell outta me," my reflection replied.

I shed my clothes and turned on the faucet to the shower. It wasn't really a shower, more like a shower head attached to the stone wall in the corner. There was no enclosure or shower curtain, but the original owner, and now Logan, didn't really have a need for privacy. As soon as the water got hot, I made quick work of getting myself clean.

Wrapped in a towel, I peeked out the bathroom door. The bedroom was empty. A moment of disappointment and longing lingered, but I pushed it aside. That's the perfect example. I shouldn't want him all the time.

A set of clothes were easy to find in my limited wardrobe, and I didn't waste any time putting them on.

"Good, you're ready."

Logan's voice drew my attention as I pulled a tank top over my head. The only thing left to put on were my shoes.

"We need to be in Reno by eight, which gives us just enough time," he continued, pulling his own shirt off and tossing it on the floor.

I tried to ignore him as he continued to undress, focusing on retying my sneakers instead.

"Why are you trying to resist this?" he asked, now standing directly in front of me wearing nothing but his boxer shorts.

Did he seriously have to ask? Was he okay with the growing need for me? Or maybe he didn't feel it the same way I did.

"The growing connection scares me," I mumbled, "and every time we're together it gets stronger. Which has only been twice since we arrived here." I stood and looked up into his eyes. A subtle red ring circled his irises. "Do you not feel it?"

"It's not much different for me now than it was before," he whispered, cupping my face in his hand.

"Well, it's very different for me," I said, leaning against his palm. "I need to slow down and sort this out."

His other hand cradled the other side of my face and his gaze pierced my heart. Was he doing that mind control thing? Something made me move closer to him and it wasn't me.

"Logan, stop," I said, placing my hand on his bare chest. "Either that or explain what you're doing to me."

"I'm doing nothing," he responded, stepping closer. "I feel the same pull you do, but I'm not resisting it."

"Why?"

"Because."

I frowned at him and tried to push away. "Because isn't an answer."

"I know. I have theories, but not answers." His thumb caressed my jaw, sending shivers down my spine. "Do you remember the emblem carved into the Magister's door?"

His sudden change in direction made me blink several times. I thought about the night Kellen and I stood outside her private rooms. It was only a few days ago, but it felt like a lifetime. A large ornate symbol was carved into the wooden surface, spreading across both doors. Symbols for the four elements surrounded a strange, winged something. I still couldn't come up with words to describe it.

"Yes, I remember," I finally answered.

"I believe there are five elements," he said. "I also believe you and I have that elusive one that no one knows about. It's why I was drawn to you the moment I saw you." His hands glided down my neck to my shoulders. "As a vampire, I should not have compassion or love. All of that should've died with me. But something keeps it tied to my soul that also shouldn't be here."

What was he trying to say? That a secret element hid among us? Did Niyol and Göksu know? Would they tell me? I was definitely asking as soon as I could.

"And you think this secret elemental is what ties us together?" I asked.

"You don't believe that stupid explanation about vampires having feelings for the one they bite, do you?"

His crooked smile made me blush. Of course I believed it, sort of.

"I couldn't think of anything else that made sense," I replied, putting more space between us. "Your feelings are very real."

"Yes, they are." His hands dropped to his sides and a flicker of disappointed washed over me.

"Damn," I muttered. "I'm not rejecting you. Please, don't ever think that. I just need time."

"I know." He turned away with slumped shoulders and disappeared into the bathroom.

"Well, shit."

I leaned over and tied my other shoe. The idea of another elemental seemed foreign and unbelievable, but my entire life fell into the witch's brew last month. Maybe it wasn't so farfetched.

"Niyol?"

Yes, princess? his voice echoed in my head, but he didn't reveal himself.

"Is there another elemental besides the four I know?"

A gentle breeze caressed my face moments before my air elemental appeared. His almost humanoid form always amazed me. It flickered each time he moved, and I marveled at the way he glided rather than walked.

"There are some things I cannot speak about, even to you," he replied, his transparent form drifting to my right towards the bookcase. "The world holds many secrets that are best left shrouded from all the species."

"So there is," I stated, joining him in front of the wall of history books.

He chuckled, his whole body fading with the movement. "I will not confirm your suspicions."

"But you didn't deny them either," I pointed out. "Is that why Logan still has his soul."

He leaned over until his face was inches from mine. "Don't run from him, princess. No matter what that stubborn brother of mine tells you."

The bathroom door opened and my elemental disappeared. Logan waltzed into the room with a towel wrapped around his waist. Water dripped from his still-wet hair and several drops rolled down his chest. The desire I'd tamped out earlier flared once again.

"I'll be in the living room," I said, trying not to run from my raging emotions and completely failing. Hadn't Niyol just told me not to? So why didn't I listen? Because I allowed myself to be lured into Kellen's trap and I wasn't keen on falling for it again. Which wasn't really fair to Logan. Kellen had lied to me and manipulated me. He never pushed himself on me romantically or sexually, he'd always just hinted at having more later. Logan didn't hide his need for me.

I plopped down on the sofa and cradled my head in my hands. I needed something to occupy my mind. Thinking about my confused emotions all the time made me grumpy and hungry. Coffee would be great.

Logan emerged from the bedroom a few minutes later fully clothed. I gawked at the blue jeans and gray button-down shirt. He'd pulled his long hair back into a ponytail and his earrings were gone.

"Close your mouth, princess," he mumbled, heading for the door. "It's not nice to stare."

I snapped my mouth closed and smiled. "You clean up nicely," I said. "I feel slightly underdressed."

"It's Marissa's fault. She told me to dress in something not gothic."

I rose from the sofa and followed him into the night.

"You don't mean Marissa, as in wolf-shifter Marissa, do you?" I asked. She was the only one I knew, but it wasn't an uncommon name.

"Yes." He knelt and held out his hand, motioning for me to get on his back.

"We are running all the way to Reno?"

"No, only to the car," he replied, then sped off into the dark.

Thank goodness. But that only gave me time to think about how Marissa was involved. I'd grown to like her during my short stay at Victor's, and her girls were great. Letting them put blue tips on my white hair a couple weeks ago made me long for a sister I'd never have. Surely she wasn't part of Jonathan's group. She had a family at Victor's lodge, and Jonathan's crew were supposed to be outcasts. It was too much to think about, and I had a feeling everything was about to get even more confusing.

I slid off Logan's back a few minutes later and squinted at the dilapidated building looming in front of us. It looked like an old auto repair shop, emphasis on 'old.'

"How is this place still standing?" I asked.

"It's deliberate," Logan replied, inserting a key into a sturdy lock on the metal door. It swung open on silent hinges. "The metal siding was confiscated from buildings scheduled to be demolished, but it's just an outer skin. The real siding beneath is fairly new and in excellent condition."

I stopped just inside the door and he pushed it shut behind me, then flipped on the lights. My jaw dropped again. This man was full of surprises. A shiny, black Mustang occupied the center bay. Right next to it was a charcoal gray Ford Explorer. A long workbench covered the back wall with rows of tools, boxes and what I assumed were parts for the vehicles.

Logan's chuckle brought me out of my stupor. "I'm shocked," I said.

"Clearly."

"You're not worried about this being discovered?" I asked, running my hand along the Mustang's fender.

"No, not really. The property is pretty far off the main road and the outside of the building looks even worse in broad daylight," he replied, opening one of the many drawers beneath the workbench. "I also paid Kellen's engineer to install similar safety measures over the garage doors as he used on the estate. Without windows, it'd be pretty hard for someone to break in."

"Wow. So we're taking the Mustang?" I really hoped we were. I knew next to nothing about cars, but even I recognized a Mustang. My foster father always talked about having more than his 1982 Ford Escort. Maybe he finally got one after he and my foster mom left me.

"No." He dangled a set of keys from his fingers and smiled. "It's too flashy."

I didn't hide my pout as he made his way towards the SUV. He opened the passenger door for me, still smiling.

"I promise to take you out in the Mustang," he said, stepping in front of me at the last second and wrapping his free arm around my waist.

He leaned into me, his lips stopping inches from mine. He was giving me the option to back away. Damnit. I closed the distance between us and ran my fingers along his chest. His kiss was just like always, passionate and unchecked. He might have hidden the Mustang from me, but his emotions were on full display.

"Any more surprises today?" I asked, breaking away from him with effort.

"Yes," he replied, that irritating smirk spreading across his face.

He pushed me into my seat and closed the door. He wasn't getting away with that short answer. Kellen constantly did that to me, creating a trust barrier I wasn't sure we could break down. Like we'd ever get past the fact that he tried to have me killed.

Logan hopped in the driver's side and turned to me before I could speak. "We'll talk about it on our way to Reno."

The SUV's engine rumbled to life, then the garage door in front of us rolled up, followed by the exterior door. He wasn't kidding about having something similar to Kellen's estate.

Once we were on the road, his headlights broke through the darkness. "I know you have a hundred or more questions, princess, but let's start with tonight's meeting." He paused and glanced over at me, but I couldn't see his expression in the dark. Wouldn't it be great to have his night vision?

"Okay," I said, when he didn't continue. "Can I ask questions as we go?"

"Like I can stop you," he replied. I imagined that stupid grin on his face and smiled. "Elaine, the woman who met us at the door, is Jonathan's second in command. She's been with him for a long time, longer than I have."

"Wow! She doesn't look that old," I said, interrupting him.

"She's a shifter. Their constantly healing bodies slow their aging. I trust her more than I do Jonathan, which is why I don't hesitate to meet with her." He tapped his fingers on the steering wheel as a car passed us. "I'm part of a four-person team. Two of the other three, I trust implicitly. The last one is a new addition and has yet to prove herself."

I noticed a slight hitch in his voice and hoped he would elaborate. If not, I'd tuck that question away for later.

"Otto joined Jonathan just after I did. He's also a mage-vampire, but his humanity is gone. Though, I believe he still harbors some hope of regaining his earth elemental. Apparently, their connection was strong and the pain of separation hasn't diminished for him. Now that I know it's equally painful for the element..." He paused again, and I wished I could see his expression. "Anyway, he is the unofficial leader of our team. Yun is a shifter and our scout. She's very outgoing and boisterous for her size." He looked over at me again. "As a matter of fact, she might be smaller than you. She frequently picks up the role of a child, who most people ignore. It works well for us."

"And the last one?"

He sighed and I suspected he actually disliked the newest member.

"Fiona is also a mage-vampire. We rescued her two years ago, so she's still very much a baby who struggles to control her basic needs. She has no humanity left, not even a desire to reconnect with her element." His right hand slid off the steering wheel. "I need to talk to Otto. I don't want her anywhere near you."

"You think she'll bite me?" I asked, trying not let my fear surface.

"Jonathan's group works because there are no humans in it," he replied. "Vampires cannot feed off shifters."

"Oh. And Fiona will be furious if she's moved to another group because of me." It wasn't hard to make the connection.

"Furious doesn't begin to describe it," Logan mumbled. "I'm quite certain she'll do everything in her power to keep from being transferred. She still seems to think she can manipulate Jonathan, and for some reason, he allows her to keep that misconception."

His disgust floated through our bond. Was it for the woman or Jonathan's lack of discipline with her? Maybe both.

"I'm sorry. Is there any way to avoid her for now?"

"That's my plan, unless Elaine changes it for us," he replied. "And don't be sorry. I will always prefer your company over hers."

A flurry of emotions assaulted me too quickly to sort, then they were gone again. Did he feel mine the same way? Did I want to know if he experienced all my indecision? Nope, not really.

I leaned my forehead against the window. I knew nothing about Logan's world, but I had a feeling I was about to be thrown into it head first. As if the last month wasn't hard enough. Going from being a nobody to overthrowing the leader of the North American mages tore my life apart. As much as I hated my life before, at least I hadn't been worried about being hunted by vampires. I closed my eyes, enjoying the cool glass on my aching forehead. It hurt to think about the things I didn't know were coming.

Chapter 4

I shouldn't have been surprised by Logan's hand on my thigh and his soft voice in my ear. I'd fallen asleep in the car, as usual. Apparently I couldn't stay awake in a moving vehicle. I hated the 'sleep button' that seemed to sprout from my ass every time I got in the car. I never had that problem until I met Kellen and dove head first into this insanity.

"Come on, princess. Let's get you some breakfast and coffee."

Logan squeezed my thigh, his fingers wrapping halfway around my skinny leg. I'd managed to gain a little muscle during my two weeks of training, but not much.

"That sounds great," I mumbled. "Which reminds me. I need to get a job. It's not fair that you have to pay for food you'll never eat." I didn't want to mention the clothes he bought me or the roof over my head.

"I don't mind," he said, waving a hand at me as we pulled into a fast food restaurant. "It feels good to be a little normal."

"Regardless, if I'm going to stay with you, I need to contribute my half," I said, waving back at him. "I refuse to be a freeloader."

He chuckled and turned off the engine. "My house is paid for. So are the cars and garage. The only thing I spend money on is traveling and now food for you. I think I can afford it." He hopped out and made his way around to my side, but I opened the door before he could and slid from the seat. "You can let me be a gentleman."

"I could, but you don't need to be subjected to the morning sun any longer than necessary," I countered, crossing the parking lot.

Once inside one of my favorite two-thousand-calories-a-meal joints, I ordered a sausage biscuit, hash browns, and coffee, then grudgingly watched as Logan paid for it. It really shouldn't bother me, but it did.

"I'm going to the ladies' room," I said as the cashier handed over his change.

"Make it quick."

I pushed open the door to the ladies' bathroom and froze. Memories of the bear I encountered in the last fast food restaurant were still fresh in my mind. Her hungry stare and aggressive stance once again made my skin break out in a cold sweat. Last time, I was supposed to be shopping with Kellen and ended up fighting with Victor. This time, I'd probably end up fighting with a vampire.

Great.

I hugged myself and shook off my fear, letting out the breath I'd been holding. The stalls were empty and the bathroom was nothing like the other one, mostly because this one was clean. I took care of business in record time anyway.

Logan met me at the restaurant's exit a few minutes later and handed me a small bag of food and a large coffee.

"Thank you," I said, letting him push open the door for me. "Where are we meeting Marissa?"

"You'll see," he replied as we crossed the parking lot. "We should be there in the next five minutes." He opened the passenger door and held my coffee while I climbed in.

Less than five minutes later, we turned into a pricey neighborhood. I tried to eat my breakfast instead of gawking at the two-story homes on large lots lining the streets with their well-manicured landscaping.

"Wow," I said, swallowing a bite of hash brown. "Should I ask who owns the house?"

"Jonathan," Logan replied. "It's one of many."

He pulled into the driveway of a large Victorian style home covered in brown stone and white trim. Not a blue house as the code name implied. The garage door on the right automatically opened, and Logan guided the SUV in. Before it closed, the one on the left rolled up and a bright red motorcycle glided in beside us. It was much quieter than I expected. I could barely hear it over the SUV's engine.

I hopped out, not waiting for Logan, and rushed to the motorbike. Marissa pulled off her helmet, revealing the hot pink hair I'd grown to love.

"AJ!" she called out, setting her helmet on the leather seat and pulling me into a crushing hug. "Logan didn't tell me you were coming with him." She loosened her grip but didn't let go, holding me out at arm's length. "If both of you need a makeover, I need to change my strategy. My girls will be disappointed that I'm covering their work of art." Her gaze drifted from me to Logan and changed to a scowl. "You should've told me."

"You know I couldn't," Logan said, making his way to the door leading into the house.

She huffed, then winked at me. I didn't realize how much I missed her winks and her smile. "At least he didn't wear all black," she whispered. "It gives me ideas." A wide grin spread across her face. "A really good idea."

I almost felt bad for Logan as we followed him into the house, secretly hoping we weren't coming out of this with fluorescent hair. Last time was fun, and I liked my blue tips, but I suspected we needed something to help us blend in, not stand out.

I tried not to ogle the salon we walked into. I'd expected a mudroom, washroom, or even a short hall leading into the magnificent home, not the elaborate hair salon in front of me. The room was easily the size of Logan's house. Four salon chairs graced one side, with two washing stations on the other. Several stainless-steel shelving units carried every hair product imaginable.

"Take a seat," Marissa said, waving her hand at us. "You're lucky I adjust so easily, Logan. Or maybe not. You won't like what I have planned for you, but I think AJ will." She turned her back to us and started gathering boxes and bottles in her arms. I had no idea what any of it was.

I sat in the nearest chair and swiveled around to face Logan. His deep frown and drawn eyebrows contrasted his flushed cheeks, making me smile. I didn't realize vampires could blush.

"Is that anticipation or irritation?" I asked quietly.

He glanced at me and his expression softened. "Her girls get their taste in fashion from their mother. She tries to blame her pink hair on them, but she loves it."

"You will not walk out of here with pink hair," Marissa said, dropping her supplies on the counter between me and Logan. "First, I need to spray AJ with a self-tanner. While it's drying, Logan will lose the long locks." She pulled the elastic band from his hair with a smile. "Any last words?"

"You're evil," Logan muttered.

I suppressed my grin. Was he really that attached to his current look? He seemed to be easing out of the all black wardrobe without any dramatics.

"Yeah, yeah, whatever," Marissa continued. "I think Logan will get dark brown, so it isn't immediately obvious when it starts to grow out." She turned to me with a mischievous grin. "You're getting a dark blonde, but rather than spiking it, we're curling it."

I wasn't sure how to feel about that, but since I'd never had any style to begin with, I couldn't knock it.

"Come on, let's get you naked and tanned," Marissa said, digging through the dozens of bottles on the counter.

I looked past her and met Logan's gaze. He shook his head and closed his eyes, but not before I saw the red ring blooming around the edges. I wanted to ask if he was okay, but I didn't want to draw attention. So I kept quiet.

"Here it is," Marissa quipped. "The lightest color we have. I'll try to keep it off Logan's truck."

My vampire's eyes snapped open, thankfully back to their normal color. Was it desire that prompted the change? Or did he need to eat? I slid off my chair and followed Marissa back into the garage. He hadn't left me in three days, which meant he hadn't eaten. How long could he go without?

Marissa positioned me in the far corner away from the vehicles and had me strip down to my bra and panties.

"I contemplated dressing you up as a boy, but I have a better idea," she said, shaking the can of spray on sunshine. "Lift up your arms."

I did as she asked and she went to work.

"You two will be a couple from very wealthy families. You'll need a new wardrobe, but I hear you needed that anyway." She moved around behind me and I frowned.

"I can't afford new clothes," I argued. "My bank account was empty when this whole thing started and I've done nothing to replenish it."

"There's no need to worry about that," she said, shaking the can again. "Logan'll need a new wardrobe too, so you can shop together. I'm giving you the name of someone who will take care of everything."

I sighed and let my arms droop. I didn't want to owe him anymore. Marissa stopped spraying and moved around in front of me.

"Don't do that," she ordered, putting her hands on her hips. "Kellen and Logan threw your life into chaos. The least they can do is buy you new clothes. They owe you, not the other way around."

Tears misted my eyes and I quickly blinked them away. I really needed a woman in my life. No one could put it all in perspective like a good friend. My thoughts wandered to Sharon, my only friend in school. She stood by me when everyone else pushed me away and didn't abandon me when we graduated. I missed her. Today's situation only reinforced all the reasons I couldn't go back, but it didn't stop me from thinking about her.

"Thank you," I mumbled. "I needed that."

"Raise your arms back up before they smudge." She smiled and leaned over to spray my legs and feet. "Kellen told everyone you were part of a secret group looking for the mages turned vampire. I assumed Logan was as well, but it's nice to confirm it."

"Yeah, I still can't wrap my head around it." I raised my arms, which were already getting tired. It was also good to confirm that Kellen hadn't sold me out. Logan was confident that whatever threat he left for my partner would keep him quiet, but I had doubts. Lots of them. I didn't think Kellen needed me anymore, so why wouldn't he make me the bad guy, or gal?

"This is going to sound stupid, because I saw you interact with your elementals, but do they really talk to you all the time?" Marissa asked, not looking up from her kneeling position.

"Yes."

She moved around the back again. "You'll be the one to bring us out of this mess, just like I always said you would."

What made her so sure? I certainly didn't have that same confidence.

Chapter 5

Three hours later, Logan and I stared at one another in the long mirror. If I saw him on the street, I wouldn't recognize him. His long black hair was now short and brown, reminding me of coffee. He refused to let Marissa wax his thick eyebrows, but she won the fight with his wardrobe. She made him roll his sleeves and unbutton his shirt, leaving it hanging open to expose the white t-shirt beneath. He looked so…preppy.

"You need colored t-shirts and more of these," she said pulling on the hem of his dress shirt. "Here's the name of the man you need to see about your wardrobe and AJ's. If you don't see him, you'll ruin everything I've done."

Logan raised an eyebrow at me in the mirror, taking the scrap of paper from Marissa. My own reflection was startling. The soft, blond curls on top of my head were pretty. Not cute like a child, but pretty. My fake tan was so light, I would never call it tan, but it was perfect. The most noticeable change were the amber eyes staring back at me. Marissa insisted on the color contacts, and she was probably right. After all, my icy blue orbs gave away my heritage. Besides the discomfort from the contacts, I didn't mind. My eyes and platinum white hair reminded everyone of my mother, something I wanted to avoid.

"You need to let your hair grow," Marissa said, swinging my chair away from the mirror. "It will give us more options in the future." Then, she pulled me into a quick hug. "And remember you have makeup on. Don't touch your face."

"I'll never be able to do this on my own," I complained. "Makeup is beyond my skills."

She handed me a shopping bag full of powders, creams, eyeliners, and lip sticks. "You only have to do it if you're going out in public."

"No kidding." I took the offered bag and frowned.

"Quit complaining and go shopping. And look up some tutorials online if you really need that much help."

I slid out of my chair and turned to Logan's, but he was already gone. The door to the garage stood open, waiting for me.

"He's so touchy," Marissa whispered. "But he's a good person. He'll take care of you."

"Thanks, for everything." I gave her one last hug before leaving her salon—and our old identities—behind.

~~~~~~~~~~~~~

Logan backed the SUV out of the garage and went the opposite direction we arrived from. The rings around his eyes swelled the farther we got away from Marissa. It impressed me that he could hide it when he had to and worried me that he didn't now.

"We can pick up our wardrobe tomorrow, Logan," I said. "I think you have other things that take priority."

"No, Marissa's right."

"And you think it's a good idea to go into the mall with all those warm bodies?" I argued, watching the hazel in his eyes disappear.

"No, I do not," he hissed, then drew a deep breath. "This isn't normal for me. I should be able to go a week or longer. It's only been three days."

"Because of me," I whispered, trying to squash my guilt. It had to be because of our connection. That was the only thing that had changed.

He pulled into a convenience store parking lot and parked at the back of the building.

"This is not your fault," he said, turning in his seat to face me. The intensity in his red eyes made me shiver.

"So, you drop me off with Marissa's guy," I offered. "While he's picking out my new wardrobe, you can do your thing." I tried not to cringe at the thought of him biting someone, then cringed again when I realized I didn't *want* him biting anyone. Shit. It's not like he could deny what he was.

"I can't leave you alone, AJ," he said, surprising me. He always called me princess.

"Of course you can. Marissa did a great job. No one will recognize me." I waved my hands at my face, but they instantly fell. His pained expression tugged at my heart.

"Fine."

He turned away from me and backed out of the parking spot. Ten minutes later, we pulled into the mall parking lot. I let him open my door and take my hand to help me out. Why was I being so nice about it? I didn't know, just like I didn't know why I felt guilty. I shouldn't. It wasn't my fault he was a vampire, but it wasn't his, either. It was just another reminder that I wasn't the only one with no control over my life, and that we could only do our best given the circumstances. And for Logan, that meant drinking someone's blood.

It only took a few minutes to find Manny, the guy who would solve my wardrobe issues, in one of the large specialty stores. He wore khaki pants and a pink pullover shirt, with brown loafers on his bare feet. His spikey blond hair looked similar to my previous style, bringing a smile to my lips.

"Welcome!" he said, wrapping me in a hug. He stepped towards Logan, then backed away. "He's a little scary."

"He's just possessive," I said, as if that explained everything. It wasn't a total lie.

Manny chuckled. "No need for that. I'm in a very happy relationship. Let's see what our friend Marissa has planned." He pulled out his smartphone and scrolled through what I assumed were Marissa's instructions. "Oh yes! This is perfect." He stuffed his phone back in his pocket and rubbed his hands together. "Who's first?"

"Me," I replied, glancing up at Logan. He did a remarkable job maintaining an impassive expression. The dark ring around his irises was barely noticeable. "I'll be here waiting," I said, brushing my fingers against his.

He didn't reply as he walked away into the rows of clothes racks. I had the irrational desire to go after him but knew I couldn't. I didn't want to witness what was about to happen and I was pretty sure he didn't want me to see it. I shook my head.

"Wow, you got it bad, girl." Manny's comment surprised me.

"What do you mean?" I asked, allowing him to lead me into another section of the store.

"You looked like a lost puppy watching him walk away."

"No I didn't," I insisted, though I knew he was right. This supernatural world was still so new to me, and I didn't feel safe on my own. I was a lost puppy without Logan around to guide me.

"Come on," Manny said, motioning for me to follow him. "Shopping will take your mind off it."

It worked for the first fifteen minutes of trying on one outfit after another, but thirty minutes later, I spent more time searching the faces around me than looking at the dresses Manny waved in front of me. I could feel Logan not far away, but I didn't see him.

"Should we move on to the men's section or wait for the boyfriend?" Manny asked, drawing my attention.

He stood in front of me with a dress draped over his arm and three shirts dangling from their hangers in his hand.

"I'm so sorry," I said. "I love everything you've picked out, and you've been so patient with me, and I've barely been paying attention."

"It's my job, girl," he said, half smiling. "Let's go pick out some stuff for the man in your life. I'm assuming he trusts your judgement, or he'd be here himself."

"You just outfitted my wardrobe, Manny. You know I have no fashion sense."

He chuckled and hung the items on the rolling rack with my other garments. "Then shame on him for not sticking around."

As my personal fashion consultant rolled my new wardrobe towards the men's department, I tried to pinpoint my vampire. *He better have a really good reason for hanging this close and not showing himself*, I thought. I was going to be really pissed if he was just avoiding shopping, because I wasn't paying for all this stuff.

We arrived in the casual-yet-professional-man section, and Manny started his pitch about what worked and what didn't. I had no idea if Logan would agree with his color selections or not, so I nodded and smiled. Manny's guess was better than mine.

"All my customers should be as agreeable as you," he said, hanging two shirts on my rolling rack, along with several ties.

"Yes, except if my boyfriend doesn't show up, I won't be leaving with it," I said. "There's no way I can pay for all this."

"It's already paid for."

That made me give him my full attention. "Really?"

"Yep. Marissa didn't tell you?"

"No, she didn't." I needed to find out who paid for all these clothes. It was one thing to have a debt to Logan—we were sort of stuck together—but not anyone else.

"Are you ready to go?" Logan asked, startling me as usual.

Manny turned from the clothes rack and smiled. "Just in time. Would you like to try on any of these items for the lady?"

"No. How long will it take to bag them?" Logan asked.

That was rude. I craned my neck to look at my vampire. His eyes were back to their normal color, but his furrowed brow and severe frown worried me. All of it should have gone away.

"Probably about twenty minutes," Manny replied, applying his own frown.

"I'll take the cart to the car and load them." Logan grabbed the metal rack and started walking to the door.

"I'm sorry, Manny. He isn't normally this cranky," I said, wrapping him in a quick hug.

"It's okay. Women aren't the only ones who suffer from PMS, but don't tell him I said that." He hugged me back and pushed me towards my vampire.

I jogged to catch up with him, reaching him just in time to open the glass doors.

"What the hell was that about?" I hissed.

"Hurry up and get to the car," he replied, not answering my question but still dragging the rack of clothes.

I couldn't believe no one stopped us from walking out with hundreds of dollars' worth of clothing. Maybe Manny took care of it for us. I hoped he did or security would be breathing down our necks any minute.

I helped Logan toss the clothes in the back of his SUV, then climbed in the passenger side. He left the cart in the empty space next to us and jumped in the driver's seat.

"Can you talk now?" I asked, trying not to sound spiteful or worried.

"Someone was following you," he replied, starting the car and turning on the air conditioning. "I have no idea who it was or why."

My eyebrows rose. I hadn't seen anyone following me and I'd been studying every face for the last forty-five minutes, looking for Logan. I guess that excused my vampire's absence and his bad mood. Being tracked by anyone wasn't good for us.

"I didn't notice anyone and I spent a whole lot of time looking for you."

"Yes, I know. You kept him really busy trying not to get caught." He turned to me and gave his full attention. "I need to find another way."

"Another way for what? To get to our meeting with your team?" What was he talking about? "And what happened to the guy following me? Shouldn't we be leaving? Won't he just follow us?"

Logan rubbed his fingers through his now short hair. He huffed and scrubbed his scalp several more times, making his hair stand on end.

"The guy following you is taken care of," he replied, wiping his hands over his face. "We'll take the scenic route to our meeting."

The slightest sense of deception drifted across the space between us. I thought about calling him out on it, but he was already a mess because of me. I couldn't add more to the pile. I almost apologized but decided not to. I didn't know what I was sorry for. Or more accurately which item on the list I was sorry for.

"As soon as we leave Elaine, we need to talk," Logan said, dragging his gaze away from me and pulling out of the parking lot.

I didn't respond to his comment. I didn't know how to, except to ask a ton of questions. I'd wait until our meeting was over. Yeah right.

"Is it something I did?" I asked, unable to stop the first question from tumbling out. "Or maybe something I didn't do?"

Logan didn't answer, nor did he turn to look at me. That sucked. It must be really bad. I ran back through the last couple days trying to remember anything that would make him this anxious, but nothing came to mind. We'd been busy making space for me in his home. Showing me the numerous traps and surveillance surrounding the property took hours. Grocery shopping at the tiny convenience store was pathetic, yet nostalgic.

The only thing that stood out was his lack of food. Did something happen to his chosen victim? Could I even ask that question? No, I didn't think so. Another thought occurred to me. He'd been spending his days awake with me. At Kellen's, Logan had slept most of the day and we trained after dark. Could the change in schedule be messing with his biological clock? It certainly screwed with mine.

We pulled into another shopping center twenty minutes later, if it could be called that. Most of the storefronts were boarded up, and only three looked like they were still in business. A pawn shop took up the left corner of the plaza. A discount tobacco store filled the space next to it. On the far-right corner was a martial arts training studio. A half-dozen minivans and family size sedans covered the parking area in front. I guessed they were having a kids' class.

"What are we doing here?" I asked.

"Meeting the team," Logan answered. "Yun is already inside, but the others aren't here yet."

"We are a little early." The clock on the dash blinked two o'clock. "Aren't we supposed to meet at four?" I squinted at the pawn shop. Was that their secret meeting place? It had to be. I couldn't see a bunch of vampires and shifters mixing in with a kids' martial art class. Unless it was one of the empty stores. That made more sense.

Logan hadn't answered me, so I turned my gaze on him only to find him staring back at me.

"What is it, Logan?"

He opened his mouth and closed it. Twice more he tried to speak, but it ended with him shaking his head.

"You're scaring me," I whispered. "What could be so bad that you can't tell me?" I knew the answer but didn't want to hear it. He killed his blood donor.

"The human who graciously provided what I needed, did not quench my thirst," he said, looking away from me. "I took as much as I dared without making him pass out, but it did nothing."

Relief flooded through me. He hadn't killed him. "Sure it did. Your eyes are back to normal."

"But I'm not satisfied. I'm missing something that my body didn't need before." His eyes shifted to a deep red within seconds. "But I can't ask you for it. I think it's what I want, but…"

Oh shit. He was talking about my blood. My eyebrows rose and fear gripped me, but it was quickly replaced by my memory of his last bite. Desire flooded my core and my face flushed. What the hell was that about? I wasn't a transitioning vampire anymore, and we weren't swapping blood. He would be *taking* mine.

"I'm sorry," he croaked. "I'll find another way. I can't do that to you."

His forehead thumped against the steering wheel and his shoulders rose and fell with each deep breath. Could I give him this? Even if I could, did I want to? If I did, would his craving become worse, like a drug addict? The thought of being his blood donor did weird things to my stomach. The desire rose again, but this time my fear and anxiety pushed it away. Just as quickly, my compassion pushed back. Would it hurt to try? Maybe it wasn't my blood he craved. Maybe he just thought it was because of our connection.

Damn. I was such a pushover. "Maybe we should test it," I started, "just to eliminate all the possibilities."

"No," Logan stated, sitting up and taking my hand in his. "I fear I'm already addicted to you. If I give in, there will be no going back."

"I thought we were already past that point anyway," I mumbled. "My life is tied to yours for eternity. What's a little blood amongst friends?"

"You are a precious gift." He lifted my hand to his lips and kissed it gently. "I'll think about it."

"Well don't think too long. I might chicken out."

"I don't believe you're afraid of anything," he countered with a chuckle.

"Then you haven't been paying attention. Everything scares me," I argued. "I'm just really stupid sometimes and it makes me look brave."

He released my hand and leaned back in his seat. "Thank you for not freaking out. That alone relieved some of my tension."

"You wouldn't leave me if I did freak out, would you?" I asked, putting voice to one of my biggest fears. If he decided to leave, I'd have nowhere to go. I certainly couldn't go back to the palace, and my old life was not an option.

"I could never leave you, AJ," he replied, turning his head to look at me. "Even if you decided to hate me tomorrow, I wouldn't abandon you."

Even though I didn't detect a lie in our bond, I wasn't sure I believed him. He'd convinced himself he would stay by my side, but he could also change his mind. I didn't want to give him a reason to do so.

"We should get back on your normal schedule," I suggested. "Being up all day isn't good for you."

"It's the best time to hide from the council," he said, surprising me. I hadn't thought of that. "Most vampires are too selfish and arrogant to change their schedule. They believe everything should revolve around them. So the likelihood of us meeting them in broad daylight is pretty slim."

"But it's also really hard on you," I argued.

"It's worth it to not have to constantly watch my back." He laced his fingers behind his head and grimaced. "Which is why I'm worried about your admirer at the mall. The council may have hired a human to watch for you."

"In Reno?"

"They're not stupid. They know you won't show up in Vegas," he replied, closing his eyes. "If I were them, I'd have people watching in all the closest cities."

"But we could be in Florida or Maine," I insisted, not really believing that my pursuer was tied to the vampires.

"Or Reno," Logan pressed. "They have the resources, so why not use them?"

"I guess," I replied. "Should we change into one of our new outfits while we wait?"

"Yes, that's probably a good idea," he responded, laying his seat all the way down and crawling towards the back. "Can you change in the car or do we need to find a restroom?"

"I'm good as long as a bunch of people don't start piling out of the studio." I laid my seat down as well and crawled into the back. I dug through the pile of clothes until I found the dress I wanted: a cute, white sundress with large yellow flowers on it. It was bright and sunny, unlike my current situation. It made me smile the minute Manny pulled it from the rack.

After five minutes, and several fights with the front seat, I sported my new outfit. During my distracted shopping spree, I hadn't noticed Manny tossed in several boxes of shoes. I slipped on a pair of white, strappy sandals and smiled. They fit perfectly. How did he do that without me trying on any of them?

I looked over at my vampire as he leaned back and buttoned a pair of tan dress pants, then buckled the leather belt around his waist. He hadn't tucked in the pale yellow t-shirt or the baby blue, long-sleeved dress shirt. It was so 'not' Logan.

"Can you roll this sleeve three times?" he asked, shoving his arm at me.

"Sure," I replied, my smile widening. "You act like you might have done this before."

He turned his gaze on me and frowned. "Some of us were adults in the '80s."

"This outfit does not look like 1980's preppy fashion," I argued, carefully rolling up his sleeve, even though it sort of did. "Did Manny stash shoes in there for you as well?"

Logan's frown deepened as he held up a pair of brown leather loafers. I didn't stop the laugh escaping my lips. "You look amazing," I said. "And no one will recognize you."

When I finished one sleeve, he slipped on his shoes and rolled his other sleeve.

An old truck pulled into the parking area, drawing our attention. "Looks like Elaine is early," Logan said. "Let's see if we can get this meeting over with before the vampires show up."

Chapter 6

Elaine's old truck parked in front of the martial arts studio, shuddering as the engine died. Jonathan needed to pay her more if that was all she could afford for transportation. What a piece of junk. The tall blonde didn't hesitate to get out of the truck and cross the few yards into the studio.

"That's our meeting site?" I asked, not hiding my surprise. "How do we avoid the people already in there?"

"The class ends at two-thirty," Logan replied. "They should be packing up and leaving anytime."

"Oh. The four o'clock meeting time makes more sense now," I said. "That way there's no chance the humans will interact with your team."

Logan remained silent as a gaggle of boys and girls swarmed out of the studio followed by a bunch of adults. Ten minutes later, the only vehicles left were Elaine's truck and us.

"How do you know Yun is here?" I asked just as Logan opened his door.

"She teaches the class," he replied. Within seconds, my door opened and he held out his hand. "If Otto and Fiona show up, do not let them bait you into anything."

I put my hand in his and he pulled me into his chest, wrapping his arms around me. What was that about?

"Especially Fiona," he whispered. "She will do everything she can to get a reaction from you." He loosened the embrace and kissed me just like always, with more compassion than any man should possess. "My heart belongs to you and no one else." He stepped back and gently pulled me from the SUV.

I paused, dumbstruck. Did he just confess his love to me... in a parking lot right before a meeting with a bunch of supernatural creatures? How did I even respond to that? I had no idea, so I remained silent as he pulled me towards the building.

He stopped at the glass door and looked inside without opening it. Elaine sat alone on a bench just inside the door, her focus on something across the room. She glanced at us for a second, then returned her attention to something we couldn't see. I almost giggled as her head snapped back to us and she rose to her feet.

Logan pulled open the door and motioned me to go in first, leaving his hand on the small of my back as he followed me in. Elaine's gaze traveled up and down Logan, then landed on me.

"Well done," Elaine said, the corners of her lips rising as if they wanted to smile, but she wouldn't allow it. "Give Marissa my regards." She reached around Logan and locked the door, then flipped the 'Open' sign over to 'Closed.' "We have a lot to discuss before Otto and Fiona arrive," she said, moving across the large room covered in small foam mats.

It smelled of sweat and pine cleaner, instantly making my stomach churn. Thankfully, we didn't linger, instead passing through another door and a short hallway that ended in a small break room.

A tiny Asian woman sat in one of the six chairs surrounding a round table. Her straight black hair stopped just below her ears and her dark eyes widened at our arrival.

"Logan?" she asked in soft, high-pitched voice as she rose from her seat. "You look so..." Her gaze drifted to me and her small hand went to her mouth. "You're the Magister's daughter, aren't you?"

I nodded, not sure what to say. Logan's fingers found mine, wrapping around them tightly. Was he trying to tell me something? Should I not reveal my identity? I thought he trusted these two women.

"AJ, this is Yun," Logan said, answering for me. "Let's have a seat."

He led me around the table and pulled out a chair. I sat and tried to smile. The tension in the room became thicker with each passing moment as if everyone here was afraid to talk.

Elaine took the chair next to Yun and Logan sat next to me. "Sit down, Yun. We had a visit from Braden yesterday."

"Oh shit," Yun said, dropping into her chair.

I felt Logan tense next to me. That couldn't be good.

"It was a very enlightening conversation," Elaine continued. "The council is looking for AJ, which we already knew. And now their search includes Logan, of course. They're also reforming their army to attack Victor again."

Logan huffed. "That's stupid. Kellen will mobilize the mages to support Victor. Surely Jack knows that."

At the mention of Jack—the leader of the vampire council—I stiffened. I'd met him once, in Vegas, before I'd even learned I was a mage. He hadn't seemed so awful then. Unpleasant? Sure. An asshole? Absolutely. But if he was in charge of this movement to expose the supernatural community, he had to be worse than I thought.

"Yes, but he also plans to eliminate the small contingent of mages still left in Australia first." Elaine's gaze settled on me. "Kellen will divert his resources to save them, leaving Victor at a disadvantage."

"Why would Kellen do that?" Logan asked, also turning to me.

I just stared at Elaine. Did she know about Kellen's family in Australia? Kellen didn't even know until Göksu mentioned it—or at least that's what he'd claimed.

"AJ?" Logan asked, putting his hand on my thigh.

"Kellen's mother's family is in Australia." I continued to stare at Elaine. "But no one knew that, not even Kellen until recently. How did Jack find out?"

"Too many people know too much," Elaine said, glancing between the three of us. "Kellen didn't know to ask, and I'd like to know how he found out."

I narrowed my eyes at her, not feeling the same trust Logan felt. She seemed to know too much, almost implying that Kellen wasn't supposed to find out about his mother's family. Or was she referring to my knowledge of his heritage? "You'll have to ask him," I responded. "Though at this point, it doesn't really matter. Can we convince him that Jack intends to use it against him?"

"Normally, we would ask Logan to intervene," Elaine said, her gaze landing on me again, "but it seems we've lost that asset."

Now I really didn't like her. She'd just accused me of taking away her line of communication. There was a very good reason Logan and I had left Kellen's estate, but I bit my lip trying to hold back the caustic response on my tongue.

"I'll talk to Kellen," Logan intervened, drawing Elaine's attention. "He's pissed at me, but he cares about his people. He'll listen. Do you have a timeline for Jack's plans?"

"No, but he has people in Australia, so it's only a phone call away," Elaine replied. "The attack on Victor's lodge won't happen until they see Kellen's forces leave."

I thought about her comment. It was layered with tons of meaning. Jack still had spies at the palace, otherwise he wouldn't know when the mages left. And there must be a portal to Australia or Kellen's people wouldn't arrive in time.

"Do the mages have a portal to Australia?" I asked. "And do you know who the spies are at the palace?"

Elaine's eyebrows rose, and her lips twitched again as she turned back to me. "She's quick. Yes and no."

"Why is Braden giving us this information?" Logan asked. "What does he gain from helping us?"

"Apparently, he is tasked with finding the princess," Elaine replied, leaning forward and resting her forearms on the table. "What surprised me was his willingness to give up the information before learning of the princess' whereabouts."

A low growl rumbled in Logan's chest. "What did you tell him?"

Elaine shrugged. "That she must be hidden at the palace." She tapped her fingers on the table before continuing, making Logan growl again. "We had no idea she was with you, not that we would've shared that information anyway. She is even more valuable now than before, if the rumors are true."

"What is our assignment?" Logan asked, his voice barely above a low rumble. Was my distrust of Elaine rubbing off?

"Keep her away from the vampires and convince Kellen to keep his mages here."

"All vampires? Or just the council's?" Logan asked, leaning back in his chair. "I notice we're missing part of our team."

"I haven't decided yet," Elaine replied.

That didn't bode well for me or Logan. This woman expected us to find a way to talk to Kellen without being noticed by anyone. Logan couldn't go to the palace or to Victor's lodge, the two most likely places to meet with Kellen. And I didn't see my vampire letting me go without him.

A slamming metal door had all three of my companions out of their seats in seconds. I turned in time to see an extremely tall man, with dark skin and even darker eyes fill the door to the break room.

"Otto, welcome to the meeting," Elaine said.

My eyes remained fixed on the man in the doorway. Even if I didn't know it in advance, everything about him screamed predator. But his appearance held nothing over the smell of fresh blood mixed with…recently cut wood? Was that his signature smell, like Logan's spearmint?

"Why is there a human here?" he asked, his voice deep and raspy. "Did someone bring me dinner?"

"Do you guys normally take turns picking up dinner?" I snapped. Yes, I should've kept my mouth shut, but seriously?

Logan's hand landed on my shoulder, and I heard him growl again. I looked up and didn't miss the red circling his hazel eyes.

Otto held up hands in surrender and a smile spread across his face. "Sorry, bro. Didn't realize she was yours. Too bad. I like 'em feisty." He strode past me and plopped down in the chair next to Yun, who let out a long breath. Were they expecting him to eat first and ask questions later? "I like the look, Logan."

"If you need nothing else from us, we'll be going," Logan hissed between his teeth, which had elongated.

"We are not done," Elaine stated. "Now, get your shit together." She dropped into her chair and glared at my vampire, who slowly lowered himself into his seat. "Otto, where's Fiona?"

"I ain't her keeper," Otto replied. "Who's the chick?"

I pulled my eyes away from Logan's brooding face and glared at the other vampire in the room. He winked at me and flashed his fangs. Seriously? I fought the urge to roll my eyes, and instead just glared back.

"That's none of your concern," Elaine replied. "When did you last see Fiona?"

"This morning," he replied, still focused on me and not Elaine. His dark eyes studied my face with intensity. If I weren't so mad at his rudeness, I would've blushed. "I told her to meet us here at four, but you know how she is about telling time."

"I need to know Jack's newest spies at the palace." Elaine slapped the table with her palm, drawing the vampire's attention away from me. "Tell me you can find out."

"It might be a little difficult," Otto stated. "Kellen didn't spare anyone." He glanced at me again. "Should we be discussing this in front of her?"

"Yes, she's fine." Elaine waved her hand at me. "What else did you find out about his culling?"

Otto glanced at me, then Logan. "All suspected allies of the Magister were imprisoned."

"Imprisoned or killed?" Yun asked.

"The official word is imprisoned, but I got a call from a buddy in Salt Lake who says they were killed." Otto's glance towards me lingered again. "Says he overheard a group of drunk mages bragging about burying the traitors alive."

A soft gasp escaped my lips. Was Kellen capable of killing them? I'd watched him open a hole in the earth during our fight at Victor's. Did the traitors get a trial to determine their guilt? It'd only been a few days since we'd left, since we'd defeated the Magister. Was that enough time to convene a trial? Unless they admitted their guilt, but even then, being buried alive shouldn't happen. People had rights even if they were guilty, but maybe that was my idealistic human side talking.

"See if you can find the spies. We need to know how close they are to the mages' new governing body," Elaine said, interrupting my thoughts. "Let me know if you need resources to travel and take Fiona with you."

"Why do we get stuck with the bitch?" Otto complained. "Logan and I can find out much quicker without her."

"Logan is not going with you," Elaine replied. "He has another task or three."

I looked up at my vampire, whose focus had not drifted from Otto. Logan's fangs had retreated, leaving his lips pressed in a thin line. Had I just tossed out his trust of Otto as well?

The door slammed open again and I dropped my head to the table. It could only be Fiona. I wasn't sure how much more tension I could take. It was already palpable in the air, making my stomach churn. I had questions, but I really would have preferred to just leave.

"And here I thought I was early." A sultry voice drifted from the doorway.

I caught Logan's chair scooting away from the table out of the corner of my eye. I decided to let him handle it. I'd be the fragile human incapable of facing down a room full of vampires and shifters. Which technically I was, even if I was a dual mage.

"You didn't save any for me," Fiona continued. "How rude."

One moment I was moping peacefully in my seat and the next my body slammed against the wall, with long claws digging into my shoulders. The pungent smell of some flower assaulted my nose as a sharp stabbing pain speared my neck. *She's biting me!*

Half a second later, a high-pitched scream pierced my ears and I slid to the floor. Fiona's body smashed into the ceiling, raining drywall onto the table. A dozen translucent shards impaled her body, securing her in place.

You did give me your blessing to protect you, princess, Niyol's voice echoed in my head.

And I don't regret it for a moment.

The room fell silent and all eyes, including the bitch on the ceiling, turned to me.

I rose and brushed down my dress, then brought my fingers to my neck. The sticky feel of my blood made me forget my fear and confusion. She bit me and no one here did a damn thing about it! My gaze fell on Logan first, whose eyes focused on my neck. I glanced at Otto, finding the same expression. Damn vampires. Yun's wide-eyed expression appeared comical on her small face. Finally my gaze settled on Elaine, whose twitching lips gave in to laughter's temptation. A soft chuckle erupted from the woman.

"Get me down!" Fiona bellowed.

I looked up at her and anger flooded over me. Her elongated fangs dripped with my blood. *My blood!*

"You will never approach me again," I commanded, taking a step towards the table. "You will not even look at me. If you speak to me, it will only be because I ordered you to." I put every ounce of power I could muster into my voice, willing the command to stick with her for eternity.

She gasped and averted her eyes, then clamped her lips closed. Several drops of blood fell from Niyol's spears where they impaled her arms and legs. Small splatters landed on the table and my bravado slipped as bile rose in my throat.

"I had no idea," Otto said, breaking the silence. "I'm sorry for my disrespect earlier, princess."

I pulled my gaze from the pooling drops and gave him my attention. He immediately looked away. Damn. I hadn't wanted him to fear me; or any of them, for that matter. Niyol was a different story, though. The vampire *should* be scared shitless by my elemental.

"I'm sure Elaine was trying to keep my identity secret. If this… thing… hadn't attacked me, you would still not know." I thought back to something Kellen told me the first time we sat down in his training room. He said I should be grateful for my small size. People would always underestimate me. And as much as I hated to admit it, he might've been right. "I'd like to keep it that way." I looked directly at Fiona. "Don't force me to make that command as well."

She nodded but didn't look at me.

"I suggest moving away from the table." I took a few steps back before calling Niyol.

Niyol, can you release her?

Well done, princess.

I couldn't have done it without you.

Without warning, Fiona's body fell from the ceiling, crushing the table with her weight. She cried out in pain and crawled away from the shattered wood, putting her back against the wall and still not looking at me. I wondered how long the command would last. Probably not as long as I wanted, but at least it would give us time to leave.

"Well, that's one question I don't have to ask," Elaine said, still smiling. She dragged her chair away from the wreckage and sat down.

Yun pulled several paper towels from the dispenser and doused them with water from a small sink. "Soak your dress in cold water as soon as you can," she said, handing me the dripping towels.

I dabbed at my neck and closed my eyes. Since everything else was out in the open, there was no reason to hide my healing.

Göksu?

Of course, child.

Thank you.

I opened my eyes as his healing warmth spread across my neck and shoulder. I had the best elementals. How did I ever live without them? Pretty fricking pathetic, that's how. Four sets of eyes stared back at me. Well, not really me, but the skin closing on my neck and shoulder.

"I assume we can go now?" Logan asked, breaking the silence that had settled once again.

"My previous order to keep her away from the vampires is no longer needed," Elaine replied. "Do what you must to get the job done."

Logan's fingers interlaced with mine and I let him pull me from the room. It felt good to be respected by people I'd been afraid of a few moments earlier. It wouldn't last, though. My command would wear off and Fiona would be pissed as hell. I'd just given her all the reason in the world to go back to the vampire council. I should've let Logan handle it. But he hadn't moved when she attacked me.

I stopped walking, halting my vampire's forward progress as well. The middle of the parking lot wasn't a good place for this confrontation, but I needed to know. He turned and looked down at me, the unasked question in his eyes.

"Why didn't you stop her?" I demanded.

"I was in shock," he whispered, closing the space between us and placing his fingers on my neck. "Her attack surprised me, but your response..." He shook his head. "I'm quick, but you reacted before I did."

"Oh." I knew he was telling the truth, even if it was hard to believe I could be faster than a vampire. But our bond showed no hint of deception. "Niyol reacted."

"Really?" His eyebrows rose and he looked over my head at the building behind me. "Let's finish this conversation on the road."

Before Logan could put the car in drive, Yun was racing across the parking lot. She no longer wore her black martial arts outfit. I knew there was a name for it, but I didn't know what it was. A long orange t-shirt hung over a pair of patterned yoga pants and her bright white sneakers nearly blinded me. Her short legs moved much faster than mine ever thought about going.

"What now?" Logan mumbled, rolling down the window.

"I'm coming with you," Yun said, rushing past his door and jumping in the backseat. She wasn't giving him the option to argue.

"Why the change in plans?" he asked, shoving the vehicle into drive and accelerating a little too fast.

"We all have resources outside our group," she replied. "I can get a message to Kellen without every shifter at Victor's knowing about it."

I swiveled in my seat and looked at the young woman. She smiled, but it didn't last. Was she also afraid of me now? I hoped not, because she was the only person in that room who hadn't immediately written me off or wanted to drink my blood. And I could definitely use another ally.

"You did nothing wrong in there, AJ," Yun said, practically reading my mind. "They need to be afraid of you. The rumors running around vary from an all-powerful mage who can wield the four elements to a powerless human Kellen recruited to look like a mage."

I couldn't hide my surprised expression. "Neither of those are even remotely true," I argued. "People don't really believe that, do they?"

"We don't, not after today," she replied. "At least not the fake mage part. I've never seen a mage react so quickly."

I looked over at Logan, who kept his eyes on the road. I knew better than reveal my true relationship with my elementals. Most mages tried to control theirs. I let Niyol do whatever he wanted and in turn, he gave me his complete loyalty. Like today. But honestly, there was no way I could truly control him. It had to be a mutually beneficial relationship. Didn't it? I needed to talk to more mages. Göksu was completely different. He helped when I asked, but only when I did it without hate. Again, I couldn't imagine controlling him.

"Can you get a message to Kellen today?" Logan asked.

"Nope, we need to go to Salt Lake," Yun replied. "Do you mind if I hitch a ride with you?"

"I didn't plan to go to Salt Lake City," Logan said.

"Did you really want to meet him at his estate?" Yun countered. "Salt Lake is neutral ground, and we can stay at the red house."

I frowned. The red house, blue house? Did they even match the colors of their code names? Probably not. The blue house hadn't been blue.

"Fine," Logan consented, sighing heavily. "We need to go home and pack first."

"Thanks. I really didn't want to stick around with the moody vampires."

"How's Fiona?" I asked. "I assume her wounds will heal."

"Why are you worried?" Yun asked. "She had it coming."

"Because, I don't want to drive a wedge through your team," I replied, watching Logan's profile. "But it looks like it might be too late."

"Nah, Fiona needed to be put in her place." The young woman waved a hand at me. "The command thing will piss her off, but again she had it coming. She would've killed you without thinking twice about it."

"And next time, she'll bring friends," I muttered.

"Her friends are nothing compared to yours," Logan said, glancing at me.

I knew he was talking about Niyol, but he was only one element. If she decided to bring a bunch of friends, I was in trouble. "What about Elaine and Otto? Are they mad?"

"I haven't seen Elaine smile in ages. No way was she mad," Yun replied. "I don't know about Otto. He's hard to read sometimes."

"Otto's good," Logan said. "He had a wakeup call, which is never a bad thing."

I wasn't so sure about that, but Logan seemed convinced. During the meeting, it seemed to me like my vampire despised Otto for just looking at me. But men were weird and vampires even more so. If Logan trusted Otto, I could at least keep an open mind.

"What are the chances that Fiona will go to the council?" I asked.

"Pretty slim," Yun replied. "She burned a bunch of bridges when she left."

"No, I burned them for her," Logan said. "I'm the one who killed her sire. Their fight is with me, more than her. If she dangled AJ in front of them, they might take her back."

"I didn't know it was you," Yun leaned forward and tried to look at him. She was too short. "I thought Otto did it."

"No, Otto was there in the middle of the fight, but I was the one who took her sire's head."

"Wow."

"So, how did you get the job of collecting mages?" I asked. Now seemed as good a time as any to start tackling my very long list of questions. Logan was the first vampire I met when all this started a month ago.

"I claimed to be seeking redemption," he replied, glancing at me. "The best way to test my loyalty was to force me to bring in the very people I was trying to save."

"Oh, I guess that didn't work out so well for the council," I said.

"No, but it worked out perfectly for me." A brief smile crossed his lips, but it faded quickly.

We wouldn't get to finish our conversation about Niyol's reaction time or how much more I should reveal to his team, not until we were alone again.

We fell into silence and the sleep button on my ass engaged a short while later.

Chapter 7

Just as the sun gave up its daily fight, Logan, Yun, and I rolled down Interstate 15 in the boring old SUV headed towards Salt Lake City, Utah. We were actually stopping about forty minutes south of Salt Lake, shortening our drive time down to just under five hours.

Logan had stretched a curtain rod across the back of his SUV to hang our new clothes. Some of his slacks were supposed to be wrinkle free, but nothing of mine was. While my new wardrobe had its perks, it was inconvenient. Sure, I liked new clothes, but I'd already ruined my sunflower dress thirty minutes after putting it on. It wouldn't feel as bad if it were a ten-dollar t-shirt. My only consolation, I was pretty sure Logan felt the same.

"You going to be okay to drive?" I asked, knowing he had less sleep than me. At least I'd caught a couple hours on the road.

"Yep, I don't need sleep like you do, princess," he replied.

I smiled at the comment, hearing the playfulness in his voice. I missed it. He'd been so moody the last couple days.

"If you're sure," I said, shrugging. "I'm going to let this sleep button do its thing."

"Sleep button?" Yun asked from the back seat.

"Yep. The one on my ass that activates as soon as the car starts rolling down the road."

She laughed, and Logan chuckled with her.

"Why don't you swap places with me, Yun?" I asked, turning in my seat. "You can poke Logan if he starts to fall asleep."

"Sure." She laughed again and we traded places.

I drifted in and out of dreamland several times, catching snippets of conversations between Logan and Yun. I remembered none of it by the time the Explorer rolled to a stop.

"Time to get up, sleepy head," my vampire said, opening the back door.

I sat up and stretched, yawning deeply before sliding off the seat. Logan had three bags draped over his shoulder before I pushed the car door closed. The smell of fresh pine greeted me along with flowers and a heavy dew that was surely covering all of it. It was wonderful. Still tired from the drive, I stumbled up the steps of a moderately sized log home. A single porch light illuminated a red door that Logan pushed open.

"There's a bed in the loft," he said, leading me through the living room to a spiral staircase. "You can sleep the rest of the night. Yun's taking her message to Kellen now. We should have our plans by morning."

"Ok," I mumbled, nearly tripping up the narrow steps. "Are you coming with me?" I couldn't believe how tired I was. But it was the middle of the night and we'd been up since the middle of last night.

"Soon," he replied, dropping the bags at the end of a queen size bed.

It looked so inviting with its fluffy pillows and down comforter. Logan caught me around the waist just before I nosedived into the beckoning softness.

"You can't sleep in this dress, princess," he whispered, tugging on the zipper at my back.

"Fine," I huffed, raising my arms over my head and letting him pull it off me. He'd already seen me naked several times, and I was too tired to really care.

"I'm going to be gone for about an hour," he said, guiding me beneath the blankets.

My brain slowly registered what he was saying. He wanted to feed again.

"Logan, why don't we try mine, just to see if it works?" I mumbled.

"No." He kissed my forehead. "You mean too much to me to use you like that."

"So, some hooker off the street is good enough to satisfy your needs, but I'm not?" I huffed, knowing I sounded ridiculous. My foggy brain just needed to go to sleep.

"I'm not looking for sex and you know it," he said.

"No, you're looking for life." I rolled over as tears pooled in my eyes. Why was I being so stupid? I didn't *want* to be his blood donor. I was his friend, maybe even lover, but not a slave to his vampire. Still, the fact that he didn't even want to try my blood hurt.

Regardless of my exhaustion, I didn't fall asleep until I felt him crawl into the bed next to me. Neither of us said a word as he threaded his arm under my head and I curled up against him. His other arm wrapped around my waist, pulling me closer. I drew in a deep breath, loving everything about him except his vampire. Was it even possible to love someone despite hating one big part of who they were?

~~~~~~~~~

Morning came way too soon along with my bladder's demand to be noticed. To my surprise, Logan was still asleep with an arm draped across my stomach. He always woke up before me. I contemplated waiting for him, knowing if I moved, he would wake. But my bladder made the decision for me and I gently rolled away from him. He moaned but appeared to stay asleep. Whew.

I looked around the space and frowned. There wasn't a bathroom in the loft. I glanced down at my bra and panties, trying to decide if I should at least put on a t-shirt. *Yeah, I better,* I thought. *Just in case Yun's up.* I didn't want to see another woman waltzing around in her panties and had to assume she felt the same. I searched the floor around the bed until I found the shirt Logan wore yesterday, pulling it over my head. The narrow staircase proved a little challenging this early in the morning, and I wondered how I made it up the stairs half asleep last night.

The steps ended in an open-concept floor space that I hadn't noticed earlier. The living room consumed the entire right side while a joined kitchen and dining room took up the left side. A small hallway ran behind the stairs with two doors, one on each side. One had to be the bathroom, right? I shrugged and picked the one on the left, the same side as the kitchen and therefore all the plumbing.

"Good guess," I whispered, pushing open the door to a small but functional bathroom.

I took my time doing my business and washing the layers of makeup off my face. It felt good to see my skin again. Marissa's work of art was beautiful, but I couldn't replicate it and wouldn't even try.

As soon as I opened the bathroom door, I knew something was wrong. A strange smell drifted towards me, like mud or the slimy stuff on drain pipes. I stopped in the open door and peeked my head around the corner. My jaw dropped, and I covered my mouth to stop the scream from erupting.

A towering creature filled the living room. Even with its back stooped, I didn't know how it came through the door. It looked human... ish. Okay, not really. It had long legs and even longer arms connected to a torso with a squat neck and bulbous head. Clumps of mud covered its green skin, and its enormous feet tracked slime across the hardwood floors.

Try as I might, I failed to tamp down my fear. Who let this thing in the house? I ducked back into the bathroom, taking deep breaths and trying to stay as quiet as possible.

Niyol? I need your help. Probably Göksu as well.

I see it, princess, Niyol's voice echoed in my mind. *It isn't alone.*

I assumed that, I snapped. *Someone had to let it in.*

There are six vampires with it.

Well shit. I bit my lip, trying to make a decision. *Is Logan awake? What about Yun?*

Your vampire is awake and panicked because you're not there, Niyol replied. *The shifter is gone.*

Can you tell him I'm down here?

A gust of wind blew my hair and I smiled. I loved that elemental more than anyone else in my life. The thought made me pause, not only because of its truth, but because Niyol wasn't even human. It didn't matter though. My smile faded with the absence of Yun. Had she not come back last night? Did the vampires kill her already? I kind of liked her, even though we'd only known each other for a few hours.

Göksu, I really need you. I don't think we can fight this many on our own.

I'm here, child.

I tamped down my frustration. He was always there, just not always helpful. I peered around the corner again just in time to see the ugly thing pick up the sofa and throw it into the kitchen. It shattered on impact, taking the island counter with it. The creature roared, forcing me to cover my ears and cower. Holy shit! The whole neighborhood would hear that thing.

A low rumble shook the floor and a tree limb shot through one of the living room windows. A fierce gale followed it, using the branch as a spear and impaling the monster's leg. It roared again, and Logan leapt from the loft, landing on the green slimy back.

I'd never seen Logan fight. He was always my gentle and sometimes moody companion, but he was never vicious. This version of him terrified me. Long claws replaced his fingers and his smooth muscles bulged on his bare back. My vampire dug his claws into the monster's neck and dropped from its back, leaving deep gouges in his wake.

Logan turned to me and I took a step back. Enormous fangs hung from his mouth and blood red consumed even the whites of his eyes. Fear paralyzed me.

"I need your help killing this thing, AJ," he slurred past his fangs.

I shook my head and stowed my fear, at least my fear of Logan. It was unfounded. I drew my long, slender spear made from compressed air, just like Niyol showed me back when I was learning the basics of my magic. Without thinking or second guessing what the hell I was doing, I sprinted towards the monstrous green creature.

It swiveled around and swung a grasping hand at Logan, who dodged it easily but kept the green machine's attention. Determined not to waste his efforts to give me a clear target, I raced halfway up the stairwell and leapt onto the creature's shoulders. I wrapped my legs around its neck, forcing my spear into the soft spot above its collar. It howled in pain and reached for the offending weapon. I grabbed hold of its large ear and unwrapped my legs just as its meaty fingers wrapped around my chest.

I couldn't breathe beneath the pressure of its grasp, and it whipped me around so we were eye-to-eye. Its wide nostrils flared and the squinty orbs bore into me.

"Put me down," I ordered between gasping breaths.

Its grip loosened and it shook its head. Blood poured from the puncture at its throat, but it didn't do as I commanded.

"Put me down, now!" I yelled.

It stumbled backward and sat in the middle of the living room but still refused to release me.

"Logan!"

My vampire appeared next to the creature, looking from it to me. "Is it still crushing you?"

"No, but it won't do as I command either."

"A strong compulsion has likely been woven over its mind. If it hasn't killed you, it's because it was instructed to capture." Logan strolled around the other side of the green monster. My vampire was no longer feral and fierce. Just my Logan, wearing a pair of boxer shorts.

"What is it?" I asked.

"An ogre."

I didn't know what to say. Kellen said there were other supernatural families, but this wasn't what I imagined. Shifters, vampires, and mages, sure, but monsters?

"Niyol said there were six vampires with it," I said, remembering my conversation and looking towards the broken window. "He appears to be handling it, though."

The trees outside the windows swayed violently and a six-foot-tall tornado raced by. If it were any elemental but Niyol, I might be worried, but I knew he had it under control.

"We need to get you out of its grasp," Logan stated, stopping at the opening to the hallway.

"No kidding."

"I cannot bite it. Well, I can, but it's a really bad idea."

"Can you get a butcher knife and cut the tendons in its wrist?" I asked.

"I can try, but it'll probably attack me again," he replied. "As long as I'm not aggressive, it'll wait until its master shows up to retrieve you."

"Wonderful," I muttered. "I'm not waiting."

I concentrated on the wind spear again, and it appeared in my hand. I stared into the ogre's squinty eyes and pulled on the magic in my core.

"Put me down or I'll be forced to kill you," I said.

It blinked several times, but otherwise didn't move.

"Okay, stupid, I'm not really trying to hurt you. Put me down now." I put as much power into the command as I could muster, but it still wasn't enough. "You stupid animal. Do you want to die?" It didn't answer me, just continued to blink rapidly. I hung my head. I didn't want to hurt this big ugly creature, especially if someone else controlled its every move. "I can't do it, Logan."

My vampire didn't answer me. I leaned over, peering around my capturer, and found an empty space where Logan had been a few seconds before. I felt for my connection to him. He was still in the house. I leaned the other way and gasped. Two men held long knives against Logan's neck. *How the hell did they catch him?*

Logan's eyes pleaded with mine not to do anything stupid, but he didn't have to. I knew our lives were tied together. I couldn't let him die.

"What do you want?" I asked.

Both men turned their heads towards the front door. My stomach lurched when a tall man with shoulder-length blond hair walked through it. It had to be Braden, the council guy looking for me. I remembered him from my first interrogation with the council so many weeks ago in that Vegas hotel.

"You are difficult to find, princess," Blondie said, strolling towards me.

"You will not call me princess," I commanded, meeting his gaze with my most hostile stare. Would I be lucky enough to boss him around the way I did with Fiona?

He cringed, stopping several yards from the ogre. "That is uncomfortable."

"No kidding," I snapped. "Who are you?"

"Braden. May I call you Alisandra?"

"Whatever. Tell this thing to release me." I added more command to my voice.

"Dearest girl," Braden said. "I'm not like your boy-toy. You cannot command me to do anything."

He thought I commanded Logan to stay with me. I nearly laughed. He knew so little about my vampire. "Tell me what you want," I ordered.

He chuckled and rubbed his temple with one finger. Maybe I couldn't make him do it, but I'd sure make him miserable.

"If you do it again, Logan will die."

I scowled at him, loathing him with every part of my being.

"That's what I thought," he said. "Now maybe we can do business. If you try to kill the ogre, Logan dies. If you attack me, Logan dies. If you try to command me again...."

"Yeah, I get it," I snapped. "Will you tell this creature to put me down? I won't do any of those things you mentioned."

The vampire eyed me for several moments, then snapped his fingers. "Put her down and leave."

The ogre dropped me, and I screamed as I fell several feet, only to land in Braden's arms just before hitting the floor. The ogre stood and ambled out the door, dripping a trail of blood along the way. I should have healed its wounds. Why didn't I think of that before now?

Braden's hands ran up my sides and brushed the edge of my breasts as he put me down.

"Don't…" I clamped my mouth shut and wiggled out his grasp. I wanted to tell him to get his filthy hands off me, but I wouldn't give him a reason to hurt Logan.

He chuckled again. "Let's sit and chat like civilized people," Braden suggested, moving towards the dining table that somehow survived the sofa's attack.

Logan's escorts pushed him that way as well and forced him into a chair. I thought about the dynamic Braden used. Did he hold Logan hostage because he thought my vampire wouldn't bargain for my life? Did Braden not know that Logan retained some of his soul, enabling him to care for me? Possibly. Most likely. Why else would he use my emotions as the bargaining chip?

I sat across the table from Logan, with a space between me and Braden.

"I'm taking a huge risk today, one that I hope I won't regret," Braden said, drawing my attention. "Your elemental took the lives of four of my men. Men I cannot afford to lose." He leaned towards me, the smell of sandalwood coming with him. Why did he have to smell good? He was an asshole. "If your elemental shows up now, you will both die."

I didn't respond to his threat. I had complete confidence that Niyol would kill Braden and protect me, but he might not be able to stop Logan's death.

"I will help you fight against the vampire council," Braden continued, leaning back in his chair and folding his arms over his chest.

This time I was stunned to silence. Why would he do that? Wasn't he on the council?

"Why?" I asked after a few silent heartbeats.

"Because there is no future for us if Jack wins," Braden replied. "None of us. I was around the last time someone tried to reveal the vampires to humanity. I have no wish to do it again."

"I thought you wanted to reveal all the supernatural families," I said. "Not just the vampires."

"Jack wants to, not me," he corrected. "What do you think will happen to the ogres when humans discover them? They're large and ugly, but they're also stupid and docile. They'll fight if they must, but they're not aggressive predators. Their entire line would be hunted and killed within a year."

I contemplated what he said. I hadn't even known they existed until today and my first instinct was to kill it even though I was sort of familiar with the supernatural world.

"Why do you care?" I asked.

"Like I said, I was there last time. Being hunted for generations is… tedious," he replied. "Those of us who managed to hide from the hunt, starved. Starvation for a vampire is worse than anything you can imagine."

"I can imagine a lot," I said. "I spent my entire life hungry."

He leaned a fraction closer to me, his deep blue eyes holding mine. "Vampires don't die from hunger," he whispered. "We just continue to starve."

I didn't want to feel bad for him, but how could I not? I averted his gaze with some effort, sparing a glance at Logan. Fear and unease drifted between us.

"What do you expect from me?" I asked, turning back to Braden.

"Leave my people alone," he replied. "When I ask for information, give it to me."

"I can't make blind promises. And pardon me," I snapped, "but how exactly am I supposed to trust you?"

"Right now, I'm the only one looking for you. I convinced Jack to give the task to me, ensuring him that I would not fail," Braden responded, uncrossing his arms. "Losing four of my men today will convince him that I'm still pursuing you. It will also force him to realize that you are stronger than he's been told by others whom he trusts. I'll continue to plant seeds of doubt and false trails." He stretched his hand across the table, palm up. "I'll provide you with information about his next attack, like the one in Australia that you're currently trying to stop."

I looked down at his outstretched hand, then glanced at Logan, who shook his head. I got it, don't take his hand.

I leaned back in my own chair and frowned. "How will I know which vampires are yours?"

He chuckled again and withdrew his hand. "Show her," he said, waving at one of his men.

The vampire on Logan's left side held out his arm. A tattoo wrapped around his forearm, but it was too far away to see the details. I sat forward and the man stepped closer. A large cross with a teardrop looping over the top covered his forearm. I could only see the entire thing if he rolled his arm from one side the other. A quick glance didn't reveal its entirety.

"And I'm supposed to do what? Hold up my hand and ask them stop charging at me so I can see their tattoos?"

"My people will not attack you, regardless of your disguise of the day," he replied, a smile playing across his face. "That will be your first clue to leave them alone."

I glanced at Logan again. Braden's men still hovered, their blades threatening my vampire. Could I trust a member of the vampire council? It didn't feel like he lied to me. Was there a way to test it? The only people who knew our location for sure, were Yun and Elaine. Possibly Otto and Fiona.

"How did you know we were here?" I asked. "Did Jonathan tell you?"

"Does it matter?" Braden countered.

"That's a stupid question," I replied. "If the shoe were on the other foot, wouldn't you want to know who revealed your location?"

"Of course, but I go to great lengths to ensure I don't have spies among my people," he replied.

"I bet you do, but that doesn't answer my question."

He was good at side stepping with his answers. I truly couldn't tell if he lied or not.

"Mr. Smith is not aware of your location," Braden finally replied. "But his people are easy to manipulate."

"Why? Because most of them are vampires?"

He chuckled again. It was really starting to irritate me.

"Do we have a deal or not?" he countered.

He wasn't going to answer my question. I couldn't make a deal with a vampire, but I could concede to cooperate if it were in my best interest.

"I'll do my best to avoid your people," I replied. "If there is information that I can give you that will be of mutual benefit to us both, I'll gladly share."

"And I will continue to lure my leader away from your path," he said. "I will also share information is that mutually beneficial."

He held his hand out again and smiled. It should have made his handsome face even more beautiful, but it only made me wary.

"I don't shake hands," I said quickly. "Too many people are interested in testing my… talent."

"Smart girl."

He stood and waved at his men. Before I could react, one of them drew his knife across Logan's neck. Blood spurted from the cut and I screamed, knocking my chair away as I raced to his side. He fell to the floor and I went with him. Logan clamped his hand over the spurting blood, his eyes meeting mine with fear. Would this kill him? I didn't know and didn't want to find out.

"Don't you dare die," I whispered. It wasn't what I meant to say, but the words fell out on their own. My heart ached and I couldn't stand the thought of not having him. I should've been afraid for my own life, and maybe I was, but my fear for him eclipsed it.

He blinked at me and tried to smile.

"Göksu, you have to do something!" I yelled. "He can't die!"

My elemental appeared at my side and placed his watery hand over Logan's. My vampire's eyes widened in disbelief.

"Move your hand, child," Göksu said in his wispy voice.

Logan did as he asked, and my elemental's translucent hand turned red with my vampire's blood. I could almost feel the warm healing saturating Logan's body. Tears filled my eyes, and huge lump swelled in my throat as the gash in his neck slowly shrank.

I was going to kill Braden, regardless of the promise I just made. As far as I was concerned, he just forfeited everything. I looked around the room and wasn't surprised to find it empty. Stupid coward.

"Your spirit calls to me," Göksu whispered, drawing my attention back. "Just as strongly as Alisandra's. I didn't understand why until now."

The elemental stood; his fluid essence only slightly pink now. Logan remained sprawled out on the floor, covered in his own blood, staring at the elemental that used to be his.

"You healed me," Logan stuttered. "I don't think I would've died from that, but you healed me anyway."

"You were already very close to death," Göksu said. "Only the blood of another would have saved you." He glanced at me and I looked away. "She would have given it freely, but I see now that you wouldn't be able to harbor the guilt when her blood didn't work."

I jerked my head up and stared at my element. "What do you mean?"

"I can't speak of gifts I did not bestow," Göksu replied. He took a step back and his form started to dissipate.

"Oh no you don't!" I yelled, jumping to my feet. "I have questions."

"But I do not have answers, child."

And then he vanished into a puddle of water and seeped into the floorboards.

Chapter 8

"How could he do that to me?" I asked no one in particular. "You don't just throw out info bombs like that and leave!" I stomped my bare feet on the damp floor boards like a child. "I know you hear me, Göksu!"

"AJ." Logan's voice halted my temper tantrum.

I slowly turned to him and tears swelled in my eyes. He stood on unsteady legs, deep red swirling in his hazel eyes. He'd lost a lot of blood that needed to be replenished.

"Would that have killed you?" I asked.

"I'm not sure," he replied. "I don't think so, but Göksu was right. My need to feed would kill everyone else."

"Braden must have known that. He did it on purpose to get rid of me." My anger flared hot and fierce.

He was definitely going to die.

"That's not important right now," Logan said. "If your blood won't quench my thirst, then no other human will either."

My eyes widened and I took a step towards him, but Logan vanished.

"I cannot be near you until this need is gone," he said, reappearing at the end of the hall. "My next victim will not survive."

Pain and guilt contorted his features, and my heart ached. Why did he have to endure this?

The front door blew open, slamming into the wall behind it. Two bodies flew into the room and landed on the floor. Niyol sauntered through the door, followed by another being I'd never seen before.

Wait... yes I had!

It's height and semi-humanoid form mirrored my air elemental, but that was the only similarity. Wide, defined shoulders supported tall wings whose bottom edges swept the floor and tops brushed the ceiling. Swirls of light and dark magic folded on each other along the wings' spines and then stretched out were feathers should have been.

Movement from the floor drew my attention. One of the men rolled to his side and moaned. Niyol speared him in the stomach, forcing a pained cry from his lips. I looked down at the tattoo on his arm. It was one of Braden's vampires; not the one that sliced Logan's throat, though. A matching tattoo ran up the other vampire's arm, confirming he was also one of Braden's. Perfect.

"Time is not our friend today," the winged stranger said, his booming voice vibrating in my chest. "There is much to tell, but let's start with your gift." He pointed at Logan, who still stood at the far end of the hall. "Don't make me wait, Logan."

Typical of my vampire, he suddenly appeared in the living room a few yards from the vampires laying on the floor.

"Human blood will no longer sustain you," the stranger said, taking a step towards Logan. My heart sank. How would he survive? "You feel the draw, do you not?"

Logan's eyes filled with blood again, the way they did when he fought the ogre, wiping out everything else. "Yes, but how?" he asked.

"The human spirit is complicated," the stranger replied. "You and the princess have managed to mingle yours, tying them together in a way that shouldn't be possible." His magical gaze drifted to me, and I almost felt guilty. "Today was the perfect example of the dangers that come with it. You cannot be allowed to crave her blood, especially when you are wounded." He closed the small distance between himself and Logan, then pointed at the vampires on the floor.

Both men stared up at the strange being with fear in their widening eyes. Niyol's spear still impaled one of them, but neither even flinched. I was pretty sure the untethered one could move fast enough to escape, so why didn't he?

"Take your fill, Logan," the stranger said. "It is my gift to you and Alisandra."

Logan's red eyes glanced at me for a second, then went back to our guest. "She cannot see this."

"It is what you are. She cannot hide from it and she doesn't fear it, not from you."

Logan looked at me again, silhouettes of white peeking out around the edges of red in his eyes. "Please, AJ. Not yet."

I nodded and completely agreed with my vampire. I didn't want to see it, regardless of what this strange being thought. "I'll be in the bathroom." I rushed down the hall and slammed the door. I knew what he was, but that part of him did scare me. How could that stranger say it didn't?

"Princess, how do you doubt yourself?" Niyol asked, appearing next to me in the small space.

"There's no doubt, Niyol. His vampire scares the shit outta me."

"No, he doesn't. You would have gladly let him sink those teeth into you, without fear." He leaned against the sink and I plopped down on the edge of the tub. Was he right?

"Who's the glowing guy with wings?" I asked, changing the subject.

"I cannot reveal his name, but he is the spirit linking you and your vampire."

I dropped my head into my hands. The image of the Magister's door solidified in my mind. Logan suspected there was another element. Was this it? Was the thing in the other room keeping Logan's soul intact?

"Will he answer my questions?" I asked, not raising my head.

"The bathroom is not the best place for a conversation," Logan replied.

I hadn't even heard the bathroom door open, but there he was, still in his boxer shorts, covered in blood, but without the red eyes. His brown orbs with flecks of green looked down on me along with his silly smirk. I jumped up wrapping my arms around his neck and my legs around his waist. Just as I knew he would, he caught me and held on.

"Never do that to me again," I demanded, my face buried in his neck.

"Which part?" he asked, sitting me down on the bathroom counter.

"The almost dying part," I replied, lifting my head and drinking in his face. "Everything else I can deal with."

"I truly don't deserve you," he whispered, his lips hovering over mine. "Your elemental is waiting for us, otherwise I'd keep you here until all your desires were met."

I glanced around the room. Apparently, Niyol left me when Logan arrived. "I'll hold you to it, later." I pressed my lips against his, but only for a moment. "Let's not keep our guest waiting."

He lifted me off the counter, but I didn't let go. Maybe I couldn't, or maybe I didn't want to. Either way, it didn't matter. His chuckle ruffled the curls on my head and made me smile.

"We're not walking out there with you hanging from my waist, princess."

I huffed, but my grin remained. "Fine." My legs released him, and he lowered me to my feet.

We walked back into the living room, but I stopped short of going in. It was a mess. Mud and bodily fluids covered the hardwood floors. The only furniture still standing was a recliner in the corner with a tall floor lamp behind it. The two vampires were gone. I didn't want to think about what happened to them, but I needed to get over that. This was my new reality, like it or not, and at the end of the day, Logan would never hurt me.

The broken sofa still teetered over the crumbling island counter. Niyol and the other elemental sat at the dining room table like normal people, in a normal situation, not the glowing beings they were. I shook my head and joined them with Logan by my side.

"Who are you?" I asked.

His wings flexed from his massive shoulders, flaring out to the sides, showing off their swirling magic. Go figure.

"I am Spirit," he replied, placing his elbows on the table and folding his hands together.

"Why does no one else know of you?" I asked, hoping he would just start explaining and not require a hundred questions. My brain wasn't really up to it.

"I'm not like my brothers," he replied. "I serve no one and will not be controlled. I'm the essence of life and death." His swirling eyes danced between me and Logan. "You two surprise me. Logan's spirit has always been strong. He had to be to calm your mother." He unfolded his hands and rested them on the table. It was such a human motion for a being made of light and shadow. "As a gift for his sacrifice to her, I allowed his soul to remain with him. She didn't deserve his loyalty or his efforts to keep her from her path of destruction, just like he didn't deserve the vampire's death she gave him."

"You're the reason I have compassion," Logan stated.

"Yes. At the time, I didn't realize the impact it would have on your future," he replied. "But in the end, destiny controls us all." He turned to me and smiled. "Your spirit amazes even me, Alisandra. Your strength is what tied you to him even before you exchanged blood. Your spirits called to each other the moment they met."

"So the vampire bond thing is fake?" I asked, not hiding my surprise.

"No, it's very real," Spirit replied. "But it's not what you share. The vampire bond is merely an undead forcing the human to yield and become the vampire's slave. It has nothing to do with love or compassion." He flipped his hands over, showing his glowing palms. "Take my hands, both of you. Logan has my gift, but he is not the only one deserving of one."

I glanced at my vampire who shrugged and reached for Spirit's hand. I followed his lead, tentatively resting my hand in the large palm reaching across the table. An intoxicating power rushed through my veins and swelled in my chest. My heart thrummed against my ribs and I struggled to breathe. Within seconds, it stopped, and air rushed back into my lungs.

"Holy shit," I mumbled, still trying to catch my breath. "What was that?"

"My gift to you," Spirit replied, releasing our hands and standing. His wings flexed again, and I marveled at the magic swirling in them. "Your shifter is here. Good luck with your hunt."

Spirit disappeared. Just vanished as if he'd never been there. Did he really just do all that and leave? He didn't even explain his gift to me. Niyol's body shifted as he rose from his chair.

"He hasn't shown himself to anyone in ages," my air elemental said. "The secret of his existence is his only protection, despite his bravado. I trust you to keep it." With a gust of wind, he was gone as well, leaving Logan and I half dressed in a destroyed house.

The front door opened and Yun stepped inside with her mouth hanging open. "I thought the outside was bad," she mumbled. "What happened?"

Logan and I looked at one another. Where should we start and how much could we reveal? Evidence of Braden's visit was splattered all over the living room. My elements would remain a secret, though. Someone told Braden where we were and Yun was one of the few people who knew.

"We had a visit from Braden," Logan said, waving an arm at the mess.

Yun's face registered genuine surprise, and I wanted to believe she hadn't betrayed us. Her gaze shifted from Logan to me, then back again.

"You guys are okay?" she asked.

"Yep, just barely," Logan replied. "He brought an ogre with him."

Yun stepped lightly across the room trying to avoid the splatters of blood and gore on the floor. "I assume you killed it?"

"No, but not for lack of trying," he replied.

Yun made it to the table and sat down across from us, in the chair recently taken by Spirit and previously occupied by the asshole vampire. My morning sucked.

The smell of roasted almonds drifted towards me. Was that Yun? I hadn't noticed it before and we'd spent five hours in the car together.

"Are you going to tell me what happened or make me pull it from you one question at a time?" she asked.

I giggled, then slapped my hand over my mouth. "Sorry. I think it's a guy thing. He and Kellen both do it."

Yun raised an eyebrow at me.

"Logan, go get dressed and I'll fill her in," I suggested. "Unless you want to tell the story and I'll find some clothes."

He looked down at his bare chest and chuckled. "Yeah, good idea." He rose and was gone before I blinked.

"I wish I could move that quick," Yun whispered. "It wouldn't have taken me all night to get my message to Kellen."

"You and me both," I agreed. "Is he willing to meet with us?"

"Yes. Six o'clock tonight at some fancy restaurant." Her tiny nose wrinkled. "I brought t-shirts and yoga pants, so of course he picks something pricey."

"I bet I have something you can borrow," I offered. "I'm only a little taller than you. We'll make it work." I looked around the room and frowned. "We need to clean up, if that's even possible."

"I'll call Elaine and tell her to send a cleaning crew," Yun said. "We'll get a couple hotel rooms if we need to stay tonight."

I hadn't considered that. We probably wouldn't stay after Kellen's visit.

"What happened here, AJ?" Yun asked.

I sighed. I needed to know who betrayed us before this conversation went any farther. "Someone told Braden we were here," I replied. "I couldn't get him to reveal who, but they're part of your team. Who else knew?"

"I swear it wasn't me," she said, raising her hands in front of her. "Elaine knew, but she'd never tell. We waited for Otto and Fiona to leave, but they could've been lurking and we didn't realize it." She dropped her hands to the table and laced her fingers together. "What did Braden tell you?"

I repeated his offer and our counter offer, leaving out Logan's near death. I still didn't know what to think of that. I needed to pick Logan's brain.

"Wow," Yun whispered. "Would he really go against Jack?"

"That's the question of day," I replied. "I guess we'll find out during our first encounter with his people. If they attack us, we'll know it's all a pack of lies."

"I guess. And the ogre did all of this?"

"Yep. Nasty creature, but I felt sorry for it." I rubbed my temple and grimaced, my fingers coming away with a sticky mess. I needed a shower. "Braden had complete control over its mind. Despite its injuries and my threat to kill it, it wouldn't disobey the vampire's orders."

"I wonder if they're controlling all the ogres." She tapped her fingers on the table several times. "They're really hard to kill. Going up against them in a battle would suck."

"Then let's hope not."

"Your turn, princess," Logan said, suddenly at my side and fully dressed. Today's fashion included a gray t-shirt tucked into dark gray slacks. A black and gray striped dress shirt hung open and untucked, with the sleeves rolled up. He looked amazing. "I might have left some hot water for you." The smirk I loved graced his lips, making me smile.

"You're so thoughtful," I said. "How about grabbing the clothes rack from the car? Yun needs something as well." I turned to the young shifter and smiled. "Pick something you think will work for both of us for tonight. I'm not picky. I actually prefer blue jeans and t-shirts."

Once they left, I stood and stretched, my muscles screaming. I hadn't done that much fighting. Or was it from the ogre's crushing grip? I shrugged. It didn't really matter now.

My first step away from table scared me, but not as much as the second. My head swam, and my stomach threatened to empty itself. What the hell? I stumbled to the broken sofa hanging over the counter and leaned against it. What was wrong with me? Spirit's gift came to mind, but this didn't feel like a gift.

I waited for my world to stop spinning and took another step. The room whizzed by. Seriously! I caught the wall and held on; this time not able to keep my stomach calm. I heaved several times, leaving more nasty things on the floor.

"Are you okay?" Logan asked from the front door, a pile of clothes in his arms.

"Nope," I replied, still leaning against the wall straddling my puke on the floor.

"I'll take these upstairs. Don't move."

"Not a problem," I mumbled.

"I'm getting a cleaning crew," Yun said from the doorway. Several hangers hung from her fingers and she struggled to lift them high enough off the ground. "We should just go to a hotel now."

"I agree. Logan, did you hear that?" I yelled.

"Yes!" he yelled back. "I'm packing up our stuff now."

I took another step and fell to my knees at the stairs, once again throwing up the contents of my stomach.

"Oh my God! Logan get down here!" Yun's high-pitched yell threatened to split my skull. "She just... I don't know, did something!"

Logan appeared at my side and I looked up at him. "What did she do, Yun?" he asked, wrapping his fingers around my arm and gently pulling me to my feet.

"She was against the wall, you know hovering over her puke," she said. "Then a second later, she was there."

I had to assume she was pointing at the various puddles on the floor, but my eyes didn't leave Logan's. He scooped me up and within seconds I was on the bed upstairs.

"Don't move," he whispered. "I mean it. This is the only clean room and I'd like to keep it that way."

I scowled at him but remained seated as he ran back and forth with our bags of clothes. With nothing left in the room but me, he knelt at the edge of the bed.

"Yun's calling Elaine for a cleaning crew, so we have a few minutes to talk," he whispered. "I think the Spirit guy gave you my speed." He grinned. "Which would be perfect!"

"Why is it making me sick?" I grumbled. "I run around with you all the time."

"Because it's your body initiating the movement, not mine," Logan replied. "But it should help you adjust faster." He stood and held out his hand. "We're going to practice walking slow, like human speed."

I took his hand and rose to my feet. He moved to my side and his arm wrapped around my waist, holding me tight. "From here to the railing, one step at a time. I'm going to hold you back so you feel the difference." He lifted his left foot and looked down at me. I hadn't moved. "Really, AJ? It's not like you've never walked."

"Yes, but walking never made me puke before either," I snapped.

I lifted my left foot and followed his lead. It felt like trying to run underwater, but we made it to the railing in one piece. He turned me around and led me back to the bed.

"Okay, now do it by yourself."

He let me go and took a step back. I focused on one slow step at a time, with Logan following right beside me. It still felt like walking underwater.

"Not bad, but you need practice," he said as we circled back to the bed.

"You should just hang on to me for a couple days," I suggested, "so I don't make a fool of myself." I thought of our dinner with Kellen tonight. "Especially tonight when we meet with Kellen."

"I planned to do that anyway." He smiled, but it wasn't nice. I suspected he planned to make Kellen very uncomfortable.

"Let's get out of here so I can shower and change."

Chapter 9

At five forty-five, we pulled into the parking lot of a large, two-story Victorian style home that was now a restaurant. I gawked at the intricate woodwork scrolling along the wrap-around porch. Small seating arrangements were strategically placed along the porch for semi-private dinners-for-two. Old style lanterns lit each table, their flames barely moving in the gentle breeze.

It was nothing like I expected. But I grew up in Vegas where everything was over-the-top and glamorous. I fell in love with the place and I hadn't even been inside yet.

"Close your mouth, princess," Logan whispered, patting my leg. "Time to go. I'm betting Kellen will be early."

Yun got out of the back seat, tugging on the clingy fabric of her strappy dress. She looked good in a 'little black dress' and black heels. It showed off her slight, muscular body perfectly, making her look like a woman and not a child.

I chose a gray pant suit, leaving the jacket open to reveal the nearly sheer white shirt beneath. I stuck with minimal makeup, knowing I'd screw it up if I did more than lipstick and eyeliner. Of course, I had to wear the amber contacts to cover my icy blue eyes.

Logan opened my door and offered his hand. I gladly took it, depending on him to keep me walking straight. I threaded my arm around his elbow and smiled up at him. He winked at me and gave me my favorite smirk.

"I told Kellen you'd changed your appearance," Yun said, walking up beside us. "But I didn't tell him how. I can't wait to see the look on his face when he sees Logan." She snickered, and I glanced over at her. "What?

My expression was priceless when I first saw him, wasn't it?"

"Whatever," Logan said, surprising me with the statement. I said it frequently, but I'd never heard him utter it. He started towards the house-turned-restaurant, pulling me back from running.

"Oh, come on, Logan. You made goth look good, but this." She waved her hand at him. "This is you. I never would've guessed it, but it is."

He seemed to ignore her, but I didn't miss the flexing of his arm beneath my fingers as we reached the steps. Everyone liked compliments.

A hostess opened the door for us, and Yun gave them Kellen's name at the podium. A pretty young girl, probably just out of high school, smiled sweetly and asked us to follow her. She led us past the main dining area, already full of guests and into what was probably once a parlor. Kellen sat at the farthest table dressed in a charcoal gray suit, looking out the window next to his seat. He looked exactly the same as the last time I saw him. Sure, that had only been a few days ago, but it felt like so much longer.

He glanced our way as the hostess approached. Kellen stood and smiled at Yun, taking her hand in his. When his gaze found Logan, his eyes widened dramatically. Then they dropped to me and his mouth fell open. Yun was right. His expression *was* priceless.

"It's good to see you too, Kellen," Logan said, breaking the awkward silence.

Yun dropped into the chair next to Kellen, and Logan pulled out the one next to her, motioning for me to sit. I struggled to take my eyes off my mage partner as my butt found the chair. I'd forgotten what it felt like to experience his emotions so clearly. Or maybe he was just in shock and forgot to hide them.

Surprise and longing outweighed everything else, but resentment and mistrust lingered in the background. I was pretty sure my own emotions were on full display, too. I didn't want to be mad at him, but my anger pushed everything else aside. Could I block my own feelings from him? I needed to; I didn't want him to feel Logan's. This was already uncomfortable enough. He stared back at me, and I imagined an invisible barrier raising between us.

His emotions vanished. I gasped and so did he, but he schooled his features quicker than I did. The impassive mask he met me with on our very first greeting over a month ago fell into place.

"Yun says you needed to talk," Kellen said, clearing his throat.

A tall young man arrived to take our drink orders. I opted for water, for several reasons. I had no money, which meant someone else was paying, and my IOU tab was already over the limit. But most importantly, I rarely drank alcohol. Doing so now would make me stupid.

I nudged Logan's knee, hoping he took the hint to talk first. He glanced at me and gave me that silly smirk. I tried not to blush.

"We have extremely good reason to believe that the council is planning a diversionary tactic to draw you away from the palace," Logan said, his smile vanishing as he answered Kellen. "Have you received any communication from them?"

Kellen pulled his gaze from me and gave Logan his attention. "No."

Lying already. Damn. How were we supposed to work together without honesty? I nudged Logan's knee again. He looked down at me and raised an eyebrow, then turned back to my partner.

"Good, then we're not too late." Logan glanced around and leaned forward. "They're planning to threaten your mother's family in Australia, expecting you to send your full contingent to protect them."

Kellen scowled, his dark brows drawing together. "Why wouldn't I protect them?"

"Because as soon as your mages leave, Jack will attack Victor's lodge," Logan whispered.

My mage partner sat back in his chair, studying Logan's face. "Assuming your information is correct, how big is the army coming for Victor?"

Logan leaned closer and braced his forearms on the table. "An ogre and six vampires attacked AJ and I this morning," he replied, keeping his voice as low as possible. "The ogre was under complete control of the vampire with it."

"What?" Kellen's dark eyes shifted to me, lingering for several moments. Was he really concerned about my safety? I was curious—because, he'd tried to have me killed—but I wasn't willing to let the wall down to find out.

"I don't know what the vampires will send to Victor's, but I have to assume they plan to succeed where they failed last time. Which they will surely do if you're not there." Logan leaned back and unfolded his napkin, placing it on his knee.

The waiter showed up a moment later with our drinks and asked for our order. I hadn't even looked at the menu. I glanced down at the thick parchment in my hand. There were only four choices, and none had prices next to them.

"What do you suggest?" I asked the waiter.

"Many of our female guests with smaller appetites prefer the salmon," he replied, pointing at my menu. The stereotype might have offended me if he weren't correct.

"That'll be fine, then. Thank you."

Yun ordered the same. Kellen order a beef something or other. I looked up at Logan wondering how he'd handle real food.

"I'll have your best beer on tap," he replied. "I have another dinner date after this and don't wish to insult the company."

I frowned at him. That was really rude, implying that Kellen's company was somehow less than worthy. I was pissed at my partner, too, but seriously? Logan and I would chat about that too. I glanced over at my mage partner to find him glaring at my vampire.

"How do I stop them?" Kellen asked in a low voice after the waiter left.

"Jonathan believes if your mages stay here, the vampires won't attack Victor."

"What about my mother's family?" Kellen growled. "I'm supposed to leave them to die?"

Logan looked away. He was trying to act like an ass, but he didn't want to see innocent people get hurt. I didn't want to see the mages slaughtered either, especially with the recent revelation from my elementals that Kellen's family was there. I remembered the look on his face when he found out. His haunted eyes would forever be imprinted on my brain.

"We'll go to Australia and protect your family," I offered, surprising myself.

Both men looked over at me as if I'd grown two heads.

"Just the two of you?" Kellen asked. "And how will you get there?"

"Through the portal, of course," I replied.

"Have you forgotten something?" Kellen asked, pointing at Logan.

"There are things even you do not know, *partner*," I replied, emphasizing the moniker. "I assume your people in Australia can fight, yes?"

He frowned at me, then looked over at Logan. I refrained from glancing at my vampire. Kellen was obviously uncomfortable about being in the dark.

"Everyone is taught basic self-defense," he replied as the waiter arrived with Logan's extremely tall glass of beer.

"Thank you." Logan nodded at the waiter, who didn't hang around.

A thought occurred to me as I watched Logan sip the frothy brew. Yes, I know, fighting has nothing to do with beer, so don't ask how my brain went there. It just did.

"What if we can create a scenario that makes Jack believe you sent a force to Australia?" I asked. "Of course you don't really, but we make him believe it. He sends his fighters to Victor, not expecting your mage warriors to be there."

"I like it!" Yun said, startling me. I'd nearly forgotten she was there. "I'll try to find out who the fiends have collected for their army, so Kellen will know what to expect."

"And AJ and I will help the mages deal with any 'fiends' in Australia," Logan added.

Kellen looked around the table at the three of us, settling his gaze on me. "Why would you help me?"

I shook my head. Even after spending nearly twenty-four hours a day together for an entire month, he still didn't know me. I wanted to hate him for the things he'd done to me, but innocent people couldn't suffer because of my hate.

"Because that's our destiny, right?" Logan replied for me. "Isn't that what started this whole thing? The desire to protect our legacy?"

Kellen braced his elbows on the table and dropped his head in his palms. Logan's hand found mine beneath the table, lacing our fingers together. I appreciated the gesture.

"I didn't mean to hurt you, AJ," Kellen mumbled, lifting his head. Was that remorse? I couldn't tell with the barrier in place. "They were supposed to detain you, but not hurt you."

I couldn't feel a lie in his words, but he hesitated. He wouldn't have stopped them from hurting me. He wasn't there to ensure they didn't. I shook it off and focused on the previous lie. His regret seemed real, but now wasn't the time to think about it.

"Who approached you about sending mages to Australia?" I asked, refusing to offer forgiveness.

Kellen chuckled. "You never miss a thing, do you? Someone I thought I could trust told me how dire the situation was, and that I had to send the full force before midnight tonight."

"Probably, the same man who said he wouldn't hurt me when he took me from the house," I pushed, not caring if it was brutal. "Do you know what he said before I escaped your room?"

Kellen shook his head, not hiding his misery.

"There were three of them in your sitting room, trying to bust down the door to the bedroom," I continued, trying to keep my voice low. "One of them, your trusted buddy, was in a really big hurry to get to me. I'm guessing he was the one who tore the door from the hinges. One of the others tried to stop him, stating it'd feel like he was 'doing the Magister.'" I air quoted the last phrase. It didn't take a genius to figure out what he meant.

Yun sucked in a breath, and I realized she hadn't known the full situation or why I wasn't with Kellen at the palace. *Too late to take it back.*

"They weren't supposed to hurt you," Kellen hissed, squeezing his eyes shut.

"But you weren't there to protect me, were you?" I countered.

Silence fell across the table. A group of servers arrived with our food, but I was pretty sure I couldn't eat. My heart lodged in my throat, and I couldn't force it back down.

When they left, Kellen looked up at me. "I'm sorry. There's no excuse for what I did."

"No, there isn't," I agreed, watching him cringe. "But I'm more concerned for our future. Jack doesn't care about our drama. There is only one thing he wants, and he's willing to kill a whole lot of people to get it."

"You are so much more than I gave you credit for," my partner said, picking up his fork and pushing around the vegetables on his plate. "I was wrong in so many things. I should've kept you by my side regardless of your situation with Logan."

"It's irrelevant now," I said. "Do you agree with the plan?"

"Yes, but I need to deal with my traitors first," he replied. "And I have something for you." He reached inside his coat pocket and retrieved an envelope. "You are the Magister, even if you're not at the palace. This is your bank account information, a debit card, and new identification."

I took the envelope from him as tears welled in my eyes. I was such a cry baby. I blinked them back, not wanting to smear the eyeliner that had taken me twenty minutes to put on.

"Thank you," I mumbled. "What time are we meeting you at the portal?"

"Before midnight," Kellen replied. "Logan knows where it is." My partner eyed my vampire. "Are you sure you can go through it?"

"Let us worry about that," Logan replied.

I tried to eat the lovely slice of salmon on my plate, but I couldn't. My emotions were running rampant, and I struggled to hold onto the invisible wall between me and my partner.

Yun cleaned her plate first and leaned towards me. "Whenever you're ready," she whispered.

"We should go," I announced, breaking the lengthening silence. "We'll be at the portal before midnight."

I stood slowly, remembering my queasiness from my new 'I can't walk at normal speed' gift. Logan didn't hesitate to take my arm and push in my chair. He pulled his wallet from his pocket and handed Kellen a hundred-dollar bill. I was surprised when my partner accepted it. Kellen had tons of money and could easily pay for our meal. I didn't think the same applied for Logan.

We walked out together, no one saying anything until we reached the car.

"Well that was interesting," Yun said as she hopped in the back seat.

I slid into the passenger seat, and Logan closed my door.

"I'm not sure I'd call it interesting," I mumbled.

Logan got in the driver's side and started the engine, turning on the air conditioner. Utah wasn't as warm as the Nevada desert, but it was still late summer. He swiveled in his seat to face me.

"What makes you think you and I can stop a vampire army?" he asked, surprising me with the harshness in his question.

I didn't really have an answer. "How else are we going to keep Kellen from doing something stupid?" I countered. "Besides, if Kellen can put on a good enough show with his mage warriors leaving tonight, the vampires will be at Victor's, not in Australia."

"Even if he does, Jack will have a small force waiting for us." Was he really mad at me? His furrowed brow and clenching jaw seemed to indicate so, but I was too overwhelmed to be sure.

"Then we'll convince the Australian mages to fight," I argued. "You know Kellen better than I do. Was there any other way to keep him from going after his family?"

"No," he huffed. "But this could end badly for us." He shifted further in his seat. "Yun, no one knows about the animosity between AJ and Kellen. I'm sure I don't have to tell you how important it is that no one finds out."

"Nope," she replied. "I was shocked when there weren't any hugs and kisses, but I understand why. What a prick!"

"Kellen's complicated, but he isn't all bad," I said, not sure why I needed to defend him. He'd made difficult choices—albeit not always good ones—and I wasn't sure I would have done things that much differently. "His first priority is the mages, as it should be."

"Yeah, but he shouldn't be willing to sacrifice his partner," she countered, glancing from me to Logan. "Anyway, I saw a side of him today I'd rather forget. I think he's got genuine regret, but is it for your safety or because he got caught?"

I turned away from Yun and avoided Logan's gaze. I didn't really want to know the answer to that. My vampire turned around as well and put the SUV into drive. My mind worked over the new information, putting it together with the old. Several things still didn't make sense to me. Like why Jack kept attacking Victor.

"What's so important about Victor's pack?" I asked.

Logan glanced at me for a moment. "Most important is the shifters' immunity to the vampires' venom. Second is they are best equipped to challenge the vampires," he explained. "Their speed and strength even the odds between the two species. Victor's pack is the strongest in North America, and his cousin leads the pack in Europe. If Jack can eliminate them, it will go a long way to derailing the shifters' support for the mages."

"Would they change sides?" I asked, surprised I hadn't thought of it myself. "The shifters, I mean. Would they really support Jack?"

Logan shook his head, and Yun snorted.

"No," she replied. "Ignoring the fact that vampires will always be our enemy, shifters are naturally tuned to the earth. Our instincts drive us to protect it. Jack's plan will result in a war no one will win."

I turned around and gave her a skeptical look. "Really? Because Logan doesn't look like the enemy to me."

"There are obvious exceptions." She waved a hand at me and blushed. "He and Otto being the best examples."

Their explanations made sense. Without the shifters' natural ability to fight against the vampires, Jack's chances of success increased dramatically.

"Anyway, we won't have time to take you back to Jonathan's," Logan said, pulling out of the parking lot and into traffic. "Do you mind taking my car home?"

"Not at all," Yun replied. "You want me to leave all your clothes in the back seat?"

"That's fine. We'll change at the hotel and take a small bag with us," he responded.

"Cool. AJ, do you mind if I keep the dress?"

I glanced back to find her smiling at me. "Sure, it looks great on you," I replied, returning her smile.

Her carefree attitude was a little contagious, but not enough to keep the smile on my face. I still had a hundred questions to ask Logan, but they would have to wait until we were alone.

Chapter 10

An hour later, Yun left in Logan's SUV with all but one backpack. I sat on the edge of the bed in a pair of yoga pants and a t-shirt; I had no need for a fancy new wardrobe in Australia. Logan dropped onto the mattress next to me.

"We'll need to pick up some warmer clothes for you," he said, tapping on the screen of his smartphone. "It looks like the average temperature in Melbourne is fifty-five degrees right now."

"Damn. I hadn't even thought of that," I mumbled.

"We'll get a taxi to drop us at the nearest department store before we go. They should have fall stuff out by now." He laid back and tossed his phone on the pillow. "Once it gets dark, I want to take you out to practice running at full speed. You're already doing much better just walking."

I laid down next to him, my legs dangling off the side of the bed. "I think I got more than just your speed," I said, staring at the ceiling. "And I think it started before Spirit did his thing."

"Really?" Logan rolled over on his side and I turned my head towards him.

"Yeah. I've been able to smell most vampires once they're close," I replied. "I think Spirit added everyone else."

"I see. I wonder if that's all."

I shrugged, giving my attention to the flat white ceiling paint. I needed to ask about his new eating habits but didn't want to. Kind of like a horrible car accident that you can't look away from, even though you should. Maybe I didn't need to know, just like I didn't need to see him fight. Yeah, right. If we were going up against a pack of vampires, I needed to fight too. It'd be better if Logan and I trained together with Niyol. It was stupid to keep jumping into fights not knowing each other's strengths, or in my case, weaknesses.

"What are you thinking about?" Logan asked, trailing a finger down my neck.

"You don't crave me anymore, do you?"

"That's a loaded question, princess," he replied.

I rolled to my side and laughed. "I suppose you're right."

"I no longer crave your blood," he said, running his fingers down my shoulder. "My vampire needs are no longer clouding my human desires."

"I'm not sure that's a good thing," I whispered, his touch making me shiver.

"How so?"

"Your vampire needs kept everything else, um, reserved."

His stupid smirk showed itself and I blushed.

"I still don't see the problem," he murmured as he moved closer to me, and my breath hitched.

Damn him! We didn't have time for this. I pushed against his chest, and he stopped, but his eyes begged for more. My heart raced, and I was pretty sure he could hear it.

"I have questions," I said, surprised at my breathlessness.

"Of course you do." A second later, he hovered over me, trailing kisses down my neck. "Do you know how good it feels to do this and not fight back the urge to bite you?"

"No, but I can imagine," I whispered, tilting my head to give him more. What the hell was I doing? I was supposed to be pushing him away. I had questions.

"Ask your questions," he mumbled as his hand swept beneath my shirt.

"I can't think when you do that." I ran my fingers through his hair and moaned as his hands became more curious. "I really do have questions, Logan."

He rolled over onto his back, taking me with him. "Fine." He laced his fingers behind his head and growled at me. I stuck my tongue out and sat up, almost regretting it. The focus of his desire lined up perfectly with mine, distracting me despite the layers of clothing between us. I rolled off him and crossed the room.

"You are a huge distraction," I muttered.

"Thank you."

I rolled my eyes and tried to put out the fire in my middle. "Seriously, I need to understand your changes," I said, collecting my thoughts as best I could. "Does taking another vampire's blood change you? Like a mage's blood is different from a human's, and a shifter is poisonous to you."

Logan sat up, his playfulness vanishing. "I felt like nothing could stop me," he said. "I think I took everything from them, not just their blood. I could feel their strength and magic infusing into me." He stood and closed the space between us again, but he didn't touch me. "It was terrifying and exhilarating. I can see me getting hooked on it like a drug."

Well *that* didn't sound good. Would he go on a vampire killing spree now? Was that really a bad thing? Probably not, considering Jack's goals, except it might make him reckless, which would get us both killed.

"Do we trust Braden after what he did to you?" I asked.

He took a step back and turned away. "I don't know. He had to know it wouldn't kill me as long as I fed immediately."

"But I was the only thing on the menu."

"Yeah."

"I assume you would've had to kill me in order to heal."

He dropped back onto the bed, putting his elbows on his knees and threading his fingers through his hair. "Not necessarily, but it would've taken a great deal of control to stop before you died."

This time I closed the space between us, sitting down next to him. "And how much effort did it take to not even start?"

He lifted his head and turned those hazel eyes on me. "So, what did he intend to prove?" Logan asked, changing the subject.

"I don't know," I replied, holding his gaze. "Did he lurk outside the window and watch Göksu heal you? Does it even matter if he saw? I can't see how Braden can gain anything from it."

No matter how many ways I wrapped my head around it, I couldn't understand what Braden had tried to accomplish. My death? Or did he just get a kick out of being cruel?

"I suppose he could have been lurking, but I don't know if it matters, either," Logan replied. "But does that mean he also saw Niyol show up with Mr. Universe with wings?"

I raised an eyebrow at him and stifled a giggle. "Mr. Universe with wings?"

"Don't tell me you didn't notice the muscles rolling across his chest."

This time I didn't stop the laugh. "Oh my God, Logan! Jealous much?"

"I wasn't the one drooling over him."

Was my vampire pouting? We played this game before and I fell for his antics.

"I wasn't drooling," I insisted, pushing his shoulder. "I was in awe over the magical wings. Didn't you see the way the magic swirled through them?"

"No, I was too caught up watching you drool."

I pushed him again, but he didn't move. "You are *not* serious."

He crossed his arms over his chest. "What if I am?"

"He's an elemental!" I exclaimed. "He doesn't have any of the necessary... tools to satisfy a woman."

"How do you know?"

I jumped up from the bed and stared down at him. I knew he was deliberately pushing me, so why did I keep arguing? "I can't believe we're having this discussion." I put my hands on my hips and glared at him. "Do you really not know how I feel about you?"

"How could I possibly know when you keep pushing me away?" Logan countered.

He was right, but I wasn't telling him that. I'd already been bitten by that snake once with Kellen. I thought he cared and look how that turned out. I had begged, pleaded, and prayed for my foster parents to love me and look how that turned out.

"You…" I pointed a finger at him as tears welled in my eyes. "No one has ever loved me, Logan."

Before I could blink away my tears, his hands wrapped around my fingers and his forehead connected with mine. "Then let me be the first," he whispered.

"I hate you right now," I mumbled.

"That wasn't the answer I was looking for."

"If I love you and you leave..."

He covered my lips with his, stopping my comment. I knew it was foolish, but I couldn't stand the thought of being heartbroken. And if he left me, my heart would shatter. I leaned into his kiss, just like he knew I would.

He ended the moment with a sigh and stepped back, still holding my hands in his. "I'm not leaving," he said.

I had to believe him. It was too late to tell myself I didn't love him. "Okay. And I'll try not to be so pitiful and insecure."

"Deal. Now, any more questions before we leave?"

"Can we learn how to fight together? I had no idea what to do with that ogre. I'm sure there was a better way if we would've coordinated."

"Yes, and hopefully we'll get some time to do that before we get to Australia," Logan replied, releasing one of my hands. "Your plan has a lot of holes."

"I know," I said, shrugging. "I just couldn't think of anything else that would convince Kellen to stay here."

"Hopefully you'll be able to convince the mages not to kill me when I pop out of the portal."

"That's the least of my worries," I said, drawing his full attention. "Vampires can't use the portal, remember? They won't know who you are. Besides, how many mages can sense a vampire?"

"I don't know if they can sense vampires as much as they notice our unnatural reflexes, which you now have."

"Oh. We need to work on that." They might think I was a vampire if I didn't get my shit together.

"It'll be dark in less than an hour," Logan said. "Let's call for our taxi, buy you a couple sweat shirts, and then go for a run. I can't wait to catch you." He winked and released my other hand, reappearing on the bed a second later to snatch up his phone.

He swung the backpack over his shoulder and held out his hand to me. I sighed, like I wasn't going to accept the invitation. Yeah, right. I laced my fingers in his and let him lead me from the room.

Ten minutes later, a taxi rolled up outside the hotel. Logan asked the driver to take us to the nearest department store as we scooted in the back seat. When we arrived, Logan paid with cash. Did he always pay with cash? He must have, because I'd never seen him swipe a credit card. I'd also never seen him stop at an ATM. Just how much cash did he carry around? I sighed, remembering the envelope Kellen had given me at dinner… which was now heading back to Logan's house, hidden amongst our new wardrobe.

"Do you know who bought my clothes yesterday?" I asked, following him into the store.

"Yes," he replied.

I waited a couple seconds, expecting him to answer me. He didn't. "And?"

"Does it matter?"

"Duh! I need to know who to pay back," I replied, gripping his elbow and forcing him to stop between two aisles. "According to Kellen, I have money now. I don't like owing someone."

"I don't want your money," he stated, stepping towards me to avoid a woman and three small children.

"You paid for all of that?"

"Who did you think paid?"

"Jonathan or Kellen." I thought back to my conversation with Manny. "Our fashion guru implied Marissa had taken care of it. I knew Victor wasn't involved, so I assumed the other two."

He looked down at me and scowled. Damn. That was the second time today I got that look. "I'm not as rich as Kellen, but I'm not destitute, AJ." He spun on his heel and headed to the women's clothing department.

I nearly ran after him but was afraid of what would happen. So I stood there like an idiot for several moments, before focusing on one foot at a time. *This was ridiculous.*

When I caught up to him, he already had three hooded sweatshirts in his arm. "We should also buy you some cargo pants," he said. "But we need to go the boy's section for that."

I almost snapped at him for making fun of my less than five-foot height, but I refrained. I'd already pissed him off once. Make that twice today.

"I'm sorry," I mumbled.

"You can make it up to me later." He offered his hand again without a smile and I took it. Of course.

We picked up a couple pair of cargo pants from the boy's section, along with socks and a pair of boots. I felt like we were outfitting for a camping trip. After Logan paid—and I remained silent about it—he called another cab. It dropped us at an old train station on the edge of town just as the sun fell behind the western mountains. I should have known the name of the mountain range, but I didn't. I was pretty sure it was some section of the Rockies but had no idea which one.

"This place is kind of creepy," I muttered under my breath.

"Yep. I'm hoping for some practice," Logan said.

I looked up at him with narrowed eyes, assuming he meant to practice on real vampires.

"Do you think you can repeat the shards of glass you used on Fiona?" he asked.

"They were Niyol's, not mine," I corrected. "But I should be able to, in theory. It can't be much different than my spear."

He raised an eyebrow at me. "That really was Niyol's doing?"

"Yep."

"Okay, we'll work on that later. Let's see how fast you are." He pulled the straps on the backpack tight around his shoulders, then held his hand out to me. "We'll start out slow and increase the speed as we go," he said. "I'm going to assume your stamina is not the same as mine, so we're only going to the end of the station." He pointed down a line of tracks leading away from the station. A dirt trail wide enough for one vehicle ran between the two tracks.

"Okay." I laced my fingers in his and took a deep breath. "Ready."

A slight tug on my hand signaled Logan's forward motion. I kept pace pretty easily, staying focused on the ground blurring beneath my feet. I didn't want to trip and fall, which would likely happen if I got distracted. I wasn't ready for Logan's sudden stop and ran into his back, rolling both of us over several times.

"Warn me next time," I grumbled, pushing myself off the ground.

"Watch something besides your feet." I looked up at my vampire to find him grinning at me. "Let's try that again. Only this time, I'm not holding your hand. Follow right behind me."

I brushed my palms on my yoga pants and nodded. I could do this without falling on my face. "Ready."

Logan took off again, and I focused on his back. He was still wearing dress slacks with his unbuttoned shirt flapping at his waist. I nearly stumbled when I realized I could see him. I'd never been able to see him when he moved this quick, and there was no doubting the speed as everything else flew by me in a blur.

He stopped suddenly, again. I would've plowed into him if he hadn't caught me.

"I could," I said between gasps of air, "see you."

He raised my arms over my head helping me take deeper breaths. I had no idea that worked so well, but it was a trick I needed to remember.

"Thank you," I said when my breathing returned to something close to normal. "I've never been able to see you when you sprint around like that. Why now?"

"Because you were moving at the same speed," he replied, lowering my arms. "We definitely need to work on stamina, but not today. I don't want you worn out before we even get started."

"How fast were we moving?"

"Pretty quick."

I felt the evasion and smacked his shoulder. "You mean slow for you and fast for me."

"Isn't that always the case?" He smiled, and I knew he wasn't talking about running. He pulled me to his chest before I could reply. "Let's refresh your basic hand-to-hand combat. We're being watched."

"How can you tell?" I whispered.

He smiled, revealing slightly elongated fangs. Damn. "Ready?"

I nodded, and he leaned down and kissed my neck. His fangs brushed against my skin, making me shiver.

"As long as you move as fast as I do, you can see me, princess."

He danced back, and I immediately followed. He swept his leg towards mine, but I leapt over it before he hit me.

"Very good," my vampire purred.

"Thank you. Do I get a weapon?"

"If you wish."

A short shard of condensed air appeared in my hand, looking a lot like sharpened glass. I flipped it back and forth in front of my chest twice, then lunged. Logan jumped back, then slipped to my left. I followed his movement, jabbing my small blade at his stomach. He twisted to the side and grabbed my wrist, swinging me around and pulling my back into his chest. I went with it. Then, I used our momentum to thrust my hip into his groin. He bent over, still holding my wrist. I dropped my weapon and grabbed his forearm, taking his weight on my back and rolling him over my shoulder. He fell to the ground with a thud, and I sat on his stomach. Like he couldn't just throw me off again.

"I like this new toy," I said, grinning wildly at his surprised expression. "I might actually be able to stab you."

"I was taking it easy on you, but I can see it wasn't necessary," he stated. "No weapons for you, little girl." He wrapped his hands around my waist and lifted me just as easily as I knew he could. Rather than standing, he sat up and lowered me onto his lap. "We're about to have company," he whispered. My smile vanished, but his didn't. "You fought like a vampire, not a human," he continued softly, kissing my neck.

"But I smell like a human," I hissed in his ear.

"They won't know that until it's too late." He continued kissing my neck and his hands found their way under my shirt.

"How can you not be worried?" I asked, scanning the empty station behind him, trying to ignore how good his hands felt on my skin.

"Because you are amazing," he replied.

Several flickers emerged from the shadows of the old building and I tensed. The sun was long past the horizon, leaving only shades of pink and purple across the sky. Logan stood, but didn't let me go.

"Did you see how many?" he asked, his gaze not leaving my face.

"Maybe five?" I answered, realizing the importance of his question. I had seen their shadows in the dark. My eyebrows rose.

"I was truly hoping that was the case," he said.

Did he mean the number of vampires or was he talking about my ability to see them? I didn't have time to ask, as four men and two women appeared about fifty feet away, fanning out in a half circle to my right.

"Well, what do we have here?" the tallest man asked, shadows concealing most of his face.

"Good evening," Logan said. "We're out for a stroll, hoping to catch the next train."

A sharp laugh erupted from one of the women, but she snapped her mouth closed a second later. A stiff breeze blew into my face, bringing with it their myriad of smells. Tangy metal, cedar, over-ripe strawberries, and something weird I couldn't place.

"You looking for a clan or just passing through?" the tall male asked, taking a step closer.

"Just passing through," Logan responded.

"Then I suggest you keep going."

I looked up at my vampire. His fully-extended fangs hung over his bottom lip and the whites of his eyes were completely gone. Shit. This was gonna get ugly. There was no way these guys didn't see that. Logan's hand slipped from my waist, and I felt his claws run across my butt. Yep, this was gonna get ugly.

My vampire really needed to get a grip.

The group across from us shifted restlessly, and I couldn't help but notice several sets of claws in the group. This was really gonna suck. Could I create several shards of glass and throw them with any accuracy? Probably not. Would I be the vampire's first target? Most definitely.

So what the hell was Logan thinking?

Niyol?

Don't worry, princess. I'm with you.

Could you tell me your plan really quick, so I don't screw it up?

My elemental chuckled, and the wind whipped around us, drawing dirt and small rocks into the air.

I'll get the two in the middle and leave the girls to you.

You're such a gentleman.

He chuckled again as Logan lunged at the tallest vampire. I didn't have time to watch them collide, as a short, stout woman and lanky man rushed towards me. So much for leaving the girls to me. I drew my spear, making it longer than normal, and dropped to my knees. My weapon swept across both their shins with a loud snap. The impact jarred my wrists, but I knew I wouldn't have time to cry over it. I jumped to my feet and spun around just in time to block the woman's claws coming towards my face.

She grabbed my spear and pulled, dragging me with it. Her lanky friend rushed to my left side, swiping at my ribs. I sucked in my gut and released my weapon. Shorty fell backward from the lack of resistance, and I blasted Lanky with a gust of air, sending him skidding across the rocky earth.

"You bitch!" the short woman yelled. "You're a mage!"

"No shit!" I yelled back, drawing on the blood in her veins and pulling it towards me.

She screamed, and her eyes grew wide as streams of blood poured from her skin. How did I not see that last time? Was it my new eyesight or had I done something different? Bile rose in my throat, forcing its way into my mouth. I clutched my stomach and heaved, falling to my knees and hoping Lanky wasn't getting ready to make me his next meal.

Shorty's scream lasted for only a second before her body fell to the ground, along with the streams of blood between us. Lanky boy stood silent off to my left.

"Holy shit," someone said from behind me. I assumed it was one of the vampires Niyol was playing with. "That's just wrong."

I pushed myself to my feet and turned around. Logan's clawed hand wrapped around one of the vampire's forearms. The other female stared past me at the corpse of her 'friend,' for lack of better term. I expected concern or sorrow, but her curled lips and narrowed brow hinted at disgust. Two more bodies lay in the dirt, but I couldn't tell if they were still alive.

"You're the Magister," the female whispered.

"No, I'm a mage trying to stop a war," I said, my voice shaking from adrenaline and fear. "You can either walk away now or die. Those are your only choices."

She looked over at the vampire in Logan's grasp who shrugged to pull his arm away. "I ain't trying to fight that," he said. "She could suck us all dry at once and we wouldn't stand a chance."

"I'm with you, man," Lanky said, making a wide path around me.

"Yeah."

The woman joined the two men, leaving the others behind without a backward glance. Did they really have no compassion for their fallen? I finally looked back to Logan and broke. I hadn't wanted to kill that woman, vampire or not. We should've been able to talk our way out of that, but no. We took on six. I wasn't prepared to fight the two that attacked me, much less six.

I jumped to my feet and stomped over to Logan, slapping him as hard as I could across his jaw. "Never do that again," I commanded.

I snatched our backpack from the ground and started walking down the tracks. I had no idea where I was going, but I wasn't staying there. How dare he endanger my life like that for no reason? We could've walked away before they'd even approached us. I was certain they'd waited in the background, knowing Logan sensed their presence. Would they have followed us if we just left? I didn't think so. For some stupid reason, my vampire needed to prove something.

There was no way I was listening to anything he had to say.

Chapter 11

We walked along the tracks for five minutes before Logan cleared his throat. I called it walking, but we were running. The trees rushed by in a blur, along with the railroad ties.

"The palace is in the opposite direction," Logan said, not even the slightest bit winded.

I stopped—sort of—stumbling several steps before coming to a complete halt. I stretched my hands over my head and took deep breaths. What was he thinking? Why would he do something so stupid? I squeezed my eyes shut and took another breath, Logan's spearmint filling my lungs. My anger flared higher and my hand shot towards him.

He caught my wrist, forcing me to open my eyes. When he started to speak, I swung with my other hand. He snatched it as well and pulled both down to my sides. I glared at him.

"The tall female followed our cab from the hotel, then again from the store," he said. I remained silent, searching for the lie that wasn't there. He continued. "As a vampire, I can feel their intentions. They would not have let us go."

"Why didn't you say so from the beginning?" I hissed, jerking my hands free from his grasp and backing away.

"I didn't realize it mattered," he replied. "They were going to try to kill us regardless, and I didn't want you to panic."

"That's stupid, Logan. You should've just told me," I said. "I thought there was some chance they would chat, and we would walk away. Until you showed your ass, then I knew we were fighting."

"I wasn't the first to show my ass," he growled.

"Are you growling at me?"

He pressed his lips together and breathed deeply through his nose.

"Go ahead, Logan," I taunted. "I could use a good fight right now. I'm really pissed at you."

"You're pissed at me?"

He closed the space between us, and I skipped back again. He jumped forward and reached for me, but I rolled to the right and slipped out of his grasp.

"AJ."

"Logan."

"Don't play games with me."

"Whatever."

I lunged forward and slapped his cheek, then sprinted away. I didn't hear him following me, but I knew he was. I called the wind to my back and nearly toppled forward as it pushed me faster.

"Gently, Niyol," I hissed.

"You're still not fast enough, princess," my elemental said, floating beside me. "Do you want me to slow him down?"

"No, this is between us."

"I assumed as much."

He disappeared, taking my helpful gust of wind with him. Logan's body slammed into mine, but he managed to wrap himself around me as we rolled through a pack of briars and stopped beneath a large pine tree. I moaned, knowing a hundred small cuts covered my exposed skin, despite Logan's efforts to protect me. He should've just let me go. I lost my temper and acted like a child.

"You are impossible," he mumbled, his arms still wrapped around me. "I think I broke something."

"Damn, I'm sorry," I said, trying to push away from him and find out what was broken. "Let go. I think Göksu will let me heal you now."

He loosened his grip and rolled onto his back. I sat next to him and sighed. His clothes were in tatters, likely from rolling through that briar patch. I ran my hands down his chest and abdomen, pushing a small surge of healing into him. A wave of pain returned my greeting, typical of the healing. I got to feel the hurt too. I wouldn't complain, though; I was healing my vampire. The one my water elemental refused to acknowledge until now.

"I don't feel anything major," I said. "At least nothing that you can't heal on your own."

He reached up and pulled me on top of him. "I just wanted your hands on me."

"You ass," I hissed, trying to push away.

"I promise to communicate better," he whispered. "I'm not used to having anyone else in my space, especially twenty-four hours a day."

I relaxed and lay my head on his chest, suddenly exhausted. Probably from all the damn running and fighting. I wouldn't be worth two cents when we arrived at the palace.

"I'll try not to second-guess your judgement, especially when it comes to vampires," I said. His fingers trailed my spine, giving me goosebumps. "And I'm sorry for turning your world upside down."

"You're the best thing that's ever happened to me."

Did he really mean that? He must believe it, because I felt no deception from him. But, had he felt that way about my mother until she betrayed him? Did he see her when he looked at me? I cringed at the thought. Had he and my mom had sex? I shuddered especially hard at that thought.

"What is it?" Logan asked, holding me tighter.

"Did you love my mom?" He laughed, and I looked up at him. "How is that funny?"

"No, I didn't love your mother," he responded, still chuckling. "She was my mage partner, but that was all."

"But Marissa said..." I remembered it perfectly – sitting at the enormous table in Victor's lodge just before our first battle with the vampires. She said my mother hadn't returned Logan's love.

"Stop. Marissa is a gossip. Her knowledge is based in truth, but she tends to add romance where there is none," he explained.

"Then why did you stay with her?" I asked, needing to understand what would make him endure her crazy.

"I made a pledge as her mage partner," he replied. "I try very hard not to break my promises."

"Oh." I guessed that made sense, and I really I hoped he meant it. He'd made a lot of promises to me in the last few days.

I found my comfortable spot just beneath his collar and drew in his scent. Knowing their relationship hadn't been romantic made me feel a little better. That would be really weird, and I definitely should've asked that question a few days ago, before we had sex.

"Are you okay?" Logan asked after several moments of silence.

"I'm really tired," I mumbled. "How close are we to the palace?"

"About thirty minutes, if I carry you," he replied.

I closed my eyes and splayed my fingers across his chest. His muscles twitched beneath my hand. I wished I had his stamina. I knew he was lying here in the dirt for my benefit, not his.

"What time is it?" I asked.

"You have time for a quick nap," he replied. "I'll wake you up."

I smiled. I couldn't believe I was already over being mad at him. He talked me out of it so easily. Should I be suspicious? Probably. Was I? Not at all. I had to trust that my elementals wouldn't leave me with him if he wasn't good for me. Niyol would surely tell me if I were being stupid.

A soft wind caressed my face and whispered in my ear, a silent answer from my elemental.

"I love you," I mumbled.

"I love you, too, princess," Logan whispered back.

I didn't correct him. I'd been talking to Niyol, but I loved my vampire too. That wasn't how I wanted to tell him, but I could always blame it on my exhaustion.

Five minutes later, or at least it felt like five minutes, Logan woke me. I was no longer lying on his chest, but he'd been kind enough to fold his tattered shirt beneath my head.

"Come on," he said, "it's time."

"This sucks," I mumbled, rolling over. A sharp stick poked my ribs and I cursed.

"Yes, it does. We probably should've spent our time sleeping rather than fighting." He fingers wrapped around my arms and pulled me up. "But we didn't. When you're done changing, we'll make our way to the palace."

I rubbed my eyes and yawned, finally noticing the backpack at my feet. Oh yeah, cargo pants, sweat shirts, and boots. "I'm guessing you're immune to the cold?" I asked, pulling off my ruined t-shirt and yoga pants. "Wow, I really need a shower."

Logan chuckled from a few yards away. He'd only half turned his back to give me privacy, but I didn't care. "Sort of. If it's really cold, it'll slow me down, but I won't suffer from frost bite or hypothermia like you."

"Do you think Kellen will have coffee?" I asked, pulling a sweatshirt over the clean t-shirt I just put on.

"I doubt it," he replied. "Do you want to keep these clothes or leave them here?"

He stood next to me as I buttoned the cargo pants now covering my bottom half. "Did you keep yours?"

"Hell, no. I lost the fight with the briar patch."

I giggled and stuffed my feet into my new boots. "I guess there's no point carrying more than we need to," I mumbled. "I hope these boots don't leave blisters. Maybe I should stick with my sneakers."

Logan zipped up the backpack and handed it to me. "You carry this, and I'll carry you both."

I took the bag from him and pulled the straps over my shoulders. One day, I'd find out how strong he really was. He lugged me everywhere like I weighed nothing, just like now. He bent to one knee and pulled me up on his back. I immediately wrapped my legs around his waist and arms around his neck. I hadn't realized it until just now, but he never tried to show off around me. He always acted like a normal person, as normal as he could, anyways. He took off running, and I recognized it was much faster than I was capable of. I never had anything to compare it to before, until now. I was really slow.

My thoughts wandered to the vampires we fought earlier. Logan said they wouldn't have let us leave, and I tried not doubt him. It was hard, though. The memory of that woman's blood hovering in the air as I pulled it from her made me queasy. How did I even do that? It's not like Göksu ever helped me fight, but maybe it was my water element. Still… he was adamant that he would only help me heal. I frowned.

Göksu?

Yes, child.

Don't act like you didn't hear my thoughts, I snapped. *How do I pull the blood from a vampire like that?*

Every mage has a small amount of magic they can use without their elemental's power, he replied. *Even Logan can use limited amounts. Though his magic is severely reduced because of his death.*

I thought about his reply. Was that what most mages did without realizing it? Did the elements only truly add their strength when the need arose?

What does your heart tell you, child? Göksu asked, answering my silent questions.

It depends on the mage, I responded. *Kellen's elements are dedicated to him, so they make him strong.*

And others will always be weak because their intentions are clouded.

So, why do you deny me? Is my soul broken like my mother's?

The thought hurt, but if everything he said was true, then I needed to know.

Logan slowed then came to a stop in the middle of the narrow path. I peeked over his shoulder at Göksu's glowing form blocking our way, his humanoid body larger than I'd ever seen him.

"What's wrong?" Logan whispered.

"We're either getting ready to hug or fight," I replied, letting go of him and sliding to the ground.

My elemental strolled towards us, the silhouettes of the trees behind him visible through his watery form. He stopped a few yards away and sat in the middle of the path.

"Sit," he ordered.

I did, but Logan didn't.

"We're sort of on a tight schedule," my vampire said. "Do we have to do this now?"

"Yes, it cannot wait."

Logan sighed and sat in the dirt next to me.

"Alisandra, I do not deny you for the reason you think," he began. "You carry more power than you're capable of wielding."

A sharp laugh escaped my lips. "You must have me confused with someone else. I let Niyol do whatever he wants because he's better at it than I am." I picked up a small pebble and rolled it between my fingers. "When I heal someone, it's you, not me. I'm merely a vessel for you to control, not the other way around."

"Do you not hear yourself, child?"

"I can't play this game right now, Göksu! I'm tired and overwhelmed," I whined. "Tell me what you need me to hear."

"You are the vessel for us," he repeated my words back to me. "Your power is only limited by the amount I choose to give you." A tiny droplet rose from the hand on his knee and floated towards me. "It is the same for Niyol. He chooses to be actively involved, doing the fighting for you. But he could just as easily give that power to you and let you wield it." The drop of water hovered in front of me, growing in size the longer it stayed. "I won't be the active warrior Niyol chooses to be, but you aren't ready to use the power I will give you, either."

"I'll never be ready if you don't make the time to train me," I mumbled. "Niyol at least gave two weeks of knowledge. Two weeks that I begged from you, but you refused." I swatted at the golf ball sized bubble in front me, my fingers swiping through it. Rather than fall apart, it grew again.

"I hesitated because of Logan, child. I should not have."

The orb of water in front me was now the size of a basketball, hovering inches from my chest. I eyed it warily, not really wanting to get my clean clothes wet.

"How does this help?" I asked. "We need to get to the palace, then confront a pile of vampires half way around the world. We don't have time for this."

"Niyol is your sword, princess, but I am your shield."

The orb of water smashed into my chest, throwing me on my back and crushing the backpack against my spine. I moaned with the onslaught of pain, but it didn't last. My elemental's warm healing magic coated my body, seeping into my sore muscles, then surging towards the well of power at my core. I rubbed my chest and sat up, shocked that I wasn't soaking wet. *How did he do that?*

"Remember, I'm your protector." He stood, his flowing form losing shape as it always did. "When you return from Australia, I'll teach you how to use it."

Then, he was gone.

"I'll never understand him," I said, shaking my head and rising to my feet. At least I wasn't tired and sore anymore, and my elemental promised to train me. Stopping wasn't a complete waste of our time after all.

"Do you realize what he meant?" Logan asked, staring down at me. "Your strength is endless."

"I heard him, but I don't think he meant it that way," I said, holding my hand out to him. "We need to get moving."

"I think that's exactly how he meant it." He knelt and helped me on his back once again. "I wonder if all the mages have that ability or is it just you?"

"I'm sure it's all of us," I replied. "Göksu confirmed that our element decides how much to give us."

Logan took off again but still tried to continue our conversation. "If it were all mages, he wouldn't have taken the time to point out your differences," he yelled back to me.

"I think you're reading too much into it!" I yelled back, but Logan's reply was lost to the wind around us.

Chapter 12

The thick forest that surrounded us for the last twenty minutes ended in a wide meadow. Logan stopped at the edge of the trees, and I slid from my perch. The faint light from the half-moon barely lit the open space. I was grateful for my new vampire-night vision.

"Let me guess," I muttered, "the palace is hidden in this field."

"Not very original, but it works," Logan whispered.

"How are we getting in?"

"There are a couple ways," he replied. "I'm going to assume Kellen reinforced the magical barrier and repaired any holes that used to be there. That leaves the underground tunnels, which are likely patrolled."

"Is there not a front door we can just knock on?" I asked. "I *am* the Magister."

He looked down at me and gave me that silly grin. "Yes, you are." He rubbed his thumb across my jaw. "We need to walk slowly, but with purpose. The guards shouldn't doubt that you know exactly where the entrance is and that you fully expect them to open the door."

And he knew where the door was because of my mother. I bit back my surging emotions.

Instead, I smiled up at him. "So, not sprinting across the field with reckless abandon."

"Exactly. Stay by my side."

"Always."

His eyebrow rose a fraction, then he started towards the not-so-empty meadow. I forced myself to take slow, steady steps. Logan's easy pace helped. We circled around the north side of the meadow and stopped, but after several seconds passed, nothing happened.

"What are you waiting for?" I asked, raising my voice and cringing as it echoed back at me.

A short, stocky man with shoulder-length hair suddenly appeared a few yards away. He wore dark pants and an equally dark long sleeve shirt.

"There are few special enough to use the gate," the man answered in a low voice.

"And your Magister doesn't fall into that category?" Logan asked.

The guard took a step closer and squinted at me.

"She don't look like the Magister," he said. "Last I heard she was still in the palace."

"I'm not required to report my whereabouts to you," I snapped. "Now open the door."

The man's eyes widened at my command. "Sorry, Magister." He turned and pulled a long sword from the nothingness beside him.

I watched in amazement as he raised the sword over his head then pressed it into the invisible wall. Magic swirled around his blade as it ripped an opening in the protective barrier.

"Thank you," I said, stepping through the hole with Logan at my heels.

A long staircase appeared in front of me, and my shoulders slumped. I'd be completely spent by the time I reached the top, and Logan couldn't play taxi for me here. Why couldn't anything just be easy? I started up the steps, mumbling to myself. Kellen should've put in an elevator or even escalators. Maybe I should've stuck around and made that happen.

Just as I suspected, I couldn't breathe when we reached the top and my thighs burned. Fricking lovely.

"Come on, princess," Logan whispered, resting his hand on my back for a moment. "It's nearly midnight. I imagine Kellen is about at the end of his patience."

"He'll have to suck it up," I hissed.

We crossed a small vestibule and entered the large courtyard I remembered from my last visit. Tall lamp posts surrounded the area, casting light across the hundreds of men and women milling around the entrance to the portal.

Kellen noticed us approaching and broke away from the cluster of people around him.

"I was getting worried," he said. "We're ready to go."

"What can you tell us about Australia's portal?" Logan asked.

"It's supposed to be protected, but I can't confirm that," Kellen said, lowering his voice. "It opens into a thick forest. The portal itself is disguised by trees and vines. A small village surrounds the portal."

"Okay, that helps," Logan said. "Where are your warriors going?"

Kellen glanced at me, then back to Logan. I didn't have my emotional shield up, but he must have. I felt nothing from him.

"Victor's," he whispered, turning his back to the crowd. "I suspect three traitors. When I approached them earlier, they had somewhat convincing stories. We'll see."

"Are you leaving first?" I asked.

"Yes." He looked down at me, his features softening from the impassive expression he held. "Please be careful."

"Never."

He and Logan both chuckled as he turned away.

"Alright, folks!" Kellen yelled over the muffled conversations. The crowd parted as he made his way towards the portal. "Let's kick some vampire ass!"

My partner stepped through the shimmering blackness without a second glance. Was I stupid for thinking I should get a hug or even a pat on the shoulder? Maybe, but it didn't ease the pain of his rejection. I thought we both struggled with that fear, or maybe it was just me.

Logan and I stood at the back of the group watching the mages disappear. When the last one fell through the inky blackness, my vampire scooped me up into his arms and stepped through. He stumbled on the other side and sucked in a deep breath.

Sunlight greeted us along with a cold breeze. The smell of wet dirt and vegetation saturated the air. Logan lowered me to my feet but didn't release me.

"Where is everyone else?"

I recognized the man's voice immediately. It was the same one looking for me when Logan stole me away from Kellen's estate. Three men stood among the trees, all of them casting suspicious glares our way. Was this the same trio who were ordered to take me last time? Why did Kellen send them here? Was it to finish the job they failed to complete?

"That's a good question," Logan replied. "I thought we were going to kick some vampire ass."

"Who are you?" the same guy asked. As his eyes drifted to me, recognition set in. "Oh, this is perfect." He glanced at the mage next to him and smiled. "It's the little Magister. Looks like Kellen is giving us free rein to take turns with the little girl before we kill her." He took a step forward, but the dark-haired man on his right grabbed his elbow.

My anger boiled just below the surface. Some people were so sick.

"I don't think so, Carson. Kellen's not stupid." The smart guy in the group warily eyed Logan. "Where are the rest of the mages? If they didn't come here, then he suspected a betrayal."

Carson frowned and looked at the third man in the party, who'd been silent. "What do you think, Stewart? Do you share his paranoia? Do I get the little bitch all to myself?"

Little bitch? What had I ever done to this man? I'd never even met him until today.

"I think I regret ever listening to you," Stewart said, dropping his chin to his chest. "She's here to take her own retribution and leave us for the vampires."

Carson laughed. "Look at her, you fool. She's the size of a child!"

Stewart dropped to one knee and met my gaze, ignoring Carson. "I'm sorry, princess. Whatever you decide, I accept my punishment willingly."

Shock swept through me as I stared at the young man kneeling in the wet leaves. His sincerity was overwhelming, and I wondered what made him join Carson in the first place. Before I could reply, a ring of fire surrounded Stewart. His cries of anguish echoed through the trees, joined by my own scream of rage. The smell of burning hair and skin wafted towards me, choking out my cry.

"No!" I called to the water surrounding me and pulled it over the flames, smothering them and Stewart immediately. He collapsed, his clothes smoldering and weak moans escaping his lips. "You bastard!" I screamed, turning to the sick asshole in front of me. "You would kill one of your own just because he disagreed with you?"

A smile crept across Carson's face, and I lost my mind. How could someone be so cruel and heartless?

"Just one less to share with," he said, then glanced at his last companion and raised his arm.

My spear appeared in my hand and I lunged at Carson, not even thinking about my vampire speed. The spear's tip drove through his heart before he could react. He looked down at the weapon buried in his chest and blood pooling around my fist. His mouth opened but no words escaped. I released the spear and stepped back, allowing the man to fall to his knees, still staring at me.

What had I done? *I just killed a man*, I thought in horror. Not a vampire, but a human being. I hadn't even thought about it; I'd just reacted with my anger. Was I becoming a monster just like the rest of them? I should heal him. That would take away some of my evil and guilt... right?

No, princess, you cannot bring him back from the death that has already taken him. Göksu whispered in my mind.

"I'm sorry," I whispered as Carson fell over. I couldn't peel my eyes from the man I killed. "Oh my God." I clamped my hand over my mouth, and tears clouded my vision.

"He needed to die," the second mage's voice drew my attention. He stood a few yards away, Logan's long fingers wrapped around his neck. "Stewart doesn't. He was opposed to this from the beginning."

I'd forgotten about the one asking forgiveness. How stupid. I crawled over to his still smoldering body and nearly lost my lunch or dinner or whatever my last meal was. The skin on his arms and face bubbled, oozing blood and other things I didn't want to think about.

"Göksu, I cannot let him suffer," I whispered, hovering my hand over the skin on his cheek.

I agree. We can save him.

The tears I'd been holding back fell from my eyes as I leaned over the helpless man. My elemental's presence settled next to me even though I couldn't see him. I focused on the pool of magic in my center, feeling it swell to the point of aching. I let it rush through my chest and down my arms, gasping at the intensity of Göksu's power as it flowed from my fingertips.

Pain replaced the pleasure of power as soon as my magic touched his wounds. Holy shit, burns sucked, but I supposed I deserved it for the life I took. I clamped my lips shut against the agony.

Pick the worst pain and move forward, Göksu whispered.

The burns on his arms appeared the most severe, so I started there, working my way to the exposed skin on his neck and face.

Logan's deft hands removed what was left of Stewart's shirt, revealing red angry blisters. "Don't wear yourself out," my vampire whispered. "We still have another fight in our future. These will heal on their own."

I fell back onto my butt and dropped my forehead on my knees. I'd killed a man, without even thinking. No wonder Göksu didn't trust me. Logan rubbed my back, but it didn't help ease my guilt.

"What was your role in this?" Logan asked. I assumed he spoke to the other mage.

"We were supposed to come here with all the mage warriors," he said.

I pulled my head from my knees and looked up at him. Logan was right; we needed answers. My self-loathing would have to wait.

"And do what?" I asked. "And I don't want to hear the mages' story."

His shoulders slumped, his gaze dropping to the wet leaves at his feet. "A group of mage-vampires will be here at dusk. They're supposed to take as many of our mages as they can and run." He paused and glanced up at me. "We were promised immortality. It's hard for you to understand as a dual mage, but the fear of going insane without a partner is real."

"So you sold out your fellow mages for a chance to become some soulless creature?" I asked. "Have you even looked for a partner outside of the US?"

He shook his head but didn't reply.

I jumped to feet, probably too quickly for a mere mage. Damn vampire speed. "Tell me you're not serious. You have a portal that will take you anywhere in the world and you haven't used it?" I raised my arms in disbelief. "Why the hell not?"

"It's not our fault," he pleaded.

"Oh bullshit!"

"Really! The Magister forbid us from visiting the other mage cities."

I rolled my eyes, but I tried to put myself in his shoes. Would I really go against my leader to find my partner? Well, duh. If the choice is insanity or pissing off a pouty bitch…

"Alright, I won't go there even though I really want to. That's the perfect example of fricking sheoples," I spat. "When this is over, we're going on field trips… like damned preschoolers." I mumbled the rest to myself. It wouldn't help to say it out loud. "Take your friend back the palace and make sure the rest of his wounds are cared for. Go ahead and spread the news about our field trips as well. Maybe it'll deter anyone else from making this same stupid decision."

"Yes, Magister."

"Wait." I held up my hand as he reached for his fellow mage. The dead body on the ground drew my gaze. "What's your talent?"

"Air, the same as you."

"Never mind then. I'll find someone to bury him."

"You're not what they said you were," he mumbled, draping Stewart's arm over his shoulder and pulling him to his feet.

"What did they say?" I asked, really looking at the mage for the first time. He was probably in his late twenties, average height and build. His plain features and sandy hair would have him blending in a crowd, totally unnoticed.

He pulled his lips into a tight line and shifted Stewart's weight. "You're nothing like your mother. Carson said you were exactly like her, but he was wrong."

I blinked back my tears, not wanting my crybaby side on display again.

"What's your name?" I asked.

"Marshall," he replied. "I'll do everything I can to undo the rumors Carson started. I imagine Stewart will help."

"Thank you."

"No, thank you." He stepped through the portal, disappearing into its inky blackness.

I fell against Logan, knowing he would catch me, and buried my head in his chest. I didn't stop my tears from soaking his shirt, and he rubbed away my shuddering sobs.

"I can't do this," I mumbled.

"I think you just proved you can," my vampire whispered. "Your people skills are amazing. If Kellen had talked to his mages like that, they would've turned away from him." He gently pushed me back and forced me to look up at him. "But I think you just created a loyalty that he never could."

"Whatever." I wiped the tears from my face with my sleeve. "I'm not cut out for this," I whispered, my gaze shifting to Carson's body again. "We need to bury him."

"We'll find a mage in the village," Logan said, stepping away from the portal and our small battle scene. "Slow and steady."

"Thanks, I needed the reminder."

He held out his hand and I took it. I needed his calming presence as well as his slow pace. Maybe one day I'd get used to my new speed.

We didn't get more than a few feet before being surrounded by dozens of dark-skinned men dressed in cotton pants and long-sleeved shirts. My skin tingled, and I realized they were feeling for my magic. I really needed to learn how to do that.

"You're mages?" I asked, hoping they spoke English. I assumed they would because we were in Australia, but that was stupid. I couldn't expect everyone to automatically speak my own language. I should've found that out before leaving the palace, but it was too late now. Instead, I made a mental note to ask those questions before the field trips I promised Marshall.

"Yes," a tall, slim man replied from the middle of the line. His dark hair hung in long braids past his narrow shoulders. His wide nose and full mouth fit perfectly on his round face, but his icy blue eyes drew my attention. "You're the American Magister?"

"That's what they keep telling me," I replied, smiling. These people were our allies, so I really needed to be nice.

He looked past me at Carson's body then nodded at the two men closest to him. "We'll bury the traitor. You'll come with us and eat."

Food sounded great, especially after he confirmed Carson's role. I had to assume Kellen had told him about possible treachery in the palace, but I didn't bother asking.

"I'd like that very much," I said. "Please lead the way."

After a short five-minute walk, the thick trees gave way to a large group of buildings. Wooden, one story homes lined a narrow street just wide enough for two cars.

Our leader and two other men, who I guessed were next in command, led the procession of mages. Logan and I were sandwiched between them, and I felt my vampire's unease grow as we made our way further into town. I hadn't thought about the risk to him, not really. Another character flaw that reinforced my argument against leadership. I wasn't good at thinking about others.

I wanted to lace my fingers through Logan's but worried about the perception. Everyone assumed Kellen and I were more than partners. Would I endanger Logan more by showing my affection for him?

The farther we walked, the bigger the crowd of onlookers grew, reminding me of my first visit to the palace. I was a spectacle then, just like now. Only I suspected for different reasons. Our escort stopped in front of a long row of buildings that reminded me of a shopping plaza. Seven or eight doors lined the front of the structure, but the center door drew my attention. The same symbol representing the elements graced the front of the carved wood. Now that I knew what those wispy wings stood for, I scoffed at the depiction. It didn't do him justice and reinforced Niyol's claim that no one had even seen Spirit in his true form.

The tall, thin mage pulled open one of the doors and motioned us inside. It was beautiful in a natural sort of way. Native plants lined the entryway and skylights allowed the sun to brighten the space. I looked up at Logan and frowned. Dark shadows hovered beneath his eyes, and I hoped the sun wasn't already wearing on him.

We passed through another set of doors, entering a large dining room.

"Please take a seat," our escort said.

"Thank you," I responded, moving to a table at the edge of the room and close to the door.

We sat down, and I scooted my chair closer to Logan, dropping our bag beneath me. The rest of the mages filed into the room, filling the other tables but not joining us.

"Are you okay?" I whispered, leaning close to him.

"Yes, just a little wary of our welcome," he replied, watching the mages.

"Can you eat?" I asked, knowing they were bringing food.

He looked down at me and winked. "Of course, but I won't like it."

I had the sudden urge to wrap my arms around him. My faced flushed and I covered it with my palms.

"Are you okay?" he asked.

"Yep, just feel like I need to sneeze."

He chuckled and nudged my ribs with his elbow. "Liar."

I looked up just in time to see our escort and his two associates heading towards our table. I needed to do proper introductions. Names were important. I stood just as they reached the table, as did Logan.

"Alisandra," I said, extending my hand.

"Jim." He reached across the table and his large hand engulfed mine, as usual. "This is Dylan and Ezekiel." He pointed to the two men with him.

"Logan, my protector."

Jim raised an eyebrow at me but shook Logan's outstretched hand. We all sat in silence for several moments. I wasn't sure what to expect of our conversation and decided to let Jim lead.

"You didn't appear to need a protector in the woods," Jim finally said.

I smiled. "You'd be surprised. I tend to bite off more than I can chew, then think about the indigestion later."

"Yes, I can see that." He rubbed his chin, his glance constantly going back to Logan. "The traitors said some disturbing things. Are they true?"

"If you witnessed our fight, then you heard the whole story," I replied. "Yes, I believe them."

"So, why are you here?" Jim asked. It wasn't an accusatory question, but I could sense the curiosity radiating off him and the others.

"That's complicated," I said, contemplating how to explain our situation. "Tons of rumors are flying around in North America right now. What I'm about to tell you is as close to the truth as I can reveal." I ran my fingers through my messy curls, reminding me I needed a shower. "Logan and I are part of a small group tasked with finding the mages who are stolen from us. Those who have not fallen to the vampire curse are returned to Kellen and the palace. The others, at least those willing to break away from the vampires, are joining us in our search."

"That answers the question of your whereabouts for the last week or so, but it doesn't explain why you're here," Jim said.

"I'm getting to that," I said as politely as I could. "In our search, we discovered the vampires were planning an attack on your home. A spy within the palace convinced Kellen that he needed to send his entire force here to protect you." I looked over at my partner and he nodded. I left out all kinds of details, but this was better than them going in totally blind. "He fully intended to do just that to ensure the vampires didn't wipe out your group. But what he didn't know was the council was using this as a ruse to pull his mage warriors from the palace. Their true targets are the shifters who support Kellen."

Several expressions raced across Jim's face. Astonishment, fear, disbelief, and anger.

"And those vampires are still coming here, but Kellen's forces are not," Jim stated, anger winning out over the rest.

"We're not certain if the vampires will come," Logan replied. "Marshall confirmed they intend to take your mages and turn them into vampires, which means they won't be here to kill you."

"We believe they will only send a small force," I added. "Logan and I will stay and fight with your mages."

"How will a tiny little girl and her 'protector' fight off a vampire army?" Jim asked, not hiding his skepticism.

"Well, I did warn you I tend to bite off more than I can chew," I replied.

He chuckled and looked over at the man on his right. "Will our warriors be ready for battle an hour before dusk, Dylan?"

"Yes, sir."

"Then let's enjoy this meal and talk of other things."

He took the news better than I expected. I wasn't sure if it made me happy or suspicious. Maybe both.

Several women carried plates of food to our table. I had no idea what I was eating, but it smelled marvelous. A roasted meat covered one side of the dish and a pile of fruits covered the other. A basket of sliced bread appeared in front of me, and my stomach rumbled. I somehow managed to wait for Jim to take a bite before I dove into my dinner.

As I swiped my bread across my empty plate, I glanced over at Logan. His plate was also empty, which surprised me. Would he be sick later? Could he even get sick? Probably not. Damn vampire.

"What's the local time, Jim?" Logan asked, breaking the prolonged silence that lingered while we ate.

"Two in the afternoon," he replied, wiping his lips with a napkin.

"Is there someplace we could shower and possibly take a quick nap?" Logan glanced down at me and I nodded. I really needed it and so did he. "We've been up for almost eighteen hours and would greatly appreciate the rest."

"Absolutely." Jim rose, leaving his plate on the table. "Follow me."

We left the crowded room and made our way back outside. Jim crossed the street to the only two-story home I'd seen so far. A sign on the outside said, 'The Water's Edge Inn.'

"Do you need two rooms or one?" Jim asked, a smile playing on his lips.

"One is fine," I replied, "As long as it has its own bathroom." I should care about his opinions, but I didn't want to be separated from Logan. I'd put him in a difficult situation. There was no way I'd leave him alone.

Jim gave me a full grin and stopped at a desk just inside the foyer, beneath a winding staircase. He spoke to a young man in hushed tones, who jumped to his feet and ran up the stairs.

"You should have about six hours before dusk," Jim stated. "Would you like me to send someone for you?"

"Only if the vampires arrive early," Logan replied. "Thank you for your acceptance and hospitality."

"I look forward to seeing our young Magister in battle." Then, Jim turned on his heel and left us alone in the foyer.

"Wow, no pressure," I mumbled.

A few minutes later, the same young man rushed back down the stairs. "Please follow me, Magister."

With a full stomach and some of the immediate drama subsiding, my exhaustion took over. I really needed to establish better sleeping habits. I traipsed up the stairs, allowing our host to open the last door in the hallway.

"Please let me know if there is anything you need," he said as I stepped past.

"Just sleep, but thank you for the offer."

After he closed the door behind us, Logan locked it, then pulled the only chair in front of the door, trying to wedge it beneath the handle.

"Do you think someone would try to come in?" I asked, dropping the backpack in the middle of the floor.

"Jim knows I'm not a mage," Logan said, giving up on the chair. "He saw us fight, so he also knows you're more than a mage."

"Damn. And I just wanted a shower and a nap," I grumbled.

"I'm probably being paranoid," he said, pulling the drapes closed and sitting on the bed to unlace his boots. "But if we do have to fight, I won't be able to hide what I am." He kicked off one boot and then the other. "I could very well become a casualty, taking you with me."

"Then I'll make it very clear to Jim that if any of his mages attacks you, I'll protect you first and ask questions later," I said, sitting beside him and pulling off my own boots. "Your life is way more important to me."

"Because it's not just my life," Logan muttered.

I looked up at him and scowled. "No, because it is your life. You put up with a lot of unnecessary shit from me and still manage to make me feel loved. It's your life I value and nothing else." I stood and pulled my shirt over my head, throwing it at him. "I'm taking a shower. I smell and I'm grumpy."

He stood, allowing my shirt to fall on the floor. "I'll join my grumpy mage in the shower and try to make you feel better."

My lip quivered, and those damn tears filled my eyes. He called me *his* mage, just like I called him my vampire, only I never did it out loud.

"That wasn't exactly the response I was looking for," Logan said, suddenly in my space, his hands cupping my cheeks.

"I'm grumpy and I stink and you called me your mage," I mumbled.

"What else would I call you?"

"Princess? AJ? Pain in the ass?"

"Come on, pain in the ass, let's get you clean and rested."

Chapter 13

I thoroughly enjoyed my shower, mostly because of Logan's attention. He relaxed me in ways I could only imagine. Of course, it wasn't like I had a ton of experience, but I didn't care. He made me feel good. The only thing that worried me was whether or not he felt the same, but I was too chicken to ask.

I crawled beneath the handmade quilt and soft sheets wearing only a t-shirt and panties. I closed my eyes, listening to my vampire hum in the bathroom. My mind wandered, his soft tune relaxing me even more.

Marshall had said the vampires planned to take the mages, not kill them. Which wasn't surprising... but was it? Someone once told me they would only keep a small number of mage-vampires so they could eliminate them after the war. Had Kellen told me that? Did it even matter who told me what?

Regardless, if they intended to keep the mage-vampires to a minimum, why kidnap more? Or was Braden behind the kidnapping? Would he use them to overthrow Jack? I sat up and opened my eyes, still playing out the conversations in my mind. Braden thought Jack would use the ogres. At least, that's what he'd implied. So, maybe Braden *was* trying to build his own army.

"What's wrong?" Logan asked as he sat on the bed next to me.

I didn't answer, my mind still searching for missing links. My mother had said she would take over the vampires with her new mage-vampire warriors. Was she working with Braden and not Jack? What if Braden planned this whole scenario with the Australia mages? No, it wouldn't make sense for him to tell us about it so we could intervene.

"AJ, talk to me."

I tapped my finger against my chin. Maybe it would help to think out loud? "Okay, I'm verbalizing thoughts, so it might sound stupid. Just go with it." I scooted over so he could join me, which, of course, he did. "Braden wants to stop Jack, so is he trying to build his own army of super vampires? He said Jack is planning on using some of the other supernatural families, so maybe Braden wants to even the odds."

Logan's eyes widened, but he didn't say anything.

"Do you think Braden was actually working with my mother? He seems to hate Jack, so maybe Braden was trying to overthrow him. And Jack found out about the vampire-mages, so Braden had to hand over some of them and come up with a stupid story to cover for himself?"

"It makes sense, sort of," Logan said, running his fingers through his wet hair. "What prompted this line of thought?"

"I couldn't figure out why the vampires would be collecting these guys today rather than killing them," I replied. "Unless Braden *is* collecting them to overthrow Jack." I shook my head. "But it *still* doesn't make sense. According to Braden, Jack ordered this attack, but Marshall said they had orders to capture, not kill. Jack wouldn't do that, would he? Doesn't he already have enough mages? Or does he plan to lose a bunch at Victor's?"

Logan leaned back against the pile of pillows, his thick brows meeting each other. "I don't know, but you're right. Something is off. There are too many unknowns, especially about Braden."

I lay back down and pulled the quilt to my chin. Something else bothered me.

"Why are we still here and not at Victor's?" I asked. "If we take these people to the palace, even for just a night, the vampires will have no one to attack."

"I'm sure they won't abandon their homes," Logan replied. "Do you want to leave them to fight this on their own?"

"That's what I'm trying to say, just not very well." I huffed and sat back up, turning sideways to look at him. "We left the palace in the middle of the night, perfect time for vampires to strike. It'll take Kellen's group three hours to get to Victor's from his estate, unless there's a portal closer?"

"No, his is the closest," Logan said slowly.

"Okay, so they get to Victor's at three in the morning, which is crazy. How will they transport all those people? I didn't see a line of buses at Kellen's." I waved my hand in the air. "Anyway, still perfect timing for a vampire attack back home regardless of who's behind it. You and I are here in the middle of the day, not a good time for vampires."

Realization slowly dawned across Logan's face. *And he's supposed to be the smart one.*

"We should pack up these warriors and join Kellen's group. Tell the families to stay at the palace for twenty-four hours until we know what the real plan is." I looked at my vampire, hoping he understood what I was trying to say.

"If we leave now, I can get you to Victor's much quicker than the others," he said, sliding off the bed. "If we're wrong, no harm done and everyone is still safe."

"But if we're right, Kellen and Victor will need everyone." I rolled off the other side and started pulling on clothes. "Have we already wasted too much time?"

"It's only been an hour or so since we arrived," Logan replied, already dressed and stuffing dirty clothes in our backpack. "If Jim can organize his guys quickly, we shouldn't be that far behind Kellen."

"Would Kellen think of this?" I asked, trying to tamp down my panic.

"I'm not sure. Are you ready?"

"Yeah, but I sure could've used a nap."

I tried not to race down the stairs and draw unnecessary questions, but I was pretty sure I failed. Logan grabbed my hand at the bottom and pulled me into a slow walk. It was probably a quick walk but felt really slow. We crossed the street and entered the same building we'd exited earlier.

Ezekiel met us in the hall. "Is everything okay?"

"No, we had a sudden realization that we'd like to discuss with Jim," I said. "Can you take me to him?"

"Of course." He turned and led us down a hall to the right and knocked on the first door.

"Come in," a muffled voice called.

Ezekiel opened the door, holding it for us to step through. Jim rose from a large sofa on the left side of the room and turned off the television.

"Magister, I thought you were getting some sleep." His eyes darted from Logan to me. I didn't miss the insinuation.

"My brain usually forbids it and today was no exception," I replied, trying not to be caustic. I felt so good ten minutes ago. I took a deep breath and repeated my concerns about Jack's plans and the timing, leaving out my mother and Braden.

"I'm inclined to agree with you," Jim said, still standing with the TV remote in his hand. "Ezekiel, gather the warriors and tell Paula to come in here."

"Yes, sir."

"Do you know where the shifter's lodge is?" Logan asked.

"No, but if you program the address in my phone, we'll be there," Jim replied. "I assume you're not waiting for us."

"We need to catch Kellen and warn him," I replied, turning towards the door.

"I have one question before you leave, Magister."

I sighed, knowing what was coming. "What is it?" I slowly turned back around, meeting his intense gaze, his icy blue eyes so much like my own.

"Your protector is a vampire, yes?"

I nodded.

"And you are as well?"

"No, I'm a dual mage with many gifts and the Magister of the North American mages," I replied, not hiding my bitterness. "While we're on the subject, I value Logan's life over everyone else's. If he is attacked, regardless who it is, I will act first and ask questions later."

"That's a dangerous position to be in," Jim said, frowning. "But I'll make sure my warriors understand."

"Thank you." I hesitated before leaving. "I'm not a weak little girl who's afraid to fight. I still have a lot to learn, but I have excellent teachers."

Jim looked over at Logan who shook his head. "She learns from her elementals who have gifted her with more power than I believed possible." Logan held out his hand. "Give me your phone, and I'll save Victor's location on your map."

Jim handed over his smartphone and looked at me. "Is this true?"

"Yes, and Logan is not just a vampire," I replied. "Which is why I value him so much."

"I thought Kellen was your mage partner?"

"He is. It's complicated."

Jim shook his head, taking his phone back. "We'll be there as soon as we can. And I'll convince the families to leave as soon as possible."

A tall woman with striking features entered the room as we turned to leave. She smiled and nodded as we walked by, but I didn't stay to hear her conversation. Jim would either take care of it or not, and I had to trust that he would get everyone out.

As soon as the small village fell out of sight, Logan picked me up and raced towards the portal. He stumbled for a fraction of a second when we landed in the empty courtyard of the palace, but he still didn't stop.

"I need you to think about Kellen's estate," he said as he made a loop around the yard.

My mind immediately went to Kellen's house and all the memories that went with it. I hadn't been back, until now. We fell back through the inky blackness. Logan stumbled again into Kellen's estate. So that's how that worked.

My vampire finally stopped and put me down in the small portal room. He leaned against the doorway, and I couldn't help but notice the dark circles under his eyes.

"Anything I can do to help?" I asked.

"No, thankfully not you," he replied, pushing away from the wall.

"Already?" I asked, following him down the hall to Kellen's kitchen.

"Yes, already. I should've taken one of the vampires we fought last night, or was it tonight? Hell, I don't know." He opened the fridge and pulled out several bottles of water. "Put these in our bag. You might need them."

I took the bottles and pulled the bag from my back. "Why didn't you take one of them earlier?" I assumed he had bitten one of the vampires at the train station. His attitude certainly implied he would.

"I didn't want to reveal myself," he replied. "I'm officially the enemy of my kind."

I froze, the bag half zipped in my hand. Once again, I hadn't thought of Logan's sacrifices. I was such a bitch.

"I'm sorry, Logan." My stupid eyes started misting up once again. Why was I such a cry baby?

"It'll be worth it if we can make this work," he said, his smile not reaching his eyes.

For a moment, my whole world went in reverse, right back to Kellen using me for his own ends. Which was total bull. Logan wasn't Kellen, and I needed to get my head out of my ass.

"It'll work," I stated, not allowing any doubt to enter my mind. I would not lose him to this nonsense.

"You're cute when you're determined, princess," he said. "Let's catch up with Kellen."

"Logan, wait." I wasn't sure exactly what I wanted to say, but I felt a shift in our relationship in that moment, just like I had with Kellen. I didn't want it going any further.

"You don't have to say anything," he said.

"Yes, I do. You've sacrificed so much for this." I waved my hand at Kellen's house, hoping he knew I meant more. "I keep asking for more without considering your needs or feelings. It's selfish and unfair. I need you to tell me what you want, need, whatever. I'm not good at seeing it for myself." I found a clump of dirt on my sweatshirt and picked at, anything to avoid his gaze. I was scared to see the accusations or pity. It had to be one or the other.

He sighed and pulled my hand into his. "I'm frustrated with the position I've been thrown into," he said. "Not that I wouldn't have chosen it anyway, but I feel like I had no choice." I looked up when he didn't continue, but I couldn't decipher the expression on his face. "That's not entirely true. I never would've picked to be a vampire." His lip curled in disgust but only for a moment as his eyes met mine. "Joining Jonathan and Kellen would've happened regardless of everyone's interference in my life. Protecting you also would've been my choice, even though it means I'm ostracized by all the supernatural families. I just hate that I have no control over any of it."

I understood completely, but I wouldn't patronize him by saying so. Everything he said was real and painful. Talking about my own experiences wouldn't help. He was there for most of it; he didn't need a repeat.

"Destiny sucks," I mumbled. "But I'll do a better job with my half of this relationship. I'm not making it any easier on you by acting like a selfish bitch."

He pulled me into his strong embrace and I melted against him. "You are not a selfish bitch, AJ. You're naïve and totally ignorant when it comes to the magical community, but I'm grateful to be stuck with you and not someone else."

"Thanks, I think," I said, pushing away from his chest, feeling just a little better. "Let's go find Kellen."

"As soon as this is done, we're going someplace where we can learn everything we need to know about each other and what we've become," he whispered, giving me that silly grin I'd grown to love.

"Deal."

Chapter 14

My sleep button must have moved from my ass to my chest because fifteen minutes into our run—well, Logan's run—I was leaning against the hard muscles in his shoulders, sleeping like a baby. How does one sleep while being carried on another person's back? Good fricking question, but I seemed to master it just fine.

I woke when Logan sat on a wide, flat rock, his chest heaving with each breath. I slid from his back and sat next to him.

"Does a drink of water help?" I asked stupidly as I pulled a bottle of water from my back pack.

"No, but thanks for asking. I shouldn't be pushing so hard. I won't be able to fight off a fly, much less a horde of vampires." He leaned over, resting his elbows on his knees and his head in his palms.

"Why didn't we just take a car?"

"Because we've covered twice as much ground going 'as the crow flies,'" he replied. "The interstate takes three hours. We're more than halfway there in one hour."

"What time is it? Will we be there before Kellen?"

Logan pulled his phone from his pocket and unlocked the screen. "Twenty minutes before three. I'm not sure where Kellen is, but we'll find out if Victor has company soon enough."

He pulled up a social media account for someone named Jolly Jeff and opened the messenger app.

"Jolly Jeff?" I raised my eyebrows. "Really?"

"This messenger thing has made it really easy to communicate without giving away my cell phone number," he replied. "Marissa knows it's me. She'll answer if she's awake." He tapped in a quick message asking if they had company and stuffed the phone back in his pocket. "Come on, let's keep moving." He motioned for me to hop on.

"Maybe I should run on my own for a little while," I suggested.

"I don't even notice you there, princess," he said. "You weigh nothing. I'm tired because I haven't had enough food or sleep."

"Well, maybe we can fix the food part when we reach Victor's," I said, trying to smile.

"I'm sure we will."

After I wrapped my arms around his neck, Logan stood, and once my legs circled his waist, he took off again. Fifteen minutes later, the rocky desert gave way to squat spruce trees and loamy earth. Another five minutes and a red haze engulfed the horizon. Logan slowed to a stop at a cluster of large boulders surrounded by the short pines.

"Please tell me that's a natural forest fire," I whispered, not letting go of him.

He pulled his phone from his pocket. I looked over his shoulder to see Marissa's reply.

"*Victor's scouts reported the vampire's advance towards the lodge*," the message read. "*Our fighters should be there momentarily.*"

"I'm guessing the fire is not natural," Logan said, slipping the phone back into his pocket. He tugged at my arms and I released him, reluctantly putting my feet on the ground. He slowly turned to face me, putting his back to the fiery glow in the distance. "I'm not sure how to enter this fight, AJ. The shifters will immediately know what I am, but so will the vampires. I'll be a target on all sides."

"Is there nothing I can do mark you as an ally?" I asked, suddenly very fearful to enter the fight. And here I thought I would be the easy target.

"If I stay with the mages, fighting against the vampires, we might be okay. I'll try to keep from transitioning fully," he replied. "But if I get separated from you, or the wolves start to mingle..." He didn't have to finish. I knew the answer.

"Then I won't leave your side," I said. "And I'll force Kellen to join us. As long as you're with us, no one would dare attack you."

"Or they'll think I'm after you."

"Aren't you?" I smiled, but it faded quickly. "Should I try to hide my new speed?" I asked, worried about how the mages would react. Would they think I was also a vampire? Or would they think I succeeded where my mother failed? Had I? I looked up at my vampire and worry consumed me. I didn't want to be like her.

"You do what is necessary to stay alive," Logan replied.

"Good idea. Let's go find the mages and see what kind of trouble we can get into."

I knew he recognized my attempt to convince myself we'd be okay, but his anxiety matched my own.

"Can you run on your own the rest of the way? It's not very far, and I'd rather show up with my hands empty, ready to fight."

I nodded, and he pulled the bag from my back, putting it on his own, then laced his fingers through mine. "I…" he started and squeezed my hand. "I can't lose you so don't do anything stupid."

"Yes, dear." I stood on my toes and kissed him. As I hoped, he returned it with his all-consuming passion.

"You're killing me," he whispered.

"I hope not," I replied, a little breathless.

He stepped back and turned, pulling me towards the fire and death waiting for us. He didn't ask if I was ready; he didn't need to. I would never be ready for this. I thought I was last time and look where it got me. I didn't want to be bit by another vampire, and I was pretty sure I wasn't the only one.

We raced between the trees, the sounds of battle reaching me faster than I wanted. Memories of the last fight among these trees assaulted me, my heart stuttering. What was I thinking? I couldn't fight these things. Would Logan be able to save me now if I did get bit? I felt my pace slow, and he slowed with me, then picked me up.

"You can do this, princess. You're not alone."

I wrapped my arms around him, burying my face in his neck as he ran the rest of the way. I was such a baby and it needed to stop. My fear and insecurity helped no one. After all, it wasn't just my life on the line. Logan needed me to be strong and brave, not a stupid little coward. I took a deep breath, drawing in his delicious smell, then kissed his neck.

"Thank you," I whispered.

He stopped and set me on my feet as soon as we saw the first group of mages battling against an unseen foe. Thick smoke from the growing fire choked the air, and the flames made an eerie back drop for the vampires darting between the walls of fire and earth.

"Stay at my side," Logan whispered, grabbing my hand and darting forward. "I'll stay slow enough for you to keep up. They won't expect it from you which will earn us a few easy kills."

My heart raced in my chest, adrenaline fueling my exhausted body. As we sped up, the other vampires slowed. Four of them seemed to be tag-teaming a group of eight mages clustered together and backed up against a tall earthen wall. Lines of fire circled their right side.

Logan headed towards a female vampire, colliding with her as her claws grazed the arm of the nearest mage. Niyol picked up the woman's tag-team partner in a swirling tornado and ran him into the fire. His dying screams attracted the attention the remaining pair. They stopped at the edge of the mages' perimeter and watched their fellow blood sucker die.

I didn't hesitate, drawing my spear into existence and lunging at a short, muscular man wearing blue jeans and a black t-shirt that barely held against his large frame.

I pulled on my connection to the air, giving myself more speed as the tip of my spear impaled the large vampire. I couldn't be lucky enough to hit his heart, but the impact did put him on the ground. Bands of rock shot from the earth and wrapped around his chest. Another man with short blond hair appeared at my side. The flickering fires reflected off the blade of his sword as it whispered past me, removing the vampire's head.

It only took a second for me to find Logan a few feet away, snapping the neck of the last vampire. As he tossed the body into the air, Niyol's tornado raced by, catching it and dropping it into the fire.

"How did you do that?" the mage asked me.

"Which part?" I asked in return, releasing my hold on the spear and watching it vanish.

"All of it, but especially the weapon."

"It's made of air," I replied. "Are any of you injured?" I looked around at the small group. Two woman and six men walked towards me. Logan's fingers found mine, and I didn't hesitate to pull him closer.

"We're fine," one of the women said. "You're the Magister?"

"I am. This is Logan," I responded, not feeling the need to explain who he was. "Why are you here by yourselves?"

"Guarding the vehicles," one of the others replied, "and taking in the injured. We have three water mages for healing." He gestured to the woman next to him and nodded at the man next to me, the one holding the sword.

It made sense, but they were a long way from the fight. I didn't understand it, but I decided not to second-guess Kellen's tactics.

"Be careful," I said. "We'll draw any lingering vampires to us, and away from you, as we head towards the main fight. The mages from Australia will be arriving within the next hour. Be sure to send them our way."

"Are there any other creatures besides the vampires?" Logan asked.

"We didn't see any," the same water mage replied.

"Let's go, princess." Logan took the first step away, and I joined his race towards the thickening smoke and screams of agony.

Another earthen wall rose in front of us, followed by a fiery tornado. We skirted around it, my heart rising into my throat. Kellen and a dozen mages were surrounded by countless vampires in full monster form. Their long claws slashed out against flaring shields of water and earth. My partner stood in the middle, and several injured mages lay on the ground, unmoving and vulnerable. His arms raised in the air, guiding the path of a wave of fire making a loop around their left flank. His sister, Kate, stood by his side raising slabs of earth to protect her brother.

Niyol, help Kellen's fire and protect Logan.

Yes, princess.

I stepped in front of Logan and gazed into his swirling eyes. He looked down at me, and I sensed waves of hunger mixing with his fear.

"I love you," I whispered, pulling his face to mine and pressing my lips to his for a fierce moment. "Do what you do best. Niyol will protect you."

My elemental's keening howl drowned out Logan's reply, but my vampire's eyes said it all. Rather than watch him as he leapt towards the nearest vampire, I raced to my partner's side, pulling on the well of magic in my core and mixing it with Göksu's strength. My first task would be healing the wounded mages. They needed to be in the fight, not lying there useless. I had to trust my elemental and my vampire to keep the monsters back. I had to.

"AJ?" Kate spun around, nearly knocking me over when I suddenly appeared at her side.

"Logan is fighting with me!" I yelled over Niyol's torrent. "Don't let the others attack him."

Kellen turned to me with a look of hatred so deep it startled me. "Why are you here and not with my family?"

"Shut up and focus!" I screamed back. "They're safe at the palace. You're welcome!" I turned my back on him and tried to swallow my anger. He just assumed I broke my promise. Stupid bastard.

Focus. I needed to focus. I knelt next to a tall man I recognized but couldn't recall his name. Long gashes ran down his left arm, and shreds of his shirt hung from his shoulder. My hands hovered over the wounds, and I pulled the water from my surroundings, coating him in a layer of healing warmth. As his pain washed over me, my world tilted. The earth rumbled at my feet, and a hot gust of air blew smoke into my face. 'Focus' my ass! Another rumble shook the ground, tossing me sideways. How did the water mages heal people during battle?

The man at my side sat up, recognition flooding his features. "Magister?"

"Yes, can you fight?"

"I can now. Thank you."

He rose to his feet and took a place next to Kellen. I searched for Logan among the vampires but didn't see him. Where did he go? I reached for our connection. He was very close, no more than a few yards away and running fast. Tingles ran down my spine and I stood. Something was coming.

"Everyone against the wall!" Logan's voice rose above the sounds of battle just before he appeared at my side. "Kellen! Back everyone up. Three ogres are inbound."

My partner's eyes widened as he backpedaled. The ground shook again, forcing everyone to their knees.

"Oh my God!" the man next to Kellen cried.

Three enormous shapes took form as they emerged from the smoky haze. Kellen didn't have to tell the mages to back up, nor did he need to instruct them grab the injured as they went.

"David, you and Rick with me!" Kellen called out. "I want a trench, now." The three men fell to their knees and pressed their palms against the blood-soaked soil. A violent shudder shook the ground. "The rest of you keep the vampires off us."

A fiery tornado raced between us and the ogres with four or five charred bodies floating in its middle. Niyol picked up two more before disappearing into the next wall of flames.

Three fiends in full vampire form rushed in from the right side, as if they'd waited for my elemental to pass. They were on Kellen's trio within seconds.

"No!" I shrieked, pushing my hands out in front of me and curling my fingers into fists. Without thinking of the consequences, I pulled the blood from their veins, jerking my arms back to my body as if I were snatching a toy and not their lives.

Their combined screams filled the night, and their shriveled bodies fell just short of my partner. Rivers of blood hung in the air, still in my grasp. What should I do with it? I wanted to give it to Logan but knew I couldn't in front of all these people.

"Logan, empty a water bottle," I said, my voice echoing in the eerie silence.

Even the ogres stopped their forward progress. I wove my hands in small circles, swirling the blood together in a thin line. The sound of liquid splashing in the dirt drew my attention to my vampire. An empty water bottle shook in his left hand as his eyes met mine. He knew it was for him. I guided as much blood as I could fit into the single bottle and he capped it, stuffing it into the bag on his back.

I continued twisting the gory fluid, thinking about the technique Niyol used to make my spears. Could the same be done with water or blood? I pressed the molecules tighter together as they continued to layer over top of each other. The thin stream of blood was now nearly two inches in diameter and three feet long, but it still wasn't solid. Could I encase it air?

"Why aren't they attacking?" Kate whispered from behind me.

"I think that answer is obvious," Kellen replied.

I looked up, trying not to lose the progress on my new weapon. How had I forgotten we were in the middle of battle? Probably because of the silence. Dozens of faces stared at me, shadows dancing across them from the still burning fires. Fear and awe, but mostly fear, consumed all of them. *I can't imagine why*, I thought wryly. Some demented witch just sucked the blood out of three vampires and was using it to make a weapon to kill the others. What the hell was wrong with me?

I dropped my hands and the weapon disintegrated, splashing in the dirt. A tall vampire, still in full monster form, emerged from the smoke. His sandy blond hair looked completely out of place above his distorted features, blood red eyes, and long fangs. Shreds of his shirt hung from his shoulders exposing the raw, tight muscles of his enlarged arms and back.

With each step, another feature softened starting with his chest and shoulders, then moving to his eyes and fangs. By time he reached me, he looked human.

"What do you want?" I asked, stepping up beside Kellen.

"You are the Magister?" he asked in a thick accent that sounded Russian.

"What do you think?" I snapped.

"I think I cannot fight against you," he replied. "My clan has already suffered too many losses in a war that has not even begun. Jack is a fool if he thinks he can win." He barked several orders in a language I didn't understand, and dozens of shadows raced away from us. The three ogres lumbered after the vampires, disappearing into the thick smoke. Their leader lingered silently for a second more before following his men into the now-quiet night.

Chapter 15

"What just happened?" I asked, suddenly feeling more exhausted than before the battle. Had the vampires retreated? Did that group just defy Jack? It sounded like it, but it couldn't be that easy.

"I believe you scared yet another member of the council," Logan replied, lacing his fingers with mine and pulling me to him. I didn't resist.

"She scared *me*," the man next to Kellen said. I wished I could remember his damn name.

"How did you do that?" Kellen asked, taking a step closer to me, his gaze darting between me and Logan.

"Which part?" I heard myself asking again.

"All of it."

"You taught me to draw out their blood, Kellen," I replied. "I couldn't actually see it until recently and hadn't even thought about doing anything with it until just now."

"How did you heal David so completely?" a woman behind me asked. "I'd been working on his injury for ten minutes. Then you showed up and took it away within seconds."

I turned to face her. A long dark braid draped over her thin shoulder. Blood and dirt covered her clothes and smears of ash ran along one side of her face. Her eyebrows drew together as she stared at me.

"I depend on my elemental to do the healing and it always does," I replied. "I guide the magic, but it's his power, not mine."

"I want to learn," she whispered.

I nodded; she needed to. They all needed to.

A hot dry wind scraped my exposed skin, and Niyol appeared at my side. The mages around us gasped, stepping back away from his towering form. "Princess, the wolves need your assistance. It appears there are two factions of vampires here."

"Is it dire?" I asked. We needed to heal the wounded and take care of the vampires I sucked dry. I could hear their hearts beating faintly, the sound making me cringe with regret.

"No, they're holding their own, but they're taking casualties."

"Kellen, can you burn those bodies while I heal the wounded? We'll need everyone with us." I turned my back to him and knelt beside one of the mages propped against the stone wall behind us.

"We'll leave the vampires," he said. "Our mages can heal the wounded. It appears all we need in this battle is you."

Was that jealousy? Bitterness? What the hell? I rose to my feet and closed the space between us, not caring that I used my new super-speed.

"The vampires are not dead," I hissed, pointing at the shriveled bodies next to him. "And we are not barbarians who would leave them to suffer." I looked over at Logan for confirmation, their faint heartbeats still calling to me. I pushed back my guilt for the woman I'd left at the train station. I'd assumed she was dead, but that probably wasn't true.

"Says the woman who sucked the blood from their veins," Kellen countered.

"Did you seriously just go there?" I whipped my head back to meet his icy stare. "Would you prefer I let them kill you? That's exactly what would've happened. Logan may have been quick enough to take one of them, possibly two, but you didn't even see them coming."

Yep, definitely bitterness and anger. It bled through our connection freely. He wanted me to know how he felt or he would've hidden it.

"We'll discuss our dysfunctional partnership later," I whispered. "There are other things happening right now that are more important."

His hand flicked out to the side, and I followed his movement. Strands of fire snaked from his fingers and wrapped around the dying vampires, consuming them in seconds. The flickering flames danced on the air, mesmerizing me. I could feel their heat and need to burn everything in their path. A longing pulled at my core. I reached for Kellen's hand, drawing his fire to me. It bowed, arching towards me in a slow, lazy loop.

Logan pushed against my arm, and I looked up at him. He shook his head, and I blinked several times. What happened?

"Ginny, stay and heal the others," Kellen barked. "Everyone else with me."

He didn't wait for me to argue or agree as he stomped off into the thick smoke, but the other mages did, including his sister. Several sets of eyes landed on me, looking for something. Approval?

"Go with him, he's your leader and knows way more about fighting than I do," I said. They nodded and ran after my partner. "Niyol, will you go with them and protect my stubborn partner?"

"Only for you, princess." His body swirled into a mini tornado then disappeared.

"It talks to you," Ginny said breathlessly.

"Yes, he does. We need to hurry and join the others," I replied, kneeling next to another wounded mage. "Reach for your element, ask its permission to use its power and help you heal."

Her eyes narrowed at me and she frowned. "Really?"

"Did I ask my wind elemental to join Kellen or tell him to?" The skeptical look remained. "Fine, keep trying it your way, then. I don't have time to argue."

I turned away from her and repeated what I knew worked for me. My healing warmth spread over the man in front of me, covering the long scrapes on his chest. As always, his pain was my reward. I clenched my teeth, holding onto the pain until his wounds closed.

"Sammy?" I barely recognized Kate's friend beneath the blood and soot. "Does anything else hurt?"

"I think I have a broken finger, but it'll wait," he responded, pushing to his feet. "It's good to see you, AJ."

"Where are the rest of your mages?" I asked, looking up at him.

"We split into several groups when the wolves showed up," he replied, rolling his newly healed shoulder. "The largest group of vampires were headed towards the lodge. We were supposed to attack from the rear and force the vampires to split."

"It looks like the tactic worked," I said, rolling back onto my butt and pressing my forehead against my knees. A splitting headache started to form between my eyes. Too much magic? "I wonder how many left with our Russian friend."

Sammy kicked the scorched earth at his feet, glancing from me to Logan. "We would've died without you here. Especially once the ogres showed up."

"You don't know that," I said, trying to reassure him.

"Our group was too small for the numbers attacking us."

I looked up at Logan, hoping for some help with a convincing argument. No such luck.

"We need to join the others," he said.

I nodded. "You've got this last one by yourself, Ginny," I said. "I don't have much left and I need to save it for the fight. Can you stay with her?" I asked Sammy.

"Yes, be careful," he replied.

Logan appeared at my side. "Help me up, and let's go," I said, offering him my hand.

"If I have to help you up, you don't need to go," Logan stated, pulling me to my feet.

My world spun and stars blinked across my vision. Maybe he was right, but I couldn't leave them to fight this on their own.

The sound of several vehicles drew my attention to the blurred headlights moving towards us through the smoke. "Now what?" I tried not to lean against Logan as we walked towards the line of vehicles. I counted six pairs of headlights snaking up a barely existent road.

When my new friend Jim jumped out of the passenger side of the first vehicle, I smiled. He waved a flashlight in the air and yelled back at the other vans. More people piled out into the darkened forest.

"I'm glad you made it," I said, approaching the leader of the Australian mages. "You're just in time. The shifters need our help just north of here. Kellen's mages are already there."

"The local fire department is on their way," he said. "The fire is visible for miles."

"Oh shit," I mumbled. Within minutes, the large group of Australians crowded around us. We didn't need a bunch of normal people witnessing a fight between vampires and werewolves. How did we stop this? "How much time do we have?"

"Maybe fifteen minutes." He shifted uncomfortably. "Several trees might have fallen on the road, but it won't take them long to clear it."

"Shit, shit, shit." I looked around at the group of men and women. "How do we stop hundreds of people from attacking each other in the next fifteen minutes?" Soft murmurs and shrugs were the only response. Great. "Leave your vehicles blocking as much of the road as possible and let's go. I'll think of something."

I mumbled the last with barely contained contempt. These people had been mages their whole lives. Why couldn't they come up with a plan? Logan and I broke into a jog, but the others still struggled to keep up. My vampire pulled on my hand forcing me to slow down. I let him. I needed to think.

Was there a way to stop the fighting long enough to put out the fire? Then the normal humans wouldn't be needed? No, they'd want to investigate and poke their noses into what started it, like the good emergency responders they were.

We raced by an earthen wall and I swore again. How would we hide those? It's not like they were natural occurrences. The closer we got, the more I realized we couldn't hide it. We had to find a way to keep the fire department from coming. Jim's vehicles would delay them, but that was it. All of this just needed to go away, but that wasn't possible either. Or was it? A brilliant, probably absurd plan drifted through my exhausted brain.

"I have a plan!" I yelled, pulling Logan to stop. Growls and snarls drifted through the trees along with flashes of light. We couldn't be more than a hundred yards from the fight, but the thick smoke prevented me from seeing more than twenty yards even with my new night vision.

Niyol, I need to get a message to Kellen.

I felt my elemental's annoyance immediately.

I'm a little busy, princess.

I know. I want to bury the vampires alive. Can you start maneuvering them so that they're sort of grouped together? I asked. *And can you convince the other wind elementals to help you?*

Niyol didn't answer, and the mages at my back waited impatiently.

"How many earth and water mages do we have?" I yelled, hoping everyone could hear me. "Logan lift me up, I can't see." He had the audacity to chuckle as he lifted me onto his shoulders. "Okay, all the earth and water mages move to the right. Air and fire to the left."

The crowd shifted and I smiled. At least two thirds were earth and water. My stupid plan might work.

"Jim, if I can get my air elemental's help, we're going to bury the vampires." It was crazy, but it would hide a lot of the evidence of our fight and protect the humans. It had to work.

Logan lowered me to the ground and I explained my plan to Jim. Dylan and Sammy stood next to us, each of them smiling as the details unfolded.

"Dylan, pass the word. All the water and earth mages stay with the Magister. Fire and wind with me," Jim said. Dylan rushed to do his bidding and the tall, dark mage grinned. "As much as I'd love to force the bastards to stay buried, you know they won't."

"We just need it to hold long enough to get the firefighters out," I said. "Maybe we'll get lucky and the vampires will surrender."

"Don't hold your breath," Logan mumbled. "This is insane. I can't believe we're going to try this."

"It's exactly why it'll work," I said. "No one will expect it."

"We're ready, Jim," Dylan said, running up to his leader.

He nodded, and the first group ran through the trees towards a battle I didn't want to see.

"Here we go," I yelled back to my group.

Dylan and Sammy were both with me. It was nice to have people by my side who weren't complete strangers.

"Sammy, can you direct the water mages?" I asked as we rushed between the trees.

"I guess so, but I've never led anyone before."

"You're just watching and coordinating. Those that can make shields to guide the vampires' movements, should do so. The others focus on putting out the fires outside of our area."

As we reached the edge of the fighting, my heart dropped. The smell of blood was so thick I could barely scent the smoke. How many people died today? I couldn't see the bodies lying in the thick, moldy leaves, but I knew they were there. Vampires in full transition fought against large wolves partnered with mages.

Niyol's fiery windstorm swept across the battlefield, running along the line between friend and foe. How did he pick up the vampires and not the wolves? Because he was awesome. The most intense fighting appeared to be in a small clearing among the thick pines. A large group of vampires surrounded an equally large group of wolves. I was surprised to see the shifters keeping pace with the vampires. Humans definitely weren't that quick.

"Are you ready, AJ?" Sammy asked, breaking me from my stupid moment of distraction.

"Yes, you know what to do."

Niyol?

Some of the others will help, but not all. Their mages are not worthy.

I understand. Thank you for trying.

Only for you, princess.

I love you, Niyol.

"Alright, here we go!" I yelled. "Our focus is the clearing in the middle. Make a crater on the southern edge deep enough that the bastards can't jump out."

The earth mages knelt, digging their hands beneath the rotting foliage, and the ground began to tremble.

"Logan." I turned around and placed both hands on his chest. "Don't leave my side. No matter what happens."

The shadows didn't hide his concern, and our connection flooded with his turmoil. He wanted to fight but knew if he jumped into that mess, he'd be attacked on all sides. We both knew it.

I joined my group of earth mages, sitting on the damp soil. Logan sat with me and pulled me into his lap. I smiled. At least I knew he wasn't going anywhere.

Göksu, I really need your strength.

I know, child. It is yours.

I also need your wisdom, I thought. *I know what I want to do, but I need you to guide me.*

I see your mind, and I have a better idea.

I could almost hear him laugh, but I wasn't about to mention it. I had his help and his strength. It was all I needed.

I placed my hands, palms up, on my knees and imagined a large dome sliding over top of my earth mages, protecting them from anything that might try to stop their progress. As promised, my elemental made it happen. The smoky air grew thick with the moisture being drawn to us. Within seconds, a liquid shield rose from the ground in a circle around my group. The sight of the water flowing up instead of down distracted several fights raging around us.

The ground shook violently, throwing the same combatants off their feet. Through my watery shield, I saw dozens of small tornados racing through the trees, picking up their targets and dragging them to the small clearing. The ground just outside my shield split open, the tear in the earth edging its way towards the hovering tornados. The fissure widened to twenty feet as it clawed its way to the clearing. Wolves and mages scattered, while fiery elementals chased the vampires and tornados tossed them in the widening fracture.

My first earth mage collapsed. I suspected it would happen, but it still broke my heart.

"Stay focused!" I yelled as the man next to him reached for his unconscious companion.

I forced a tendril of water from my shield to extend to the exhausted mage. It snaked around his torso, then covered him in a healing warmth. The mage's exhaustion wrapped around me, draining the energy from my limbs. Damn, I wasn't expecting that, but I should've been. Healing always worked that way. I fell back against Logan, grateful for his presence.

The somewhat revived mage resumed his position, digging his hands back into the dirt. Torrents of air pushed more of the vampires into the crevice. Finally, a wave of fire blanketed the hole – just like I imagined the gates of hell - our cue to close it up.

"Close it, now!"

The ground shook violently, and I was grateful I was already sitting. Those who weren't were thrown off their feet as the crevice slammed closed. The mages around me collapsed in various phases of exhaustion.

"This is going to hurt," I whispered. "Don't let me go, Logan."

I released my shield and asked my elemental to heal those who gave so much of themselves. Rather than sliding back into the earth, the dome collapsed, soaking the men and women around me. With each contact, another wave of exhaustion siphoned my consciousness. I let it, knowing we just neutralized an enemy that would've killed dozens more of the people we needed to protect.

Logan's arms tightened around me as my eyes fluttered shut.

Göksu, I'm relying on you to keep me alive.
Of course, child.

Chapter 16

A soft click followed by a light humming interrupted my bizarre dream. Beautiful blond men grew from the dark soil beneath my house. I'm not sure how they got there or how I saw them under the floor boards, but they were magnificent with their bulging naked bodies. One spoke to me in a harsh language that sounded like it had no vowels.

My eyes snapped open. What the hell was that? I didn't own a house, nor did I know any beautiful blond men. I pulled my hands out from beneath my favorite quilt and rubbed my eyes. It only took a second for me to remember that my favorite quilt had been left at Kellen's.

I sat up and my head swam, forcing me to lay back down. Peeling one eye open, I looked around and sighed. I was back in my room at Kellen's house, covered by my favorite quilt. I lifted the blanket and found a tank top and panties covering me. At least it wasn't one of Kellen's t-shirts. That might have pissed me off.

I fell back against the pillows and glanced around again, this time with both eyes open. The dresser across the room was still right where I left it. The same sheers covered the windows, and the same nightstand sat next to the bed. The bathroom door stood ajar, and I heard the shower running. I hoped it was Logan.

Could I get up without falling on my face? Or should I wait for Logan to get done in the shower and yell for him? Whatever. I wasn't helpless, just tired. Ever so slowly, I pushed myself into a seated position, squeezing my eyes shut as the dresser multiplied across the room.

"Wow, that really sucks." My voice cracked, my throat burning from thirst.

I sat completely still for several moments as my stomach ran in circles. I refused to be sick on my favorite quilt, and I knew I wasn't making it to the bathroom. I thought about using a little healing, then thought better of it. Magic was likely what brought all this on in the first place.

Inch by inch, I scooted backwards and leaned against the headboard. My stomach rolled again, and I pulled my lips into a thin line. I was not getting sick.

"There's a small garbage can next to the bed, if you need it." Logan's voice made me smile.

I ran my tongue over my lips. "I don't think I can move to get it," I whispered.

A cold glass met my parched lips, and I greedily sipped the water from it. I peeked through my lashes at my vampire. His hazel eyes stared back at me beneath his thick brow. My gaze followed the drops of water rolling down his neck from his wet hair.

"Are you okay?" he asked.

"I have no idea," I replied. "Nothing really hurts, I just feel queasy."

He held the cup to my lips again, and I wrapped my hand around his, feeding my thirst.

"You scared the hell out of me," he said. "You've been asleep for eighteen hours."

"That would explain why I'm so thirsty." I tried to smile, but Logan's frown stamped it out. "What happened?"

"You'll have to ask Kellen. I brought you here as soon as you passed out."

"How many did we lose?" I was afraid to ask but needed to know.

Logan looked away and sat the glass on my nightstand. "Too many. Victor's small group lost half of their wolves. Thirty mages were killed, and dozens more are injured."

"And the vampires?"

"Kellen said they didn't allow any to escape the pit you dug for them."

Guilt and shame washed over me. I should've seen that coming. It's not like we were taking prisoners, and Jack intended to wipe out Victor's entire pack. So why did I feel guilty? Because of my vampire. We killed every one of his kind, mercilessly. I twisted the quilt around my fingers, something I hadn't done in a while.

"I'm sorry," I whispered. "That's not what I intended."

"It was the only possible outcome," Logan said, standing and walking around the far side of the bed, flinging the blankets back. "You shouldn't be sorry." He crawled beneath the covers and scooted next to me. I let him pull me beneath the quilt and hold my back tight against his chest. His strong embrace eased some of my guilt.

"What can I do to help you?" I asked. "I can feel your emotional pain."

"There's nothing you can do," he whispered. "I need to find my purpose." His huff ruffled my hair. "That's not true. I have my purpose. I just need to accept it."

I hadn't felt the lie he claimed. But I knew he didn't feel like he'd found his purpose, and in his mind, he needed to be more than just my protector. He was a predator, and I kept him from hunting. We needed to find a way to have balance or be without each other. Could I stay here with Kellen and help rule the mages? More importantly, could I let Logan go? He certainly couldn't stay.

"I think we need to decide where to go from here," I said, pulling the edge of the quilt between my fingers. "I know the mages expect me to stay at the palace, but I'm not sure I can."

Silence lingered between us, making me worry. He couldn't stay at the palace. He knew that just as well as I did. Was he contemplating leaving me there alone? Would he tell me I couldn't go with him? I needed to know what he was thinking. I rolled over, forcing him to loosen his hold on me.

"I need to know what you're thinking," I said, resting my hand on his chest.

His eyes met mine, delving into my soul. "My mind tells me you should stay with Kellen and help put the mages in a good place, especially after their losses last night." He reached up and brushed a loose curl from my forehead. "But I can't stand the thought of not having you with me. I keep telling myself it's because I need to know you're safe. My life is tied to yours and I can't protect that if you're not with me." His fingers trailed down my face, stopping on my neck. "But my heart tells me different. I don't know what to do."

Relief flooded through me. His thoughts mirrored my own.

"I think you promised me a vacation," I said, unable to stop the smile spreading across my face. "And Göksu owes me training time."

"You're okay with leaving?" he asked. "I can't give you the luxuries you would have at the palace."

I rolled my eyes and pinched his chest. He flinched and growled at me. "Since when have I ever lived in luxury? Which reminds me, we need to get back to your place and set up my finances. I still have no idea how much money Kellen put in my account."

"I think you need to meet with Kellen and the mage council first and let them know your intentions," he said, pulling my fingers away from his chest. "They may decide to take away your finances if you don't stay."

I hadn't thought of that. I rolled onto my back and frowned. "That would complicate things. I need to have a way to support myself."

"Don't let finances impact your decision. If they think they can hold you hostage with money, they will," Logan said. "I have everything you need, if you really don't want to stay."

I glanced over at him, but he looked away. There was something else he wasn't saying. Should I push him? We didn't seem to get much time to have these conversations. I flipped back onto my side, propping my head in my hand. He still avoided my gaze, his eyes following my movement instead.

"What else is bugging you?" I asked.

Rather than look at me, he rolled onto his back and threaded his fingers behind his head. Wow, did I really want to know?

"If you decide to come with me instead of staying here," he paused and bit his bottom lip. "Feeding was much easier for me before and my appetite was not as voracious." He glanced at me, but quickly looked away. "I'll be spending a lot of my time hunting, leaving you alone."

In the back of my mind, I knew that would be the case, but hearing it said made it reality. Could I stay alone in that tiny house? I already knew that answer.

"How much is 'a lot of your time?'" I asked. "If it's a couple days a week, I can make that work. I need time to train with my elementals. When you're not hunting, you can keep teaching me how to fight a vampire."

He turned his head and looked at me with widening eyes. "You really don't want to be at the palace?"

"My people skills suck. You know that," I replied. "I can't stand the thought of being trapped there with a bunch of people I don't trust. Kellen hates me. He made that very clear last night."

I rolled onto my stomach and buried my face in the pillow. I'd avoided thinking about Kellen's emotions. His anger, resentment, and jealousy hurt. I didn't ask for anything of this, but he did. He was one who threw me into this mess. I gave him the mages, just like he wanted. Why was he mad at me about it?

Logan's arm wrapped around me and pulled me against him again. "He doesn't hate you, princess. He hates that you're stronger than him. In one night, you proved that he is less than you. A tiny girl who's only known her magic for a month outdid the best mages on the field."

"But I didn't," I argued, wiping the tears of rejection from my eyes. "My elementals did that, not me."

"They didn't see your elementals," Logan countered. "They only saw you."

I knew he was right, but it still felt awful. At some point in the future, I would need my partner. Destiny didn't do anything without a reason. Kellen and I were meant to work together, not hate each other.

"I think you're the only one who really sees me," I mumbled. "Which is why I want to be with you and not them."

His lips brushed against my neck and trailed down my shoulder, sending shivers all the way down to my toes.

"We'll visit your mage council and hopefully leave on good terms," he said quietly. "But we should probably come up with a believable story of what you intend to do while you're away."

I rolled towards him, trying to keep my tears in check. "You can't go to the palace, Logan."

"I can't let you go alone." His thumb wiped away a rebellious tear running down my cheek.

"I don't deserve you," I whispered.

His laugh made me smile. "I was just thinking I didn't deserve you," he said. "No one else would agree to live in that extremely tiny off-the-grid home with a moody vampire."

"It's a huge upgrade from my apartment," I quipped. "But you really do need internet."

"I'll see what I can do."

His fingers threaded into my hair, and I didn't resist his efforts to close the space between us. I probably should've felt guilty about having sex with Logan in Kellen's house, but I didn't. Kellen never wanted me, only the leverage I gave him with the mages.

An hour later, I emerged from my room with Logan at my side. Voices floated down the hall from the kitchen. It sounded like Kellen and Kate, and it wasn't pleasant.

"Don't be stupid, Kellen," Kate hissed. "We need her with us. Just because you're jealous, doesn't give you a right to be an ass. Besides, the council has already voted on it."

I looked up at Logan and frowned, slowing my pace as we got closer. What had the council decided without my consent?

"The council cannot decide her fate," Kellen argued. "She has some say over her life."

My eyebrows rose in surprise. Did he just defend me? That didn't sound like Kellen being an ass.

"I agree, but we need her," Kate insisted. "She did things none of us even thought possible. I want to know how. Let's not forget the mages from Australia. Jim said they're leaving."

"You expected them to live in our courtyard?"

"Well… no."

I tugged Logan's elbow and pulled him into the room. At the very least, our eavesdropping was rude. At its worst, it was a breach of trust. Yes, Kellen had already crossed that bridge, but it didn't make it right. I tapped on the door frame as we entered, giving away our presence.

"AJ!" Kate jumped down from my favorite barstool and rushed towards me, wrapping her arms around my neck. "I was worried you wouldn't wake up."

"I'm fine," I said, trying to gently pull away from her embrace. "I'm a little woozy, but I think I'm just hungry."

"Well, we have leftover spaghetti," she said. "I'll warm it up for you."

"Thanks."

I took her place on my stool and Logan sat on the one next to me. Kellen leaned on the island counter. I could feel his eyes scouring my face and looked over at him. Yep. He didn't look away.

"How are the Australians doing?" I asked, resting my forearms on the granite counter. "Are they still at the palace, or did they go home already?"

"Jim insists on talking to you before they leave," Kellen replied. "You made a rather lasting impression on him."

"He's a good guy." I shrugged. "Cares about his people and didn't hesitate to drop everything to help us."

"Apparently, you went out of your way to help him as well," my partner said, still holding my gaze. "He told me about your conversation with Stewart and Marshall. He wants to have a private discussion with our council, but only if you're there."

I looked away. This is how it would start, forcing me into a position to make decisions.

"Well, let's take care of that, shall we?" Kate slid a plate of spaghetti in front of me, and a tall glass of milk followed it. "After I eat."

Vampire's Crucible

Chapter 17

Kellen and Kate disappeared through the portal, but I held Logan back.

"Don't let me be convinced to stay," I said. "I know that's their plan, and it's not what I want."

He scooped me up, and I wrapped my arms around his neck. Logan didn't say a word as he stepped through the portal. The world shifted uncomfortably, and pain radiated from my chest before we landed hard on the stone courtyard. Logan released me and we both fell to the ground. Crawling to him, I placed my hand on his neck.

"Are you okay?" I whispered.

"I can't do that again," he murmured.

I nodded and pushed myself to my feet. A strong hand caught my arm and pulled me the rest of the way. I looked up to find Kellen staring down at me. Concern filtered through my connection to him.

"I'm okay," I mumbled, pulling away from his grasp.

He dropped his hand with an awkward motion and looked over my head. I followed his gaze to see Jim helping Logan stand. My vampire's eyes met mine. Was that fear? I understood why. Using the portal had never been painful, so why now?

Soft muttering drew my attention to the growing crowd around us. I recognized Dylan and Ezekiel right away as they approached their leader. The other mages drifted in behind Jim, all staring at me and Logan.

"I'm glad you made it, Magister," Jim said. He didn't mention our graceless entry.

"So am I," I agreed, brushing off my blue jeans. "I owe a debt of gratitude to your mages. Their performance last night was exceptional. We couldn't have succeeded without them."

"You tested their endurance. Many of them feared for their lives." He raised his eyebrows, his icy blue eyes holding mine. "Any debt you feel owed has been paid with your own life. Everyone saw how much of yourself you gave to them when it was finished."

"What was I supposed to do?" I asked, blushing. "Leave them unconscious in the middle of a burning forest with local fire fighters breathing down our necks?"

"It was certainly an option," Jim replied. "One your previous Magister would have considered taking rather than risking her own life."

I wasn't sure how to respond. I knew my elemental wouldn't let me die, but my mother wouldn't have had that same reassurance. She also wouldn't have been able to do what we did.

"I don't know what my mother would've done," I said carefully. "I can only do what I know is right." I took a step closer to Logan. "I believe we have a meeting to attend?"

"We do." Jim turned to Dylan. "Take a scouting party back to the village and make sure we won't have any unexpected visitors."

"Yes, sir." Dylan turned back to the crowd, pointing at several men and women.

"Shall we?" Kellen's deep voice drew my attention.

I nodded but didn't start moving until Logan did. I could feel his anxiety and fear. Had Kellen done something to the portal? Was that why I felt so much pain when we fell through it? Surely my partner wouldn't sabotage the portal. He was one of the only ones who knew mine and Logan's lives were tied together. I needed to know what changed before we used it again.

Our small group made our way through the first set of large wooden doors, entering the palace's foyer. The black and white tiles stretching the length of the hall amazed me just as much today as they had they had the first time I saw them. Their shiny surface reflected the lights along the walls. The palace was everything I expected it to be: regal, elegant, and luxurious.

We passed by the doors leading to the Magister's Hall and entered the council's meeting room. The twelve council members were already seated at the far end of the long table, talking quietly amongst each other.

Two strangers occupied the chairs closet to the door. An older man with thin white hair covering his perfectly shaped head looked up as we filed in. He rested his hand on the other man's shoulder and pushed himself to his feet with effort. My eyes widened as he stood. Even hunched over from age, he was tall. His well-cut suit fit perfectly, giving away his wealthy status. Normal people couldn't afford a personal tailor.

The man next to him stood as well, meeting his companion's height. As soon as he turned towards us, I knew they were father and son. They both had the same long pointed nose, narrow face, and square chin. The only differences were their eyes and hair. The son's light brown eyes matched his short, sandy hair. The father's blue eyes settled on me, a smile splitting the wrinkles on his face.

"It's good to finally meet you, Alisandra," the older man said with a clipped British accent. "My name is William, and this is my son, Thomas." Though the father and son bowed, neither offered to shake hands. Not that I minded. I hated when people tested my magic.

I returned his smile. "It's nice to meet you, too."

Kellen cleared his throat and pulled out the chair directly across from William, motioning for me to sit. "This is King William and Prince Thomas," Kellen said. "They are the European mages' royal family."

My face flushed with embarrassment. He could've told me that before we walked in the room. I'd made a complete idiot of myself.

"Please excuse my rudeness," I said, trying not to scowl at my partner. "My knowledge of the mage families is extremely limited, including my own ancestry." I bowed slightly and took my seat, my face still flaming.

Kellen sat on my right, directly across from Thomas, and Logan sat on my left. Jim and Ezekiel filled the two chairs separating us from the rest of the mage council.

"Consider it forgotten, my dear," King William replied, taking his seat. "We are not here to judge your etiquette. We were invited by your partner to discuss your proposed... field trips."

His smile deepened along with my embarrassment. I clasped my hands in my lap to keep from slapping Kellen. I'd expected Marshall to repeat the conversation we had, but I'd also expected Kellen to clean it up. Just one more reason I shouldn't be leading the North American mages.

King William chuckled. "You are a joy to watch. I would've loved to hear that conversation coming from you." He glanced at my partner. "Kellen lacks the required facial expressions."

I suppressed my grin. Even though William was right, I wouldn't publicly demean my partner. "I might have been a little too harsh," I said, "but I believe many of our problems could be solved by socializing our mages with the others. Am I correct in assuming that you also have single mages who are unable to find partners?"

"You're correct, princess. My son has been single for much longer than is suitable for a prince." He laughed, the wrinkles on his face bouncing with the movement.

My face flushed again, the heat reaching my ears and neck. I'd meant mage partners, not romantic partners, though I had a feeling King William knew that and was toying with me. Thomas coughed and I glanced at him. The edges of his mouth twitched, his eyes gleaming with humor.

"I apologize, my dear. It's refreshing to have someone speak to me like a person and not a king. Too many of my court watch every word that flows from their mouth." He ran his bony fingers through his thin hair. "But you are correct. We need to coordinate times for our mages to meet. The vampires' offer of a life free from insanity is too tempting. You are not the only ones to suffer from it."

"Forgive my ignorance, but would it be too difficult for our first meeting to be one great big party?" I turned to Jim. "Would that be acceptable for your people?"

"I think it would put a target on our backs," Kellen replied before anyone else. "Having that many mages together in one place would put our strongholds at risk."

"Do we have that many single mages without partners?" I asked, frowning at him.

Kellen shifted in his seat, angling his body to face me. "No... I assumed you meant a party for everyone."

"Oh, I guess I should've clarified that." I tried not to sound trite, but I was pretty sure I failed. "If the number isn't too large, do we have a facility to accommodate it? Do we have the resources to make it happen?"

"Why wouldn't we start with smaller groups?" Thomas' deep baritone surprised me. It was melodious and so unexpected from his thin frame.

"Forgive my bluntness, but Jack is going to retaliate after last night's losses," I replied, giving my attention to the prince and trying to sound more refined than I really was. "We need to convince our mages that there's an alternative to the vampires' offer. They have to know that we're fighting for them." I shifted my gaze to Kellen. "That their lives have more meaning to their mage family than the vampires who wish to take them."

My partner's impassive stare softened, and the man I followed blindly a month ago emerged. His people had his heart, which was exactly why I relinquished my leadership to him. Kellen was an ass, but he still cared about what mattered most.

"I wish I had found you years ago, princess," William said, drawing my attention. "But we can't languish in the past. We'll plan a party at the castle for all the single mages. It will be a three-day event, which will hopefully be enough time for their elements to find each other." He turned to Jim. "Please be sure to pass the invitation to those in your care. I'll send messengers to our Asian and African counterparts."

"I'll send word to our South American friends," Kellen offered. "I also have several people here who excel at coordinating large events and would likely abandon me if I didn't offer their services to you."

"We'll gladly accept their help," William said. "Now, tell me about this battle. It's beyond me why everyone refuses to tell me anything when every mage here witnessed it."

"I was late to the party, so I'll let someone else tell it," I mumbled.

"Pardon me, Your Highness, but we have some very important items on our agenda that need to be discussed." An older gentleman at the far end of the table raised his gravelly voice to be heard. "We would be honored if you'd stay while we make these decisions."

"By all means," William waved a hand at the older man and smiled. "I didn't mean to monopolize your time." He leaned back in his seat and folded his arms over his chest. I didn't miss the smug look on his face. He enjoyed people kowtowing to him. Why wouldn't he? He called himself a king.

"Thank you, Your Highness." The older man turned to me, his lips pressed into a thin line. "Magister, the council would like you to stay at the palace and teach our water mages how to create the enormous shield you created. Several have also requested your healing knowledge." He paused and looked around the table at the other members. A young man with green eyes nodded. "We'd also like to discuss your air elemental."

"May I ask a question?" Thomas interrupted, leaning forward and looking towards the older gentleman.

I needed to find out his name but couldn't think of a way to do it without making myself look stupid. As Magister, I should know my council members.

The old man nodded. "Of course."

"You're asking for the expertise of a young woman who has only known her magic for a month?" the prince asked.

Several of the council members blushed, but the young man with green eyes spoke up. "I was at the battle last night. We don't possess the knowledge to do what she did."

"But you do," I argued. "Please don't be offended, but I believe your ignorance is born of outdated traditions." I scooted my chair back and stood, leaning over the table so I could see everyone. "As you all know, I have very little training. Kellen and Logan did the best they could in the few weeks they were given. What I do have is the humility to listen to my elementals. I don't command them, even though I could." Not. There was no way I'd command either of them.

I looked down at my vampire. "I love and respect them. I ask for their help and trust their decision when they say no." Logan winked at me and I smiled, then turned back to the group. "The shield we created last night was not only my doing. Jim's water mages helped." I pointed at the dark-skinned mage next to Kellen. "Without them, it couldn't have happened. The rift in the earth was the same way. They worked together and pooled their strength to create a crevice deep enough to swallow hundreds of vampires. Without the fire and air mages, the crevice was nothing more than a hole in the ground. The fiery tornados raging through the battlefield drove the vampires to the death that waited them."

My gaze landed on my partner. "You have all you need except a new perspective. Everything that happened could've just as easily been coordinated by you." I chuckled. "Actually, you probably could've done better. I was flying by the seat of my pants hoping nothing fell apart."

I dropped back into my chair. The following silence was deafening, and too many eyes stared at me with looks of disbelief.

"Does that mean you will not stay?" the old man asked.

"I have a training schedule with my water elemental," I replied. "After the power he sacrificed for me last night, I won't deny him my time. I've also made promises to continue the search for our stolen mages. None of that can happen here in the palace."

"Your elemental is training you?" Thomas asked, not hiding his surprise.

I narrowed my eyes at him. After my conversation with Göksu, I assumed all royal families had the same relationship with their elements. "Yes. And most everything I know about using air came from my air elemental."

He started to ask another question, but his father interrupted. "Who will rule your people if you leave to do these things, Alisandra? Your place is here, leading, not doing the work of a common mage."

There it was, the superiority complex of someone born to wealth and privilege.

"There is no one more qualified to rule our mages than my partner," I replied, glancing at Kellen. "I trust his decisions completely. Our new council provides guidance and relieves some of the burden required of a single ruler. I don't wish to insult your method, as it obviously works well for you." I looked down the table at the group of council members whose names I should I know. "But our people need to have confidence that their interests are being considered. My mother failed to do that. Her selfishness nearly led to our demise. I have complete faith in our council to remember the Magister's shortcomings and make the best decisions for our people."

Smiles of gratitude spread across the faces of the council. They needed to hear that their hard work mattered, even if I wasn't around to see it.

"As for my absence, I've been granted gifts that I can't and won't discuss with you. Staying at the palace doesn't allow me the freedom to learn how to use them." I leaned forward, trying to keep my expression polite. "Jack's retaliation will be brutal. Our fight with him has only just begun. In case you hadn't heard, he's using the ogres to fight in his army. It would be wise for us to recruit the other supernatural families before he takes them as well."

A hostile look crossed the king's face for the briefest moment, instantly replaced by a smile. A fake smile, one born from years of practice. "Such wisdom from one so young and ignorant of our ways. We will assist in every way possible, princess."

It was impossible to miss the implied insult, but I ignored it. "I never doubted your dedication, Your Highness." I stood and turned to the old man at the end of the table. "Is there anything else on our agenda?"

"No, Alisandra, nothing that cannot wait until our next meeting."

"You don't hear it enough, especially from me, but none of this would be possible without you," I said. "The quick mobilization of our warriors yesterday and the continued functioning of our people is a testament to your dedication and sacrifice. Thank you."

Murmurs of acknowledgment followed as everyone stood. I placed my hand on Kellen's arm, and he looked down at me. "I need to talk to you in private," I said.

He raised an eyebrow at me and nodded. I remained by my chair as the others filed out of the room. King William corralled Jim, asking him to tell the story of last night's battle. Jim glanced at me. Was he asking my permission?

"I trust you to tell what needs to be told, my friend," I said, smiling. I had to trust that he wouldn't reveal Logan. I wasn't sure how King William would react to a vampire in his midst.

The two leaders left, leaving me, Kellen, Logan, and Thomas. I suspected the prince had questions about my elementals, questions he should already know the answers to but didn't. He stood behind his chair, towering over the rest of us. His lanky frame eliminated any sense of intimidation.

"There's something you want to ask," I stated, breaking the silence.

"I don't know where to begin," he said, gripping the back of his chair. "Anything I say will disrespect my family."

"Then let's find a better place to talk," Kellen suggested, "where there aren't unwanted ears."

"Thank you."

Thomas' obvious relief worried me. Maybe this wasn't about his elementals.

"My home or the Magister's rooms?" Kellen asked, looking down at me.

"The Magister's rooms would be best," I replied, trying to hide my frown. I hated those rooms, but I wasn't leaving Logan here, and he wasn't using the portal. "Let's go."

Chapter 18

Kellen led the way to the rooms that used to belong to my mother. Logan and I fell in line behind the prince. My heart raced as we traversed the winding staircase and stopped in front of the double wooden doors. So much happened behind those doors. My entire life changed in so many ways. We fought my mother and won, releasing the mages from her grasp. Logan revealed the truth of our bonding, creating an unhealable rift between me and Kellen. I glanced at my vampire. He'd also give me his friendship and love, something I'd never had before.

My partner pulled open the left-hand door and waited for us to enter. My feet wouldn't move. I hadn't been in there since we fought my mother and her mage-vampires. Had Kellen cleaned up our mess? Did he replace the broken furniture? I had to assume so or he wouldn't have offered the room to the prince. Logan gently pushed me forward, and I crossed the threshold.

A smile slid across my face once I entered. The gaudy pink wallpaper was gone, replaced by a soft sand-colored paint. Hardwood floors ran the length of the room and two dark leather sofas faced each other beneath the undressed windows. Paintings of green meadows and waterfalls hung on each of the walls, adding splashes of color to the room. Everything was now a reflection of Kellen.

"Please have a seat," Kellen said, motioning to the sofas. "Can I get you something to drink?"

"Wine would be wonderful," Thomas replied. "Red, if you have it."

Kellen nodded. "AJ? Logan?"

"Water is fine," I replied, appreciating his efforts to protect Logan.

"Whiskey," Logan answered. "You know my favorite."

I sat on the sofa facing the door, and Logan joined me. Thomas sat opposite of us, a frown marring his pointed features.

"What's on your mind, Your Highness?" I asked.

"Please just call me Thomas," he replied. "I'm not my father."

"Fair enough. I'm AJ."

A faint smile replaced his frown, but only for a moment. "We've heard so many rumors about you and Kellen," he said. "Then the talk of last night's battle." He looked out the window at the fading light. "I don't know what to believe. Does your elemental really talk to you?"

"They both do," I replied. "But I'm beginning to think I'm an exception and not in a good way. Kellen would argue differently, but only because I haven't shared with him everything that's happened. The more I learn, the more I realize that some higher being controls every part of my life."

Kellen handed out drinks and took the space next to Thomas. "Please share, AJ. I'm all ears," he said, painting on that impassive expression that seemed to become his norm. Before my mother's death, I got to see his smile frequently.

I sighed but couldn't be mad at his resentment. "When that ogre attacked Logan and I the other day, it became obvious I wasn't equipped to handle what was coming. Not just the physical fight but the strategic one as well. There are too many players and not all of them have our best interest in mind. I fear some of our allies are really the enemy. The story about the attack on Jim's people doesn't add up. Compound that with the attack on Victor's lodge, and, well, there are too many inconsistencies. We have traitors we don't know about."

"And that answers none of Thomas' questions," Kellen said.

I narrowed my eyes at him. "After our near death with the ogre and its vampire master, my elementals gave me gifts to help fight against them," I explained, knowing I couldn't tell the whole truth. "As well as Logan. I'm pretty sure they come with a price. At some point, I'll be expected to use those gifts to protect us. In order to do that, I need to learn how to use them. We can't do that here."

"So last night was a result of your gifts?" Kellen asked.

"Yes and no. Everything I said in today's meeting was the absolute truth," I replied. "What we accomplished could've been done without me, except maybe the healing part at the end. That was another gift from my water elemental."

"The increased speed I noticed last night is yet another gift?" My partner gripped his glass of whiskey with both hands, but didn't drink it, giving away his efforts to maintain his impassive expression.

I glanced at Thomas, then back to Kellen. I had to assume the prince would tell his father everything we said. Is that why he asked for a private audience? Did he try to make us feel comfortable, hoping we'd reveal more than intended?

"One of my gifts was increased speed, to level the playing field when the vampires get antsy," I answered. "It's proven to be extremely useful."

"How many times have you been attacked?" Thomas asked.

"Once is too many and several is overwhelming," I replied, evading his question.

"Yes, I suppose you're right. Why was Logan given these gifts and not your partner?" the prince questioned. "Would your partner's magic not be stronger?"

"When someone gives a box of chocolates, do you question why or just say thank you?" I responded. "I can't begin to understand an elemental's logic. The typical response is, 'Princess, there are things I cannot tell even you.'" I tried to mimic Göksu. No one but Logan would know I failed miserably.

"I'm amazed they speak to you." Thomas sipped his wine, rolling his glass between his fingers. "I'm also jealous. But I'm willing to change the way I use my magic if it will bring me closer to them. My father will object. He hates change. We've taught our mages to command their magic for generations and have prided ourselves in our success." His soft brown eyes met mine, pleading with me to understand. "Listening to your mages talk about you with awe and respect makes me want what you have. How does someone so new have all that power?"

"I told you in our meeting. I respect my elementals and ask for their strength," I replied, trying not to pick at my clothing. Why was that so hard to understand for other mages? "Honestly, if I tried to boss my wind elemental, he'd laugh at me and toss me across the room. I don't know how you command yours. I certainly can't." I looked at my still-closed water bottle and twisted the top off. "And my water elemental will do nothing for me unless I come to him with love and compassion. When I do, he gives me the strength I need."

The prince shook his head and turned to Kellen. "And what of your partnership?" he asked. "Will you be married?"

Kellen and I looked at one another with similar expressions. I didn't want to have that discussion. He took a long drink of his whiskey, emptying the glass.

"That's a personal conversation that AJ and I need to have," Kellen replied. "And it's really none of your business."

My mouth dropped open at Kellen's rudeness. Not that I didn't appreciate it, I was just surprised.

"I meant no offense," Thomas said, raising one hand in the air as if to wave off the sudden hostility. "My father is pushing me to court the princess." He blushed but refused to look at me. "But I have no desire to force myself on someone who is already taken."

I couldn't stop the smile tugging at my lips. A new level of respect for this man just entered the picture. I didn't want to be pursued by anyone.

"Thank you," Kellen said. "The last few weeks haven't left us much time to think about anything other than fighting for our people." He glanced at me, his expression unreadable and for good reason. Logan and I found plenty of time to get to know each other after Kellen chased me away. We'd become close friends even before that.

"If that situation should change…" the prince paused, leaving the rest unsaid. At least he had the decency to blush again and look me in the eye.

A low growl rumbled from my vampire, but the other two men in the room didn't seem to notice.

"Seriously? I'm sitting here," I grumbled, hating that my face flushed with embarrassment. "Don't we have other things to discuss?"

"I should find my father," Thomas said, finishing his glass of wine and standing. "I hope to see you at the party, princess,"

"It was good to meet you, Thomas." I stood with him and offered my hand. Logan rose with me. I refrained from looking up at him, knowing his expression wasn't friendly.

Instead of shaking my offered hand, the prince kissed my fingers. It was weird and flattering. I blushed again. Damn!

Kellen stood as well, escorting the prince to the door. They mumbled softly, and I snuck a glance at Logan. Sure enough, jealous daggers soared from his eyes into the back of Thomas' head.

I brushed my fingers across his chest, drawing his attention. "You have nothing to worry about," I whispered. "Now relax. The hard part is next."

The furrow between his eyes relaxed along with his clenching jaw, but he didn't smile. "You handled that much better than I would have," he whispered back to me.

I smiled. "I heard you growl."

"No you didn't. Did you?" He reached down and swept back a wild curl falling across my forehead.

"Yeah. Was I not supposed to?"

"No."

That was interesting.

"You want another drink, Logan?" Kellen asked from across the room.

"Yes, thanks."

"AJ, you want something other than water?"

"No, its fine. It'll just make me stupid and I don't need any help with that."

Kellen snorted, and I couldn't help but laugh at his expressive gesture after being so cold.

"You have been the only intelligent one here," Kellen said, pouring two more glasses of amber whiskey.

"I doubt that." I fell back into the sofa, some of my anxiety slipping away with my partner's self-deprecation. Hopefully, this wouldn't be an 'AJ bashing party' by the time we were done. There was so much we needed to get out in the open, and regardless of our past, I needed to trust the man who would be leading our mages.

Kellen sauntered back over to the little seating arrangement and handed Logan a glass.

"To the future."

He extended his cup to my vampire who graciously accepted the toast.

"To the future."

They both emptied their glasses and sat. Kellen's eyes drifted from me to Logan several times. I waited for him to put his thoughts together. There was so much I wanted to say, but I needed him to initiate this.

"Apologizing won't change the past," Kellen finally said. "I regret so many things. I should have just been honest and open with you from the beginning, AJ." He rolled the small glass in his hands, watching it rather than looking at me. "Of course, hindsight is twenty-twenty. My biggest regret is my reaction to your bonding. I hated Logan for doing it, but there weren't any options. You would've died or become a vampire. While I could hope you would retain some humanity the way Logan has, there was no guarantee."

He looked up at me, his brown eyes softening. "But our mages wouldn't accept you as a vampire any more than your mother. So that wasn't an option. At the time, I thought being tied to Logan was the same thing. I realize now that we can keep it secret." He set his glass on the narrow table next to the sofa and leaned towards me. "I've told no one. After I got over being pissed off, I quit trying to find out how it happened, realizing it would expose the two of you. The people love you, AJ. After last night, they'll overlook a lot of inconsistencies."

I didn't know what to say. His admission was so far from what I expected; I could only sit there with my mouth hanging open.

"Close your mouth, princess," Logan said. "There's a 'but,' isn't there?"

Kellen nodded. "You can't spend all your time away. They'll forgive many things, but they need their Magister here." He raised a hand in the air to stop my argument. "Not all the time. We can explain your need to train and look for the others, but you need to spend some of your time here with your people."

Kellen cleared his throat and braced his elbows on his knees. "You and I need to act like we enjoy each other's company. Anyone with eyes can see the wall between us. Thomas was polite just now, but there were all kinds of subliminal messages in that conversation. He said he'll not pursue you, but it's not what he meant. If we aren't officially engaged soon, he's moving in."

My mouth fell open again. He couldn't possibly be serious. There was no way I was getting engaged to the man who tried to kill me. I could forgive him and maybe even try to understand his reasoning, but marriage? Hell no! I snapped my mouth closed and jumped to my feet.

"How dare you! You never cared for me! You used me to get my mother off the throne and take her seat of power. Then you tried to kill me when you thought I would threaten that seat." My voice grew louder with each thought, tears clouding my vision. "There's no way in hell I would ever marry you."

"AJ, wait."

Logan's voice forced my tears to fall. The man who was supposed to love me better not defend Kellen. I turned towards him, crossing my arms over my stomach, daring him to side with my traitorous partner.

"You know my heart better than anyone else," Logan said, remaining seated. "As much as it disgusts me to think about it, Kellen has a point."

"Stop. Don't say another word." I took a step away from him, slamming into the doors across the room before I realized what happened. "You don't get to break my heart, remember?"

He hovered over me seconds later, his hands on each side of my head and my back against the door. "He doesn't need you to love him," my vampire whispered.

"The two of you would force me into an arranged marriage?" I asked, my anger pulsing through my veins. "Get away from me."

Logan's forehead dropped to mine. "I won't force you to do anything, AJ."

"But you won't stop him from doing it." I pushed against his chest, but he wouldn't move. "Logan, get out of my way."

"You can't leave here mad. We need to talk about this."

"No, we don't."

"AJ, think about it. You're the ruler of the North American mages, basically a queen in the eyes of the other ruling families," Logan whispered. "And you're single."

"No, I'm not," I muttered.

"No one knows that but you and I."

I tilted my head to look up at him. His hazel eyes swept across my face, stopping at the tears rolling down my cheeks. We could never have an open relationship, could we? It would always be hidden behind closed doors. Moments stolen in secret.

"I can't do this."

"How many times have you said that and still found a way?"

He took a step back, giving me space. I looked over at my partner and sighed. His pained expression mirrored my own. I pushed myself away from the wall and walked back to the sofa, plopping down on it and tucking my legs beneath me.

"Tell me what brought on this decision," I said, wiping my tears away.

Logan took his place beside me, and Kellen collapsed into the sofa across from us.

"Jim asked to take you home with him," Kellen said. "So did King William."

My eyes widened in surprise. "That's ridiculous."

"No, not really. You control the North American mages." Kellen shifted in his seat, uneasiness radiating off him. "If you think of it on a political scale, each region would benefit greatly from a marriage with you."

"But none of them love me," I said bitterly. "Including you."

My partner glared at me, his anger filtering through our bond. "I will allow Logan free passage to come and go as he pleases. I'll let you build your strength and teach our mages how to connect with their elements." He took a deep breath and closed his eyes, rubbing his temples for several moments. "Thomas will treat you like a princess, but he won't let you to leave the castle. Jim would treat you well, but he'd never allow Logan near you."

He leaned forward, resting his elbows on his knees and lacing his long fingers together. "I expect my uncle to approach me next. Women in his culture have nothing. He would give you to one of his sons for breeding, in the hopes that you would produce another powerful mage."

"So you're the lesser of all the evils. Is that what you're saying?" I regretted it as soon as the words left my mouth. It was a harsh and calloused thing to say even if it felt like the truth to me. His face fell into his hands. Damn. "I'm sorry, Kellen. It's really hard for me to see the silver lining in this. Why can't I just hand this over to you?"

He looked up at me. His whole face pulling into a deep frown. "Because I am the usurper trying to steal North America from you," he replied, his lip curled in disgust. He rose from his seat and paced towards the window. "Do you know why my parents came to America?"

He didn't turn around, so I didn't answer.

"For the same reason thousands of others do. The freedom to raise their kids without fear of persecution." He ran his fingers through his dark hair and turned to me. "Kate and I were both born in Egypt. But when my parents realized my sister only had one element, they packed up their stuff and moved here. Single mages under my uncle's rule are executed at thirty years old if they don't find a partner. They believe it's more humane than allowing the mage to suffer insanity." He bit his lower lip, and I found myself twisting the end of my shirt. "I never understood why it surprised my parents that she only had one, until your elemental revealed my mother's ancestry. Kate should have had two elements. We moved here hoping she would find a partner, but she hasn't."

He turned back to the window. I felt guilty for my impatience, but he really needed to get to the point. His parents' choice made sense. I wouldn't have stayed either had I been in their position.

"My parents fought against the corruption the Magister sowed deep within this palace. They dedicated so much of their time and resources trying to fix what was broken." His breath hitched, but he didn't turn around. "The Magister had them killed for it. I didn't know she was responsible until years later when I was part of her court. I should've known she wasn't capable of kindness or compassion. I'd heard about Logan's fate and the rumors around her involvement with the vampires." Kellen shook his head. "But I needed someone to care about me and take care of Kate. I was so stupid. Regardless of my blindness, I grew to love this place. It's my home, and I've given up everything in my fight to keep it."

I glanced at Logan, suspecting I held the same pitiful look on my face. Kellen didn't need pity, though.

"That doesn't make you a usurper, Kellen," I said.

"No, but it makes me a foreigner trying to rule a people who are not mine to rule." He turned towards us, his brows nearly meeting each other. "You can leave, granting the mage council leadership, but they aren't strong enough to keep another royal family from coming in and taking over. The mages have always been led by royalty. We can change it, but it needs to happen in phases or it'll never work."

"So you and I need to be the ruling party until the council is strong enough to keep the others out?" I asked.

He nodded. "I don't hate you, AJ. I'm stupid, selfish, and arrogant, but I promise to treat you with kindness and respect. I promise I won't take your freedom from you."

I looked down at my fingers now tangled in my shirt. "I can't love you, Kellen."

"I don't expect you to. It's obvious your heart belongs to Logan, and I won't keep you apart." He walked back to the sofa and sat down again. "I told you, he will have free access to the palace. I only ask that our secrets remain between us."

We both looked at my vampire. It wasn't just my decision.

"AJ and I will never be able to have an open relationship," Logan said. "It's probably better if we keep it to ourselves anyway. It's already been used against us once. We only put our lives at risk if we carry our emotions in public."

"What exactly did we just decide?" I asked, fearing I'd just agreed to everything I said I wouldn't.

Logan and Kellen looked at one another and shrugged. Men! How did they accept these things so easily? Or did they just hide it?

"We'll announce our engagement in the next couple days," Kellen said. "We don't have to set a wedding date any time soon. I'd like to expand this suite to include two bedrooms, giving each of us our own personal space." He paused and settled his gaze on my vampire. "I'd like to continue our efforts to collect information about Jack's plans. I think it's even more important now than before."

"I agree," Logan said. "But you need to fix the portal first. I can—or could, until today—use the portal as long as AJ was with me. Something changed today."

Kellen frowned. "We haven't done anything to the portals. Changing one would force a change in all of them, and I assure you that hasn't happened."

I gaped at Logan. If it wasn't the portal, it was him. Could it be his recent change in diet?

"Is it your lack of human blood?" I asked.

"I wouldn't think so, but that's the only thing that's changed."

"What are you two talking about?" Kellen asked.

"It's not like you can keep it secret forever, Logan," I said. "And it might be better for him to hear about it before he sees it in battle."

My vampire rubbed his hands across his face, then looked over at Kellen. "To prevent me from trying to bite AJ in dire situations, I was given a gift. It's turned out to be more of a curse, though." He took a deep breath and let it out slowly. "I no longer need human blood to survive. Vampire blood has replaced it."

Kellen's eyebrows raced to his hairline and his eyes darted back and forth between me and Logan. "No shit?"

"Yeah. I don't want to discuss the details." Logan ran his fingers through his hair. "The portal only allows the living to pass through. I've successfully used it several times as long as AJ was with me. Her body created enough of an illusion of a living being to keep the portal's magic from killing me."

"Okay, I need a minute to think about how the portals work." Kellen stood and tapped his finger on his chin, mumbling to himself and pacing back and forth. I didn't realize he was that familiar with the portal's magic, but it made sense. I was certain he fixed the one at his home after our last escapade. "I don't think that's it," he said after a few moments. "You're still a vampire, regardless of your diet. You didn't become even more dead. It has to be AJ." He stopped his pacing and looked at me. "What's changed for you?"

Time to let it all out of the bag, or at least some of it. I would never speak of my spirit elemental.

"I can move faster, see in the dark and hear really well, but I still like pasta and coffee," I replied. "There is no blood in my diet, not even rare meat."

"Are you willing to test a few things?" Kellen asked.

"No!" Logan and I answered together.

"Today's experience was painful," Logan said. "I was pretty sure my heart stopped. I'm not willing to risk AJ's life."

"I felt the same pain," I added. "I'm not willing to risk our lives either. If one of us doesn't make it, we're both done."

Kellen's perpetual frown deepened. "I can't change the portal's access, because we'd have to change all of them. Not only is that a security risk, we'd have to explain ourselves. I'm not prepared to do that."

"So, we'll be traveling the normal way," I said. "I hope you have a passport, Logan."

He smiled, but it wasn't very convincing. "I've never been able to use the portals, princess. Of course I have a passport."

"That'll complicate things for AJ, though," Kellen stated, giving me his attention as he sat down again. "They'll expect you to use the portal to attend your field trip at the castle."

"I'm not willing to chance it, Kellen," I argued.

"Even if I create the illusion of a live body around you?" Kellen asked. "If your tiny body could fool the portal's magic into thinking Logan was alive, surely mine can protect you. Especially because you're very much alive."

His logic made sense, even if it didn't explain why our method no longer worked with me and Logan.

"What about Logan?" I countered. "Will he be boarding a plane the day before in order to get to our field trip on time?"

"I won't be going," Logan replied.

My eyes searched his, finding the same sadness. I should've guessed as much. If King William discovered a vampire at his castle, we'd both be dead. A tiny crack in my heart beckoned the beginning of our separation from each other.

"It'll take time to plan this event," Kellen said, pulling me away from my morbid thoughts. "It's not happening tomorrow or even next week." He rose from the sofa once again, reminding me of one of those bouncy toys. Up and down, up and down. "We should make sure the king and his son are given a proper send off. Jim will likely entertain them with his tales for a while, but even he has his limits."

I unfolded my legs and stood, trying to straighten my shirt where I'd twisted it in knots. "Lead the way," I mumbled, still tugging at my clothes and not at all comfortable with the decisions we'd made. My future didn't look very bright, not that my past was full of sunshine either. But it would've been really nice to meet a great guy, get married, and raise kids. None of that was in my future.

William and Thomas weren't ready to leave when we found them in a full dining hall. The Australian mages mingled easily with ours, surprising me. They were all native Aborigines. I guess my naïve brain assumed there would be prejudices, but the mages proved me wrong. They ate and drank until long past midnight.

The royal father and son seemed to enjoy the stories running rampant around the room, each of them expressing genuine interest. Thomas' interest lingered on me more often than I liked, but I played along, smiling like it mattered.

We bade them farewell at the portal just after one in the morning. I collapsed in Kellen's new room shortly after, with Logan by my side. A twinge of guilt poked at my conscience for kicking Kellen out of his space and filling it with my vampire. It was rude and heartless, but it didn't keep me from snuggling next to Logan and falling asleep.

Chapter 19

The sun rose over the courtyard, chasing away the chill air that had settled in the early morning hours. The dark swirling portal stood in front of me, again. Its murkiness could never look innocent, not in my eyes, regardless of Kellen's reassurances. I rubbed my chest, the memory of our last attempt still very fresh in my mind.

Logan's hand brushed against my lower back, and I pulled my eyes away from the portal.

"We'll be okay," he said. "It's better to test it now than find out later."

"Yes, I'm so anxious to throw…" I stuttered, almost saying his life, "my life away." It was unlikely anyone was listening, but I didn't want to chance it. The courtyard appeared empty, but there had to be guards patrolling.

"We'll be right back," Kellen said. He scooped one arm under my knees and the other behind my shoulders, then stepped through the portal without waiting for me to object.

The world spun around me like it always did, but nothing hurt as we arrived at Kellen's estate. There was just a brief tightening in my chest. He lowered me to my feet, but his hands stayed on my shoulders, his dark eyes searching my face.

"I'm okay," I said. "No pain, not even any nausea." I rubbed my chest. Something was different.

A look of relief washed over his features. "Good. I was worried you were no longer human."

I took a step away and glared at him, his hands falling to his sides. "Did you think Logan turned me and we didn't tell you?"

"What was I supposed to think?" he answered with his own question. "You have these new vampire traits without being a vampire."

I put my hands on my hips and glared at him. "I explained that."

"Yes, but you have to admit it's rather unbelievable." A rare smile lit up his eyes, reminding me of a time when I thought I loved him. "You've changed so much."

I looked away, not sure what he meant and really not wanting to know. "Let's get back so Logan isn't standing in the middle of your courtyard by himself." He reached for me, and I took another step back. "We need to find a way to do this that doesn't involve me being carried like a child."

He closed the space between us and replaced my hands with his on my hips. "Wrap your arms around my neck, that way it looks more like an embrace and less like a carry."

An uncomfortable feeling wiggled in my stomach. This was the same man who tried to have me killed, and now I was supposed to pretend that I cared for him. Life was so unfair.

I took a deep breath and placed my hands on his chest. Before my fingers reached his collar, he pulled me tight against him and stepped back through the portal. Logan's low growl greeted us, and I hoped I was the only one to hear it. Kellen didn't immediately let me go, and I dropped my head on his chest to hide my frustrated emotions. Was he going out of his way to piss off Logan?

"There are several mages in the courtyard," he whispered in my ear.

Kellen didn't linger, though. He released me and walked away. I followed his path to two men walking towards us. I recognized one from the battle the night before. His name might have been David or Daniel or something. He smiled at me, then gave his attention to my partner. I had the sudden urge to run away really fast and never look back.

"Let's get you some breakfast," Logan said, taking my elbow.

We stopped next to Kellen, and I looked at my worn-out sneakers. I should buy a new pair.

"We're getting breakfast, then going to pick up AJ's stuff from the house. She also has a training session with her water elemental," Logan said. "Do you need anything while we're gone?"

"No," Kellen replied. I couldn't force myself to look at him. "When can I expect you back?"

Neither of us answered, and I reluctantly drew my attention away from my shoes. Kellen looked at me expectantly.

"Probably tomorrow evening. I'm not sure how much time my elemental needs," I replied.

"Be safe," he said, his expression softening for a moment.

"Never." I couldn't stop my lips from smiling, despite my efforts. Nothing in my life was safe. It was ridiculous that I found it funny.

David snorted, and his companion laughed. At least I wasn't the only one.

"Sorry, Magister," David said. "It sounds a little funny coming from such a small person, even though I got a firsthand demonstration of your strength."

"It's okay, being underestimated has turned out to be good for me," I replied. "Just like someone said it would." I gave Kellen a smile, and he returned it. Maybe he remembered that conversation as well as I did.

"Are you sure you don't want a bigger entourage to protect you?" David asked.

"No, it's easier for two people to disappear in a crowd," I replied. "And I will be careful. Logan won't let me do anything stupid."

"Yes, because I'm so immune to your commands, princess," Logan said, eliciting laughs from the mages. Apparently, they didn't carry suspicions about my vampire, or Kellen had already given them orders to act normal. Probably the latter. Either way, it was thoughtful and appreciated.

"Take your phone in case I need you back earlier," Kellen stated.

"Yes, dear."

Logan and I walked away, with him holding my elbow to make sure I didn't sprint. He led me to the dining hall and waited our turn to order food. My heaping plate of eggs, bacon, toast, and fruit looked odd next to his single cup of coffee.

"How are we getting back to your place?" I whispered, just in case someone was trying to eavesdrop.

"We're running to the outskirts of Salt Lake," Logan replied in an equally soft tone. "Yun will have a car waiting for us."

"Okay, good." I stuffed a forkful of eggs in my mouth.

"Your hearing gets better every day. You shouldn't be able to hear me."

"Just like I shouldn't be able to hear you growling?" I raised my eyebrows at him and popped a piece of bacon in my mouth.

And there was my favorite grin. I washed down my breakfast with orange juice and took the cup of coffee he hadn't touched.

"What if I wanted to drink that?" he asked, obviously pretending to be offended.

"It's awful when it's cold," I replied. "And it's already lukewarm."

He chuckled, standing up from the table in one fluid motion. "Let's go before too many people are out of bed."

~~~~~~~~~~~~~

As promised, Logan's SUV waited for us at the same train station where I thought I'd killed the female vampire. Her body was nowhere to be found. Logan gave me a funny look when I voiced my guilt over leaving her.

"Hi guys! Long time, no see." Yun's cheerful voice forced me to smile.

It felt good to be away from the palace and the responsibilities threatening to squash me. In the two days I'd been there, the place had smothered me.

"It's good to see you, too," I said, accepting her hug. It was also good to find someone my own height, but I wasn't saying that out loud. Short people tended to be sensitive about their shortness.

"I need you to drop me off at the red house," she said, hopping in the back seat. "They're delivering new furniture today."

"That was quick." I pulled myself into the front passenger seat as Logan adjusted the driver's seat before getting in. "They've already repaired all the damage we did?" I asked.

"Yep," she squeaked. "It was mostly just a mess, except for the furniture and kitchen island."

"Do you have a ride back to the desert?" Logan asked, steering the vehicle onto the highway.

"Yep," she said again. "Otto is bringing the furniture. He'll take me home."

"Okay, good. AJ and I have a lot to get done." He glanced over at me, and I didn't miss the anxiety darting between us. So much for getting away from my stress.

"We'll start with my bank account," I stated. "I'm tempted to automatically transfer the funds to another account just in case someone changes their mind."

"I planned to suggest that," Logan said.

"I agree," Yun added from the back seat. "It's never a good idea to have all your eggs in one basket."

"Can I use your mailing address, Logan?" I asked, turning sideways in my seat. "Or should I pay for one of those mailbox-store-things?"

He glanced at me again. "Of course you can use mine, but I also have one of those mailbox-store-things."

I laughed, letting the humor drain away some of the tension from the last two days. I didn't want to think about Kellen or the vampire council or anything that had to do with a war between supernatural families. I needed a break; an escape from my reality. If I didn't force myself to take one, there would never be time.

"Can we go to the movies?" I asked.

"What?" Logan asked in return.

"You know, a theater that plays movies with actors," I replied, rolling my eyes.

"There's a great new chick flick out!" Yun exclaimed. "Been at the theater for a week, but I'll never get any of these guys to go with me."

I turned further in my seat, my smile growing. "That sounds great. For two hours, I can forget about everything else and just be normal."

Logan just shook his head and remained silent as Yun and I planned a girl's night out. Smart man. I wasn't taking no for an answer. A break from reality was exactly what I needed.

"So, tell me about this battle the rumor mill is burning up," my new best friend said after we made a date for the evening.

"I'd prefer to hear the rumor mill version, first," Logan said.

"Well, according to Marissa, who heard it from her brother, our little mage single-handedly killed over a hundred vampires from Ernesto's clan," she explained, her eyes simmering with excitement. "I know Marissa exaggerates. So which part is true?"

"I didn't realize they were Ernesto's," Logan said, not really answering her question. "It's interesting that he and Sergey were both there." He tapped the steering wheel with his fingers. "I'd say one hundred is about right, but AJ didn't do it by herself."

"Just a sec," I interrupted. "Who are these men? Members of the vampire council?" I asked, needing clarification.

"Yes," Logan replied. "Sergey is leader of the Russian clan and Ernesto has the South American."

I frowned. Jack *really* wanted the shifters out of the picture.

"I hadn't heard that Sergey was there," Yun stated, her enthusiasm waning. "Between the two, there should've been closer to three hundred vampires." She leaned forward across the center console, craning her neck to see Logan.

"Do you know if Ernesto survived?" my vampire asked, glancing at her.

"Pretty sure he did," she replied. "What happened with Sergey?"

"AJ sent him packing, along with three ogres."

Yun transferred her focus to me. "What did you do to scare the Russian? He's fierce."

I looked away from her needy eyes and picked up a penny from the cup holder. "I drew the blood from several of the vampires' bodies and attempted to make a weapon with it."

"With their blood?"

"Yeah."

"That's gross, but I'm surprised it had any effect on the Russian." She leaned back in her seat. "Like I said, he's fierce. I've heard some really nasty stories about stuff he's done to folks."

I shrugged, not having an answer for her. My thoughts drifted to Braden and his desire to overthrow Jack. Was Sergey trying to do the same thing? Did he use my display of power as an excuse to back away? Another thought struck me.

"Yun, was Sergey also responsible for the first attack on Victor's lodge?" I asked, trying to connect my thoughts.

"Yeah...." Her eyes lit up. "He retreated then, too, after your elemental tossed them about like ragdolls."

"Is he trying to sabotage Jack's plans?" I asked. "He ran from both fights when he didn't really need to. Or is he just a coward?"

Logan glanced at me, his thick brows drawing together. "As Yun said, he's not a coward. We need to consider his loyalty compromised," he said. "Although, Jack might not see it that way, not yet. If Sergey hadn't left when he did, most of his soldiers would be dead alongside Ernesto's." He tapped his fingers on the steering wheel again. "Jack will initially applaud the Russian for recognizing an overwhelming threat, until he hears the rest of the story. I'd love to be a fly on the wall in Jack's office."

The SUV slowed to a stop, and I recognized the cedar cottage with a red door where that nasty ogre nearly suffocated me. Trees surrounded the cottage, and the nearest house was at least a mile away. No wonder none of the neighbors reacted to our destruction. There were no neighbors.

A moving truck filled the dirt driveway, and Otto leaned against the front fender. Yun immediately hopped out. Logan followed her, but I hesitated. My last confrontation with Otto hadn't been good. The two vampires shook hands, and the little shifter unlocked the door to the cottage. I sighed and got out of the car.

"You bring two tiny women to unload the truck?" Otto asked as I approached. "Yun might be some help, but not this one." He smiled at me. "But it's good to see you again, little mage. I've heard some great stories about you."

"Don't believe everything you hear," I mumbled.

"Lies are always more entertaining." He laughed and moved towards the back of the truck, winking at me as he strode by. "Especially when the enemy's trying to guess which part's true."

His words made sense. I'm sure Jack was pretty unpleasant to be around right now, with Sergey deserting and a hundred or more of their soldiers dead. "I'll be inside with Yun," I said, making my way up the steps and leaving the heavy lifting for the vampires who wouldn't notice it anyway.

New wood floors spanned the entire living area, including the dining room and kitchen. Fresh paint covered the walls, and a new window replaced the one that Niyol tossed a tree through. A blank space occupied the spot where the kitchen island should have been.

"Why didn't they replace the island?" I asked, moving farther into the living room.

She shrugged. "They ordered a larger dining table," she replied. "I would've preferred the island, but it wasn't my decision."

Logan and Otto deftly maneuvered a large sofa through the doorway, setting it down against the far wall. They didn't hang out, leaving immediately to get more.

"Do you think Logan and Otto will go with us to the movie theater?" I asked.

"Logan, maybe. Otto, definitely not." Yun hoisted herself onto the counter, swinging her legs back and forth. "But if I don't go back with Otto, you guys are stuck with me."

I sighed. We needed to go back to Logan's to get my stuff, but I really needed time with Göksu as well. A movie really shouldn't override my promise to my elemental, especially after all the shit I gave him for not training me sooner.

"It's okay," Yun said, as if reading my mind. "I understand the whole 'being a responsible adult' thing." She air quoted and smiled. "But we're definitely having a movie night, just not tonight."

"You're the best," I said. "You know that, right?"

"Yeah, whatever." She waved her hand at me as the boys brought in two recliners. "How much you got left in the truck?" she yelled across the room.

Otto placed his chair next to the sofa and shot a glare at Yun. "You could be helpful," he spat. "There are several lamps and shit you can carry."

She jumped down off the counter with a grin. "You should've said so, stupid."

"I shouldn't have to, tweety-bird." He stopped in the middle of front doorway, with his hands on his hips, blocking her way.

"You'll pay for that, blood sucker." Yun sauntered up to him, her chin barely reaching his chest.

I suspected the barb about the bird was directed at her animal form. I didn't know she was a bird, but it felt rude to ask.

"You're not quick enough," the vampire taunted, staring down at her, his lips twitching into a smile.

"I don't have to be quick." She poked his chest with her finger. "Now move or I'm not helping."

Logan appeared by my side, chuckling softly. "Otto never wins," he whispered. "He thinks he does, but Yun's too clever for him."

"Do it again, tweety-bird," Otto jeered, swiping her hand away.

Of course she did, thumping her small finger against his hard chest. I would've. In pure vampire style, Otto swept her off her feet, tossed her over his shoulder like a bag of dogfood, and carried her out the door. Yun screamed, slamming her small fists against his back.

"Reminds me of someone else," Logan said, following them.

"That's not funny," I mumbled, knowing exactly what he referred to. He'd done the same to me when we first met at Jack's casino.

"Yes it is," Logan called over his shoulder.

"Damn vampire hearing," I muttered again.

Their playful banter eased some of my concerns about Otto. I hadn't expected the easy relationship between them. The vampire seemed so abrasive towards me last time, like I was nothing more than a snack, until I'd attacked Fiona. Did he treat all humans that way? I didn't remember Logan treating humans with such indifference, but I hadn't really had the opportunity to watch him interact either. It probably didn't matter now anyway.

Maybe I needed to watch his interaction with Otto. Was his craving for vampire blood making it hard for him to be around his team? That would suck. How could you work with someone you constantly felt the need to consume? No wonder there were no humans in Jonathan's group of vampires.

I shook my head as the men maneuvered a large oval table through the door. Yun followed with a chair that matched. Why wasn't I helping? Because I was being stupid. I walked out to the back of the truck and picked up another chair.

Yun and Otto left thirty minutes later, leaving me and Logan alone in the cottage. I stood in the space between the living room and dining area, now fully furnished. I shouldn't feel awkward around Logan, but I did. The new stuff with Kellen made it hard to be comfortable, and I hated it. I didn't want to lose our easygoing relationship.

"Where to next?" Logan asked, leaning against the back of the nearest recliner. It rocked with his weight. "And what made you decide to cancel movie night?"

"I don't know," I replied, crossing my arms over my stomach. "And I don't know."

"You need a break from reality, AJ," Logan said, surprising me. "This might be the only time you get it. As much as I want to believe Kellen, you're going to get sucked into the role of Magister."

I blinked, and his arms wrapped around me. His love and longing embraced me, and my crybaby showed her ugly head. I knew what was coming next, and I didn't want to hear it.

"I never should've gone back to Kellen's." I mumbled.

"We had to go back," Logan said. "We can't win this fight without him and the mages."

"Fine. I don't want to argue with you."

"Let's go see your chick flick," he offered. "And maybe explore the nightlife afterwards."

"And what about my training with Göksu?" I sniffled. "I was supposed to use this time with him."

"Make Kellen show you the training rooms," he replied, pulling me closer. "It's the best place to practice anyway."

"And what about my vampire training?" I mumbled against his chest, not wanting to accept what was coming.

"I'm sure I can be there for that," he responded. "But I can't stay at the palace." His fingers trailed up and down my spine. "We need information about Jack's plans. I won't sit idle while he plots to destroy everything we've fought so hard for."

I hated his words, regardless of their truth. But I also knew the things he didn't say. A vampire couldn't stay at the palace, no matter what Kellen said. I would be putting us both at risk by asking him to be with me. Kellen knew it too, the bastard. My partner only made those promises to lure me in, and it worked. The crack in my heart widened.

"You'll come see me as often as you can," I commanded. "That isn't a request. I need to be reminded that someone loves me."

His lips brushed against mine. "Yes, princess."

"I'm also leaving with you as often as I can."

"Be quiet and let me help you forget your responsibilities for just one night."

"You'll also keep the short haircut. I really like it," I said, running my fingers through his hair. I wanted more than one night. I wanted a lifetime, but I wouldn't get it. "I also liked the earrings, so if you wanted to add them back, I have no objections."

His kiss stopped my blabbering, and he swept me off my feet. He stopped and locked the front door before taking me up the steps to the queen-sized bed in the loft.

Chapter 20

Logan and I followed the crowd of excited women and bored men out of the theater. I was surprised he sat through two hours of sappy love story. It was hokey and completely unrealistic but also exactly what I needed. The couple in the movie had a happy ending, something I was sure I wouldn't get.

The cool night's breeze felt great when we finally made it to the parking lot. A crescent moon hung low in the sky, and its adoring stars sparkled around it. I took a deep breath, enjoying the fresh air filled with car exhaust and sandalwood. Well, shit. How many vampires could possibly smell like sandalwood? Hopefully a ton of them, because I only knew one. Braden.

"We have company," Logan whispered.

"You could have lied to me about it," I complained.

"No, not really."

The parking lot's flood lights reflected off Braden's black sedan parked right next to Logan's Explorer. My new vision gave me a spectacular view of the offending vampire leaned against the driver's door smiling at the women walking by. I could only imagine the stupid female responses he received. He was extremely good looking with his blond hair and handsome features. The ridiculously expensive suit he wore hung perfectly from his muscular build. Whatever.

"Good evening, Alisandra," Braden purred my name, making the hairs on my neck stand straight up. "Logan, I'm surprised to see you."

Logan grabbed my arm, holding me in place. I hadn't forgotten our last visit from this monster. I really wanted to suck the blood from his body and give it to my vampire. Maybe I would, then leave his shriveled ass laying in the parking lot. Yep, sounded like a great plan to me.

"What do you want, Braden?" Logan asked.

The blond vampire's eyes landed on me, and I pulled away from Logan. Well, I tried to pull away from Logan, but he stepped behind me and wrapped both arms around my chest.

Braden chuckled. "Don't hold her back," he said. "I'd love to see her on a rampage."

"Not if it's directed at you," I hissed.

"Especially if it's directed at me," he countered. "Pain is a beautiful aphrodisiac. You should try it sometime."

This man was truly sick. "Why are you here?" I asked. I would not be baited by him.

"I heard a rumor that I thought you might like to share," he replied, pushing away from his car. "But it's not something I'll discuss where anyone could be listening." His voice dropped significantly, to a point that a normal human couldn't hear.

I looked up at Logan, not wanting to give away anything to this monster.

"He wants us to go for a ride," Logan said.

"Oh, hell no!"

"My thoughts exactly," my vampire agreed. "How about you join us?" Logan suggested. "I'm sure your minions can follow me easily."

"Only if the beautiful young lady sits in the back seat with me," Braden purred, his eyes drifting down my body.

"Not happening," Logan growled.

"Alisandra?" Braden asked. "I'll be alone and at the mercy of your wishes. You have nothing to fear from me."

"Yeah, right, and I was born to a wealthy family who loved and pampered me my entire life," I retorted. "Quit the bullshit. It doesn't work on me."

"My, my. You *are* a treasure." Braden pulled his eyes from mine, piercing Logan with an icy stare. "Last chance, or the information goes elsewhere." His voice was once again too low for a normal person to hear.

Logan grabbed my shoulders and turned me around, his hazel eyes boring into mine.

"I got this," I mouthed. I really didn't think Braden would kill me, not yet, anyway. After he wrested control from Jack, my life was probably forfeit. Until then, he needed me alive.

"Fine, get in," Logan grunted.

"Follow him," Braden said to the man driving his car, then he opened the back-passenger door of Logan's SUV and disappeared into the dark interior.

"This is a bad idea," Logan whispered, opening the back door on the driver's side for me.

"Probably."

I slid into my seat and glanced at Braden, wishing I hadn't. His eyes roamed my body, making me wish I had anything to cover it with. I flipped him off and buckled my seatbelt. He laughed and leaned towards me.

"You will one day be mine, my dear," he whispered.

"You will be dead before that day," I whispered back, knowing I shouldn't have. I wasn't supposed to hear his comment.

His pale eyebrows rose, and he drew in a deep breath through his nose.

"Personal space is a thing," I said loud enough for everyone to hear and held his widening gaze. "And sniffing people is rude."

"You are definitely not your mother," he said, sliding back out of my space.

"You just now noticed?" I jeered. "Tell us what you have to say."

"My friend Ernesto is devastated by the loss of his men," Braden said, surprising me with his matter-of-fact tone. "Jack is concerned about the disappearance of Sergey and his entire army."

"You'll have tell me who these people are in order for it to mean anything to me," I said, turning slightly in my seat to face him.

"Really? Logan has not explained the vampire hierarchy to you?" His gaze landed on the back of Logan's head. "Interesting. We have six members of the council, not counting our illustrious leader." His focus turned back to me and he crossed one leg over his opposite knee, leaning back against the window. "I lead the European vampires. Our history predates any others, and it's believed we are the forefathers of our kind."

I didn't miss the note of pride in his voice and the slight uptick in his smirk. Why was he sharing so willingly?

"Simon leads Africa's vampires. As much as I detest the man, he does a remarkable job. The native African tribes carry deep superstitions about vampires and are relentless when they find one. Yutaka, slimy little bastard that he is, brilliantly handles all of Asia and the eastern islands of Taiwan and the Philippines." He leaned forward for a moment, tapping Logan's seat. "Turn right up ahead and stop at the third building on the left."

The bastard winked at me before leaning back again. "Then there is Vail, a young and promising new member. He somehow convinced Yutaka to give up Australia and New Zealand. Neither will say a word about the agreement. And finally, our two leaders in question.

Ernesto is vile, even for a vampire. He leads the South American clan and is completely onboard with Jack about revealing our secrets. He wishes to enslave humans and breed them like cattle for his own consumption. Any idiot should realize that humans will go to extremes to keep that from happening, including nuclear options. I don't understand why Jack can't see this."

He rubbed a hand across his jaw, but I noticed he avoided touching his long, blond hair. Was it a vanity thing? Was he afraid to mess it up? It was beautiful, certainly the envy of many women.

"Lastly, Sergey," he paused and glanced out the back window, probably to make sure his cronies were still following. "My Russian friend controls his own country as well as the Baltic States and unruly Middle East. I don't how he manages it, but he does. Quite the accomplishment. His disappearance is disturbing, though."

Braden's eyes fell on me, capturing mine in his. "Ernesto cannot confirm whether or not Sergey's men fell into that fiery pit you created for them." He paused, no doubt waiting for me to provide an explanation.

I smiled.

He smiled back. "I thought we agreed to share information, Alisandra."

"I agreed to share information that would be beneficial to us both," I said. "You haven't demonstrated how my knowledge of Sergey's demise will benefit either of us."

"Have I said you're a treasure?" he asked, his smile widening. "Of course I have. If Sergey is dead, someone will need to take over his region. I might consider taking Russia, but I want nothing to do with the others. Yutaka might consider it."

He glanced through the back window again, and his brow furrowed. He put both feet on the floorboards and leaned towards my vampire. "You didn't stop where I instructed."

"No kidding?" Logan asked. "I must have missed it. I know a nice little park we can visit. It should be empty this time of night."

"Don't toy with me, child," Braden growled.

"Don't threaten my vampire," I warned. "Not everything you heard from Ernesto was exaggerated. And if you haven't talked to Sergey, you missed the best part."

If Ernesto was siding with Jack, but Sergey was going rogue as Yun, Logan, and I suspected, then it made sense that nobody had seen Sergey since he ran. But Braden didn't need to know that.

"Are you threatening me?" Braden twisted in the seat and invaded my space. "I'd love to battle with you, little mage."

"I would kill you now if I didn't need your info," I barely spoke. "If you pull another stunt like you did last time, you *won't* walk away."

"You honestly believe you can kill me," he whispered back, sitting so close to me I could feel his breath on my skin. "I can feel no hesitation or deceit, only anger." He reached up and ran a finger along the left side of my jaw.

My anger flared with his touch. A razor-sharp shard of air appeared in my hand, and I stabbed his open palm. I expected fury or retaliation, maybe even fear. I got neither. How could I be so stupid? His hands cupped my face, and his lips pressed against mine. Passion that I couldn't handle slammed into me from this monster. For a split second, I responded with way too much enthusiasm. Luckily, the vehicle swerved and brought me back to reality. I forced another shard of glass into his chest, but his tongue continued its exploration of mine. What the hell? I bit down hard on the intruder, his blood filling my mouth instantly. I swallowed before I thought about what I was doing, then I gagged. The vampire jerked away from me, but not far enough for my liking, until Logan slammed on the brakes. If not for my seatbelt, I would've face-planted into the back of his seat.

My door opened seconds later, and Logan reached for the buckle to release it. I glared at Braden. Blood dripped from his smiling lips, and his eyes danced across my face. The taste of his blood lingered in my throat.

"You'll have to do better than that, my dear," Braden said, his words slurring from his injured tongue. "I already warned you that I enjoy pain. Your little knives will only make me want you more. And those pleasant little teeth."

Logan pulled me from the vehicle and raced to the opposite side of the street.

"Why the hell would you bait him like that?" my vampire hissed.

"He threatened you, Logan," I hissed back.

"And you gave him more ammunition against you." He looked over my head towards his vehicle. "He will never stop hunting you now, not until he has you for his own."

I heard a car door slam and the soft rumble of an engine fading into the night.

"You cannot be alone with him, AJ. Do you hear me?" Fear radiated from my vampire. "He will turn you or kill you to keep anyone else from having you."

I dropped my head against his chest. I was so stupid thinking I could go up against Braden. *That's what happens when people go on and on about how powerful someone is. It all goes to their head.* I should've been immune to that. I'd been walked over my whole damn life. How did I let my confidence make me stupid?

"I'm sorry," I mumbled. "I didn't think this could get any more complicated, but somehow I succeeded in making it so."

He hugged me close but didn't contradict me. Nor did he tell me not to worry or that it wasn't my fault. All of it would've been a lie, and we both knew it.

Chapter 21

The next evening, Logan and I showed up at Kellen's estate with most of my new fancy wardrobe. I'd left a couple things at Logan's in the hopes that one day I'd go back. We'd also set up my alternate bank account and the automatic transfer of funds. I left enough money in my 'Magister' account to buy whatever I needed. I couldn't believe how much money they thought I required to survive. It was absurd.

When we arrived, Kellen was waiting for me, along with David and Kate.

"Wow! You look great!" Kate exclaimed, wrapping me in a hug.

I wore sky blue capri pants with a pale yellow tank top covered by a sheer white blouse. My new favorite strappy sandals pretended to protect my feet. It wasn't practical, but it was fashionable.

"Thanks," I mumbled.

I didn't feel great. Logan and I had already said goodbye before we left his house. I didn't look at him as David and Kate picked up my luggage. They disappeared through the portal a few moments later.

"Don't let her out by herself," Logan warned. "Braden has taken an unhealthy interest in our princess."

Kellen's dark brows furrowed as he glanced between me and Logan. "Thanks for the warning. Be careful, Logan. I assume his interest extends to you as well."

"It does, but I know how to avoid him," Logan assured my partner, but I heard the deception in his voice. "I'll be back in a few days."

I forced myself to meet his hazel eyes. Tears blurred my vision, distorting my favorite grin.

"Turn off the lights in the fire room to practice your vampire skills." He closed the space between us and took my hand in his. "The next time I see you, I expect to get stabbed."

I laughed and wrapped my arms around his neck. "I love you," I whispered so only he could hear.

"My heart will always belong to you," he whispered back. He loosened my grasp and stepped away. "See you in a couple days."

He didn't linger, just turned and left the portal room. My heart ached watching him leave.

Kellen's arm slipped around my waist and gently pulled me towards the portal.

"He'll be okay, AJ," Kellen said. "He's kept himself alive for almost forty years as a vampire." He tipped my chin with his finger, forcing me to look up at him. "He now has your life to consider, and he won't do anything to risk it."

I wanted to believe him, but there were too many other people pulling the strings. I sighed, then shook my head. My life seemed like a never-ending sigh.

"I'm ready." I rested my cheek on his chest as his arms wrapped around me and lifted me off the ground long enough to step through the portal. Tingles raced across my skin, and my heart ached. I missed my vampire already.

I didn't move when we arrived and neither did Kellen. Maybe he felt my overwhelming sadness or the despair that threatened my collapse.

"Do you want me to take you upstairs?" he asked, quietly. "It's late enough. No one will care if you go to bed early."

I nodded, unable to speak past the lump in my throat. What the hell was wrong with me? Logan would be back in a couple days. I was supposed to be safe here in the palace. Kellen could show me the training rooms where I could hide as long as I wanted.

My partner scooped me up and I buried my tear-stained face in his neck. Brown sugar and cinnamon assaulted my nostrils, and I choked back a laugh.

"What's so funny?" Kellen asked, striding easily across the courtyard with me in his arms.

"I forgot how good you smell," I whispered.

His face flushed as he smiled. "So, what does my partner smell like?"

"Jasmine, according to Logan," I replied. "But I wouldn't know. I can't smell myself."

"And everyone else?" He bypassed the large doors leading to the main entrance and put me down next to the private stairs to the Magister's quarters.

"I can only smell you and other vampires," I replied. "Everyone else is just soap, perfumes, or unpleasant body odor."

He stood next to me with his hand on the doorknob, his brown eyes searching my face. "Your luggage is already in the room," he finally said. "Will you be okay alone, or do you want me to join you?"

I looked down at my sandals. I didn't want to be alone, but I didn't want Kellen's company either.

"I can't kick you out of your own space," I replied. "I'll leave it up to you."

He laughed. I looked up, frowning at him.

"How is that funny?" I asked.

"It's definitely not my decision," he said. "And you're the Magister. You can kick me out anytime you wish." His smile didn't fade with his words, adding to my confusion.

"I still don't get it," I mumbled, looking away from him and reaching for the doorknob.

"I thought I made all the decisions, lining out each plan with intricate details." He pushed open the door and motioned for me to go in. "You have proven that I control nothing," he continued as I made my way up the winding staircase. "I laugh because I've already exhausted all the other emotions."

I stopped mid-stride and spun around. Two steps above Kellen put me at eye level with him. "Well, I haven't made it past pissed off yet," I said.

"But you're getting through the sadness and pain," he said, his smile fading. "My anger came first, then jealousy, then despair."

"And where are you now?" I asked, not sure I really wanted to know.

"Resignation, mostly," he responded. "Possibly leading into determination to finish this."

"I have no control over any of this, either," I muttered, continuing my trek up the steps. I wanted to say I wouldn't be here if I had any say in it, but it wouldn't change anything, nor would it help. "I'd like you to show me the training rooms in the morning."

"I'd like to give you a full tour in the morning," he said, still following me. "You need to know where everything is without getting lost."

"That's probably a good idea," I said. "Thank you."

I finally reached the top of the steps a little out of breath. The large wooden doors greeted me with their symbols for the elements. Spirit's wings drew me in, and I placed my hand over them. A small amount of peace washed over me.

"Your mother said her parents refused to tell her what that symbol was." Kellen's voice made me jump, and I turned around to face him.

"I didn't realize it represented anything," I said, trying desperately to hide the lie. "It looks a little like bells with wings."

He raised an eyebrow at me then glanced at Spirit's symbol. "I don't see bells."

I followed his gaze, grateful for the redirect. "Really? Those don't look like bells to you?" I traced what I now believed was a bad representation of Spirit's face.

"No, not at all." He laid his fingers over mine and traced the wispy wings. "These are definitely wings, but this looks more like an abstract face to me."

"Hmm." I pulled my hand away and stuffed it in my pocket. "Still looks like bells."

He chuckled and opened the doors. The new muted tones calmed some of my anxiety over being back in this room. I should've gotten over it after our little meeting the other day, but I hadn't. Memories of being choked by my own mother assaulted me, along with the mage-vampires who attacked us. I pressed my palms against my eyes, trying to make them go away. The image just heightened, and I sank to my knees.

Logan's face appeared before me, his hands cradling my head as he gave me the memory of our bonding. My shock and anguish from discovering the truth forced sobs from my throat, yet again. I tried to tell myself it wasn't real, that all of it was in the past, but it didn't lessen the pain. I wanted to be the tough girl, the one who could take a beating and keep fighting, but I wasn't. I was on the floor falling apart like a child.

Kellen's arms wrapped around me again, picking me up off the floor. "I'll stay with you tonight," he whispered. "I promise to be a gentleman."

Just what I wanted. Not.

But, true to his word, my partner helped me shuck my capris and took off my sandals, then pulled my favorite quilt up to my chin. When had he brought it here? Why would he do that? He didn't even like me.

I lay in bed with Kellen by my side. He was close, but not touching me. Reassuring but not demanding. What the hell? Why the mixed signals? He admitted to telling his goons to kidnap me and lock me away. He had to know that bastard Carlton or Carson or whatever his name was would do more. People like that didn't become disgusting pigs overnight.

Was he being nice to make our situation easier to deal with? It couldn't be easy being nice to someone you hated. I wasn't doing a very good job of it. He said he didn't hate me, but his actions told a different story, didn't they?

"Since we aren't sleeping, you want to tell me what's on your mind?" Kellen's low voice interrupted my thoughts.

I opened my eyes and stared up at the high ceilings. My new vampire sight let me see the intricately carved wood work crossing the beams over my head. Repeated patterns traced the beams: water, fire, earth, air, and spirit. I squinted, trying to get a better look at the spirit symbol. The round emblem circled the elemental's magical wings and the same blurred bells graced the center. Had there been a time when Spirit interacted as much as the others? The symbols implied there was.

Kellen shifting on the mattress drew my attention. He rolled to his side and looked my way. I could see him straining to make out my features in the dark. The blankets rested at his waist, showing off his wide, chiseled chest, much wider than I remembered. The scars from our challenge at Victor's contrasted wildly against his dark skin. Did he lay there half naked knowing I could see him?

"Tell me what you're thinking, AJ," he said, propping up on his elbow and resting his head in his palm.

"Why are you suddenly being nice to me?" I asked. "You can't honestly want me around."

He frowned and started drawing a circle on the sheet with his finger. Would he do that if he knew I could see him? "When I sent Carson and Marshall after you, I was pissed. I thought you ruined everything I worked so hard for. We defeated your mother, but I needed you on the council, and I felt like you betrayed me with someone I considered my best friend."

I snorted and looked up at the ceiling. He and I remembered that entire series of events differently.

"I didn't say it was rational, AJ," he continued. "It's how I felt. When Carson said you escaped, I was so relieved, but that was quickly replaced by guilt."

He paused, and I rolled to my side to face him. Kellen never poured his heart out, and here he was trying to explain it all a second time.

"Self-loathing consumed me for days after I found Logan's threat," he whispered, still drawing a circle on the sheets. "I'd pushed away the one person who made all of this possible. You."

I wanted to argue with him about my importance, but I couldn't. I knew my heritage alone made a difference. The fact that my elementals liked me sealed the deal. But I didn't know what he expected me to say. Did he really think his confession would make it all better? That I'd just forgive and forget?

"What can I do to show you how sorry I am?" he asked. "I don't expect forgiveness. I want it and my heart needs it, but…" His hand reached for mine, stopping short of touching me. "If I were in your place, I never would've come back. The fact that you're here gives me hope."

I wasn't sure how to reply. What did I expect from him? Honesty, trust, friendship? All of the above.

"Remove your emotional barrier," I said. "I can't trust anything you tell me, when I can't feel the truth through our connection. And where's Sparky?" I hadn't realized how much I missed the mischievous little connection between our elements.

The pain in his eyes when he turned his head towards me melted some of my reserve. I could almost see his shield dropping like a curtain falling to the floor. His emotions slammed into me, the rawness of his regret and self-loathing bringing tears to my eyes.

"I haven't seen Sparky since you left," he replied, his voice harsh and wavering. "I assumed you took him with you." He sat up, not bothering to pull the quilt over the boxers covering his important parts. The muscles in his thighs bulged when he folded his legs in front of him. "I thought I'd lost your connection. Carson said you escaped, but I couldn't feel you. For days, I truly thought you were dead." He ran his fingers through his dark hair, then scrubbed his face with his palm. "The horror of telling the council of your death haunted me. What could I say? It was all my fault, but how could I tell them that?"

I sat up and faced him, folding my legs in front of me with our knees almost touching. He had to see the significance of my gesture. We'd sat like this so many times in his training room, it became natural for us to do so anytime we entered the large stone space.

"When did you find out I survived?" I asked, almost ready to offer a tiny piece of forgiveness.

"When Yun contacted me and said Logan wanted to meet," he replied, placing his hands on his knees, palms up. I recognized what he did. "She told me you were with him, and I put the pieces together. He was the only one capable of taking you from my estate and hiding you so thoroughly."

"You didn't act like you were glad to see me at that fancy restaurant," I said, placing my hands on my own knees.

He looked away from me, and I felt his jealousy. It confused me. Was he seriously jealous of Logan? Kellen never wanted a romantic relationship with me, so why would he care if Logan did?

"At first, I was too shocked by your change of appearance to respond properly," he replied. "Then I couldn't help but notice the closeness between you and Logan. When you blocked me from your emotions, I let my anger take over. Not anger at you, but at myself for being so stupid."

I sighed. The story of my life, it seemed. "Why would you be jealous of Logan?" I asked. "You made it clear you weren't interested in a relationship with me, despite the feelings you knew I had for you."

He raised both hands to his head and pulled them through his hair. His frustration battered me. "You're relentless, AJ."

"Maybe, but I need to be thorough," I said. "You're still my partner, and I should be able to trust you when everyone else in my life betrays me. You're supposed to be that person who supports me and makes me stronger. I need to know if that's you or not."

He blew out a long breath. "When we first met and I realized we would be partners, I hated it," he replied. I was grateful he couldn't see my hurt expression but suspected he could feel it. "You were so small and defenseless, naïve about the magical community, and the complete opposite of everything I wanted in a woman."

"Wow, and I'm relentless," I scoffed.

"Sorry, I'm trying to be honest, and that's how I felt," he said, rubbing his palms on his thighs. "You look so much like the woman who killed my parents, and I couldn't see past that. I didn't *want* to see past it." He sighed, his shoulders drooping with his effort to speak. "As we got to know each other, you forced me to see parts of you I didn't want to believe existed. I put you into a special little box that you kept jumping out of. When you walked into that restaurant looking nothing like your mother, my brain shut down."

He extended his hands to me once again, resting them on his knees a few inches from mine. "It's unfair of me to do that to you. You've proven time and again that you are not your mother. I need to be the man you expect me to be."

Well shit. How did I not forgive him after all that? He'd left his emotions open to me the entire time, and I couldn't feel any deception in his words. The brutal honesty hurt, but it also healed some of my own pain.

I reached for the connection between our elements, that little thing I'd nicknamed Sparky not that long ago. A tiny light glowed in Kellen's chest, racing away from his heart and down his arm, finally popping up in the palm of my partner's hand.

"Long time, no see, troublemaker," I whispered. "Come here."

He bounced into my hand but stayed on the surface of my skin. I felt his apprehension. "I'm still the same person," I said, watching the little spark slowly move up my arm. "Sort of. But you can't tell anyone." I looked up at Kellen, suddenly realizing he might find out about my connection to Spirit. Could I keep it from him?

Göksu? Niyol? Do I keep Sparky out?

No, child, my water elemental replied.

Are you sure? Can I trust Kellen?

You can trust the spark, Niyol said.

Sparky probably couldn't reveal anything to Kellen. It's not like it talked to me, either, but would it tell my partner's elementals? Did it matter? They should already know about Spirit. I hated being undecided.

Sparky moved a little faster across my shoulders, and I put a finger in front of him, stopping his progress. "Wait." He stopped, and I looked over at Kellen, his confusion plain on his face. "I'm sorry. I don't know if I can share this. I was sworn to secrecy, and I think the consequence for revealing it is pretty fricking bad."

My partner's eyebrows rose. "What did they do to you?"

"Sparky, go back to Kellen until I find an answer," I said. I swear the little spark moped all the way down my arm. "I told you. I can see better, hear better, and move faster than before." I blushed and tried not to smile. "You've been working out."

He looked down at his bare chest and grinned. I expected him to snatch the quilt and cover up, but he didn't. Men.

"I also have a special hatred for Braden, regardless of the information he's provided to us," I continued. "He revealed the true nature of vampires to me, 'cause let's face it, Logan is totally an exception."

"Logan said Braden had taken a special interest in you," Kellen said. "What happened?"

I told him about our fight with the ogre, repeating some of the same stuff Logan had during our fancy dinner. Then I described Braden's treachery when his men slit Logan's throat. Anger boiled in my stomach for that fiend, and I didn't hide it from Kellen.

"I can't believe your water elemental healed Logan," Kellen said.

"Yeah, well if he hadn't, Logan probably would've killed me. I still can't figure out Braden's intentions." I turned and laid back down, staring at the ceiling again. "When Logan recovered, my elementals decided he shouldn't crave my blood. That's when all the changes happened."

"Damn, AJ," Kellen whispered. "I think craving vampire blood is worse. He can't just go downtown and get a snack, leaving the human unaware of what happened."

"You think I don't know that?" I snapped, looking over at him. "Logan has suffered more than any of us. First by my mother forcing him to become the monster he despises, and now my elementals. It's a wonder he doesn't hate me."

"You're difficult to hate," Kellen said.

I waved a hand at him. "Whatever."

"What happened that's made Logan believe Braden will come for you?" he asked

"I'd rather not talk about that," I mumbled. "I stupidly baited the asshole and will now pay the price. Hopefully Logan doesn't pay it with me."

"You won't tell me?"

I heard the disappointment in his voice and felt it through our connection. Damn men.

"Don't get pissed off and don't say I didn't warn you." I waved both hands at the ceiling, mumbling, "Stupid men. Like I want to admit my ignorance." I sat up but didn't face him, pulling the blankets over my lap. I waggled my finger at him. "If you hadn't just bared your soul to me, we wouldn't be having this conversation. I didn't know he's a sadist. I should have. He hinted at it, but I was too over-confident to listen." I repeated my episode with the bastard vampire, choking on my words and swearing the taste of his blood resurfaced. "The only good thing to come out of that was his news about Sergey and Ernesto." I continued retelling our conversation about the vampire council, trying hard to redirect Kellen's attention. It didn't work.

"He'll never stop wanting you, AJ," my partner said, his voice rising with concern.

"No shit, Sherlock," I muttered. "I was so stupid."

I fell back into the pillows and pulled the quilt over my head. The mattress shifted from Kellen's weight, and his body moved in next to mine. I flipped back the blanket and looked at him. He stared back at me, his face only inches from mine.

"He can't have you," Kellen whispered. "I will be the partner you need. Your strength, support, and friend. We'll grow together like we were supposed to all along."

His words scared me, and I slammed up my mental barrier. His eyes narrowed for a moment, but then he scooted back, giving me space. I'd always wanted more from him, but his rejection and threat to my life ended those feelings. Right? So why was my heart racing?

"I'm not sleeping," I mumbled. "Will you take me to the water training room?"

"Of course." He rolled off the opposite side of the bed, and I took a deep breath.

This was going to suck.

Chapter 22

The training rooms lined an entire wing of the palace, each one specially designed for its element. Four fountains grounded the four corners of the water room. The hushed sound of flowing water relaxed me as soon as I entered, kicking off my shoes out of habit. The cool stone felt wonderful on my bare feet, bleeding away more of my stress.

"I might come here every day," I mumbled.

"Why is that?" Kellen asked, startling me. I hadn't expected him to follow me into the room. But here he was by my side, bare toes flexing on the dark gray stone.

"It's relaxing," I replied. "The element soothes my mind. I think I could actually meditate here."

Kellen looked around, pausing at the four fountains for a few seconds each. I followed his gaze, wondering what he thought. He'd also replaced his mental barrier, blocking me out. I could hardly blame him. I was the one who started it.

"What are we learning today?" he asked, his long legs folding beneath him as he sat.

"I didn't mean to drag you with me," I said. "Göksu and I have a date."

"He told you his name?"

Did Kellen really not know? I tried to remember when my elemental revealed it. At Logan's house? Or was it in Kellen's estate?

"Yes, he's been extremely helpful the last week or so," I replied, sitting down in front of my partner, again out of habit, and folding my own legs.

"Mine haven't spoken to me since that first time," Kellen muttered. "I want to learn how you do it."

"There's nothing to teach, Kellen. I told you all I know at the council meeting with King William." My tone softened, and I placed my hand on his knee. "You introduced me to my magic, showed me how to use it and where to find it." I tapped my sternum, the spot where my well of power resided. "You are the one who dragged me into all this six weeks ago. Now you want me to teach you?"

"When you put it that way, it makes me feel like an idiot."

"Well, if the shoe fits…" I smiled at him, and he narrowed his eyes at me. "You're not an idiot. You're just a control freak. I've never had control over a damn thing, so I'm used to everyone else bossing me around. Listen to your elements." I removed my hand from his knee and laced my fingers in my lap. "Now be quiet, I'm easily distracted."

He grinned, then leaned back resting his weight on his elbows. "I can't believe you said you don't boss people around."

I stuck my tongue out at him and closed my eyes. The moisture in the air called to me and a small breeze whispered by my face. Niyol. I smiled, leaving my eyes closed. I loved that wispy elemental, so devoted and loyal.

You are my favorite mage, he whispered in my ear, ruffling my hair.

I giggled. "Niyol, are you supposed to be doing something besides occupying Göksu's training room?"

"No, princess. My sole task is protecting you."

"Yes, about that," I said. "Where the hell were you when that bastard attacked me in the car?"

"I was outside the car." A gust of wind knocked me over, and I opened my eyes. Niyol's transparent body hovered right next to me. "I thought you had it under control, princess."

I sat back up and tried to glare at him. I couldn't be mad at Niyol, though. I was the one who screwed it up. "Yes, until I didn't."

"It won't happen again," my elemental stated.

"I'm afraid it will," I mumbled. "But I'll be ready next time. Anyway, I'm here to talk to Göksu."

"Yes, I know," Niyol said, drifting around behind my partner.

My gaze dropped to Kellen, who turned halfway around to look at Niyol. My partner's astonished expression would've been funny in any other situation. I suspected my air elemental was antagonizing him on purpose. Niyol had already made it clear he didn't trust Kellen's elementals.

Göksu?

Yes, child. I'm almost there.

You're traveling? I didn't know that was even a thing.

His fluid form rose up from the stone floor on my right side. He too moved around behind my partner, his body losing shape as he did.

"I see what you mean, brother," Göksu said in his soft voice. "He has changed, definitely for the better."

I tried not to let my mouth fall open. They were analyzing Kellen? I thought they were trying to intimidate my partner, not judge his worthiness.

"Shall we include him in the training?" Niyol asked, circling around me.

"Yes, I believe we shall," Göksu replied. "Alisandra will need his strength."

My two elementals stopped, one on each side of me, both staring at Kellen. His wide eyes looked like they would pop from his head. I was right there with him, but for a different reason.

"Did they just judge whether or not I'm worthy to train?" he asked.

"Kind of sounded like it," I replied, trying to keep from smiling. My elementals' arrogance surpassed my partner's, and it somehow surprised him.

He leaned forward and wiped his hands on his jeans. "Alright. I'm ready."

"I'm sure you're not," Niyol purred. "You will be the target. Be sure to defend yourself, but you are not allowed to attack the princess."

Kellen's stare widened, but he remained silent.

"On your feet," Niyol commanded, then turned to me as I stood. "Your attempt to create the weapon from the vampire's blood was admirable, but the technique was wrong, which is why it remained fluid."

"You must freeze the water, then compress the molecules," Göksu added.

It made sense in theory. "How do I freeze the water?" I asked. "I didn't realize I could change the air temperature."

"You cannot, child," my water elemental said, drifting towards the nearest fountain. "But your partner can call on fire, which removes the heat. The two of you together can create a weapon."

"But only you can wield it, princess." Niyol picked up the instruction, following Göksu. "Your partner's fire will damage its stability."

I looked at Kellen, finding the same shocked expression I knew spread across my face.

"I guess you didn't know either," I said.

"Nope, but I'm anxious to try it," he replied.

"This knowledge cannot leave this room," Niyol stated, rising into the air. "It would be best to practice it elsewhere, but I'll keep watch tonight to ensure there are no unwanted guests."

With a gust of wind, he disappeared, leaving me and Kellen staring at Göksu.

"Let's begin."

I rolled my shoulders and held out my hands, pulling a stream of water from the fountain. It came so easily in this room. Was it enchanted or just the abundance of moisture? I didn't know and, at the moment, didn't care.

I thought about the weapon I wanted to make and remembered the long sword Kellen carried in our first fight against the vampires. He needed to teach me to use one. I twisted the stream over itself several times, creating a sword-sized cylinder.

"I want to make a sword," I said, continuing to manipulate the water. "I'm not sure if I can make the edges sharp though. I know I can do it with air, but…" I bit my bottom lip as I tried to flatten the rounded shape.

"I'm not sure how to draw the heat off your weapon," Kellen said. "I can't pull fire from water, can I?"

"You're the fire mage. Don't ask me," I retorted. "Ask your elemental."

I heard him huff and mumble a request about fire. I didn't expect his elemental to show up right away, but apparently Kellen did.

"This is impossible," he muttered.

I dropped my strand of water and turned to my partner as it splashed against the stone. How dare he talk about the impossible? My entire life was impossible, but here I was.

"I never want to hear that come from your mouth," I said. "You've taught me nothing is impossible. Six weeks ago, vampires and ogres were impossible. And werewolves. And magic!" I placed my hands on my hips and glared at him. "If you want your elemental's knowledge, give him a good reason to share it with you. 'Because I said so' isn't a reason."

A smile crept across his face. "You've changed so much."

"Whatever. We've already been down that road." I turned to Göksu and a wave of understanding and love washed over me. "I don't want to go back to a life without them," I said, pointing at my elemental. "Not just for the power they give me, but the friendship and loyalty. I've never known love, and I'm grateful theirs was first. It fills my soul like nothing else can."

Göksu's fluid form puddled and reappeared in front of me. "How can I not love someone who sees me that way?" he asked. His hand pressed against my chest, his warm touch filling me with magic.

"I want to feel that," Kellen whispered. "I want that relationship."

"Then you must convince your elemental that you deserve it," Göksu said. "When you do, this lesson will wait for you."

I expected my partner to run to the fire room immediately, but he didn't. I snuck a glance at him. His squared shoulders and pursed lips spoke of his determination. With each passing moment, my trust in him bloomed.

"I understand," he said.

"Good. Protect yourself so the princess can do some target practice."

I chuckled and took a few steps back. "Don't worry, Kellen. I'll aim for your walls of dirt, not your head. You can't heal like Logan."

"That's not very encouraging," he said, frowning and backing up. "Are you using your new speed?"

I pulled a splinter from the air, making it about seven or eight inches long, with points on both ends, but no bladed edge. I'd become so good at it; the effort hardly required any thought. It rolled between my fingers, and I smiled at Kellen's surprised expression.

"I don't think I can keep from going fast, but you're right. I should try to look more human and less vampire. It scares people."

"No, child, you should not," my elemental interrupted. "Battles are not fair, and your partner needs to prepare to fight against something quicker than himself." He flowed to one of the fountains and perched on its edge. "I will heal his wounds when you're done, so don't hold back."

My partner licked his lips and narrowed his eyes. I could almost feel his nervous tension, which surprised me again. I expected arrogance, not anxiety. He was afraid of me. I shook the thought away and drew three more small spears, holding them in my left hand. I pulled my right arm back and drew a breath, aiming at my partner. I nodded, hopefully giving him a cue that it was coming. Before I could release my weapon, a pool of ice formed under my feet, and I scrabbled to keep my balance.

"Oh shit!" I screamed, swinging my arms as I tried not fall on my butt. "Göksu! That's cheating." I scanned the room looking for my element. He was gone, but his puddle of ice remained.

"I think your elemental is going to challenge us both," Kellen said. The rock around his feet trembled, bouncing small fragments of stone on its surface.

"So it would seem," I snapped. "I guess I asked for it." Irritation flitted over me, but I couldn't be mad. It was what I wanted. I'd begged my elemental to teach me how to use water and now he was.

My feet slid to the right over the ice, doing a silly shuffle. When I reached the stone, I let my first weapon fly. A wedge of rock rose into the air shattering my small, glass missile. Damn. Kellen smiled. I smiled back and grabbed another from my left hand. As soon as I released it, a swell of water crashed into my back. Rather than throwing me to the ground, I barely balanced on a wave surging towards my partner. I squealed with excitement and terror, launching another weapon at Kellen.

He rolled to the side, and a short wall of rock sprang from the ground, redirecting my new surf board. I launched my last weapon at him but didn't get to see it hit its mark. The water vanished, and I tumbled head-over-heels across the stone, screaming the whole way.

That shit hurt.

My elemental was getting a piece of my mind.

When I came to a stop, I sat up and looked around for Kellen. He was sprawled out on the floor about ten yards away, blood oozing from his shoulder. His gaze met mine as he sat up. My anger melted. I'd hit him, and it had to hurt. I rolled to my hands and knees, every one of my joints aching from my wanna-be acrobatics.

"You and I are going to fight, Göksu," I mumbled. "That hurt."

Halfway to my partner, and still crawling on my hands and knees, a deluge of water fell over me. I gasped, expecting another attack, then cursing as the all too familiar warmth of healing washed over my body. I loved it when my elemental did it. There was no painful trade-off.

Kellen's laugh drew my attention. He was now laying on his back, soaked in water, the puddle around him seeping into the cracked stone. I crawled to his side, leaving my own watery trail. His soft chuckles became infectious, and I giggled.

"What's so funny?" I asked.

"Everything," he replied, reaching over and rubbing his now healed shoulder. "I need to train with you more often."

As he sat up, water dripped down his face from the hair plastered to his forehead. His soaked t-shirt clung to his chest, as I imagined my own did. The smile on his face brought back too many memories of a time when I actually liked him.

"I never imagined using my elemental the way you just did," he continued. "You need to work on the dismount, but that was brilliant."

A barked laugh escaped my lips, and I rolled back to sit on my heels. "You thought I did that?" I asked. "Göksu totally tossed me around. My screaming like a little girl should've given that away."

"Probably, but you still managed to hit me," he said, his smile not fading. "I need to practice throwing up shields, and we need to take you surfing."

"You're not funny," I mumbled, but I couldn't hold back my grin. Riding around on that wave felt awesome and terrifying. I didn't think I could recreate it, though. My elemental controlled all of it, which was fine with me. There was no way I could hold onto the wave, create my little weapons, and attack someone all at the same time. Thinking about it made my head spin.

A blast of hot air sent me and Kellen both falling over onto our backs.

"Thanks, Niyol," I muttered. "I've already been tossed around enough."

"You're welcome, princess."

I stuck my tongue out at my element. He didn't miss my sarcasm; he just chose to ignore it.

"We have company," he continued. "Your British admirer wishes to speak with you."

"King William is here?" Kellen asked, rising to his feet. He held his hand out to me, and I let him pull me to my feet.

"The prince is waiting for you in the Magister's Hall," Niyol replied. "Your guard is on his way to your sleeping quarters to wake you."

What could the prince want in the middle of the night? Couldn't he just call? Surely he had Kellen's number.

"Thanks, Niyol," I said, trying to smooth my wet clothes and push back the hair sticking to my forehead. "I need to change before seeing anyone."

"I agree," Kellen said, heading for the door. "I'll tell the guard to offer Thomas refreshments while he waits for us. He can't expect us to be awake right now anyway."

I chuckled, following him out into the hallway. "He certainly wouldn't expect to see us traipsing down the hall, soaking wet."

We reached the door to our private stairwell and humiliation washed over me. Prince Thomas stood at the door, wearing tan slacks and a white shirt opened at the neck. His sandy blond hair was combed to perfection. His wide-eyed stare made me hide behind my partner's shoulders. I looked like shit right now and had no desire to embarrass myself in front of royalty.

Kellen straightened his posture and rolled his shoulders back. "Thomas."

"Kellen, it's good to see you again."

"If you'd like to wait in the dining room, I'm sure we can wake up one of the cooks to provide refreshments," Kellen offered.

Still hiding behind my partner, I didn't see Thomas' expression. A large puddle of water had pooled at our feet, and I stifled a giggle. *We must look ridiculous.*

"It's not necessary," Thomas replied. "I didn't come to inconvenience your staff. In all honesty, I forgot about the time zones. I would come back in a few hours, but I have a meeting that will suck up my entire afternoon."

Well that was rude. 'Let me show up in the middle of the night and expect my hosts to jump out of bed to accommodate my need to chat.'

"As you can see, we aren't exactly ready to entertain company," Kellen stated.

"Yes, and I apologize for my rudeness, but this really can't wait," Thomas insisted.

Silence filled the small corridor for several seconds. I assumed the two men were in the middle of a stare down. Would Kellen give up first? I counted the seconds as they ticked by. Men. I wasn't standing here any longer. My wet clothes were chafing places they shouldn't, and my toes were pruning.

"Men are so stupid," I mumbled, pushing Kellen aside and trying not to race up the steps. "You two keep arguing. I'm changing into something respectable," I called over my shoulder.

"She's refreshing in an irritating sort of way," I heard Thomas say even though he probably didn't know it.

Kellen, on the other hand, was probably well aware that I could hear them. "No, she's someone to be treasured."

Chapter 23

When I finally emerged from the bedroom, Kellen and Thomas were in the small seating area. My partner must have changed in another room because he was no longer soaking wet. I took my time selecting my outfit, a red broomstick skirt with a white camisole and sheer black blouse over top. I slipped my feet into my favorite white strappy sandals. I didn't want 'Prince Thomas' remembering me as a wet rat, even if it was the middle of the night.

The two men sat across from one another, each on a separate sofa. I shook my head, fighting the urge to roll my eyes. *Like I would choose to sit with the prince.* They rose when they noticed me, and Thomas offered his hand to me. I hesitated, not wanting to endure the magical inquisition that came with it. But it didn't matter; he'd already done the finger kissing thing last time.

I gave him my hand and sure enough, his lips brushed against my fingers. I pulled my hand away as soon as I could without seeming rude and sat down next to my partner.

"Kellen tells me you were training," Thomas said as soon as he sat.

"Yes," I replied to the obvious question even though he made it sound like a statement.

"Can I ask with what?" he pressed.

"I would think it was obvious," I replied, flashing a smile.

He chuckled. "Yes, I suppose so."

"You said your visit was urgent," Kellen said, leading the conversation away from our training.

Our guest shifted in his seat and looked around the room at everything but us. Something made him uncomfortable. Surely he wouldn't show up in the middle of the night to ask about my engagement to Kellen. Would he?

"We had a visitor last night," he began, clasping his hands in his lap. "That was about six hours ago. She demanded that we apprehend the princess as soon as you showed up at our door for the party." His nose wrinkled and his top lip rose into a sneer. "My father allowed a *vampire* to make demands. He should have had the monster killed on the spot, but he didn't."

I glanced at Kellen and wished Logan were here. He might know the right questions to ask about vampire's magic.

"Which vampire are we talking about?" I asked. "And do I assume that your father agreed?"

Thomas finally met my gaze. The single lamp in the room cast shadows across his pale skin but didn't hide his disgust.

"She is the ambassador for the European vampires," he spat. "I've always suspected she had my father under her thrall, but last night's conversation merely proved it. He agreed to hand you over after the party this weekend."

This weekend? I thought it would take longer to prepare, but apparently not. More importantly, it sounded like the king was in league with Jack or was this emissary working for Braden?

"Interesting," I mumbled and tapped my chin, thinking about the reasoning behind the ambassador. Did Braden send her to the king? He'd admitted to being the leader of the European vampires. But why would he kidnap me now? He needed me here fighting against Jack, not locked up in his dungeon.

"Alisandra, you can't really be considering attending the party," Thomas' panicked voice interrupted my musings. "My father's men obey without question. We won't protect you from the vampires."

Heat rose up my neck and my face flushed. "First, no one tells me what I can or can't do," I said, pointing at him. "Second, the vampire's actions confuse me. How long have you had an ambassador? Do you also have a mage ambassador with the vampires?"

The prince rubbed his hands across his face. "I can't believe you're not even reacting to this threat."

"I *am* reacting," I argued. "Just not the way you expected. Will you answer my questions?"

His eyes searched my face. "I cannot. I wanted to warn you of the danger because my instinct tells me we need you in this fight. But I can't betray my father."

"I understand and appreciate your concerns." I leaned over and reached across the narrow space between us, offering my hand to him. He tentatively wrapped his fingers around mine. "Don't worry for my safety. I think the players are showing their cards, and I won't be the one to fold."

I squeezed his hand and sent a wave of warm healing through him. Hot spikes of pain shot through my hand, and a small squeak escaped my lips.

"Are you not well, Prince Thomas?" I asked, before thinking about how rude the question was.

His face flushed and he pulled his hand from mine. "It's nothing," he replied.

"If it becomes something, I'm happy to help," I offered, rubbing my palm. The pain still lingered, and I wondered what would do that. I'd have to ask Göksu.

He nodded and reached into his pocket, retrieving a small, gilded envelope. "Your invitation to the party."

Kellen took it and glanced at me, obviously wanting to know my thoughts. Had Thomas answered my questions, I might have shared with him still present. Not now.

"Thank you for coming all this way, Prince Thomas," Kellen said. "We'll see you at the party."

"I hate that you're not taking this more seriously," the prince said as he rose from his seat.

"If we don't show up, your father will know we were warned," I said. "Who do you think he'll suspect? I assume there were very few people in the room for the meeting with your emissary."

He blushed again. The poor guy just wasn't cut out for all the subterfuge, not that I was either, but at least I saw the obvious. Most of the time.

"Thank you, Princess. I'll help you if I can." He bowed and started for the door. Kellen rose, laying his hand on my shoulder as he passed by me.

"I'll be right back," he whispered.

I watched the two men leave, then collapsed into the sofa pulling my legs beneath my skirt. Was Braden orchestrating this game, or did his ambassador take instructions from Jack? I was almost certain Braden wouldn't try to take me, not yet. If it was him, what could he gain from planting that story? Was he testing King William's loyalty or maybe the ambassador's? Maybe he was seeing if I had a connection to the European mages.

My thoughts rolled around in my head until Kellen returned. He dropped onto the cushion beside me and handed me the envelope. He'd already opened it.

"When is our next appointment with death?" I asked, rubbing my fingers on the thick paper.

"Saturday at six in the evening, London time," he replied, throwing his arm over the back of the sofa. "So, Saturday morning for us."

"Two days," I mumbled. "How do you coordinate a party that big so quickly?"

"Money and magic, my dear," Kellen answered.

I pulled my gaze from the pretty paper and looked at him. His furrowed brow made his flippant comment seem out of place.

"I'm not sure if we should go," Kellen said. "We can't let them take you."

"If Braden is involved, they won't," I countered, hoping I was right about the vampire's intentions to overthrow Jack. "He needs me in the fight, just like everyone else does. After Jack's defeat... I'll be worried." I folded the edge of our invitation. "Maybe I'll ask Logan if Mr. Smith has heard anything new."

"You're so certain of Jack's defeat?"

"Aren't you?" I smoothed my skirt over my knees and raised my eyebrows at him.

"I want to be," he replied. "But nothing is certain."

"You better keep that uncertainty in this room," I warned. "Your people don't need to see it."

A faint smile replaced his frown. "Yes, Princess. So, what do you think Braden's planning?"

"Again, if he's behind all of this, I think he's testing his information flow," I replied. "If we don't show up, Braden will know that either the prince or the king blabbed. If King William doesn't take me, he'll know his little bitch didn't carry through or that the king is no longer under her control." I turned to face my partner and leaned against the back of the sofa. "If the king does try to take me, Braden gets to watch me escape."

"You think the vampire will be there?" Kellen asked. "And you're also certain of your escape?"

"If I were him, I'd be hiding in the background," I replied. "The only way I don't escape is if the vampires are chasing me. Evading King William's men will be easy."

"Your new vampire skills?"

"Yep, just make sure you get back to the portal and don't think to rescue me," I warned. "They'll use you to make me cooperate."

He frowned. I understood. Even in the little time that I'd known Kellen, he didn't run from a fight.

We sat in silence staring at one another for several moments, both of us lost in our thoughts. Braden's reluctance to reveal his clan to the world made a lot more sense now. He had a forced peace with the European mages. Was the king truly under the vampire's control? Thomas seemed to think so. But was it Braden's control or Jack's? I shouldn't just assume it was Braden, even though it appeared that way.

"I was considering announcing our engagement at the party, but I'm not sure that's a good idea now," Kellen said.

I tried not to cringe. "I don't know. It's supposed to be about the single mages. You and I shouldn't overshadow that," I said. "Just being there together will likely confirm any suspicions about our relationship. I'll be sure to shun the prince at every opportunity."

My partner chuckled. "I was going to suggest that you flirt with Thomas in order to win over the loyalty of his mages. Maybe then they'd think twice about taking you."

"You're an idiot." I smiled to soften the insult. "I'd rather you make some rousing speech about mutual cooperation and continued efforts to find partners for everyone. I don't trust Thomas. What if he's the one under the vampire's control and not his father?"

"I hadn't considered that." He rubbed his jaw, then ran his fingers through his hair. "It's certainly possible. The young prince should be married already, unless he's been spelled by the female vampire. What made you think something was off?"

I thought about the fake vampire bonding. It was a way for the vampire to control the human. Could Thomas be part of one? Was the pain I felt from him a result of a vampire bond?

"When I took his hand at the end, something felt off," I replied.

"That's why you asked if he was okay?"

"Yeah, but I shouldn't be jumping to conclusions like that," I said. "He could be really sick and not want anyone to know."

A jaw-cracking yawn surprised me. It shouldn't have. It's not like it wasn't well after midnight.

"I'm going to bed." I stood and stretched, another yawn forcing itself on me.

"Do you mind if I join you?" Kellen asked. "I hate sleeping in the other room, but I will if you insist."

He stood beside me but didn't invade my space. I looked up at him, trying to read his expression.

"Just stay on your side of the bed," I said.

Without waiting for a response, I raced into the bathroom to get out of my silly outfit and into one of Logan's t-shirts. It hung loosely on my narrow frame and smelled heavily of spearmint. I took a deep breath and crawled into bed, trying to ignore my partner. The fears and memories from this room faded from my mind. Honestly, there wasn't any room in my tiny brain to really think about it. I had two days to mentally prepare myself to be kidnapped.

Another yawn escaped me as I pulled the quilt to my chin.

"Thank you for bringing my quilt," I mumbled.

"You're welcome."

Chapter 24

I didn't see Kellen at all the next morning, but several of the council members found the time to track me down. The first was at breakfast while I enjoyed my steaming pile of pancakes soaked in maple syrup. A large cup of coffee accompanied my outstanding meal that wasn't eggs or cereal. For some reason, it still mattered to me.

"May I join you?"

I looked up to see the young councilman with green eyes smiling down at me. A tray of food balanced easily in his hands as he waited for my response. *I really should remember his name*, I thought. But I didn't, which meant I'd have to look like a fool and ask him.

"By all means," I replied, waving at the chair next to me.

"Thank you."

I watched with fascination as he removed his plate of bacon, eggs, and toast from the tray still balanced in one hand, adjusting the plate of food several times. Next came the cup of orange juice set just above his plate and to the left. Then his cup of coffee right next to it. He snatched his utensils, still rolled in their paper napkin, off the tray and set it on the empty table next to us.

He looked over and caught me watching him. I blushed furiously and returned to own food as he laughed at me.

"My mother beat it into my head as a child," he said, still chuckling. "I haven't managed to break the habit."

"No need to explain it to me," I said, stuffing pancakes in my mouth. "I have enough oddities all by myself to make fun of anyone else's."

I saw him unroll his napkin out the corner of my eye and strategically place his utensils. Somehow I knew he would, but I didn't want to get caught staring like an idiot. I kept eating.

"I doubt anyone would call your talents an oddity, Magister," he said after everything was to his satisfaction.

"Please, call me Alisandra," I requested after swallowing the sweet gooey bite I'd just taken. "The Magister was my mother, and I wish to distance myself from her in every way possible."

He rested his forearms on the edge of the table, and I couldn't help but notice his stillness. I set my fork on my plate and turned to him. He studied his food, but I didn't think he really saw it.

"What's on your mind?" I asked, trying to figure out a way to ask him name without sounding foolish.

He looked over at me and sat his utensils down. "Your words at the meeting the other day meant a lot to us," he said. "Many of us have spent hours in the training rooms since then trying to connect with our elements." A small smile lit up his face. "Mine talked to me late yesterday evening. It scared the shit out of me when its voice echoed in my head. I haven't been able to stop smiling ever since."

I took a deep breath, trying to force down the lump in my throat. Elation washed over me in waves, as I suddenly realized I'd doubted my own words. It was certainly possible I was an anomaly, but it felt good to be wrong.

"I can't tell you how happy that makes me," I said. "I truly hope you continue to grow with your element. You have water, correct?" I assumed so, based on his eye color. Most water mages seemed to have green eyes, just as most air mages had blue or grey and earth had brown. It'd be embarrassing if I was wrong, though.

He nodded. "I'm trying not to bug it all the time. I don't want to seem like a silly child."

I laughed, and his smile faltered. "My water elemental calls me a child every time we speak," I explained. "Of course, I really am just a baby mage."

He picked up his fork again. "Thank you for giving me that. I never would've found it on my own."

He turned his focus to his food, and I returned to mine. It felt really good to make a difference, to see the happiness on his face. He'd given me a gift as well, the hope that all my frustrations and heartache mattered.

We sat in silence as we finished eating. Several people walked by saying hello or nodding, but no one stopped or asked to join us. I smiled and replied politely to everyone. I hadn't received this much attention with Kellen around. Was it his presence that kept them away? Or were they breaking out of their shell? I'd have to test my theory later.

"I have several things for you when you have a few minutes," my breakfast companion said. "The palace has its own internet connection and network you can use, but we need to set up your account. I also have a smartphone programmed for you."

"I have time now, actually," I said. "But I have a question first that's going to seem very rude and embarrassing for me."

"Okay?"

"I don't remember your name."

He laughed, then wiped his hand on his napkin and held it out to me. "I'm Brian."

I shook his hand and smiled. "Thank you, Brian. I might have you make a list of the other council members for me as well. I'm terrible with names."

"You're welcome. Let's go to my office and set up your stuff." He stood, piling all his dishes on the tray he'd used earlier, then adding mine to it as well. We stopped at the nearest trash receptacle before leaving the dining hall.

I followed him across the courtyard and down another corridor on the opposite side. I tried to remember the layout as I went, but doubted I would. I'd never learn my way around if I didn't spend more time exploring. Another thing to add to my list.

Brian's office was just as meticulous as his meal. White built-in cabinetry lined two walls from the hardwood floors to the ceiling, and a long counter supported by more cabinets covered the third wall. The countertop was empty with the exception of a large laptop strategically placed over a small cut-out in the cabinets. A rolling chair was pushed all the way in, leaving the center of the room completely open. Every cabinet had a label, and I was pretty sure nothing would be out of place.

Brian opened a door on the top right side labeled 'laptops.' *Imagine that.* I smiled as he put a slim laptop on the counter. The computer even had a label with my name on it. I couldn't imagine what this guy's house looked like. He pulled open a drawer, retrieving a smartphone also with my name stuck across the box.

I leaned against the counter while he did cool stuff with my new electronics that I didn't understand. "Just make it so I can find the internet really easy," I said after he explained all the apps on my laptop. "I'm not very tech savvy."

He programmed my phone and handed me both. "If you ever have questions or stuff stops working, just come see me," he said. "Also, putting on my council member hat, we'd like you to keep your phone with you at all times. It has a tracker in it. Just in case something should happen to you, we'd like to be able to find you."

My good humor faded. At least he told me. "Thanks. I'll be sure to take it when I leave the palace."

"Great!" He made a sweeping motion with his hand as if he threw his hat away. "Thanks for not getting mad about it. It's for your safety and our sanity."

I waved away the concern, acting like it meant nothing even if I didn't like it. Because I wouldn't be taking his phone with me when I left with Logan.

"Last but not least, let's make a list of people you should know," Brian said.

"That would be amazing!" I exclaimed.

As soon as I walked out of Brian's office with my new toys, the heavy-set woman from the council greeted me. We just went over the damn list that was now in my pocket. Hettie, I hoped her name was Hettie.

"Magister, I'm so glad I found you," she said between ragged breaths.

"Alisandra, please." I requested. "You can walk with me to my rooms to drop off the new toys Brian graciously set up for me." I gave her my best smile.

"Thank you, Alisandra."

I waited for her to move forward, hoping to set my pace with hers. She obliged, and we strolled back across the courtyard towards my private stairwell. Two guards stood sentry at the door. They hadn't been there before, and I narrowed my eyes at them. They shifted nervously, but I decided now was not the time to address their presence. Kellen likely put them there.

The guard on the left opened the door for me, sparing a glance at Hettie.

"Hettie and I will be back down in a few minutes," I said, glancing at my new friend to see if I got her name wrong.

"If it's all the same to you, Magis…. Alisandra, I'd rather not make a trip up those steps," she said.

I felt guilty for not having considered the winding steps that left me out of breath. I turned to her, my face blushing.

"Forgive me," I said. "I don't want to climb these steps, so I shouldn't expect anyone else to be excited about it. Maybe we can have an elevator installed."

"That would be splendid."

"I'll be right back." As soon as I rounded the first bend, out of sight of the people below, I raced up the stairs. The double wooden doors at the top made me stop and not just because they were closed. Spirit's symbol seemed to call to me. I brushed the wings with my fingertips before opening the doors and putting my stuff on the low table next to the sofa.

A few minutes later, I rejoined Hettie at the bottom of the steps.

"That was quick," she squeaked.

"Well, I just dropped my stuff and ran back down," I said, pretending to gasp for breath. How was I not sucking wind? Too many times up and down the damn steps. "So, what did you want to chat about?"

"Oh, we got our invitation to the party," she said, a smile spreading across her round face. A glimmer of pride twinkled in her blue eyes. "His Highness insisted on this Saturday, and somehow, we managed to get everything together in time to make it happen."

She stopped in the middle of the courtyard, beaming at me. That explained the question I hadn't asked Thomas last night.

"Wow! I'm impressed," I said, pretending like I hadn't already received my invitation. "I can't imagine how much work went into making that happen so quickly. How many people do you expect to be there?"

"At least five hundred," she replied, rubbing her hands together. "You wouldn't believe the volunteers we had from the other mage families. Everyone is so excited to make this happen. And we couldn't have done it without you."

She bounced on the balls of her feet and squeezed her hands together. I could almost feel the hug struggling to be contained. Her enthusiasm was almost contagious.

"It sounds to me like we couldn't do it without you." I smiled and offered her my open arms. She engulfed me in a tight embrace, and I heard her sniffle.

"My daughter has been helping with decorations," she continued, releasing me from her smothering hug, but still clinging to my arm. She led me across the courtyard again and pulled me into a large room a few doors down from Brian's office. "She's still looking for a partner. I think she found hers with one of the volunteers from China."

Hettie squeezed my arm and stopped between a tall stack of boxes and folding tables lined up in rows with matching chairs. "I can't tell you how much it means to me. I don't care where her partner comes from as long as I don't lose her." Tears welled in the woman's eyes. "We've never known the fear of losing our children to the madness until your mother took over. She refused to let us visit the other families. You've given us a beautiful gift."

She wrapped me in another quick hug and sniffled again. I struggled to hold back my own tears. Hettie had no idea the gift she gave me with her own story. She and Brian filled an empty spot in my heart. Maybe being Magister wasn't all bad. The satisfaction of seeing their happy faces was worth it.

"Anyway, I wanted to show you what we're contributing. King William won't care, but some of his court will expect you to know." She pointed out the rows of tables and chairs, along with boxes of tablecloths, napkins, decorations, and tons of other stuff I was not remembering. I should've brought a notebook to write it all down.

"So we're basically doing set up and decorations," I said, trying not to make it a question.

"You got it," she replied. "King William's court is providing beverages. Everything you can possibly imagine, I'm sure." She led me back the way we came. "The other families are providing food. Everyone will be demonstrating their own cultural music and dance."

I was astounded. "And you guys set all this up in less than a week?"

"Seems kind of crazy, doesn't it?" Her smile grew. I wasn't sure how, but it did. "We had so many people willing to give their time. And the woman coordinating from King William's court is amazing." She paused and pressed her hands together again. "Well, I've taken enough of your time." She tugged on the hem of her blouse, and her face flushed. I wasn't sure how much more emotion I could take, but I smiled and waited for her. "I had severe reservations about you when Kellen first told us of his plan. I'm glad I was wrong. You're exactly what we needed."

My face burned with embarrassment. "I'm not so sure about that," I mumbled. "But I'll do my best, and I'll depend on the council way more than I should."

"That's why we're here." She waved her hands towards the door. "I'm sure you have a ton of stuff to do. Don't let me monopolize anymore of your time."

"Thank you, Hettie," I said. She gave me another big smile and headed back into the rows of boxes.

I once again entered the courtyard in a whirl of emotions, the sun now beating down from its midday position. Had I really spent all morning with only two people? Obviously. Where to next? I wanted to talk to Logan. I missed him, probably too much. Maybe he could help me prioritize which emotion needed to be first. Happiness, relief, fear, anxiety. There were too many to sort through on my own.

However, the two guards standing at my door reminded me I needed information from them. They both wore the same outfit: black cargo pants, black t-shirts that hugged their muscular frames, and black leather boots. The only difference was the patch on their shoulder. The man on the right wore fire's symbol and the man on the left wore earth. That made it easy.

"Good morning, gentlemen," I said as I approached.

They nodded and eyed me warily.

"Will you always have the pleasure of wearing out your boots on my steps or does it get passed around?" I asked.

They looked at each other and shrugged.

"A detail of six has been assigned to you, Magister," earth guy replied.

"I see," I said, tapping my finger on my chin as if I really needed to think about it. "I assume my fiancé arranged this?"

Their eyes widened but only for a moment. "Kellen is in charge of security, ma'am."

"Then, yes." That was easy. News would spread like wildfire about our engagement without having to make any official announcement, which would be uncomfortable. "Who is allowed in our quarters?"

"You and Kellen," fire guy answered. "And any guests who accompany you."

Interesting. Did that mean I had to escort Logan? Not a chance. I'd just open the door and let him zip by unnoticed. Could I also zip by? I needed to test it.

"And can guests be unaccompanied?" I pressed.

"Absolutely not," fire guy replied. "They will remain here while one of us announces them."

"Excellent." I smiled at their obvious relief. "I don't suppose you could warn me when Kellen arrives?" I asked, leaning closer and lowering my voice. "I'm rearranging his furniture and he probably won't like it."

Fire guy snorted and smoothed the smile from his face. "I can try, ma'am, but he'll know something's up if one of us runs up the steps as soon as we see him."

"You're probably right." I shrugged. "Hopefully, I get it done before he returns." Halfway through the door, I stopped. "I'll come up with a special code or knock or something." I winked at them and continued up the steps, not missing their smiles as I turned.

As soon as I heard the door close, I raced up the steps. When I reached the top, I ran back down, then sprinted up again. Still not tired. What the hell? Not that I wanted to complain, but changes weren't always good. My body didn't feel any different, but something was.

I pulled both wooden doors and left them open and welcoming, then crossed the room to the tall windows. After a few tugs, they raised on their sashes, allowing a cool breeze to waft across the space. I turned in a slow circle. We needed a reading nook, with a big fluffy chair that would swallow me whole. Possibly even a writing desk and more light.

I picked up my new tablet and phone and went into the bedroom. It had a desk, but Kellen's stuff stretched out across it. The phone Logan gave me sat on the bedside table, plugged into its charger. I picked it up and unlocked the screen. Nothing. Was he waiting for me to initiate a conversation? It'd only been a day. I couldn't expect him to text me every hour giving me updates about where he was. Besides, I hadn't sent anything to him, so I could hardly be mad about not hearing from him. Was he mad because I didn't text and tell him good night?

I huffed and tapped on the keypad.

AJ: You aren't in trouble, are you?

Logan: Did you download a surveillance camera on my phone?

I smiled. He'd texted back immediately. Maybe I was just overthinking things.

AJ: You know better

He was well aware of my technology allergy, but I imagined he had my favorite goofy grin on his face with his reply. He knew how to make me smile.

Logan: I miss you

A lump swelled in my throat. Did he have to go there already?

AJ: No you don't. You just miss my stupid comments and my knack for getting us in trouble.

Logan: Oh definitely

I plopped down on the bed and leaned back against my pillow. I really did miss his constant company.

AJ: Can you call me?

My phone rang a few seconds later. "How's my vampire?" I asked as soon as the call connected.

"Better now," he replied.

"Don't lie. You're grateful you don't have to carry me around like a sack of potatoes."

"Well, maybe that." His chuckle made me smile. "Any news about your other favorite vampire?"

"Wow, can we not talk about work already?" My bottom lip pushed out and trembled. *Don't be a crybaby, AJ,* I thought. *Not now. You were smiling two seconds ago.*

"Let's get work out of the way, then I'll cheer you up."

"If you insist," I mumbled. I repeated our late-night conversation with Thomas along with all my theories. He listened with the patience I'd taken for granted. God, I missed him.

"I'll see what Jonathan knows about Braden's plans," Logan said after several moments of silence. "I don't like you being there, especially when I can't go with you, but I agree. You need to be at that party."

"Be careful, Logan. Braden's not stupid. He'll use you against me."

"I know, princess. I'm good at being careful."

I wasn't, and my vampire knew it, even though he wouldn't say it out loud. For the next twenty minutes we talked about plans for training with hand-to-hand combat using my vampire skills. Then his promise to take me for a drive in the Mustang. Then the conversation devolved into sexual innuendos and hints at our next night together.

Kellen's brown sugar and cinnamon drifting on the constant breeze warned me of his imminent arrival.

"I gotta go," I said reluctantly.

"Be careful, princess."

"You too."

My phone went silent as my partner entered the room with a puzzled look on his face.

"Welcome home," I said, swinging my legs off the bed and stretching.

"Thank you," Kellen muttered. "Have you been here all day?"

I pushed past him, carrying my laptop with me.

"Don't ask questions you already know the answer to," I replied.

His boots clomped across the floor behind me. I dropped into one the sofas and opened my laptop. I wasn't sure why I felt the need to antagonize him, but I did. Maybe because of my babysitters downstairs or the role he brilliantly pushed me into once again.

"Touché. You want a drink?" He moved to the bar, retrieving a short glass from the cabinet. I expected it to be full of whiskey in two seconds.

"Nope, I'm good." I opened my internet explorer and typed in office furniture. All kinds of stuff popped up on my screen, and I started scrolling through it.

"You created quite the stir this morning," he said, walking towards me with his glass of amber liquid.

"I did? That seems unlikely. I only spoke to Brian when he gave me my laptop and phone." I held up my toy for him to see. "Then Hettie, whom I really like. She gave me the scoop on Saturday's party."

"You didn't speak to anyone else?" he asked, sitting down across from me.

I tried not to smile. Had my guards already spread the news? It seemed unlikely, but not impossible.

"Nope, just the babysitters downstairs," I replied. "I needed to know who was allowed in our space."

"They aren't babysitters, AJ," Kellen hissed. "They're there for our protection. No one should be up here but us."

"Of course. So what's got your panties in a bunch?" I waved a hand at him, knowing I was fueling the fire.

He downed half the whiskey in his cup and glared at me. "Half the palace is talking about our engagement, and the other half will know by sunset. I thought we would announce it together."

"I didn't announce anything," I said, not looking up from my scrolling list of desks. "I told you who I talked to this morning. Are you sure you didn't mention it to someone?"

I glanced up, looking at him through my lashes. He studied the whiskey in his glass.

"I did, but I also swore him to secrecy, explaining the importance of it coming from us and not rumors."

"It's really hard to keep something like that secret, Kellen," I said, closing my laptop. "Gossip is tasty, and that kind of gossip is sinful. Don't be mad at your friend. He likely made the same threat and promise you did. That person did the same and so on. You're smart; you get the picture."

"I wanted it to be special," he mumbled.

"And I didn't. I hate being the center of attention. It feels awful," I said.

He looked up at me, his frown replaced by his impassive stare. Damn.

"Now we can just be us, without all the expectations and fanfare," I insisted. "It's easier for me, which should make it easier for both of us." Was I being selfish? Absolutely.

He grunted, then nodded towards my laptop. "What are you looking for?"

Grateful for the change of subject, I opened it and turned it towards him. "I'd like a desk out here and one of those big fluffy chairs that I can't get out of."

He raised an eyebrow at me and smiled, probably imagining me rolling around like a turtle trying to get out of said chair.

"We can do that." He moved around to the space beside me. "I prefer this vendor for furniture," he said, his fingers dancing across the keyboard. "It's better quality."

We spent the next hour picking out new furniture and talking about design ideas for the expansion of our suite. It felt good to get away from the impending war, even it meant making this space my home. I wanted none of this, but once again, I had no choice. Except my furniture, and I'd take full advantage of that.

Chapter 25

Saturday morning, I stood in front of the mirrored wall in Kate's bedroom, staring at my reflection. I'd changed my clothes five times already, going back to the first one I tried on. A knee-length dress in shimmering material, somewhere between slate gray and sky blue, hugged my torso and fell over my narrow hips. Slender straps draped over my shoulders. It was pretty without being cute. I didn't want to look like a child, and my chosen dress was just classy enough to pull it off.

"If you're done admiring yourself, let's put some makeup on that cute little face," Kate said, standing behind me with her hands on her hips. A wide grin softened her comment. "You look great. Quit fussing over it and come here."

I sighed and let her guide me onto the small stool in front of her dresser.

"I think muted shades of pink and pearl is best," she mumbled. "We don't want to make your skin look washed out." She fumbled in her makeup kit pulling out a bunch of different eye shadows. "Maybe a little silver around the edges though to make your eyes pop."

Her soft muttering faded, so I let my mind wander as she worked. In less than an hour, I'd be in England. It seemed unreal, even more so because I'd be in a *castle* in England. The thought made me giddy with excitement.

"Have you ever been to the castle?" I asked.

"You weren't listening to anything I said, were you?" Kate replied with her own question.

"Sorry. I'm a little nervous."

"I'd tell you not to be, but I understand." She brushed a light powder over my cheeks. "I'm nervous too, but probably for different reasons."

"I'm excited for you guys. I know it's wishful thinking, but I really hope everyone finds their partner today." I paused while she coated my lashes with mascara. "No one should have to worry about not having one."

Kate leaned back, tilting her head back and forth. "I really like the silver eye shadow. Let's soften it with a little pearl and call it good." Her eyes met mine, shimmering with tears. "We've never been to any of the other regions, AJ. You've given us a beautiful gift. Even if I don't find my partner today, I know the opportunity is there. Something we wouldn't have without you."

"Nonsense." I waved my hand at her and blinked away my own tears. "Kellen would've done the same thing."

"Eventually, but his mind is so wrapped up in our security and politics. It might have taken a while." She dabbed more color on my eyelids and stepped back. "You've improved both without even trying."

I understood her comment. Eliminating the single mages' fears also reduced the chances of them betraying us to the vampires. That alone would improve our security. Hopefully, it also improved politics, something I sucked at. Or maybe I didn't. My conversations with Hettie and Brian had suggested I had at least a little skill with people.

"Alright, shoes and a pocket book and we're ready," Kate said, dumping her stuff back in her makeup kit. "Do you even own a purse?" She hesitated and turned to me. "I don't think I've ever seen you with one."

"No, not really," I replied, hoping the layers of blush and powder covered my embarrassment. "I always carried a backpack before."

She abandoned her task and opened one of the dresser drawers. Dozens of small purses filled the drawer in every color imaginable.

"Wow," I whispered.

Kate pulled two out of her stash and held them up to my dress. A silver one and an off-white one. "I'm torn. Your sandals are off-white, but I really like the silver," she said, biting her lip. "I think we have to go with white, though."

She handed me the tiny bag, and I gave her a confused look. "What am I supposed to put in it?"

"Your phone, lipstick and a change purse," she replied, digging through her drawer of purses again. A small silver bag hanging from a delicate chain emerged. "For the cash you must carry with you, just in case."

"Thank you, Kate, for all your help," I said, rising from the stool and going in search of my blue jeans. The phone from Logan and my debit card were still in my pockets. Being with Kellen meant I didn't need the other phone, but I wasn't about to miss a text from my vampire. I hadn't heard from him since the day before, and I tried not to think about it. He knew the party was today, and I hoped to at least get a 'break your leg.' But I hadn't.

I transferred the items to my new purse and glanced in the mirror one more time. Memories of my first visit to Kate's room six or seven weeks ago resurfaced. A time when I was still covered by the magical veil someone placed over me, a veil I'd endured my entire life until Kellen removed it. The only thing that remained of that woman was my scrawny body and icy blue eyes.

"Let's go. I bet Kellen was ready an hour ago. I'm surprised he hasn't started banging on the door." Kate opened her door and disappeared down the hall, not waiting for me.

"Pull your shit together girl," I mumbled. "It's just a party."

"One I'll truly hate missing."

I jumped and spun towards the sliding glass doors leading to the patio garden. Tears welled in my eyes, and I ran to my vampire. He caught me as I jumped into his arms, with total disregard for my dress.

"Stop crying," he whispered. "You'll smear your makeup."

"You can't leave me again, Logan." The words tumbled from my mouth before I could stop them. "I can't pretend to be someone I'm not, and everyone expects me to be happy with the situation I'm forced into." I hadn't realized my insecurities and doubts until I saw him, and now they poured out in waves.

"You're much stronger than you give yourself credit for, princess," he said. "You've got this." He loosened his hold and looked down at me, giving me that silly grin I loved so much. "I'll be waiting for you at the palace when you get back."

"There are guards at the bottom of the stairs," I sniffed.

"Let me worry about that." He kissed my forehead and drew in a deep breath. "Have fun and be careful. I assume you and Kellen have already established a plan of escape?"

"Yes, Kellen is leaving before me," I replied. "When the king's guards try to take me, I'll easily evade them with my new vampire speed."

His eyebrows rose. "Kellen agreed to leave without you?"

"No, I made him promise he would after a thirty-minute argument." I ran my fingers along his jaw and down his neck. "I'm still not sure he'll do what he's supposed to."

I traced the hem of his button-down shirt all the way to the bottom where it hung open just below his waist.

Logan trapped my wandering hand in his. "Save that for later."

I smiled and stood on my tiptoes, brushing his lips with mine. "You better be there."

"How could I refuse?" He looked past me and his smile faltered. "Your partner's ready."

I didn't turn away, needing to memorize every part of his face for just a second longer. "See you tonight," I whispered so only he could hear.

"Be careful."

"Never."

He grinned, turned on his heel and disappeared into the garden. I followed my connection to him until he was too far away, then shook my head, trying to focus on the day ahead. Thoughts of Logan would have to wait until tonight.

I slowly turned around to face my partner. His emotional shield must've been tightly bound; I didn't feel a thing coming from him. The impassive expression I hated rested easily on his face.

"You clean up well," I said. "I might have to carry a stick to beat back the women who'll be falling over themselves to get to you."

His lips twitched and his eyes softened, but only for a moment. He did look good in the charcoal gray suit that was obviously tailored to fit him. A silver tie shimmered against his white shirt. Kate must have suggested it to match my dress.

"Flattery doesn't work on me," he said. "We both know you wouldn't defend me against them."

I strolled across the room, picking up my small purse along the way. His comment hurt, but his current status was his fault, not mine. "Flattery works on everyone," I replied. "A few weeks ago, I would've stabbed anyone who even looked at you, if I thought you'd return the favor. But now...." I shrugged. "You'll have to work really hard to convince me that you care."

"I am working really hard," he hissed, grabbing my arm as I tried to push past him. "And I do care. I thought spilling my heart to you the other night would mean something."

I glared at him. His confession the other night had meant a lot to me, but I couldn't just forget. What happened the next time I pissed him off? Would he react the same way?

"It meant the world to me," I said, hoping he could sense my honesty. "But why don't you put the shoe on the other foot? Would you forgive me if I stabbed you in the stomach and left you to die?"

He seethed at me, his lips drawing into a thin line.

"That's what I thought," I snapped. "And if I came back five minutes later and completely healed your wound, would it all of a sudden make everything better?"

The fingers around my arm loosened, and his head drooped with his shoulders.

"I'm sorry, AJ," he whispered.

"And I'm trying to forgive you," I responded. "But it doesn't happen overnight or even three or four nights. I need to know that I'm not a target the next time I piss you off or ruin your plans."

"They weren't supposed to hurt you, dammit!" he yelled, his eyes darkening with each word. "They had strict orders to subdue you and bring you back to the palace. I planned to keep you in my old room until my mind was rational enough to make a decision."

I wanted to believe him. I really did. Maybe I could talk to Marshall or Stewart and verify the story. Stewart! I'd saved his life, so he owed me one. I made a mental note to talk to him once we got back from the party.

"I'll try harder not to antagonize you," I conceded.

"I'll do my best to make you feel loved and appreciated," he said.

I wanted to tell him not to bother if it wasn't real, but that would fall in the 'antagonizing' bucket, so I let it go.

"Shall we try this again?" I asked holding my hand out to him. "I need an escort through the portal, and I'd appreciate if you did the honors."

He accepted my hand, some of his tension fading. "I'd love to."

We made our way to the portal room, hand-in-hand. Kate waited at the shimmering black hole, smiling as we entered. She winked at me and stepped into the darkness. Kellen pulled me to the portal's edge and drew me into a hug.

"I can't tell you how much I want this to work between us," he said softly.

I didn't respond. My heart belonged to Logan, not Kellen. My partner said he knew that, but did he? Would he try to separate me from my vampire? I hoped not. He'd even promised to let Logan into the palace anytime. If he broke that promise, I'd be leaving. Or would I? Not through the portal.

"I'm ready," I mumbled into his chest, trying to keep my makeup from smearing on his suit.

He stepped in, and my world lurched. Pinpricks of pain raced across my skin, and my heart stuttered in my chest. I gripped the lapels of Kellen's jacket, sucking my breath through my teeth. His arms tightened around me, and I found myself not wanting to let go. What was *that*? I'd felt it the last time, but assumed it was my heart breaking for Logan. This time was stronger.

"You okay?" he whispered.

I nodded, knowing he wouldn't believe me, but it was the only acceptable answer. I released my grip on him and took a step back, looking around at my new surroundings. Two guards dressed in navy blue suits flanked the portal, one on each side. I caught one glancing at me, but it was the only movement from either of them. What did they think of our arrival? An intimate moment or did they notice my pain? Hopefully the former and not the latter.

Kellen laced his fingers with mine and led me from the small, darkened room. We emerged into a similarly lit hall, meaning not very well. Sconces hung from the stone walls every ten feet or so, casting a soft light across the gray floors. I tried to act like I wasn't enthralled by the uniformed guards spaced evenly between the lights or the high arching ceiling with its dark wooden joists.

The ache in my chest ebbed away with my excitement. I was in a fricking castle, complete with castle guards and stone walls. It took every bit of self-control to cage my giddiness. I refused to look like a fan girl, no matter how true it might've been.

My shoes tapped along the stone, echoing in the silence. I'd expected more people. It's not like we were early, and where was Kate? Why didn't she wait for us? Two more guards eye-balled us as we passed by. How many did that make between the portal and our destination? I resisted the urge the turn around and count. It might make a difference in my mad dash to escape the king's plans. I should've paid better attention. There had to be at least eight, possibly ten. As long as none of them saw me, I'd be okay. How did I go from excitement to paranoia in one breath? *Focus on the excitement and enjoy the evening,* I told myself. *You'll still be able to escape.*

A large wooden door to our right slid open. Loud music preceded another guard, almost spitting the man out with the burst of noise. The man and the music startled me after the unusual silence in the hallway. The sound proofing in the rooms was astonishing. As soon as the door closed, the music disappeared again. They could be torturing people and no one would know. I drew in a sharp breath.

That would be another snag in my plans.

I'd have to take off my shoes to avoid anyone hearing me sprinting down the stupid hall. Damn. This was getting more complicated by the second.

"I guess we found the party," I mumbled, my enthusiasm waning quickly.

Kellen didn't reply to my meaningless observation. He nodded at the guard recently expelled from the noisy room, then gently squeezed my fingers and opened the door.

Chapter 26

Once I forced myself past the loud music, a smile spread across my face. Hettie and her crew did a marvelous job on the decorations, and I hoped our mages were proud of the beautifully adorned tables. Clusters of multi-colored candles centered each table, surrounded by a thin bed of tiny white flowers. Tall, metal abstract art rose from the middle of each centerpiece, providing the groups with something to talk about if their conversations got awkward or just died out. The long tables covered with food had the same beds of flowers between each serving dish and tiny lights edging the dark table cloths.

Too many tables to count covered each side of the room, leaving the center open. Groups of men and women already filled the dance floor, making me smile. I'd never been part of that crowd, the one that danced and partied then went home with their favorite treat of the night. I'd always dreamed of one day receiving that invitation to be part of the 'fun crowd.' It never happened. Even now, the invitation was obligatory. I was the Magister. They had to invite me.

I let Kellen pull me along the edge of the dancefloor towards the back of the room. As we passed by the long row of food tables, my stomach rumbled. Thank goodness no one could hear it past the music. It seemed weird to have dinner for breakfast, but I didn't really care. Everything looked and smelled marvelous. I couldn't distinguish one scent from the others; they mingled together perfectly. Diced potatoes and fancy carrots wrapped around whole roasts, thinly sliced and dripping with perfection. Every salad imaginable stared back at me, calling my name. My stomach growled again in return. I licked my lips, remembering my lipstick at the last second and hoping I hadn't smeared it.

Kellen stopped in front of me, and I nearly bumped into him. He squeezed my hand and I slid to his side. My appetite vanished immediately. Standing next to Thomas was the one man I couldn't see, not tonight. Braden. I'd expected him to be here in hiding, not as a guest. His straight blond hair hung loose over his collar, framing his chiseled features. The dark suit framed his shoulders and narrow waist, outlining his muscular form perfectly. He winked at me and I pulled my gaze from him, trying to school my features.

"It's good to see you, Princess," King William said with a smile, extending his hand to me.

"And you as well, Your Highness," I replied, giving him my hand. He lightly kissed my fingers. "Thank you for hosting our mages in your beautiful castle."

"The pleasure is all mine," he said, his smile unwavering as he turned to my partner. "Kellen, thank you for bringing her to my humble abode."

"It was a pleasure I wouldn't allow anyone else to have," Kellen said, bowing slightly.

"No, I imagine not." King William chuckled. "Introductions are in order."

He waved his hand at the group of people standing just behind him spouting off names as he went. I wouldn't remember any of them and hoped that Kellen would. Maybe he already knew them, making it that much easier. When he got to the blonde-haired fiend, I held my breath.

"This is Branden, an influential business associate who begged to experience tonight's party."

William's smile was genuine and lacked any fear or deception. Did he not know that one of the vampire council was in his midst? How could he not after Thomas' revelation the other night? And where was the female ambassador? I'd been certain she worked for Braden—or Branden, the crappy alter ego he'd adopted—but maybe I was wrong.

I looked up at my partner to find him smiling and shaking hands with the other leaders of the magical community. Did he not recognize Braden? Maybe he'd never seen him in person. I should've asked, but I assumed he knew. An Indian woman with soft brown eyes greeted me with a glowing smile, pulling my focus back to what I should be doing. I offered handshakes and accepted hugs and smiles from complete strangers for the next few minutes. 'Branden' kept his distance, but I could feel his eyes on me.

"Alisandra." Thomas' voice drew my attention. He moved towards me from his father's side. "We took the liberty of reserving seats for you at our table." He motioned towards a large round table at the corner of the dance floor opposite the food tables. "If you'd like to make yourself comfortable."

"Thank you, Thomas," I replied. "I'd like to get a plate of food before I find my seat."

"Allow one of my servants to do that for you," he insisted, now at my side with his hand brushing my elbow.

Against my better judgement, I acquiesced. I wouldn't embarrass myself by arguing with him.

"I'll take care of it," Kellen offered, apparently hearing our conversation.

"Thank you." I gave him my best smile, mostly because I was truly grateful for his presence. Regardless of our dysfunctional relationship, I thought I could trust him. At least he had some idea what I liked to eat. He released my hand, and Thomas guided me across the room.

"Would you prefer to sit next to me or Branden?" the prince asked as we approached the table.

"Are those my only choices?" I asked in return, trying to smile like I was kidding. His face flushed, and I thought I saw the all too familiar pain of rejection. Damn. "I was kidding, Thomas. My only preference is to not have my back to the dancefloor."

He wound his way to the far side of the table and pulled out a chair for me. "Then, this will be your seat."

"Thank you. And you'll be sitting next to me?" I asked.

"No, I'll be on the opposite side of my father," he mumbled. I suspected it wasn't really loud enough to be heard over the music.

"I'm sorry, I didn't hear you," I insisted, patting the seat next to me.

He sat sideways in the chair, a frown pulling at his thin lips. "Our ambassador was supposed to be here tonight," he said, leaning towards me and taking my hands in his. I let him, knowing he was trying to tell me something important. He kept his deep voice quiet. "I'm not sure why she isn't, but I suspect Branden had something to do with it."

I looked at our joined hands, trying to compose my thoughts. How much did Thomas know? Should I tell him I recognize who 'Branden' really was?

"How well do you know him?" I asked.

"Not at all," he replied, now whispering loudly. "My father has talked about their business dealings for years, but this is the first time I've met him."

"Then what makes you think he's involved?" I pressed.

"Just a hunch," he replied. "Branden is here and she is not."

That answered most of my questions. "Maybe I can loosen his tongue for you," I suggested with a smile.

"Be careful, Alisandra. I know nothing about him."

"Careful is my middle name." I squeezed his fingers, then released his hand as Braden's signature scent drifted towards me. It was going to be a very long day.

"Prince Thomas, thank you for the beautiful dinner companion," Braden said, standing behind his chair.

I avoided looking up at him as the prince rose. I didn't want to see the smug look on the vampire's face. I needed to make sure Kellen knew who it was, but how? Braden would hear everything I said to my partner.

"Certainly," Thomas said, moving to the opposite side of the table and taking his own seat.

The king sat between them and gave me his ever-present smile. My jaw hurt just watching him. It must have taken years of practice to keep that thing painted on his face.

"Your council did a marvelous job with decorations, Alisandra," the king said.

"Thank you," I responded. "I'll be sure to pass along your praise. It'll mean a lot to them. They're already grateful for the opportunity they've been given tonight."

"Yes. It looks like several have already found an interest." His gaze swept the dancefloor, and I followed it.

The music slowed, and couples swayed together. Some of them kept an appropriate distance from each other, but many didn't. Their bodies melded, making me long for Logan. Everything about it felt wrong, except the rightness of it. Was I supposed to have a romantic relationship with my mage partner? When we'd first met, Kellen said we could be partners and not lovers.

I pulled my eyes from the dance floor and glanced around the tables. Mages sat together in pairs across the room. Some both men and others both women, along with the male and female pairings. It shouldn't matter. My magic shouldn't need a romantic love to work.

A plate of roasted vegetables and possibly chicken appeared before me. I looked up into my partner's dark eyes and smiled. He grinned and sat down.

"I played it safe," he said, "but I think there are several dishes up there you would love to try."

I stabbed the chicken and it shredded easily with my fork. I swallowed the pooling saliva in my mouth and replaced it with a small bite. It was heavenly. I had no idea what it was, but it melted on my tongue in a burst of flavor.

"Oh my God," I said. "You need to learn how to cook this, Kellen."

"Do I?" he asked, grinning at me. "What do I get in return?"

I swallowed the delicious morsel and stuck my tongue out at him. His smile widened and I blushed. "You're awful," I hissed.

"I know." He winked and leaned back as a young man placed glasses of wine on the table.

I tried to avoid looking at the vampire on my other side. The slices of rare beef on his plate were not his normal diet, and my curiosity wanted to see his reaction to eating it. But I wouldn't give in. He would know, and his insufferable smirk would just piss me off.

Kellen looked past me, and I swallowed hard, trying not to choke on my vegetables. He wasn't going to engage in a conversation with Braden, was he?

"Branden," my partner called over my head. "What type of business are you in?"

"I'm a partner in a trading firm in London," he replied. "We deal mostly in new technologies."

I focused on my plate, with the occasional glance at Braden. Was that true? It could be, I supposed. The magical families still needed money to operate.

"Ah. I'm surprised we haven't met before," Kellen said. "My own company deals in marketing techniques for large tech firms."

"I should have my people contact yours, then," the vampire stated. "Our current marketing plan isn't as effective as it should be."

"I'd be happy to assist," Kellen said. I didn't miss the enthusiasm in his voice. "I didn't bring business cards with me, but I can give you the contact information for our European office before I leave."

"That would be splendid."

Just fricking splendid, I thought. I needed to tell Kellen who he really was. Creating a business relationship with this vampire was not a good idea.

"I'm getting dessert," Kellen said, placing his hand over mine. "They have a luscious chocolate cake. Do you want some?"

"You know I'm not saying no to chocolate," I replied. "I'll come with you."

"Nope, I got it," he smiled and rose from his chair.

I watched him until he drifted out of sight between the swaying bodies.

"Is there something we should know, dear?" King William asked, drawing my attention.

Was he talking to me? I gave him my best 'Who me' smile.

"The rumors are running wild about you and Kellen being engaged," Thomas finished for his father.

A choking sound erupted from Braden, and I turned to him. His eyes pulled me to him, and that smug grin erased my blush.

"We are," I replied, "but we didn't want to announce it until after tonight. This event is about our mages, not Kellen and I."

"Very noble of you," the king said. "I'll be sure to congratulate your fiancé."

"So young to be tied to one man," Braden whispered, his smile growing. He knew I was the only one hearing him, making it so I couldn't reply.

"Thank you, Your Highness."

"Just make sure I receive an invitation to the wedding," William said, chuckling.

"I better be on the guest list, as well," the vampire whispered.

"You'll be on the top of our list." I tried to ignore the fiend next to me, but it was becoming impossible. "Just maybe not the list you expect," I added in a soft whisper of my own, meeting Braden's gaze. He held me in his deep blue eyes until Kellen showed up with cake. How did he do that? How did these people not see him doing it? More importantly, how did I stop him from drawing me in like that? *Don't look at him, stupid.*

I picked at my cake. It was delicious, just like everything else, but I struggled to keep my thoughts from veering towards the night's end. With Braden sitting next to me, would the king even need to do anything? The vampire could scoop me up and run, and no one would even see him. He was too fast for me to avoid, and unless I killed him in the first strike, attacking him was pointless. Our plan for escape was quickly falling apart, and I wasn't doing a good job trying to come up with something better. Maybe we should just leave early and unexpectedly. Maybe the guards down the hall wouldn't try to stop us. And maybe the ones at the portal would just let us go through. And maybe I was higher than a kite and dreaming with my head in the clouds.

The music slowed again and Kellen took my hand. "You want to dance?"

"I would love to," I replied, pushing out my chair and standing. It would be the perfect opportunity to spill the beans on Braden.

"Kellen!" Kate's voice drifted towards us as she bounced towards her brother. Her face glowed with a permanent smile. "Dance with me! We need to chat."

Kellen glanced at me, his own smile widening. His sister found her partner. It would be the only thing to cause that much happiness.

"Go ahead," I said, releasing his hand. "If she doesn't tell someone, she'll burst."

He leaned down and kissed my cheek. "I owe you so much," he said.

I blushed and watched them walk away. Kate threw her arms around her brother's neck, and he half carried her onto the dance floor. This was why we were here, to find this happiness.

"May I take his dance?" Braden's breath rustled the hair at my ear, and I tried not to react. He crushed my moment of happiness. Why was he here? I wasn't that important in the grand scheme of things. It had to about the king. Or was it? Did he want to see how many mages were no longer on his list of recruits?

"I'm not asking again," he whispered, the implied threat obvious. I didn't want him in my personal space, but I had no doubt he'd make a scene if I denied him. Did I want him to make a scene? Maybe revealing him to a roomful of mages would help me. Probably not. He'd run, taking me with him.

I slowly turned my back to the table and pushed in my chair. "Only if you keep your teeth to yourself," I hissed, cringing as he chuckled.

"Excuse us, Your Highness," Braden said as his hand brushed my lower back.

This was going to be really hard. I should change my mind. The thought of his hands on me made my skin crawl. What the hell was I thinking? Maybe I could get Kellen to interrupt our dance. Yep, that was a good plan.

He guided me to the dancefloor as another slow melody started, snaking his hand around my waist and grasping my right hand in his other. He pulled me into his hard body, regardless of my efforts to keep him away.

"You know I like it when you fight," he purred.

My blood boiled. Someone needed to kill this prick.

"Why are you here?" I snapped, keeping my voice low enough that the conversation would stay between us. "And how do these people not know what you are?"

"Smile, princess. People are watching," he replied, not at all answering my questions.

I pulled my gaze from his almost perfect features and glanced at our fellow dancers. I recognized a few of the mages but didn't know any of their names. Kellen and Kate wandered off the dance floor with another woman. Their smiles should've made me happy, but my current company stifled everything. I didn't see anyone watching us.

"What are you doing here, Braden?" I asked again.

"Would you believe me if I said I wanted to apologize to you?" he replied.

My head snapped up and his eyes caught mine. Nope, not doing that. I pulled them away and looked at his lips. They, too, were perfect.

"No. Don't waste your lies on me," I answered.

"I have never lied to you." His lips parted revealing his white teeth. Too perfect. Fangs hid behind that beautiful smile.

"Whatever," I snapped. "Insincere apologies are meaningless." He released my waist and spun me around, then immediately pulled me back to him. My eyes met his again. I needed information, but would he give it to me? "Where's your little tramp?"

"My tramp? You must be referring to the ambassador Thomas couldn't wait to reveal to you," he replied. "She found herself on the wrong side of my kindness."

I tried not to bite my bottom lip as he moved us deeper into the throng of dancers. Did that mean he'd orchestrated Thomas' visit with us? Was I right about the vampire searching for a traitor?

"So, you flushed out your traitor, then?" I asked.

He pulled me closer as the floor around us became even more crowded. Another slow ballad started. The DJ was good at picking up on the party's vibes.

"Mine and yours," he replied.

He released my hand and wrapped both arms around my waist, leaving my free hand hanging in the air. I didn't want to touch him, but knew it looked awkward. I lightly placed it on the lapel of his jacket and tried not to appreciate the softness of the expensive material.

"Bastard," I mumbled.

"I actually have a well-established bloodline, princess," he corrected.

"Tell me about 'our' traitor," I insisted, not wanting to hear about his family.

"Your command doesn't work on me," he replied. "But I'll comply because it benefits us both."

My eyes roamed from his black tie up his neck. "Please don't let me keep you from talking."

He leaned his head down next to my ear. "It would be easier if I thought I had your attention."

"Quit trying to entrance me and I might give you my attention."

He chuckled, the sound grating my nerves. It was so insincere, almost like a nervous tick.

"Fair enough," he conceded. "You force me to do this the hard way."

I looked up into his eyes and immediately noticed the difference. The pull to stay locked in them was gone. "Nothing worthwhile is ever easy," I said. "Surely you've heard that before."

"Your prince is aligned with Jack," Braden said, apparently ignoring my comment and eliciting a small gasp from me. "Smile. We're being watched."

I snapped my mouth closed and forced a smile. "How can you know that?"

"My tramp confirmed their duplicity a few hours ago," he replied.

The press of bodies against us made movement almost impossible, forcing us to sway gently from side-to-side. I stepped onto the tops of his shoes and stretched, putting my face closer to his. His eyebrows rose, and he smiled. I huffed. He was accusing the prince of conspiring against his father. We didn't need to be overheard.

"Does the king know?" I whispered.

"No. I haven't decided if I should tell him."

"Why should I believe you?" I searched his face looking for any sign of deception. Would I see it? Probably not, but it didn't hurt to try.

"I already told you. I'm here to apologize for my behavior the other night," he replied. "You caught me off guard, which won't happen again." He dipped his head closer to mine. "I need an alliance with you if we are to defeat Jack. I can't have that if you fear me."

Did I take the chance and believe him? Could I afford not to? Maybe there was a way to verify his claim. "Do I need be concerned about the king's men not allowing me to leave tonight?" I asked, baiting him to reveal his knowledge of that plan.

"Yes and no." He lifted his feet and mine spinning us in a half circle. I suspected he was avoiding someone's attention. "The king's guards won't stop you, but the prince's men plan to take you."

That really sucked. Not that Kellen and I hadn't anticipated it, but his confirmation just made everything worse. I sighed and leaned into him. His sandalwood smell wrapped around me, calming some of my nerves and pissing me off at the same time. I didn't know what to do, and I didn't want to ask this vampire.

"Thank you for telling me," I whispered, lifting my head and meeting his gaze.

"So I am forgiven for the other night?"

"Hell no!" I hissed. "You attacked me."

"I believe you attacked me first," he countered.

"I don't remember it that way," I argued. He'd taunted me, but I'd stabbed him first... not that I would admit it.

His lips curled up into a genuine smile, not that stupid smug expression he was so good at. "How was your trip through the portal?"

His sudden change of subject made me frown. "Fine, why?"

"You haven't noticed a difference trying to use it?"

"What are you getting at, Braden?" Worry settled in. He knew that I couldn't do it by myself, which meant he also knew why. How would he know that?

"That's what I thought." His head dipped closer to mine once again. His breath against my skin made me shiver. "My blood is running through you, little mage."

He kissed my neck, and I felt a small pinch. Did the bastard just bite me? And what did he mean his blood? I gasped. I'd bit the vile tongue he'd forced into my mouth. How much blood had I swallowed? Shouldn't I just piss it away or something? My body wouldn't retain it, would it?

A drumroll quickly followed by 'I love Rock-n-Roll' interrupted my panicked thoughts. Braden released me and took a step back, my feet sliding off his. His gaze held mine, but not involuntarily. I had more questions, and he knew the answers.

"Shall we get a drink?" he asked, running his tongue across his lips.

I brushed my fingers against my neck, and he laughed. The skin was smooth, my fingers coming away clean. I glowered at him. He grabbed my hand and pulled me towards a bar in the back corner of the room. I glanced at the dozens of faces around me, looking for Kellen. I hadn't seen him since Kate and her new friend led him from the dancefloor. I still couldn't find him, and I really needed to.

"Two margaritas, please," Braden said, dropping my hand.

I continued to scan the room looking for Kellen. I didn't see Kate either. Where had he gone? Could I assume he was with his sister? It made sense, but an uneasy feeling settled in my gut. A few moments later, a drink appeared in my hand.

"I'm going back to the table," I said. "And I still need answers from you."

"Any further information will come at a price, little mage," Braden said, sliding past me. "Let me clear a path for you."

He didn't wait for me to argue. Instead, he politely pushed his way through the crowd to our table. Six empty chairs greeted us. Someone had already cleared away the dinner plates, leaving only fresh glasses of water. I took my chair before Braden had a chance to pull it out for me and swept my hand beneath it looking for my small purse. I found it after several attempts and pulled out my phone. I forgot it was Logan's phone. I'd left Kellen's at the house. That wasn't a very good idea.

Braden sat next to me, turning sideways in his chair to face me. "Your partner left with his sister and another woman during our dance."

"I assumed as much," I mumbled. My brain caught up with my ears, and my head snapped up. "How do you know so much about my partner when he didn't recognize you?"

He draped his arm over the back of his chair and smiled. "There's a price for the information."

"Is there?" I set my purse and phone on the table and mimicked his pose. "What is your price?"

His smile faltered and he leaned forward, resting his elbows on his knees. "I don't deal in trivial things."

"I would be a fool to assume you did." I refrained from moving from my wanna-be-relaxed pose. "Tell me your price and I'll either accept or not."

"You're mine when we defeat Jack."

I stared at him in disbelief. No way was that happening. Absolutely not.

"No."

"I will tell you why you can no longer use your portal," he said. "As well as Thomas' plans and how they will affect your mages. I'll also reveal my knowledge of your clan, including the identity of your father." He leaned back again, assuming his original pose.

Holy shit. No one else had even hinted at knowing my father. Why did it have to be Braden? "Why would you tell me all that?" I asked, knowing he was luring me into what he wanted. But why me? What could he gain from having me? Not a leaderless North American mage community. Our own council and Kellen would be strong enough by then. The people would trust my partner if we defeated Jack. Braden had to know that.

"Because you need to know," he replied. "I've been around a very long time. Information is the only power needed to defeat my enemies."

"And I'm your enemy."

"I'm trying to make you an ally," he replied.

"By making me a slave to you." I bit back the profanity trying to escape my lips.

"No. By giving you everything you desire and even things you don't know you desire." He leaned towards me again, his eyes drawing mine but only for a second. I knew the moment he released me. "I need someone..." He frowned and looked down at his hands. I followed his gaze to his long, bony fingers. His perfectly manicured hands clamped together, turning his knuckles white. "You will never suffer at my hand or anyone else's if I can prevent it."

I wasn't sure what to think. I stared at him, dumb-founded. What could he possibly need from me that he couldn't get from anyone else? He had to know I'd never sleep with him or willingly be a blood donor. I'd take my own life before letting him turn me into a vampire.

"Why me?" I asked, leaning towards him.

"Agree to my terms and I'll tell you," he whispered, barely loud enough for me to hear.

Was that pain in his eyes? Sadness? Regret? "I can't give myself to someone who is incapable of love," I whispered back.

"Then we're done talking." He turned in his chair and picked up his margarita, taking a long sip.

I bit my lip, considering things I shouldn't. His offer wouldn't be temporary. I'd be his forever, unless I could kill him. The consequences for taking his life would not be good, assuming I could even do it. Shit, shit, shit. Curiosity was about to kill the cat.

"Twenty-four hours," I said. "I will be yours for twenty-four hours, but only if we defeat Jack."

He glanced at me and set his glass on the table. I expected his smug expression, but it wasn't what I got. His brows furrowed and a red ring circled his blue eyes. "This oath is unbreakable, Alisandra. Don't go into this lightly."

"Will you tell me what you intend to do with my twenty-four hours?" I asked, my composure slipping rapidly. I still had time to back out. Did I really need to know everything he offered? No and yes.

"I will only bring you pleasure," he replied.

I scoffed, searching for any sign of the lie that had to be there. I couldn't find one.

"So, a full day of pleasure for me along with all the information promised by you?" I asked. "Someone's getting the wrong end of the stick, and I'm pretty sure it has to be me."

"You won't be the only one being pleasured."

His smile finally emerged, and it didn't take a genius to figure out what he meant. Okay, maybe it wasn't worth it. Would I seriously whore myself out for a whole day just to get information from this guy? No, I wouldn't. Logan would hate me, and I'd despise myself even more.

I glanced around the room. The center was still full of dancing men and women, but most of the tables were empty. Thomas and his father were nowhere in sight, neither were my partner or Kate. That still worried me. He wouldn't leave without me, would he? That had been the plan, but he was supposed to let me know before he went. Was Braden keeping me distracted while Thomas arranged my kidnapping?

"I can't," I finally said. "I wouldn't be able to look at myself in the mirror if I whored myself out just to gain information."

Braden laughed, his amusement reaching every part of his face. I blushed. That wasn't funny. My image of myself was important. I'd finally started liking the person in the mirror. I wasn't about to destroy all that.

"I wasn't talking about sex," he said, still smiling. "I wouldn't object to it obviously, but there are other forms of pleasure that are just as satisfying."

"Really?"

He laughed again, and my frown deepened. What the hell was he talking about?

"Do we have an agreement, now that your virtue will still be intact?"

"I still don't know what I'm agreeing to," I said shaking my head. "What do you expect from me for twenty-four hours?"

He stretched his hands towards me across the table, palms up.

"You already know what I like," he whispered. "I will give you a full day to torture me anyway you wish. With only one stipulation. You cannot kill me."

Holy shit. Could I really stab this man for an entire day? Maybe. Probably. My eyes danced from his hands to his face and back again. I was trying to find the downside. Having an outlet for my rage and frustration would be amazing. But that would also make me a demented sadist, wouldn't it? Maybe not. We wouldn't be having sex, just torture. I shivered. No, I don't think I could hurt him without a reason.

"Last chance," he whispered, pulling his hands back. "I've already revealed more than is good for me."

Damn. "Alright." I held my hand out to him intending to seal our deal with a handshake.

He placed his palm on his knee just below the edge of the table. I choked down my gasp as he drew a strange symbol in his palm with the single claw from his opposite hand. My eyes widened as I looked up at him. Would he do the same to me? I was allergic to pain. He nodded, and I gave him my shaking hand.

He lifted my palm to his lips, then his fangs sank into my skin. I clamped my mouth shut, expecting pain. There was nothing, not even a pinch, just an odd sensation from the intrusion. How did he do that? It only lasted for a moment before he lowered my hand. Two small punctures remained, my blood pooling from them. He closed his bleeding palm over mine and bumped my chin with his free hand. His eyes drew mine.

"I will tell you about your father and your clan. I will also reveal what I know of Thomas' plans with Jack. And I will tell you why you cannot use your mage portal."

I stared at his blue eyes, wondering what the hell I'd gotten myself into. Where the hell was my partner to stop me? He's supposed to keep me from doing stupid shit. Like this.

"Tell me what you are giving me, little mage," Braden whispered.

I blinked several times. "I will gladly inflict pain on you for twenty-four hours, after we defeat Jack," I whispered.

The whites of his eyes disappeared, swallowed by a red so dark it was nearly black. It consumed his blue irises, and fear replaced my indecision. I was in so much trouble.

Pain surged through my palm, raced up my arm, and slammed into my heart. It stuttered several times, and I gasped.

"Come, we have much to discuss." Braden pulled me to my feet, and my knees gave out.

"What did you do to me?" I tried to sink back into my chair, but he wouldn't let me, holding me up by my arms.

"It's a blood oath, and my blood is very strong," he replied, like I should know what he was talking about. Whatever.

"I need a minute," I hissed. My legs felt like jelly, and my heart still stuttered.

Göksu?

I can't help you with this, child.

You should've interrupted the whole thing and told me not to be a dumbass!

I thought I heard him chuckle. Stupid elemental.

"We really need to go if you intend to save your partner," Braden said, shifting his weight and gripping my arm.

"What do you mean, save my partner?" My heart stuttered again, and I clamped my hand over my chest. Damn, that hurt.

Braden scooped me up in his arms, and the room blurred by. "Thomas has betrayed his father and kidnapped your partner," he whispered, racing from the room and down the long corridor. We sped past the portal room and through a narrow archway. "He plans to kill Kellen and force you to marry him. As soon as the union is complete, he will kill his father."

"What makes him think I would ever marry him?" I asked. "I can rule our mages without Kellen. I don't need Thomas."

We quickly descended a flight of steps and Braden stopped at a solid wooden door at the bottom. "He will take Logan and force you to cooperate." He set me on my feet but didn't let go. "He'll use your love as a tool to weaken you."

Several emotions flickered through me. Had Logan and I been that obvious when Thomas was at the palace? "Does Thomas know what Logan is?"

"No."

"I'd like to keep it that way," I said.

"I agree. Revealing myself or my people has never been part of my plan." He reached for the old, metal door knob, but paused.

The pain in my chest surged again, and I couldn't stop the whimper escaping my lips. "Is it supposed to do this?"

"No. I can hear your heart struggling." His hand hovered over my chest, and his eyes met mine. "May I?"

"Whatever," I muttered. "Why does it hurt?"

"Have you had another vampire's blood?" he asked.

My thoughts immediately went to Logan. I assumed Braden knew, but maybe not.

"Yes, but it's been awhile," I answered, the warmth of his hand on my skin made me shudder. I forced myself to take slow breaths.

"How much did you drink?" He tilted my chin, forcing me to look at him.

"I don't know. I wasn't exactly coherent when it happened."

His eyes danced across my face and I suspected he looked for a lie. "My blood should be strong enough to override his. Not many vampires are as old as I am." He reached for the door again. "Your heart rate has settled. Let's go."

I wasn't sure what to think of his comment. Did that mean my bond to Logan would be broken? I hoped not. Would it kill us if it did? I *really* hoped not. Man, was I stupid.

"You and I should have no difficulties freeing your partner. Thomas and his crew are not very strong," Braden said. "But we should avoid using any vampire traits on the guards that will be with him."

"I don't want to kill anyone," I said. "We'll disable them and let their justice system take care of the rest."

A raised eyebrow was his only reply before he pushed open the door. A dank hallway greeted us, the smell of mold and urine included. The same intermittent sconces hung from the walls.

"A dungeon? Seriously?" I shook my head and followed Braden down the hall.

The dirt floor covered the sound of my shoes, and the moss-covered walls dampened everything else. Braden didn't have to warn me about the voices filtering through the thick air in front of us. One was definitely Thomas, but I didn't recognize the other.

"Is he secured?" Thomas asked.

"Yes, Your Highness," the man answered.

"Good, we'll deal with him after I escort the princess home."

I grabbed Braden's jacket and pulled on it as I backed up. We passed by several doors on our way down the hall. We could hide and let the little bastard pass, then rescue Kellen. Braden didn't move.

Damn vampire.

Chapter 27

I pushed past the stubborn vampire. I needed to try to settle this with words before we devolved into violence. Braden might have the self-control to fight like a normal person, but I didn't. Not to mention, I didn't want to kill a fellow mage.

"Thomas," I called out, the damp walls swallowing my voice.

He stopped a few yards away, blinking and squinting at me. "Alisandra?"

"We can stop this now, before it goes any farther," I said, not advancing towards him.

"Is that Braden with you?"

I didn't miss the fact that he called the vampire by his real name. I should've known better. If he was working with Jack, then he would know Braden. How did I not see his lies? Did that mean Jack also knew about Braden's intentions?

"Does it matter?" I asked. "Will it change anything you're doing?"

"No, but it will change my report to Jack," he replied, a sneer spreading across his face. "He knew there was a traitor, but he couldn't figure out who." Thomas stepped towards me, and two men followed in his wake. "I never would've suspected him, though. He's the golden boy."

The kindness I once connected to Thomas was now gone, but so was the modicum of trust I'd placed in the vampire at my side. Jack's golden boy? I hesitated in my decision, something I really needed to work on. Braden's fingers wrapped around my arm, and he wasn't gentle.

"What makes you think Jack would put his trust in a simple human?" Braden asked. "Had it not occurred to you that I was keeping her busy while you and eight others secured her partner?"

Thomas snorted. "So, what, you're here to make sure the job is done?"

"Again, why would Jack trust you with something so important?" Braden sneered. "Besides, it's not like you can kill them."

"And you can?" The prince's voice rose with his indignation. "She destroyed Sergey's entire army and half of Ernesto's!"

"One doesn't become the favorite by accident," the vampire hissed. "Where is Kellen?"

Thomas pointed back down the hall. "Last door on the left."

Before I realized what happened, Braden tossed me over his shoulder and raced down the hall. My mind raced with him. Was it all an act? Had our blood oath meant nothing to him? If he killed me, did it erase the oath? I should've asked that. Fear seeped through my stupidity. Braden implied he would kill us both. Were we sprinting to my death?

I gasped.

It would be Logan's too and he wasn't even here to defend himself.

"Thank you for playing along," Braden whispered, setting me down in front of the last door. "Keep it up for a few more minutes."

I nodded, but my fear didn't subside.

"I promised not to hurt you, remember?" he asked.

I nodded again, but had a hard time believing him. I didn't feel any deception from him, but I hadn't felt it from Thomas either. And look where that got me.

"You should try to resist being captured," he suggested.

Duh. What the hell was wrong with me? I was scared to death, that's what.

I kicked his shin, making him roll his eyes. He grabbed my arm and spun me around, pinning my back against his chest. "Make it beautiful, little mage," he breathed in my ear.

My stomach folded into a million knots. He wanted me to hurt him, but could I?

"Don't force me to make you angry."

"You'll have to," I hissed. "I can't just stab you."

"Do you know what happens if I bite you and inject my venom into your veins?" His lips brushed my neck, and I tensed.

"Of course I do."

"Then why aren't you trying to stop me?" His breath on my neck made my heart race and not in a bad way. *What the hell?* His fangs punching through skin and muscle snuffed out everything except my fear and memories of the last vampire who tried to turn me.

I drew forth my short spear and drove it through Braden's thigh, but he didn't release his grip or his fangs. I pulled another weapon from the air, stabbing his other leg. His mouth withdrew from my neck with a howling laugh and he threw me into the air. I squealed as my head brushed the low ceiling. Before I realized I was falling, his arms wrapped around me again, this time pinning my elbows at my sides. My face was inches from his, and there was no missing the dark red eyes piercing mine.

"More," he whispered.

I hadn't released the first two weapons still protruding from his legs. I was tempted to pull the blood from his body but couldn't bring myself to do it. If he really was an ally, I shouldn't kill him, but there were too many mixed signals. This man was demented, yet somehow I was supposed to trust him. No, I was cooperating, not trusting.

Do you need my help, princess? Niyol asked, a strong breeze whipping down the damp hall. It was probably the first time the dungeon had seen fresh air in ages.

I don't think so, Niyol, but if it looks like he's going to hurt me, then by all means, jump in.

As the wind settled, I focused on creating a protective shield between me and Braden. A thin bubble of water rose from my feet, surging up my legs. It stopped when it reached the resistance between me and my capturer. I pushed harder, forcing it between us. Braden's eyes widened when he finally noticed the thin barrier.

"Impressive," he murmured a smile spreading across his face.

"Hold her, Braden!" Thomas yelled, finally catching up with us. "Oh shit! Unlock the door. Hurry before she gets away!" he shouted at the nearest guard.

The man fumbled with the keys, and Braden's grip loosened around me, probably on purpose. I summoned two small shards of air, fisting one in each hand. My half-assed barrier fell away, leaving a puddle on the already damp floor.

"Do your worst, princess," the vampire whispered, then licked the side of my neck.

Heat raced across my skin, and I pulled back both my arms as far as he would allow, then drove my weapons into his sides. They sliced through his jacket and shirt with ease, finding his flesh beneath. His head fell back as he screamed, but rather than let go of me, he crushed my body against his, driving the small weapons deeper. There was no way to avoid noticing his obvious desire pressing against my middle. He didn't scream in anguish, but in ecstasy. My face flushed, but I wasn't sure if it was anger or embarrassment. I twisted my weapons deeper into his sides, hoping to derail his passion. No such luck. His bulge throbbed against my lower stomach. What had I agreed to? Would I ever hurt him, or would it always be pleasure for him?

"Quick, take her inside!" Thomas yelled.

The panic in his voice almost made me laugh. Who was he afraid of? Me or the monster carrying me?

Braden stomped into the cell, not stopping until we reached the back wall. He slammed me into it hard enough to be convincing, but not really hurting me. His arms took most of the impact.

"My timeline just moved up," he whispered. "I will have my full day with you sooner rather than later."

"You're disgusting," I hissed.

He smiled, revealing the fangs hanging below his lip. "I'm a vampire," he purred.

He snatched both my wrists with one hand and pulled them over my head, then turned towards the prince still lingering at the door. "You have restraints for her, I assume?"

"Oh, yes." Thomas waved at the guards who slowly made their way across the room. A single torch hanging beside the door lit the space, leaving dark shadows in the farthest corners. The thought of being chained to the wall terrified me. I'd be at their mercy. Would Braden really allow them to do it? I struggled against his hold, kicking out at him but failing to connect. His grip tightened and he pulled me higher. My feet barely touched the ground, and my shoulders screamed with the strain.

"I will kill you!" I bellowed. "How dare you think you can do this to me. Where is Kellen?"

Thomas' eyes darted to my left. I followed his gaze, and my heart dropped. My partner hung from chains connected to his wrists. The beautiful suit he wore to the party was mostly gone, and what was left was ruined. The only thing that remained was his dark trousers and leather shoes. Deep cuts crossed his exposed chest and dark bruises circled his waist. His chin rested against his collar, and he didn't move despite my yelling.

"You better hope he's still alive," I warned. "Because if he's not, my wrath will be unending."

"You'll do nothing when I bring your vampire lover down here to hang next to him," the prince snapped, raising his chin as if his fight was already won. Arrogant bastard.

"Did you hear nothing I said to you at the palace?" I asked.

His haughty look wavered. "If your elements cared for you the way you claimed, where are they now?"

The guards stopped halfway across the room, uncertainty wavering in their expressions.

"Do you really want that answer?" I asked in return. "I'm giving you a chance to walk away alive, except for him." I kicked at Braden's legs, but he dodged it easily. "He will die. I'll give you the opportunity to change your ways and prove your loyalty. But that offer ends in ten seconds."

"You don't understand, Alisandra," Thomas suddenly pleaded. "There's no way to win against them." He pointed at Braden, his finger shaking wildly. "We need to join the winning side or be slaughtered with the losers."

I shook my head. Was there anything I could say to change his mind? Not likely, especially with Braden in the room pretending to be the enemy.

Niyol? Göksu? Will you help me?

Of course, child. I assume the vampire is an ally? my water elemental asked.

Just for today, I replied.

The cell door slammed shut and a thick layer of ice sealed it. The three mages jumped and spun towards the door.

"Last chance, Thomas," I said.

The tension on my shoulders eased as Braden moved behind me, pulling my hands and his down around my waist. Did he just make me a human shield?

"You aren't supposed to kill her, vampire," Thomas squeaked, frantically glancing between me and the frozen door.

"You think to command me?" Braden asked. "Your heart is too weak to command your own men. You could never control me."

The vampire's grip tightened around me as my elementals took form. The prince's pale face blanched to white when Niyol bore down on him.

"Protect your prince, you fools!" he screamed.

A rock wall sprung from the ground between Niyol and Thomas. I laughed at the idiocy. Niyol vanished, three tornados taking his place. The mages ran in opposite directions while my elemental chased them around the large cell, corralling them into a corner.

Göksu went to Kellen, and I elbowed Braden.

"Let me go," I hissed.

"We will have to kill the prince and his minions," the vampire said, relaxing his hold but not releasing me. "They cannot tell Jack what has transpired here."

"Whatever, you can just erase their memory." I said, elbowing his ribs again. Logan had done it to me, surely Braden could do it to them. "Now let go."

"And your elementals will not harm me?"

"No, not unless you piss me off," I grunted, nodding in Niyol's direction. One by one, the mages slammed against the wall and stuck like fly paper. "Why do you think he's just toying with them? They aren't a threat."

"Just toying?"

Braden's arms fell away, and I rushed to Kellen's side. He still hung from his chains, but it didn't stop Göksu from healing the lacerations across his skin.

"He has broken ribs and possibly a concussion," my elemental said.

"Then we'll heal his ribs before we release him," I stated, placing my hands against his dark skin.

Göksu's watery hand covered mine, and we pushed waves of healing into my partner. Loud cracks and pops elicited a pained groan from Kellen. My eyes darted from his chest to his face. He looked down at me beneath heavy eyelids.

"AJ?" he mumbled.

I ran my fingers up his neck and gently cupped the sides of his face. Bruises covered his left cheek, and I swallowed my anger for the prince.

"I'm here, and we're taking you home," I said.

His eyes closed for a moment then popped open again. "Thomas did this."

I placed my fingers over his lips. "I know. I'll take care of it."

He laughed softly. "My little partner saving my ass."

"Well, we can't all be perfect," I quipped. "Now be still so we can get you out of these chains."

"Yes, princess," he murmured.

His eyes drooped again, and I spun around, running into Braden's chest.

"Move!" I commanded, pushing against him and looking for Niyol and his prisoners.

He took half a step and stopped. I huffed and looked up at him, immediately frowning at his stupid grin.

"I said, move."

He stepped back and bowed. "Of course, princess."

I mumbled a curse and crossed the space to the three mages plastered to the wall by Niyol's torrent.

"Give me the keys." I commanded again, holding my hand out the guards.

"I can't move," one of the men said through the corner of his mouth.

"Which pocket?" I asked.

"Right thigh," he replied.

I closed the space between us and opened the cargo pocket on his thigh, retrieving a key chain with only two keys. I sprinted back to my partner and quickly realized I couldn't reach the lock above his wrists.

"Well, shit."

I turned back to Braden, just as he pulled his jacket from his shoulders. Blood stained his white shirt just above his belt. A moment of guilt assaulted me, but it didn't last. He'd asked for it, then enjoyed it.

"Unlock his chains," I said, holding the keys out to him.

Before he could protest my command, the ground beneath us shook. Braden was by my side instantly, keeping me from falling. Why? It's not like he was capable of caring.

"The vampire will not touch him," a low, rumbling voice said from behind me.

Braden's eyes widened. Was that fear? I slowly turned to find the wide stone form of Kellen's earth elemental standing between me and my partner. Everything else in the room was immediately forgotten.

"Really? Where the hell were you when these mages beat the shit out of my partner?" I bellowed. "You and that damn fire elemental abandoned him when he needed you! You should feel nothing but shame for your actions."

The accused fire elemental flared into existence at earth's side, brightening the room. "How dare you insult me!"

"How dare you let this happen to your mage and then have the audacity to deny someone who would help him." I glared at the two of them, allowing my anger to overrun my fear of the two deadly beings standing in front of me. "Get out of my way."

"I will release my mage, princess." The earth elemental reached up with his stone hand and forced apart the iron links of Kellen's chain. My partner fell into the elemental's waiting arms. "We are not allowed to act against another mage without consent," he rumbled.

"Are you telling me Kellen forbid you to protect him?" I asked, not believing that bullshit.

"No, he was unconscious the entire time. He could not give his consent."

My hands fisted at my sides, my neck growing hot. I swiveled around to face the prince with nothing but death on my mind.

"You did this to him while he was unconscious?" I asked, closing the space between myself and the other mages. I shook with uncontrolled fury. "You cowards! You filthy, disgusting, cowards!"

Tears pooled in Thomas' eyes, but I knew it was fear, not regret or remorse. Two shards of glass appeared in my hands, the edges slicing my palms from my grip. Who does that shit? How can someone be so heartless? A vampire, sure. Not a mage.

"Please Alisandra," the prince whispered, his eyes darting from my hands to my face.

Too quick for him to see, I embedded the blades in each of his palms, shattering the bones. He screamed in agony, and I spun around on my heels. My entire body trembled with my rage. What was wrong with these people? The mages, the vampires, and even the damn elementals.

"All of you disgust me!" I roared. "Whose consent do you need to protect him? His or mine?"

Kellen moaned, and my anger abated. I rushed to him, still in earth's stony arms.

"Kellen?" His eyelids fluttered with my voice. "Tell them to protect you, please." I ran my fingers over his brow and kissed his cheek.

"Why the hell would I have to tell them that?" he mumbled, his eyes barely opening. Definitely a concussion, probably severe.

"That was my thought, too, but apparently they can't think for themselves," I replied.

"Yes, protection is good." His eyes fell shut again, but his hand reached for me. I took his fingers in mine, and he sighed.

"Get him to the palace and make sure they do whatever is necessary to heal him," I commanded, not taking my eyes from his face.

"Yes, princess," the earth elemental said, moving toward the door. Kellen's fingers slid from my hand.

Large chunks of ice crashed to floor, then the door swung open. The stone giant with my partner disappeared into the hall. He would be okay. He had to be. Despite the nonsense I spouted to Braden, I couldn't lead the mages without Kellen.

A wave of heat brushed my back, and I spun around just in time to see a wall of fire smashing into Thomas and his two guards. The flames consumed them before they had a chance to cry out. I twirled again, looking for Braden and was surprised by my relief to see him standing by the door. He raised an eyebrow at me but remained silent.

"We needed them alive," I spat, turning my rage on the fire elemental.

Flames surged around its humanoid form and its black eyes narrowed at me. "No, you don't. Four other mages participated in this," it said. "They will confess to their king when they realize the prince is dead."

"You will protect my partner," I ordered. "Just don't be stupid about the threat."

"If Earth had not stopped me earlier, all seven of them would've died before my mage sustained those injuries." His intensity waned. "But I might have misjudged your elder vampire."

"Yeah." I glanced over my shoulder at Braden. "I'm still on the fence about that one, too, but he's kept his word so far. Until that changes, he isn't a threat."

Braden leaned against the broken door frame with his jacket draped over his arm and smiled. How did he find any of this humorous? I shook my head. This whole day sucked. Why couldn't I just enjoy a great party? Because I wasn't destined to enjoy anything, it seemed.

"Go with your mage and make sure he arrives at the palace. I still have to deal with the king."

"Thank you, princess." The fire elemental disappeared in a puff of smoke, leaving me alone with Niyol, Göksu, and Braden.

Niyol's wispy form fluttered around me ruffling my hair and cooling the stifling air. He solidified in front of me and tilted his head. "I wasn't included in your disgust, was I?"

I smiled, exhaustion replacing my anger. "No. I love you too much for that," I replied. "I'm sorry for losing my head."

He wrapped his arms around me, and I fell into his soft touch. It was like hugging a fluffy pillow. Göksu's soothing embrace joined Niyol's, and my anger fell away.

Thank you, I said to my best friends.

What do you need from us, child?

Where is Logan? I asked, needing to know he was safe.

I believe he's at home, Göksu replied.

Can you stay with him? I knew it was an unfair question. My water elemental shouldn't be my vampire's keeper, but I couldn't help it.

Of course, child.

Thank you. I can't tell you how much it means to me.

You don't have to. I already know.

Our little huddle broke up, and Göksu cascaded into the floor. Niyol looked over my shoulder, and I turned to face Braden.

"I can kill him for you, Alisandra," Niyol said, drifting towards the vampire.

Braden's eyes widened, but he didn't back away.

"What's wrong, Braden? Don't like the thought of being tortured by my elemental?" I teased, letting a smile cross my face.

He glanced at me, then Niyol. "Not especially, no."

My elemental disappeared in a violent gust of wind, dragging the burned ashes of the three mages into the air. I covered my face with my hands and held my breath. I did not want to inhale someone's ashes. The thought made me queasy and I headed for the door.

"That's not funny, Niyol," I grumbled. "We'll find something to kill later."

"A blood-thirsty elemental?" Braden mumbled, following me into the hall. "I didn't think anything could surprise me, but you've proven me wrong several times today."

"That's me," I muttered. "Full of surprises."

"Do you always take him out to satisfy his need to kill?"

"No," I replied, hurrying along the musty corridor. "He's just grumpy because I denied him a perfectly good vampire. He'll feel better when I give him another."

Braden's intake of breath made me stop and spin around. His surprised expression was laced with concern.

"Truly?" he asked.

I giggled. "No, but seeing your expression was so worth the lie."

"And you call me demented."

"You are demented."

I quickened my pace down the hall and away from the death behind me. Being out of the immediate area forced me to think about what happened. The prince was dead. It didn't matter that someone else killed him. I still carried the guilt. How was I going to tell the king what Thomas had done? Would he believe me? I wouldn't if I were in his shoes. I shivered, not just from the dampness surrounding me, but from having to tell a father that his son was a traitor.

Without realizing it, my pace slowed to a stop before I even reached the wooden door leading to the stairwell.

"We need to discuss the story we present to the king," Braden said, draping his jacket over my shoulders. "I know you want to leave, but this is probably the best place to do that."

I almost tossed his coat on the floor, but its warmth felt good. It'd be stupid to suffer just because I despised this man. I'd already made enough stupid decisions for one day.

"How do I tell the king that I killed his son?" I asked.

"You didn't kill him," Braden replied. "The fire elemental did in defense of Kellen."

"And your stab wounds?" I glanced at his blood-stained outfit. "We aren't hiding that."

"Obtained while defending you, of course. I should've known I didn't stand a chance against a mage, being a mere human myself. You healed me before we left the dungeon," he responded. "The only lie we tell is my involvement. I'd like to keep my business association intact. It's quite lucrative."

I pulled his coat tighter around my shoulders. I wasn't good at this part. Kellen was supposed to be the political guru, not me. And I hated depending on a vampire I didn't trust. I'd already made too many bad decisions where he was concerned. The violence I inflicted on him tied my stomach in knots. I shouldn't be capable of that.

"Shit," I mumbled, leaning against the slimy wall behind me, unconcerned with the mold rubbing off onto my clothes. Braden's blood covered my dress, and clumps of stinking mud clung to my no-longer-white shoes. "You and I still have stuff to talk about. I'm just not sure I have the energy to do it today. This discussion with William won't go well."

"It'll go better than you expect," he assured me. "I believe he already suspected his son's traitorous nature, but there are two things that worry me. First, is the king's early departure from the meeting. Did Thomas already kill his father?" He waved two long fingers in the air. "The second is his decision to reveal his son's actions or cover them up."

"Oh, God. So how is that smoother than I expect?"

"I don't think he'll immediately strike out against us." He held his hand out to me, the same one we'd made our bargain with. I stared at the smooth skin that showed no signs of our blood oath. "Let's take care of the king, then we'll talk."

I pushed away from the wall and ignored his hand. His fake kindness worried me. I'd seen how vile he could be. I didn't want to fall into a sense of ease with him. He chuckled, that irritating laugh that meant nothing.

"Back to cold acquaintances again, are we?" he asked, following me the short distance to the door. "After all the passion we just experienced together."

I spun on him, my anger surging to the surface again. "I have no passion for you," I hissed, "only loathing."

He licked his bottom lip, deliberately showing his fangs. "Your body said something different."

"Whatever!" I snatched the door open and raced up the steps. I'd felt nothing but disgust and anger when we fought. Maybe a tiny of bit satisfaction being able to stab someone I despised without him trying to kill me for it. Definitely not pleasure of any kind, though. The thought of finding pleasure in doing something so morbid made me sick. It was not who I wanted to be.

I didn't slow when I reached the main hall still lined with guards. It would be a good opportunity to find out if they saw me. I sped by them, not stopping until I reached the door to the party room, flinging it open and stopping just inside the door. Yet again, another bad decision. The guards next to me startled, then wrinkled their noses at the lovely smell I knew wafted from my filthy clothes. I should've just kept running. Braden flew past me into the room.

"Princess, are you okay?" the nearest guard asked, his eyes roaming up and down my body.

I looked down at Braden's bloody coat hanging almost to my knees. "No and yes," I replied. "Where is King William?"

"He went to his chambers earlier."

"I need to see him immediately," I said. "I prefer to keep our conversation private for obvious reasons." Braden appeared at my side, emerging from the party room. Gasps and loud voices followed him. I rolled my eyes. "As soon as possible."

The guard's expression turned fearful at the vampire's blood-stained shirt. "Is he okay?"

"Yes," I snapped. "Take me to King William, now." Braden let me push him into the hall and close the door, sealing out the curious onlookers. He held out my purse, and I couldn't stop the gratitude in my brief smile. He didn't have to do that, damn vampire.

"Yes, princess," the guard stammered. "Follow me."

Chapter 28

I paced across the large anteroom the guard left us in. Braden leaned against a darkened windowsill. The entire space felt like a museum. Anything I touched would've been ruined, and I couldn't even think about putting my filthy butt on the antique furniture.

"Calm down, little mage," Braden murmured. "It's only been five minutes."

"Whatever. I just want to get this over with," I grumbled. "I need a shower and clean clothes and a soft bed to sink into and forget any of this ever happened."

I rolled my phone over in my hand looking at the blank screen, like I'd done a hundred times already. I'd texted Logan as soon as we got in this room, but he hadn't replied. My anxiety ratcheted another notch. He always replied right away. Had the prince's goons already taken him? I doubted it. A couple mages wouldn't catch Logan.

"No word?"

"Obviously."

"Logan is too smart to get caught," he continued.

How did he know I texted Logan? I hadn't said anything. I glowered at my companion and started pacing again. I really needed to get past my bad mood before the king showed up. I couldn't have this conversation as scatterbrained as I was right now.

I plopped down on the floor and folded my legs beneath me, not caring if my dress covered anything or not. Okay, I did care. I smoothed out my rumpled skirt, then closed my eyes. The air in the room had a faint floral scent mixed with wood polish and sandalwood. My own musty dirt and blood tainted the pleasant smells making my nose wrinkle. I pushed away the distasteful thought, completely closing my mind to the unpleasantness.

The guards mumbled outside the door of our room, but I couldn't make out their words. Heavy footsteps and slamming drawers came from the king's chambers along with muffled complaints. The sound of shifting fabric and soft leather against the carpet gave away Braden's movement.

I think the king may know more than he lets on, Niyol's voice whispered in my mind.

Really?

Yes, he and his guard are discussing his son's disappearance into the dungeons. He doesn't know his son's fate but expects bad news from you.

Lovely. Thanks, Niyol.

I opened my eyes, not surprised to find Braden standing in front of me.

"The king is suspicious," I whispered as quietly as I could.

"I assumed he would be," the vampire said. "We should not be sitting when he finally joins us."

"You can stand if you like, but I need to clear my mind," I disagreed. "I'm stressing out and I don't' care if he knows it. I've had a really shitty day."

"It's all about perception, Alisandra. He is still king, and you are a queen. Don't allow him to see you weak."

I looked up at him and frowned, hating that he might be right. Stupid vampire. I pushed myself to my feet and shrugged his coat off my shoulders. "Here." I held it out to him and leaned into his space. "And my name is AJ, especially to someone I have to torture mercilessly."

He took his jacket and smiled, that genuine smile that only showed up when he thought he was winning. I wasn't sure how I figured it out, but that's exactly what it was. When he made that stupid comment about my mysterious father, that smile showed up, then again when he knew I'd finally given in to his blood oath.

The opening door made both of us turn. King William finally graced us with his presence, dressed in khaki pants and a light blue shirt buttoned all the way to the top. A spotted bowtie would've completed the look, but I guess the king didn't think so. I found it odd that he wasn't wearing the beautiful suit from the party. We hadn't been gone that long.

His eyes widened at our less than stellar appearance. "Are you hurt?"

"Not anymore, but my partner wasn't as lucky," I replied. "He's returned to the palace for further care."

William's eyes drifted to Braden, then back to me. "And my business partner? Why is he part of this?"

"Do you know what *this* is?" I asked, not answering his question.

His white eyebrows drew together and the wrinkles on his face sagged, making him look very old. "Let's sit."

He didn't wait for me to acknowledge him as he moved to a seating arrangement facing an enormous stone fireplace. He dropped into a wing-backed chair, leaving a small settee available for me and Braden.

"Are you sure?" I asked, standing next to the beautifully upholstered sofa. "I'll likely ruin your furniture."

He waved a hand at me as if the furniture were irrelevant. "Is my son dead?"

His question startled me, making me sort of hover over the cushion. Braden poked my leg, and I sat.

"Yes," I replied. I should've added condolences, but I couldn't bring myself to utter the words. I wasn't sorry that the stupid shit was gone.

"He did this to you?" William asked, staring at the empty fireplace.

"Yes." I considered what to say next. The man kept his emotions tightly controlled. The permanent smile I'd grown used to seeing was nowhere in sight. "Do you want to know what happened?"

"No, but I have no choice," he replied. "I know he's betrayed his people and his family."

I gave him an abbreviated version of our discovery in the basement and the ensuing fight. William's head fell back against his chair when I finally got to his son's death at the fire elemental's hand. Silence blanketed the room, and I glanced at Braden. For once, his smug expression was gone, and he at least pretended to grieve for the king.

"I'm sorry, Your Highness," I said quietly. "This was supposed to be a happy day for our people."

"This is not your fault, Alisandra." He turned his head towards me and tears swelled in my eyes. "These events have been brewing for decades. You just happened to be the catalyst for all of it to unravel." He leaned forward, dropping his head into his palms. "I think today was happy for our mages. I've heard of so many finding their potential partner, Kellen's sister included. She and my niece are spending tonight in the castle. Like many others, they hope to do their bonding ceremony tomorrow."

"Wow, that soon?" I didn't hide the surprise in my voice.

"Did you not know immediately that Kellen was your partner?" he asked, pulling his face from his hands and looking at me.

"That's debatable," I replied. "In hindsight, yes. At the time, I was too stubborn to admit it."

His genuine smile only lasted a moment. "Humility is so rare nowadays, yet you put yours on full display."

I blushed, pretty certain it wasn't a compliment. "Is there anything I can do for you before I leave?"

"No, but please give my apologies to your betrothed," he replied. "I hope we are able to get past the treachery my son has wrought."

"Do you wish for me to stay, Your Highness?" Braden asked, surprising me with the amount of sympathy in his voice.

"Branden, my apologies extend to you as well," William said, his despair deepening. "I truly hope this doesn't threaten our professional relationship."

"You've always been more than generous with my representatives, Your Highness," Braden replied. "Had one of them been here, the outcome may have been different. In which case, I might not have been so understanding. Most of my associates are not aware of your special abilities." He dared to put a hand on my knee, and I forced myself not to react. "But, had it not been for the princess, I would have died tonight. I owe her a great deal."

I wasn't sure what to make of his little speech. I didn't miss the implied threat, nor did I miss the importance he put on my well-being. Men were so confusing.

Braden rose, and I stood with him.

"Can I have your guards send someone in?" the vampire asked.

"No, but thank you."

Braden bowed slightly and took my elbow, pulling me towards the door. The king didn't stand or see us out, not that I expected him to. I wasn't sure how I would handle the news he just received. Life was so unfair. I let my escort pull me through the long hall, then down the sweeping steps leading to the next floor.

My phone buzzed in my purse and I fumbled to get it out. Logan's name greeted me, relieving some of my anxiety.

Logan: Where are you?
AJ: Still at the castle.
Logan: How are you getting home?

"Well shit," I mumbled.

AJ: I'm working on it. Where are you?
Logan: Not at the palace.

"Can you walk and text?" Braden asked, grabbing my elbow. "We still have a lot to do tonight."
I glared at him.

AJ: Give me ten minutes. Be safe. Bad shit happened tonight and you're part of the threat.
Logan: I know.

The impatient vampire at my side jerked my arm, pulling me farther down the hall.
"You could be nice about it," I hissed.
"We need to leave, before William decides this is your fault," he hissed back.
My eyes widened. I wanted to deny his claim, but anger was part of grieving. William would want to blame someone eventually. We hurried down another flight of stairs opening into a beautiful foyer. Shiny hardwood floors blanketed the space, and tall portraits covered the walls. My escort pulled me away from them and nodded at the guards posted on each side of two large doors. One of them nodded back and let us out.

A cold, wet wind smacked me in the face, and a burst of lightning lit the night sky. A peal of thunder quickly followed. How did we not hear this storm inside the castle? Was the whole thing soundproof, or was that some kind of magic? Probably magic.

"You better have a car here," I muttered. Freezing raindrops pelted my skin, instantly making my teeth chatter. When Braden's warm coat covered my shoulders, I didn't protest.

"Keep up, or I'll carry you," Braden said, walking along a wide circular drive.

A hundred yards away, two headlights broke through the darkness closing the space between us quickly. Braden opened the back door when it stopped beside him and all but threw me in.

"Take us to the penthouse," he ordered. "I need to get out of these clothes."

I huffed and pulled my phone back out of my purse, then scooted to the far side of his fancy sedan.

AJ: Are you okay?
Logan: Yes, I'm home.

Relief flooded through me. He should be safe at his house. There was little chance Thomas knew where it was. The house may have been small and remote and may have needed a damn TV, but at least it would keep my vampire safe.

AJ: Good. I'll get there as soon as I can
Logan: Be careful. There are too many people looking for you right now. I don't think you should go back to the palace.

What was he saying? How was the palace not safe for me? Duh, because Thomas' men had free access to the portals. Shit! Kellen wasn't safe either.

AJ: Is Kellen okay?
Logan: Yes, he's under guard in our medical facility.
AJ: Ok, good. Don't trust anyone coming from the castle.
Logan: Don't text me where you're going, princess.

I stared at his text. What was he trying to tell me? Was someone monitoring his phone? Or was he not really at home? Wait, he would never call the palace his. Whose medical facility were they at?

AJ: Be careful. I love you.

Saying I loved him through a text felt cheap and impersonal, but I needed Logan to know how I felt. I had a feeling our situation had grown even more dangerous after the party's end.

Logan: I love you.

I tucked my phone back in my purse and glanced up at Braden. He stared at me with that stupid smug grin.

"How do you manage it?" he asked, folding his arms over his chest.

"What?"

"To get so many people to do whatever you want?"

I snorted, a very unladylike noise that I didn't apologize for. "Where are we going?" I asked in return. His question didn't warrant an answer. I had no control over my life or anyone else. Tonight's events should've made that obvious.

"To my apartment in London," he replied. "We'll get cleaned up and decide our next move. Unless you'd like to stay with me." He winked, and that irritating chuckle filled the back seat.

"I need someplace to think," I said. "And sleep would be great." Logan's text meant something, but my brain wasn't putting the pieces together. I needed a quiet place to talk to my elementals. Could I trust Braden to let me stay at his apartment for a few hours?

Braden raised his eyebrows and glanced at his driver. Great. Did that mean he didn't trust the driver? I thought he worked hard to flush out any traitors. Or maybe he just kept them all ignorant. Probably the latter. It's easy to be loyal to someone when you don't know just how evil they are. My brain seriously wasn't functioning. All vampires were evil. Except Logan. I rubbed my temples.

"Really?" I mouthed, not allowing the words to actually form.

He shrugged.

"Can I stay the night?" I asked, playing along, knowing he was manipulating me. Damn vampire.

"Of course," he replied. "The spare room should have everything you need."

I leaned my head against the cool glass and closed my eyes. Big mistake. The sleep button on my ass activated immediately.

~~~~~~~~~~~~

"Wake up, little mage," Braden's voice interrupted a very deep sleep.

"No," I mumbled, knowing it was ridiculous.

"Yes, or I'll I have the driver carry you upstairs."

I forced my eyes open and stretched. The car rolled to a stop, and Braden opened his door. Within seconds, my door opened too, and I nearly tumbled out.

"Bastard," I muttered, standing with effort. My whole body ached, and my head pounded. I grabbed my purse and left the car, following Braden across an underground garage to an elevator. The driver didn't join us, which sort of surprised me.

He pushed a keycard into a slot by the elevator doors. When they slid open, Braden motioned me inside. I went without argument. Just add one more stupid Braden-related decision to the pile.

He inserted the keycard into another slot but didn't push any of the little round buttons. The elevator started moving, and I glanced up at the smug smile I hated. When the doors finally opened, the vampire motioned me forward.

I stepped into a small foyer and immediately felt like I violated the space. Its sparse simplicity was elegant, beautiful, and spotless, almost like the dust was afraid to settle on the highly polished table next to a solid wood door. My dirty shoes would definitely offend the shiny floors beneath my feet. A bouquet of freshly cut flowers scented the small space, chasing away my disgusting odor.

Braden pushed open the door and held it for me. "The bedroom on the right side is for guests," he said, following me in and closing the door. "You'll find clothes in the closet and all the toiletries you need in the bathroom."

"Thank you for telling me I stink," I grumbled, taking off my shoes and leaving them at the door. My feet weren't much better.

Braden didn't wait for me, so I followed his path down the hall that opened into the most elegant room I'd ever seen. Almost everything was white: the walls, the large sectional sofa, the fluffy rug in the center of the living room. The not white parts were dark, contrasting colors of deep reds and greens so dark they were nearly black. It was stunning and spotless. And the bedroom I needed to get to was all the way across the room.

"I can't reach that room without ruining your carpet, which would be a horrible shame," I said. "It's absolutely beautiful."

Braden chuckled, then scooped me up and dropped me across the room at the bedroom door. I spun around panicked, knowing he left prints on his carpet and feeling stupid because I was wrong. Of course he didn't.

"Thanks," I mumbled, pushing open the door. "I'll see you in two hours."

"Two hours?"

"It'll take that long to scrub off everything I had to endure today." Which was a lie. I'd never be able to wash it off. I removed his jacket and handed it to him. "Thank you."

"I still have my part of the oath to fulfill," he said. "So, don't fall asleep."

"Two hours," I insisted. I wanted time to talk to Niyol and sort my thoughts.

"One and I'm coming in."

"Bastard."

"We've already had this discussion," he called as he laughed and disappeared in a blur of speed.

The door on the opposite side of the room opening and closing was my only indication of where he went. His bedroom, I assumed. Didn't matter, I was locking myself in this one. Yeah right. I closed the door and cursed. No lock. Fricking vampire.

I tugged at the zipper on the back of my dress, which was likely ruined, and looked around the room. A queen-sized bed centered the wall on the right, with a nightstand on each side. The white comforter covering it had to be goose down, and it called my name. I let my dress fall off my shoulders to the floor and looked to the left.

"Oh shit!"

A wall of windows greeted me along with a fit of vertigo. I could see the entire city from this height. I was immediately grateful I hadn't turned on the lights or anyone interested in looking would've had full view of me in my bra and panties.

The city below took my breath away. I'd seen Vegas at night many times, but this was so much better. I had to assume it was London, unless Braden had been lying to me earlier. He was going to point out everything as soon as we got past our other conversation. I frowned. Maybe before. I needed something positive first.

I tiptoed across the hardwood floor, avoiding another soft, fluffy area rug. It called my name too, almost convincing me to bury my toes into its heavenly fibers. I resisted. I needed a shower.

The bathroom was just as luxurious as everything else and, as promised, was stocked with shampoo, conditioner, and body wash. I shed the rest of my clothes and went to work scrubbing away the layers of dirt and guilt.

A half hour later, I found a man's long sleeve dress shirt in the closet next to the bathroom. It also had women's clothing, but nothing fit except for the one-size-fits-all yoga pants and a lacy camisole. I pulled the shirt over my cami, buttoning all but the top button, then went to work rolling up the sleeves. The man's shirt swallowed me. No surprise there, but at least it sort of hid my bra-less chest. I refused to wear anyone's panties other than my own, so I scrubbed them in the sink and left them on the towel rack to dry with my bra that also received a severe scrubbing.

I had half an hour to sort my thoughts, or let my elementals sort them for me. I sat on the oh-so-soft carpet with my legs folded in front of me. I thought about the bed but suspected I'd just fall asleep. The city's lights stretched out in front of me in a myriad of colors, vaguely reminding me of home. Maybe my life as a shunned, deformed nobody was the better option.

Niyol? Göksu?

What have you gotten yourself into now? Niyol asked.

I was hoping you knew.

I cannot enter the vampire's home, so don't do anything stupid.

That wasn't what I wanted to hear but important to know.

Göksu, do you know where Logan is?

He is at Mr. Smith's compound, he replied. *And yes, Kellen is with him.*

What about the palace? Is the council okay? Have the European mages taken over our home? I tried to tamp down my panic but failed miserably. With Kellen and I both gone, who would be there to make sure the people were okay? Or worse, were they being lied to about what happened?

Calm down, child. Kellen explained the prince's attack. Your council is aware of his treachery, Göksu explained. *But they've closed the portal, isolating themselves from everyone.*

I took a deep breath and opened my phone, re-reading Logan's text. He didn't want me to go to the palace, but he didn't want Jonathan knowing my location either.

It's probably best for now, I said. *They're being targeted for some reason.*

No, you're being targeted, child. You are the unifying force.

Yeah, whatever. I waved my hand in the air like they could see me. *Logan thinks I should stay away from both the palace and Mr. Smith's, but I don't want to stay here. Braden and I will end up killing each other.*

You cannot go to Victor's either, Niyol said, preempting my next question. *You need to find a way to get to the other mage families and explain what happened to Prince Thomas. As much as I dislike the elder vampire, he's right. William will need to blame someone, and he won't want his son's name tarnished.*

Shit.

Can I not get Kellen, and then the two of us can make house calls together? He can tell his part of the story and I'll tell mine. I don't want to put my trust in Braden.

When neither answered me, I started to worry they wouldn't. I bit the inside of my cheek and twisted my fingers in the tail of my shirt to keep from asking again.

I'll stay with Logan and Kellen, Göksu finally said. *Convince the elder to take you to one of the mage families. When you get there, I'll find a way to let Kellen know.*

And he can find a way to get to me, I finished, rubbing at the tears pooling in my eyes. *I could never do this without you two.*

You'll never have to, Niyol said. *And don't feel guilty about cutting that vampire to pieces. Use his willingness to learn how to fight against him.*

I will give you the strength to heal yourself, if he should hurt you, Göksu added. *Just don't take any more of his blood.*

That reminded me of my bond with Logan and Braden's effect on it.

What happens to my bond with Logan if Braden's blood is in me?

I don't know, child, Göksu answered. *We aren't privy to vampire secrets.*

I thought my bond to him belonged to Spirit, not the vampires?

It's both. Don't take any more of his blood.

A knock at my door interrupted the conversation.

"It hasn't been an hour yet!" I yelled.

"We have to go." He opened the door, the lights from the other room silhouetting his tall frame. "King William has acted sooner than expected."

I rose to my feet and grabbed my phone and tiny purse. "He's accusing me of killing Thomas, isn't he?"

"Yes."

I pushed past him, my bare feet slapping against the hardwood floor. "My mages know differently," I said. "They saw Kellen when he arrived and heard his story." I stuffed my phone in my purse and took one last step to curl my toes in the soft carpet. "I assume William knows this place or we wouldn't be leaving."

"You assume correctly." He glanced at my attire and shook his head. "Did nothing in there fit you?"

I held a leg out in front of me. "The yoga pants. Is every woman you know five foot seven and a hundred and forty pounds?"

"Possibly. None of the shoes fit?"

I rolled my eyes and made for the door. "I'm also without underclothes, but I do have a credit card. Let's go."

So much for my tour of London's skyline.

Chapter 29

Braden's driver didn't join us this time, and I didn't want to think about why. I sat in the front passenger seat of his Mercedes, wrapped in a coat the vampire threw at me on the way out the door. It should've been the driver's side, but it wasn't. We were in England, so the driver sat on the right side, not the left. It felt weird, but I refused to complain. Rain pelted the windshield, and the wiper blades struggled to keep up with the torrential downpour. Between that and the darkness, it was nearly impossible to see the passing scenery.

"We have a long drive ahead of us," Braden said, not looking at me. "Do you want to sleep or talk?"

"I'm not tired right now, so let's talk," I replied. "Let's start with what your blood is doing to me."

"Interesting that you would choose my secrets first, rather than ask about yours," he said, still not taking his eyes from the road.

I hadn't actually thought about it that way. I was more concerned about Logan than revealing vampire secrets, but I wasn't telling him that.

"Well, spill it."

He chuckled. "An elder's blood is different than most vampire's," he said. "I should've been angry when you took mine the other night, but I was too consumed by... other desires." He glanced at me. "No one dares to attack me. Yet this tiny mage did so without hesitation. You've awakened a part of me that I haven't enjoyed in ages."

I squirmed, edging closer to the passenger door. "That doesn't explain my inability to use our mage portal."

"No, I suppose it doesn't," he conceded. "My blood will linger in you. Its presence is strong enough for others to detect. Like the magic in your portal."

"So the portal thinks I'm a vampire?" I asked.

"I wouldn't go that far, but it certainly recognizes my blood in your veins."

I pulled my feet into the seat and hugged my knees. Logan's blood hadn't done that to me. I'd actually been able to protect him going through the portal. But after Braden's blood, even Kellen's large body wrapped around me wasn't enough to fool the portal's magic.

"How long will it linger?" I asked. "Especially after our thing with the blood oath?"

"I'm not sure," Braden replied. "Weeks, possibly months."

"Fricking lovely," I mumbled. Maybe having the portal to the palace closed was a good idea. No one would know why I wasn't using it. "Are there long term affects? What if our blood mingles during my twenty-four hours of torture?"

He glanced at me again, this time his smugness faded completely. "We should avoid swapping blood again," he replied.

I frowned. Göksu had said the same thing. "I'm not sure I can hurt you unless I'm provoked," I said. "Don't get me wrong, I despise you. But my dislike doesn't automatically turn into violence."

"Your honesty is so refreshing," he murmured.

The highlights from a passing car highlighted his frown. There was no way I'd offended him, was there? Maybe my disrespect pissed him off. I should at least try to be nice.

"Sorry," I said. "I'll try to get a tighter rein on the filter that should be over my mouth."

"No. I prefer your honesty," he said. "It's just difficult to hear. Most of the people I encounter on a daily basis say what they think I want to hear, even if the truth would benefit them more."

Was this another manipulation? I didn't want to see him with normal insecurities. I needed to keep him in the 'enemy of my enemy is my friend for a moment' category. Hopefully, we wouldn't be spending too much time together. He would take me to the nearest mage family and we'd be done. Sure, because all my plans worked out that way.

"I'd like the same truth from you," I said after the moment of silence.

"Agreed."

That was too easy. I needed someone smarter than me in these conversations with him.

"Okay, so next topic," I said, taking a deep breath. "Your knowledge of my 'clan.'" I air quoted clan, even though he didn't look at me.

"Still not your father?" he asked.

"I'm not ready for that yet," I replied, keeping to the honesty. Right. I really wasn't ready.

"Your mother killed Kellen's parents because they discovered her connection to me," he began, tapping his finger on the steering wheel. "I was surprised when I heard of your partnership with him and wondered how he felt about that. I never would've accepted the woman who was the mirror image of my parents' murderer." He glanced at me, then back to the road. "But he's human. You do things I'll never understand."

"You were human once, weren't you?" I asked.

"It's irrelevant. Stop taking me off topic."

Another passing car highlighted his face, revealing the deep frown. I might have preferred his smugness over his current mood.

"I thought I could use your mother to recruit mages into my ranks," he said. "It worked for a while. I spent a great deal of time watching the training of new recruits. Their strength was impressive and gave me hope to stop Jack's stupidity. But when Logan killed his sire and ran, there was no hiding it from Jack." His lip curled. I wasn't happy that he'd confirmed my suspicions. "I hated giving up my secret weapon, but I had no choice. Everything spiraled out of control after that, including your mother. Even after her transition, she was unstable."

The sound of the rain beating against the car filled the silence that followed. He'd been fighting against Jack's plan for a long time. A new thought surfaced from my subconscious, something Thomas had said in the dungeons.

"How are you keeping Jack's loyalty?" I asked. "Does he really consider you his golden boy?"

Braden laughed, a genuine belly laugh, and looked at me. "That is not part of our oath, little mage."

"Can't blame me for trying," I said, smiling.

"I'd be disappointed if you hadn't tried." He turned his attention back to the road. "Are you ready for the last topic?"

"No, that can't be all your knowledge of my clan," I replied. "You're old. Surely you knew my grandparents."

"Thank you for that wonderful assessment of my age." He laughed again, and I blushed. "And yes, I knew your grandfather but not your grandmother. He wouldn't allow me near her."

"Smart man," I said, grinning at him. "So, tell me what you know." I pulled the long coat around my knees and leaned back against the door, giving him my full attention.

"Your grandfather and I had a working relationship much like King William's," he said. "Only he was aware of my heritage, where the king is not."

"So just business?"

"It's always business," he replied.

"And you had nothing to do with his falling out with the mages?" I pressed.

"I did not," he said. "His downfall started with his marriage and ended with his daughter. His situation was not unique, though. Royalty is forced into rules that everyone else can ignore. Many rulers have endured his fate."

The car slowed, and we turned off the highway onto a narrow, two-lane road. The rain hadn't let up.

"Yes, I've already encountered that," I muttered, thinking of my engagement to Kellen. Braden confirmed my partner's feelings about me and added to my guilt. I didn't want to admit that Kellen's resentment was justified, but maybe part of it was.

"Love is so inconvenient and has destroyed many lives throughout history," the vampire said. "I'm grateful not to have it."

I studied his features with a frown. That perspective hadn't crossed my mind. I'd been without love and it sucked. But now that I had it, everyone used it against me.

"Yet you don't hesitate to use it against me," I growled.

"Of course not," he said. "It's an efficient tool."

"Yes, and a stipulation I should've included in our blood oath," I muttered.

He chuckled, and I glared at him.

"The first time I received word of Lily with your father, I thought nothing of it," Braden said, starting the subject without asking.

I twisted in my chair and looked out the window, not ready to hear what he had to say. I hated confronting my mother's rejection; I wasn't sure I could handle my father's as well.

"It was after her failure with Logan," he continued, "and after her new arrangement with Jack. I kept tabs on her because information is power." He shook a finger at me. "My men didn't recognize Cedric for what he really was, they only saw a man the Magister was finally interested in. I thought it odd that she never took him to the palace, only setting up clandestine meetings with him."

A prolonged silence forced me to look at him. I just knew he'd have that smug smile tugging at his lips. I was right.

"Just spit it out," I hissed.

"I should've known she was up to something." He shrugged, that stupid smile not leaving his lips as he turned his attention back to the road. "I don't think Cedric realized what she was up to until it was too late." He paused again and an urge to stab him swept over me. He was doing it on purpose, and I knew it.

"What was he?" I asked.

"He is a unique creature that is so rare, I haven't seen one in centuries," he replied.

I didn't miss his correction. My father was still alive. I doused the drop of hope that wanted to surge. He'd never looked for me either.

"Stop being an ass and just tell me," I commanded.

"No matter how hard you try, you cannot command me," he said. "But I did promise information. He is a fae, or fairy, which in itself is not unusual, but males are. The females will mingle with humanity occasionally, but never the males. I'm not sure how your mother found him, but I believe her plan was to have an immortal child who she could use to find her own immortality."

He paused, letting the patter of rain fill the silence. I knew nothing about the fae, but I didn't miss his breadcrumb about immortality. It didn't make sense, though. She could've had me at her mercy by just pretending to be happy about being united with her daughter. But she tried to kill me. *Might as well ask*, I thought. *Wasn't that the point of this stupid blood oath?*

"I don't understand," I said. "My mother tried to kill me. It would've been easy for her to use me anyway she way she wanted. I would've done anything for her love."

"She tried to kill you because she was angry," he said. "By the time you entered her life, she was already a vampire. Though, she would've killed you regardless. She needed your blood for her immortality."

I stared at him horrified, not able to think about what that meant.

"I'm not an expert in fae magic. None but the fae themselves know it," he continued. "If memory serves me correctly, there is a ritual that would trade your life for hers."

Tears welled in my eyes, and I looked out the window. I knew I wasn't ready for this story. I'd accepted my mother's rejection and thought I was past it. Apparently not. And I couldn't even wrap my mind around being immortal. It sure didn't feel that way. And how did my elementals not know it? Surely, they would've told me. Or maybe not. They hadn't said anything about Spirit until it was forced on them.

"Where's my father?"

"I don't know," he replied. "After he stole you from your mother at birth, he was never seen again. Neither were you until a few months ago."

"But I don't remember him at all," I argued. "If he stole me from her, he turned right around and gave me to the state."

"Do you know how old you were when the state took custody of you?"

"Not more than a few days, according to their records," I replied. I'd looked during that desperate time in my childhood that I thought I could find my parents.

"I'm not sure what happened," he said. "The pieces I can fit together lead me to believe that your father placed the veil on you and created your binding."

The car slowed and pulled off the road. I refused to look at Braden, giving all my attention to the water dripping down my window.

"Alisandra, I think he was trying to protect you from everyone," Braden whispered even though we were the only ones in the car. "The only reason we found you was because the veil started to fade and for some reason, he hadn't renewed it."

My head fell against the cool glass, my finger tracing a droplet of water. I choked back a sob. "The binding was meant to kill me if it wasn't renewed," I whispered. "How does that protect me?"

"It protects all of us," he replied. "If your fae magic is activated, I can only imagine the power you will possess."

I huffed and wiped my nose with the back of my hand. "Which is why you want me as your ally." I turned towards him, studying his reaction.

"Yes."

At least he didn't lie to me or try to make excuses. I was beginning to think the blood oath was worth it.

"Who else knows about my dad?" I asked.

"No one."

"What about your men who found me and followed my mother?"

"The ones who followed Lily are dead," he replied. "Logan found you, but he doesn't know why your veil weakened or who placed it." He shrugged and shifted to face me. "Unless Lily told someone—which is unlikely—no one else knows."

I rubbed my hands across my face. Could he be lying to me? I didn't think so. If my father was still alive, he must know I'd taken over as Magister. Would he look for me now? Did I want him to? Not really. He'd probably try to kill me, just like everyone else. My life sucked so bad.

"I have books at the estate about the fae," Braden said. "You should read them while we're there."

"Thank you," I mumbled.

"I fulfilled my end of the oath, as promised," he stated. "There is no reason to thank me."

"I disagree." I curled up in the seat, facing him. "You didn't have to include that in our oath, but you did."

"I wanted your cooperation," he countered. "Telling you the truth ensures I will get it."

I chuckled and thought about my recent conversations with Logan and my elementals. "I'm not sure anything secures my cooperation."

"Your love for Logan will be your undoing, little mage," he said, his seriousness scaring me. "Don't let yourself love Kellen, too."

I sat up and wiped away my tears. "You would still use him against me?"

"If you think of betraying me, yes."

"You know I won't betray you to Jack," I spat, "and you'll get your twenty-four hours of pain, you sick bastard.

Logan never needs to enter the picture." I seethed at him. Just when I thought he might be nice, he proved me wrong.

"There's my girl."

He put the car in drive and pulled back onto the deserted highway. Sometime during our little chat, the rain had stopped. My mind mulled over the new information. I needed more information about the fae and possibly my dad. If males were that rare, maybe I could find something about him. But if Braden couldn't find him, how would I? I reminded myself I didn't want to. His binding had intended to kill me.

I turned my back to the vampire and laid the seat back. I needed sleep, if my brain would slow down enough to let it happen.

Chapter 30

A slamming door startled me awake. I smashed my knee on the bottom of the dash and cursed. A bright light shined in my window, making me squint. The green and orange striped awning above me glowed with its fluorescent lighting. I sat up, pulling the back of the seat with me. A gas station. Braden stood beside the car on the opposite side, refueling the tank.

I stretched and pulled my phone out of my purse. Four-twenty AM and five percent battery. Had I been thinking, I would've plugged it in before I fell asleep. I dug around the center console, finding a smartphone already plugged into the charger. Luckily it was the same model as mine. I swapped them out and looked back at Braden. Still pumping gas.

I pushed open the door and stood, stretching again. The seat was not comfortable and my body was letting me know exactly how unhappy it was about it. My bladder also reminded me it was full. Turning slowly, I found the small store I hoped would be open. It was.

"I'm going to the bathroom," I said, gingerly stepping across the pavement, the loose stones assaulting my bare feet.

"You could wait for me," Braden stated. "You won't want to go in their bathroom without shoes."

"I don't want to go to the bathroom with you either," I countered.

He laughed, and I blushed.

"I imagine they will have some sort of sandal or touristy type flipflop," he said.

"Oh." My blush deepened. I should've thought about that. Most convenience stores in the US had silly souvenirs, including t-shirts and sandals.

A few moments later, he was by my side, picking me up and carrying me into the small store. An old man with thick glasses covering his wrinkled eyes waved at us. I waved back, smiling and still blushing. I felt like an idiot being carried around by the blond beauty.

Braden stopped at the wall nearest the door, the one covered in screen printed t-shirts with pictures of "Big Ben." On a low shelf just beneath them was a crate of fluorescent green and pink flipflops.

The vampire slowly lowered me to my feet. "Stand on my shoes and pick something," he whispered. "And make it quick. I'd like to be home before sunrise."

I reached down and selected the smallest hot pink I could find that weren't children's and slid my feet into them.

"Thanks, I'll be right back." I rushed to the bathroom, grateful for his help. My mind still lingered on his revelations earlier. Now that my brain was awake, I wanted more answers, but I wasn't sure I'd get them.

Braden waited at the door with a bag in his hand when I finished, not even trying to hide his look of impatience. I quietly followed him back to the car assuming he paid for my new shoes.

"Take this." He shoved the bag towards me as soon as we were back in the car.

I took it and unfolded the top. Two bottles of water, a wrapped sandwich, and several candy bars greeted me. Not the breakfast of champions, but food.

"Thanks, again," I mumbled. "How close are we?"

"Fifteen minutes," Braden replied, pulling away from the gas station and back onto a two-lane road. "There will not be any food for you at the estate, for obvious reasons."

I unwrapped a chocolate bar and took a bite. My stomach rumbled loud enough for Braden to hear.

"How long will we be at this estate?" I asked, taking another bite.

"I need information and you need clothes," he replied. "I want to be gone this evening." He glanced at me, a deep frown crossing his face. "Hopefully, everyone will be in bed when we get there."

I swallowed my chocolatey goodness and contemplated his increasingly bad mood. Was it because he'd fulfilled his part of the oath and didn't find the need to be nice anymore? Maybe he was tired or hungry. I cringed.

"Is there anything I should know before we arrive?" I asked.

"Don't speak to or look at anyone, and don't leave my side." He glanced at me, and I couldn't help but notice the red ring around his blue eyes. "Don't react to any threats. I mean it. You *do not* react. Keep your head down and stay with me."

Fear crept along my spine. What the hell was I walking into?

"Should I just stay back at the gas station?" I asked.

"I thought about it, but no," he replied. "My blood should keep you safe. The others will smell it and leave you alone."

I raised an eyebrow at him. "Then why all the warnings?"

"Because you've demonstrated that you lack the common sense to follow quietly," he snapped.

"I guess we're definitely back to cold acquaintances then, aren't we?" I asked, needing to know where we stood before walking into the lion's den.

He jerked the wheel and skidded to a stop on the side of the road, slamming the shifter into park. My fear inched higher. I wasn't trying to piss him off, but clearly I had.

"When a human is brought to the estate, it is for one purpose," he said. "I've never brought home dinner. There will be questions and possibly challenges unless I get lucky and everyone has retired for the night."

"I'm never lucky," I mumbled. "I'm okay with waiting at the gas station."

I could see the indecision in his eyes as they shifted from red to blue and back again. He picked up his phone and tapped it, then held it to his ear.

"Yes, Master Braden," a man's voice said on the other end.

He must have known I could hear his conversation.

"Who's still awake?" Braden asked.

"The guards and I, possibly a few others who came in late," the man replied.

"I need names," Braden demanded.

The vampire on the other end spouted out six or seven names. Braden's frown deepened.

"I want you, Bryce, and Paxton in the library in ten minutes," he said, hanging up before the vampire on the other end could respond. He stared at me with his shifting eyes for several moments. "How do you feel about killing a vampire for me?"

"Not happening," I replied. "If you have another traitor, you need to take care of it. If I attack one of your guys, I'm pretty sure I'll have the whole place on me."

"I'm going to give him the opportunity to submit himself willingly," Braden explained. "He won't, but I'll make it his choice. The vampires at the estate know my stand with Jack. Paxton is trying his hand at blackmail. He thinks to make a new position for himself either in my clan or Jack's. His self-importance will be his undoing, today."

"And what do you accomplish if I kill him?" I asked, knowing there was something for him to gain. Always.

"Loyalty," he replied, running one hand along the steering wheel. "My personal guard knows of my efforts to ally with you. If the others see the alliance, their confidence in our success will grow and prevent more deserters."

I drew a deep breath. I could see his point but didn't like the idea of killing a vampire in the middle of a vampire camp.

"Will you protect me if the others decide my murderous ways are unacceptable?"

"Of course, you have an oath to fulfill," he replied, then smiled, the red in his eyes fading.

"And how would you like your traitor to die?" I couldn't believe I was agreeing to this. Where were my elementals? Someone was supposed to keep me from these stupid decisions.

His smile widened. "How many ways do you know?"

"Only one that's truly affective, but it's gruesome and more than a little scary." I bit my bottom lip and frowned. "Actually, I forgot. It doesn't kill the vampire. It just leaves their hollow husk behind, still alive."

Braden's eyes widened, his smile waning.

"Forget it," I said, waving a hand at him. "I'll stab him in the heart and cut off his head."

"You cannot throw that out there, then not explain."

"Yes, I can."

"Tell me now," he growled.

"Let's make a deal," I suggested. Two could play the information game.

He leaned back against the door and looked at me. "Okay, little mage. What is your request?"

"Why are you Jack's golden boy?"

"Not worth it," he replied. "Try again."

"I don't believe you," I countered. "I can see it on your face. You want to know how I could leave you a dried-out husk but not dead."

"I don't believe it's possible."

"There are dozens of vampires from the last battle who witnessed it," I said. "Maybe some of your own have even heard the tale. I actually considered doing it to you in King William's dungeon before I realized you were playing games with Thomas."

We stared at one another, but I wasn't backing down. I wanted to know why Jack's Boy would betray him.

"Jack is my brother," Braden finally said, his lips twisting in a sneer. "It used to be common knowledge, but too many of our clan were lost during the last hunt. Jack left England with our strongest warriors and went to America, leaving the leftovers to me. I made an empire out of the trash he left behind."

"And you continue to provide him with information he needs for his plans," I finished for him.

"Yes," he replied. "I've proven myself to be the most cunning and resourceful in our council. I've also delivered several traitors to him in the past."

I narrowed my eyes at him, and he winked at me.

"You delivered people who were made to look like traitors," I corrected.

"Perception is everything."

I didn't stand a chance against this man's brilliance. As soon as Jack was defeated and my oath fulfilled, I needed to run from him as fast as I could.

"I'll demonstrate my technique," I agreed. "It'll be your decision to kill him or not. It'll also be your decision to share the threat with your people or not."

"You're ruthless, little mage," Braden said, his features softening.

"I wasn't always this way," I mumbled. "I'd like to go back to hiding in my apartment and being alone."

"I don't believe you." The vampire straightened in his seat and pulled the car back onto the road.

We spent the remainder of the short trip in silence, my mind analyzing the information I had. Braden had tons of reasons to hate Jack. The fact that he hid it so well scared me. I remembered him in my first interview with the vampire council. He was so laid back and nonchalant about everything in the room. I never would've guessed he harbored these feelings.

I was also surprised he shared it with me. My ability to suck the blood from vampires wasn't a secret. Or was it? Sergey's vampires witnessed my ability, not Ernesto's. Had the Russian really disappeared with his army? Could I find a way to ask Braden without revealing my own knowledge of his survival? Or should I just tell Braden? Sergey could be another ally. I didn't know the answer, and our arrival at a large iron gate took my opportunity to ask.

The gate slid open as we approached, then slid closed after we passed through. The pre-dawn twilight silhouetted a sprawling estate. Several brick homes made a half circle around a two-story mansion that had Braden written all over it. Its long lines, square windows, and tall spires on the corners fit their owner perfectly.

"It's Elizabethan architecture," Braden said. "It was my least favorite era, but they built the most beautiful homes."

"That surprises me about you," I commented. "You didn't strike me as a neat freak."

He wrinkled his nose and parked in front of the sweeping steps leading to a dark wood-paneled door.

"Remember what I said. No confrontations."

"Got it, but it's hard to look like the mage queen when I'm being an obedient little follower."

"You lost queen status when you put on those leggings."

I laughed, and he smiled. I didn't wait for him to open the door as I slid out, grabbing my phone from the charger on the way. I fell in step beside him and tried not to look like a tourist as the door opened into a grand foyer. It was the only appropriate word for it. The room made the castle's foyer look like a cheap hotel.

Dark parquet wood floors stretched the length of the room. Sand-colored walls provided a muted backdrop for dozens of colorful paintings. All landscapes. Not a single piece of furniture obscured the beauty.

"Master Braden, this is a first," a deep voice echoed across the empty space. A tall, muscular man emerged from an open door at the far end of the room. "You've never brought us dinner."

Two other men followed him. As he got closer, I noticed his fangs protruding from his lips and his deep red eyes ran the length of my body. I tried to contain my fear but was pretty sure I failed.

"Not dinner, then," he continued. "Has our illustrious leader finally found a pet?"

Braden growled, drawing my attention. A deep furrow ran between his red eyes. "In the library, now," he ordered.

I stayed by his side as we entered the first door on the left. Library was too modest a description. Like everything else 'Braden,' it was beautiful. Dark gray stones covered the floor. Strategically placed seating arrangements filled the corners of the large room, with a white fluffy carpet beneath each of them. Most importantly, every wall was covered with books.

A hand on my lower back brought me out of tourist mode. A dark-skinned man with long braids pushed me towards the settee where Braden dropped his elegant butt. Was I jealous of his wealth? Yep, and maybe just a little bitter. I felt like a clown in a room full of royalty. The men around me wore tailored shirts and pants with leather shoes. Everything about them said, 'Look at me. I have tons of money.' While I wore yoga pants, no panties, and a man's dress shirt with the ugliest pink flip flops on the planet. I sat down next to Braden and scowled.

"What's happened since yesterday?" Braden asked after the other three men joined us.

"King William has threatened to withdraw from our trade agreements," the man with dreadlocks said. "Your CEO has managed to convince him it would be a financial disaster if he did, but I'm not sure William is listening."

"Thank you, Gordon. Bryce?"

The man sitting next to Gordon nodded, the thick, dark curls on his head bouncing with the movement. He glanced at me, then Braden. "Sergey wants to speak with you today. I tried to put him off until tonight, but he insists his information cannot wait." Bryce looked at me again.

"Yes, this is the Magister," Braden said. "You can speak in front of her. I'm sure she already knows everything about Sergey's position."

My eyebrows rose. Apparently they did know the Russian survived.

Bryce cleared his throat and nodded again. "He's concerned about King William's stance. He has reason to believe that William and Thomas were working together."

That little tidbit should've surprised me, but it didn't. It would explain why William left early with his son and why he'd changed his clothes. Did Kellen know the king was part of the attack? I had to assume not, or he would've told me.

"Paxton?" Braden turned to the large man sitting in a chair between me and Gordon.

"Jack won't be happy about Thomas' death," the big man said.

"You haven't already told him?" Braden asked.

"No, I was waiting for you to return so I could make a proper report."

"Stop toying with me, child," the elder hissed. "Make your demands." Paxton glanced at me much like Bryce had, and Braden chuckled. "I told you, she already knows, and her knowledge didn't come from me. She is adept at getting people to talk to her."

Paxton straightened his shoulders and stood. "I want the Mediterranean."

"Of course you do." Braden waved his hand in the air. "The ports control most of our trade. What will you do when I refuse?"

The big man pushed out his chest. "I'll tell Jack all of your plans."

The elder vampire leaned back and stretched his arm across the back of the settee behind me. "Why wouldn't I just kill you?"

"Because you need me to coordinate the shipping channels," he replied. "No one else has the connections to make it happen as efficiently as I do."

I stifled my snort of disbelief with a sneeze. His reason sounded stupid even to me, and I didn't know anything about trade or shipping. Anyone should be able to learn how to do it.

"I see we are in agreement," Braden said, his fingers rubbing my neck. Tingles ran down my spine, and I knew I blushed. "Tell me, Alisandra. What do you find so funny?"

I looked at him and raised my eyebrows. He nodded.

"Well, I'm not an expert in trade, but coordinating shipments shouldn't be that difficult," I replied. "Anyone with decent training and a modicum of intelligence should be able to pick it up pretty quickly. People come and go in that field pretty regularly, don't they?"

"Our trade partners are not typical," Paxton hissed.

"But you have a product they want," I countered. "I suspect they'll deal with whoever they have to in order to get it. Your boss isn't stupid. He'd likely handle the partners himself until a suitable replacement for you is found. No one is irreplaceable."

The big man growled, his fingers elongating into claws. "You bring her here to insult us?" he asked, the seams of his shirt straining against his widening shoulders.

"No, I'm testing her fortitude and intelligence," Braden replied. "And so far, she's done very well pointing out the obvious despite knowing very little about our business."

Paxton's frame continued to grow, and his expensive shirt ripped across his chest. Gordon and Bryce tensed but didn't move from their spot on the sofa across from me.

"I will not be insulted by you or this stupid little girl!" the vampire bellowed, his words slurred by the protrusion of his long fangs.

He lunged at me, and I rolled into Braden's lap, flinging my arms out. Paxton hit a wall of air and fell back. I reached for the blood pulsing in his veins and pulled, yanking my hands down to Braden's knees. Streams of deep red oozed from his body, and the vampire howled in pain.

I thought about Göksu's instructions for creating a weapon with the blood. I needed Kellen to solidify it, but my vampire friends didn't know that. Braden would have his demonstration. I wove my fingers together, twisting the streams of blood into a slender spear as Paxton collapsed on the floor. Gasps from all three men made me smile. I held my new weapon above Paxton's shriveled body, slowly turning it in a circle to point at the elder vampire. Braden chuckled. Yep, a nervous twitch.

"He's still alive, barely," I said. "I can't put the blood back into his body, but you might be able to feed it to him."

"And you call me a monster," Braden whispered.

"It's all in the eye of the beholder," I said, scooting back into my side of the settee. "The first vampire who tried to bite me created this monster. Where do you want his blood?"

"Gordon, empty a vase for our mage. I don't want to ruin the carpet."

A few minutes later, I funneled the gory mess into a beautiful waist-high vase, trying to avoid the mummy on the floor. Soft moans drifted from Paxton. I hated doing that.

"You should end his suffering," I said, trying not to make it a command.

"You care if he suffers?" Bryce asked.

"I'm human," I snapped. "Of course I care. It's an unnecessary cruelty to leave him."

Gordon frowned. "Then why did you do it?"

"Because I asked her to," Braden replied before I could speak. "I didn't believe the rumors coming from Sergey's men." He pointed at the dying man. "Kill him."

Gordon pulled a long knife from a pocket at his knee. I hadn't even noticed it until he reached for the blade. I looked away but couldn't block out the sound of his blade slicing through the hardened flesh.

"What is our next move?" Bryce asked.

"We need to get the Magister home," Braden replied. "Then I need to report to Jack."

"I can't go home," I said, drawing the attention of all three men. "William cannot convince the other mage families that I killed his son. If he does, he ensures we're divided." I tried not to play with the buttons on my shirt under their intense gazes. "If he is in league with Jack, he'll try to convince the others to join him."

"Where would you go?" Braden asked. "By yourself, no less."

"To the nearest mage family who might be influenced by William. I need to reach them as soon as possible," I replied. "I won't be alone. Kellen has agreed to meet me as soon as I tell him where I'll be."

"I've monitored your phone, little mage," he continued, a smile spreading across his face. "When did you make all these arrangements?"

"Shall we make another deal?" I asked in return.

"No, my dear, we will not." He laughed and turned to his men. "She is almost as devious as I."

"So, where to?" Bryce asked, not smiling.

"Egypt would be best, if Kellen is meeting you there," Braden replied to his vampire but didn't look away from me. "You can stay with his family."

"I'll have the plane ready tonight," Bryce said, standing. "Is there anything else you need from me before I retire?"

"Yes. Tell Sergey he's welcome to come to the estate anytime, but we're not meeting until six this evening." Braden pointed at the shriveled body on the floor. "Take that with you, when you go."

"Thank you, sir." Bryce was gone before I could blink and so was Paxton.

Gordon stood as well, but Braden wasn't done with him. "I need you to go with her," he said, remaining in his relaxed pose.

Gordon's nostril's flared. He obviously wasn't happy about it. Neither was I. Having an unknown vampire hanging around wasn't my idea of fun.

"It's not necessary," I said. "I don't need a protector." Which was a lie that Braden surely recognized.

"He will stay with you until Kellen arrives."

"Like Kellen's family will allow a vampire among them," I argued. "I'll be fine."

"No, you won't," Gordon interrupted. "A woman should not be unescorted there. We'll stay at the safe house in Alexandria until your partner shows up."

"Thank you," Braden said, pushing himself from the settee as if the matter were settled and I had no say. "The library is yours to peruse, Alisandra, until this evening. Gordon will stay with you to ensure no one disturbs your studies."

My new babysitter flared his nostrils again, but Braden ignored him. The door slammed shut, leaving me with a hostile vampire who had no desire to stay up all day. I sighed.

"You can sleep on one of the sofas if you like. I'll put a chair in front of the door so we have warning if someone's coming," I suggested. "I don't need a keeper, but I understand the rank structure."

"Braden will kill me if I sleep." He eyed the spot where Paxton died. "Or give me to you."

"We're already stuck together," I said. "I'm not stupid enough to wander around the estate. Besides, I love to read, and there's more than enough here to keep me busy."

He eyed me warily, then picked up the nearest chair, bracing the edge under the door. I wandered around the shelves, looking for books about the fae. He'd either lay down and sleep or not. I couldn't make him. Well, maybe I could, but I wouldn't.

It took me half an hour to find what I wanted. A smile spread across my face when I stumbled into an entire section about supernatural beings. "Perfect." I pulled six books off the shelf and looked around. Only one of the seating arrangements had a table. I crossed the room and dropped my treasures.

"What are you looking for?" Gordon asked, startling me.

"Don't do that," I hissed. "I know nothing about the supernatural families. Since I have all day, I figured it was the perfect time to educate myself." I smiled and headed back to the bookshelf. "I don't suppose you know where the stuff about ogres is, do you?" I called over my shoulder. "I also want the shifters, and oooohhhh!" I stopped at the shelf just before the fae. "Elves? Really?" My babysitter laughed and I turned on him. "What?"

"You are not at all what I expected," he said.

I waved my hand at him. "Whatever. I get that a lot. Reach up to the top shelf and get me those five," I said, trying not to make it a command. It might not work on Braden, but it definitely worked on Fiona.

"These?" he asked, reaching the top shelf easily.

"Yep. Thank you much." I added them to my pile. Who didn't want to read about elves?

"Anymore top shelf items before I relax?"

I ran back to the fae section. They were all on the bottom shelves, but several books about merfolk were on the top.

"Those ones," I pointed up at them and he took them down without comment. "Thank you for your help. I'll try not to bug you."

I took the books from him and went back to my new pile of reading material. I didn't want to open the fae books first, so I picked one about the elves and got comfortable.

"How did you do that?" Gordon asked, still standing next to the book shelf.

"Do what?" I asked, thinking back over our last few minutes. What had I done?

"Mages don't move that quick," he replied.

"Yes, well, that's a long, complicated story," I replied. "I'm usually better at hiding it."

"I see."

He leaned against the bookshelf, his dark brown eyes staring at me. I stared back. He wasn't lean like Logan, but he wasn't wide and muscular like Kellen either. His braided hair fell below his shoulders, but he pulled it back with a wide band. It looked good on him.

"Does Braden know of your little talent?"

"Is there anything he doesn't know?" I countered.

Gordon smiled. "I suppose not."

"Get some rest and I'll get educated," I suggested.

He pushed off the bookshelf and settled into a sofa in the nearest grouping. I went back to my book about elves. It didn't take long for me to get sucked into the elves' lore. An hour passed quickly, and I looked up to find Gordon's legs hanging over one end of the sofa and his head resting against the other. His eyes were closed, but I wasn't assuming he was sleeping. I swapped out books, picking up the first one about the fae. The vampire didn't stir with my movement. Maybe he was sleeping.

I dug through the titles looking for something that didn't have pictures of little fairies. Even in my ignorance, I was pretty sure my dad wasn't a little pixie with wings. Two of my selections looked promising, so I flipped through the first one. It had pictures every few pages, making me stop to read the descriptions. Trees with faces, deer with human torsos, little bugs with shimmering wings, dark shadows with long claws and sharp fangs. I got lost in the book.

Regardless of the fairy's form, its magic was similar. They could communicate telepathically and had a natural affinity to nature. They were all immortal, sort of. They could be killed, but without a fatal wound, they would live forever. They were also closely connected to the elements. The trait that worried me the most was one I didn't want to accept. They could change their appearance at will into whoever or whatever they wanted. My dad could be in my life right now, and I wouldn't know it.

I sighed. None of that explained why I would be so dangerous, though. I already talked to my elementals in my head. I couldn't imagine anyone being closer to them than I was. Immortality was cool, but not dangerous. Being able to change my appearance would also be cool and good if I were into espionage, but still not very dangerous. It didn't add up. I was missing something.

Which brought about other questions. Why didn't my elementals tell me? They had to know about the fae, if they were also connected to the elements. Did they know I was part fae, or did Braden lie about it? I didn't think he had, but I knew nothing about a blood oath. Maybe I should look for a book about that, too.

I stood and stretched, watching Gordon for any sign of awareness. A soft snort escaped his lips, but he didn't move. Would he even hear if someone were at the door? It didn't look like it. I removed my flipflops and crossed the room in my bare feet. Braden wouldn't tolerate a dirty floor, so I didn't worry about stepping in something.

All the texts about supernatural families seemed to be on the same side of the room, which was convenient for me. I looked through the fae stuff again, flipping through several books and putting them back. Finally, one caught my eye, but only because it had a picture of a man. He looked a little like an elf but was too short and muscular.

I sat on the floor and started reading. Not only could these fae change their own appearance, but others as well. They easily manipulated others into their way of thinking. They also channeled the elements, allowing the power to flow through them, making them exponentially stronger than other magic users. I already did that, didn't I? Göksu said something similar, hadn't he? Was he preparing me to use my fae magic? It sure sounded like it. But I couldn't change my appearance, or anyone else's for that matter. Braden insisted I convinced others to do what I wanted, but I'd never noticed it. Destiny seemed to dictate my entire life.

I huffed. Regardless, it still didn't make me some super powerful being that Braden feared. And fear was the only explanation for his reaction. He wanted me on his side because he didn't want to fight against me. But he also said everything I needed was here in the library.

Göksu?

Yes, child.

Tell me what you know.

You would already have my knowledge if I could. The regret in his voice rang out loud and clear.

That's bullshit, I snapped. *This is my life we're talking about!*

It's everyone's life. I already told you I'll do whatever I can do to protect you, but my ultimate loyalty is to this world.

Whatever! My ignorance is somehow better?

For now, yes.

Because I was the enemy. Some super-secret nuclear weapon.

Tell Kellen I'm going to see his family. I'll be in Alexandria tonight, waiting for him.

Göksu didn't reply, but I didn't expect or want him to. He probably felt it. These magical beings were so stupid. Throwing all this out there and then refusing to give me details only drove my curiosity. Admitting the danger would scare the shit of me and keep me away from it. Why couldn't they see that?

Braden said the answers were here. If I didn't find it, I'd get the information from him. I stood and ran my fingers along the spines of the remaining books. They looked like children's bedtime stories.

"You already got through that entire pile?" Gordon asked, startling me again. He hadn't moved from the sofa too small for his long legs.

"No, I found references to other things that led me back here," I replied. "I had no idea so many myths were actually real. How do they keep it all hidden?"

"Because the alternative is death."

Chapter 31

The chair propped under the door handle rattled. Gordon zipped across the room in seconds and removed the barrier. The door opened revealing a scowling Braden. My new friend dropped his head and stood to the side.

"Come with me," the elder said.

I had hoped he'd be in a better mood. I needed more information. I retrieved my shoes and purse, then stood at Braden's side. "Thank you for all your help, Gordon, and the company."

His brown eyes met mine with a smile. "The pleasure was all mine, Magister."

"Call me, AJ," I corrected.

"Are we done with the niceties?" Braden snapped.

I never thought I'd see someone bristle, but that was the only description for Braden. What had his panties in a bunch? At least he was wearing them. I giggled, then clapped my hand over my mouth. He turned his scowl on me.

"Sure," I replied. "Let's go."

Back in the foyer, I fell back into tourist mode. The beauty was amazing, regardless of the fact the room was devoid of any furniture or the potential enemies lurking all around. Braden grabbed my elbow, pulling me up a wide staircase along the wall.

"This is beautiful, Braden," I whispered, running my fingers along the wooden banister.

His grip on my arm loosened, and I looked up at him. Dark circles lingered under his eyes, but a ghost of a smile appeared on his lips. Something had happened, and I was pretty sure I wasn't going to like it.

He pulled me into the last room along the hall at the top of the stairs. I expected a bedroom but was surprised by an office in typical Braden style. Clean and elegant. He crossed the room and opened another door, then motioned me inside.

"We need to talk," he said.

His lack of 'let's make a deal' worried me. I chose to remain silent rather than asking the dozens of questions running through my head. I got the impression he was sharing without any prompts. The room I walked into was dark and windowless, the only light coming from the open door. Braden flicked a switch on the wall and several lamps brightened the space before he closed us in his bedroom. Also elegant and clean. The temptation to wrinkle the white bedspread nearly overwhelmed me, but I refrained. The only thing in the room was a large bed and two long dressers with mirrors hanging over them.

"I don't suppose you have a bathroom I can use?" I asked. I'd been holding it most of the day, not wanting to interrupt Gordon's nap.

He pointed across the room. "The door on the left. Make it quick."

I did. His anxiety was infectious, and the curiosity over it was killing me. A few minutes later, I sat on the edge of his bed while he leaned against the nearest dresser.

"Gordon will take you to our private airstrip in an hour and travel with you to Alexandria," he said, crossing his arms over his chest. "There will be clothes and a passport for you on the plane. Do not leave his side until your partner shows up, and don't convince him to take you sightseeing. That's not his job."

"What's happening?" I asked. "We weren't supposed to leave until tonight."

He shifted his weight to one foot and looked at his shoes. Was that uncertainty from this arrogant man?

"Jack will be here at sunset," he replied. "He's demanding Sergey's presence."

That wasn't good news and could mean all kinds of things.

"Does Jack normally come here?"

"No. He always makes us come to him."

I scooted back on the bed and tucked my legs beneath me. I didn't think I knew enough about Jack to draw any conclusions.

"What do you think happened?" I asked. "How did he find out about Sergey?"

"I was hoping you'd know," he answered.

"What? How would I know? I've been with you the entire time."

"Can I see your phone?" He held out his hand and I laughed, pulling it out of my purse and tossing it to him. He caught it easily. "This isn't funny, Alisandra."

"No and yes," I said. "You can't figure out how I'm communicating with Kellen, so you assume I'm spilling your secrets. What the hell do I gain from telling Jack anything?"

"The lock code for your phone?" he asked, ignoring my question.

"Jackass," I replied. "All lowercase."

He raised an eyebrow at me and typed it in, shaking his head when it worked. "I won't ask what prompted that." He scrolled through my texts with Logan, continuing to shake his head.

While he scoured my personal messages with my love, I racked my brain, trying to think of who knew about Sergey's retreat. All the mages involved saw him walk away, and the rumor mill at the palace was prolific. Elaine and

Yun knew, which meant Jonathan did as well. Had they told Fiona and Otto?

"How does Kellen know where to meet you?" Braden asked, interrupting my thoughts.

He cradled my phone is his hand but stared at me. Could I chance offering another deal? Yep, because I was stupid like that.

"The knowledge will cost you," I responded.

His eyes glowed red and he dropped my phone on the dresser. "You would play games with me?"

My heart raced with fear. I tried to convince myself he wouldn't hurt me. Scare me, sure, but not hurt me.

"You started it," I quipped.

He crossed the room and pushed me onto my back, hovering over me with his hands on the mattress beside my head. His red eyes bored into mine, long fangs protruding from his mouth.

"Tell me," he slurred past his fangs.

"What makes my fae magic so dangerous?" I asked, trying to keep my voice from shaking. "I read all your books and nothing indicated some super-secret nuclear weapon you believe me to be."

He leaned down and placed his fangs on my neck. I stifled my scream, but it still emerged as a tiny squeak. "I'll bite you back," I threatened, remembering his warning about mixing our blood and ignoring my elemental's warning not to.

He pulled away but not very far, leaving his face inches from mine. His sharp teeth receded with his red eyes. "I think you'll be the death of me," he whispered.

"Let's hope not," I breathed back. "Let's at least wait until Jack is defeated."

He rolled off me and sprawled out on the bed. I unfolded my legs and rolled onto my side. He did the same and propped himself up on his elbow.

"You found the part about channeling the elements, correct?" he asked.

"Yep."

"That doesn't scare you?"

"Nope."

"Mages cannot channel the elements," he continued. "They command them. I realize you're trying to convince them otherwise, but that is a fae trait, not a mage one."

"And how does that make me dangerous?" I asked. "Dangerous enough that my father would rather see me dead?" I realized that was the question I needed answered. What was so bad that my own father wanted me dead?

"Blood magic is also fae," Braden replied. "Mages don't do that."

"That doesn't make sense," I argued. "Kellen was the one who told me to do it the first time."

"No, Kellen told you to take the water from the vampire's body, not his blood."

I narrowed my eyes at him. "Who told you that?"

"Are we trading information?"

"Obviously," I spat.

"Then let's draw clear lines," he said. "I want to know how you're communicating with Kellen."

"I want to know why you fear me," I stated. "Which apparently includes your knowledge of my first kill."

"Then I want to know how many of your fae traits are already activated," he countered.

I wrinkled my nose. "I might not know that."

"But you'll tell me when you do." He made it a statement, rather than a question.

"I'm not sure I can," I answered. "There are some things that cannot be shared."

"Then there's only one piece of information to trade," he replied. "If you can repeat your performance this morning with the power of all four elements, what would happen on the battlefield?"

I frowned, dropping my eyes to the white coverlet beneath me. I only had two elements, not four. The book said the fae were tuned to the elements. Did that mean all of them? If so, where were these mythical creatures with so much power? Why weren't they in this fight?

I didn't know that answer, so I went back to Braden's question. I could probably kill a lot of vampires. No, they wouldn't be dead, just suffering in an almost dead state. Bile rose in my throat, and I swallowed it with effort. I could never do that.

Could I?

"I won't do it, even if I could," I replied.

"Not even to protect your mages?" he questioned, lifting my chin with his finger and forcing me to look at him. "If it meant freedom or slavery for humans, what would you choose?"

"I hate you," I grumbled.

"As you should," he whispered.

"Why don't we just kill Jack today?" I asked, pulling my mind from the grotesque visual he'd created. "We could end this whole thing by killing him now."

"It wouldn't end with Jack's death. There are too many others with the same desires," he replied, running his thumb along my jaw before dropping his hand to the bed. "They'll pick up the reins and keeping running."

I failed to suppress the shivers running down my spine from his touch. "Is there no way to avoid a war?"

"I've been trying for decades," he answered. "I should've killed him years ago before he sowed his seeds of insanity."

"Why aren't you onboard with him?" I asked. "Human slaves would be ideal for you and your clan."

"Who will provide my wealth if humanity is enslaved?" he replied, surprising me. "The supernatural community cannot sustain our current lifestyle. Most of them hide in the wilderness from humans. They have no money."

"I hadn't thought about it that way."

He sat up and smoothed his shirt. "I've lived in poverty and squalor, feeding off rodents to keep from starving. I'll not allow my people to endure that."

I pushed away the pity that rose for him. It accomplished nothing.

"What will Jack do here tonight?" I asked, sitting up next to him.

"He will make an example of Sergey and pick another to take his place," he replied.

"Does he suspect you? Is that why he's coming here?"

"Probably. I'll redirect his suspicions, but it'll make everything that much harder." He fisted his hands in his lap then stood, crossing the room again. "He'll make the entire display in front of my people, which will create doubt in my ability to lead them."

"Are you sure we shouldn't just kill him?" I asked again. "It'll take time for someone else to take charge. Time we can use to solidify our alliances."

He turned to me as I slid from the bed. "Elder vampires are not easy to kill, little mage," he replied. "You cannot kill me without your fae magic."

My eyes widened at the revelation. That was twice now he shared information without asking for anything in return. "Can Jack kill you?"

He smiled at me and shook his head. "Get out of my house before I tell you all my secrets." He tossed me my phone and opened the door.

I stopped in front of him and tapped my temple with my fingers. "I talk to my elementals all the time and they pass the information to my partner," I whispered. "You've seen my relationship with them. I'm surprised you didn't already know."

He laughed and pushed me out the door. "I should've known."

~~~~~~~~~~~~~

An hour later, I buckled my seatbelt on the most luxurious private jet I'd ever seen. Okay, it was the only one I'd ever seen, but it was still amazing. Gordon sat across from me. He'd been silent the entire trip to the airport and even now, he wasn't interested in conversation. It left me plenty of time to think about how much my life had changed in the last couple of months.

I was no longer a weak little girl rejected by everyone. I didn't like the fact that my enemies wanted me just as much as my allies, but I had to admit that it felt good to be wanted and accepted. Having the power to protect myself felt just as good, even if it did carry the weight of my responsibilities.

Despite all the good feelings, apprehension and fear cast a really long shadow. I had a feeling I'd be facing my father soon. The old fear of rejection twisted in my gut. He'd abandoned me once already. Any reunion between us would struggle to get past my resentment.

And my deal with Braden was only the beginning of that nightmare. I still couldn't believe I was stupid enough to make an oath with him, an oath I knew nothing about. Why did he want to keep me forever, not just twenty-four hours? There had to be a reason beyond his sadistic pleasures. He knew way more about what was happening than the little bit he revealed to me.

It wasn't just a little, though. I'd learned a lot from him. Would I have another opportunity to learn more? Maybe he'd let me spend another day in his library. So much information sat on those shelves, information I needed about the supernatural families.

My thoughts wandered to Kellen. How would we convince his family to believe us over King William? Kellen had admitted he hadn't talked to his uncle in ages. Would they trust his word? If we did manage to convince them, where would we go next? I couldn't use the portals, so we'd have to fly. Did we have time for that? Maybe Kellen could go without me.

The thought of being alone scared me, which was ridiculous. I'd been alone my entire life, so why was I afraid now? It had to be all the people who wanted me. I didn't want to spend my life looking over my shoulder for the lurking vampire.

I stared out the small window next to me into the setting sun. My life would never go back to anything resembling normal. I just hoped it didn't end in my death or the death of someone I cared for.

Vampire's Crucible

Epilogue

Braden watched his newest toy slide into the black Cadillac with more grace than any human should possess. Her fae blood would give her those traits, but they weren't activated yet. Not yet. The small clues to her heritage shined like a beacon to anyone who knew what to look for, but her other skills were a mystery to him. He hated not knowing. Knowledge had proven its worth so many times in the last few centuries. He would discover her secrets, hopefully before their war with Jack.

Braden's lip curled in disgust at the thought of his brother. The moron would ruin everything for them. How did he not see their destruction? Nothing good could come from this war. Jack had lived through the last hunts. He'd witnessed their near extinction, starvation, and suffering. Braden shook his head.

He'd made his argument too many times already. His brother wouldn't listen.

The Cadillac pulled out of the drive and into the sunset. If he was lucky, Jack's car wouldn't pass them on the road.

"Sergey and his personal guard are in the main hall," Bryce said. The man had served Braden loyally for over a century, and the elder rewarded him handsomely for it.

"Let's not keep him waiting." The soles of his leather shoes tapped on the hardwood floors as they entered the main hall. "Sergey, it's good to see you alive."

"I don't have time for games, Braden," the Russian sneered. "My life is forfeit when Jack arrives. I'm trusting you to ensure that Shaw takes my place." He waved at the man to his right.

The elder settled into the nearest chair and leaned back. "Who shall I offer as a distraction?" he asked. "Jack will not pick my suggestion."

"I don't care," he rumbled.

"Who is your least favorite?" Braden suggested.

"Hans is completely incompetent and disrespected by my men," he replied.

Perfect, Braden thought and smiled at the Russian. "What did you need to tell me before Jack's untimely visit?"

"He knows of your betrayal," Sergey replied. "I don't know who told him, but he knows."

Braden's smile vanished. Alisandra had been right. Was it too late to call her back? He palmed the phone in his pocket as the door to his hall opened. His brother entered the room with two dozen men following him, including the other council members. He sent a quick text to Gordon, the code to evacuate. One of his people had to survive.

"All of my traitors in one room," Jack slurred, already taking his full vampire form. "Let's make it fun, boys."

Thank you for reading *Vampire's Crucible*, the second book in *Call of the Elements* series. You can continue the series with *Elemental's Domain*.

Please leave a review on Amazon or Goodreads.com. Reviews are very important for both readers and authors.

Feel free to contact me on Facebook.com, Twitter @YvetteBostic or my website (www.yvettebostic.com), where I post updates for new releases, along with non-essential information about my books.

Join my newsletter to receive fantastic opportunities for free books and prizes. Go to my website and wait for the lovely popup asking you to join.

Made in the USA
Monee, IL
04 April 2023

31339293R00239